STARS WILL GUIDE YOU HOME

JAMES MCGUINNESS

ISBN: 9781079605914

DEDICATION

To my daughter Addison (any other children down the line)— May you never forget about what your great grandparents and millions of others went through. I hope you never have to deal with a crisis like theirs.

To the veterans of and people affected by World War II all over the world—Thank you for your sacrifice and strength. I'm sorry for all that you endured.

To my dad, thank you for encouraging me to complete my dream, thank you for sharing multiple stories, for believing in me. I miss you so much.

To my wife Jamie thank you for supporting me in following my dreams.

FOREWORD

In the 1930's, Hitler rose to power in Germany with his Nazi party. Despite warnings from European allies of France, Russia and Great Britain not to invade Poland, in 1939 Hitler instigated the invasion. As a result of this the allies were left with little choice other than to declare war on Nazi Germany.

The British government was worried about the rise of the Nazi party and there was a deep fear that Britain could also be invaded. Therefore, the government honored their agreement but Great Britain was not ready for this. The British Army and Navy had been depleted by the Great War 30 years earlier. While they were still regarded as a global force, many of their ships, tanks, and equipment were of a poor standard.

They were still a dominant global empire but the global economic crash of 1929 had also left much of Britain's population poor. Many from the older generation feared war and felt that it would be better to let Germany continue with their annexation and growth and become their ally. But the majority of the public were in full support of this and many of the younger generation were keen to do their part. Given how little work there was available, many young men quickly signed up to join the armed forces.

By 1940, the war was quickly draining all of the UK's resources and man power. Plus, the strength of the Nazi army had caught everyone off guard. They were steadily advancing through Europe; Britain was a likely next target. Paris would soon fall to the Germans who were advancing to the UK.

CHAPTER 1 - 1940

Eddie and Mac were walking up the steep hill towards the football field. They had met at the Trevanston market at a quarter past ten. They'd planned for ten o'clock but Eddie was late which was typical of him. Trevanston was a tiny village in Hertfordshire, England with a canal that swept through it. Apart from the small idyllic town centre with its few shops and one pub, the majority of the town was rural countryside. Eddie had grown up there, along with his two brothers and two sisters. For him, this was home. Eddie's dad had passed away when he was young so the villagers had watched him grow up and all therefore knew and loved him. He was late because he had just walked through Trevanston market and had stopped to talk with all of the market vendors, many of whom he'd known for years. He'd even managed to obtain a couple of free apples and plums, one of which he had given to Mac when they met.

Eddie was a young looking teenager with blonde hair and sparkling blue eyes. He was closer to five feet than six but always acted as if he was the latter and he walked that way to boot. His hair was cut short and what little he had was scruffy. He was very fit and healthy but had a little potbelly, which he believed was due to all the beer he drank.

Stephen MacPherson was known as Mac. Mac was the opposite of Eddie in so many ways. He'd moved to Trevanston six years ago and was a little socially awkward. He was very methodical and that was apparent in his unwavering need to be early. He'd been there for five minutes and had not said hello to anyone on the way to the market. Mac was taller than Eddie— over six feet— with brown hair and dark brown eyes. He was the kind of lad that could easily grow a beard if he wanted to but often kept his face smooth; but occasionally, he become stubbly and today was one of those days. He was tall and skinny and walked with big strides. People in town often joked about how odd the two of them looked walking together.

Since there were two others on the football team also called Stephen and an additional two in his class, Eddie had decided to call him Mac from the day they'd met, Mac's second day in the village. He had not initially been fond of the village when he arrived as it had been hard for him to leave his life in north London. Eddie was the best thing for Mac since moving to Trevanston and the two had hit it off instantly.

Mac was a decent footballer but back in North London, where footballing talent was as common as leaves falling from a tree, he'd been considered less than average. Despite that, Mac loved the game and his father, feeling guilty about moving the family there, had arranged for him to try out for the village's club. He passed the test and Eddie, who was captain of the team and one of the best footballers Mac had ever played with, became an instant best friend.

They'd now been playing together for six years on junior teams and now Trevanston's senior team. Being a small town, Trevanston didn't have an abundance of players so the younger members had become starters. Mac—who was sixteen—and Eddie—about to turn seventeen—were some of the youngest on the team.

It was March 1940 and there was a crisp chill in the air while the sun was beaming down. Mac had feared that their game would be called off because of a frozen pitch, but he was now fairly confident the game would go ahead. Both of them wore sweatshirts covering their team kits. Mac could clearly feel the chill on his knees.

Mac's father had been in the Army and fought in World War One. Afterwards, he had become a teacher and taught math. The war had been horrific for him and he had experienced nightmares because of it. Loud noises had affected him terribly, so he had moved his family to Trevanston. His mother was also a teacher and they taught at Trevanston School. Both were very disciplined and had insisted that Mac stay at school until he was sixteen and pass his qualifications. Mac had done so with flying colors and had completed his final exam yesterday. He was an intelligent child and had the option to go to university that summer, earlier than most. Eddie, on the other hand, had basically given up on school when he was fourteen.

Eddie had had trials for a number of English football clubs. At fifteen, he was signed to play for Watford and for him being a professional footballer along with any supplemental work— construction, painting, or whatever work he could get his hands on—was the ideal life. He earned more money at fifteen than most of his friends and loved being able to go down the pub and buy a round. However, last year he'd broken his leg while playing for Watford.

Now, he simply played for Trevanston and focused on construction work. He still earned great money in his estimation and loved his life. Despite their differences, Eddie and Mac had been inseparable for the last six years. Most evenings they were either playing football in a field, using shirts as goal posts, or at Mac's house where Mac would be studying while Eddie distracted him with the latest football news. Mac's parents never really liked this but loved that their son had a best friend. Mac had even worked for Eddie in construction last summer, earning extra money. They were also seen down at the King's Arms, the town pub several nights a week since Eddie's brother Bill ran the bar.

"So...what's next?" Eddie asked Mac as they walked up the road to the football field. Mac was waiting for this question; it was a regular conversation between the two of them.

"I've applied for several universities in London and then several others."

"What others?"

"Sheffield, Manchester and Cardiff; Penny's family is originally from near there so that might be an option."

Penny was Mac's girlfriend. She lived in London and they had been together for two years. They'd met when Mac worked in Penny's family business a few summers ago and they'd dated ever since. She often took the train up to watch him play football and spend the weekend in Trevanston. It was just a thirty-minute train ride. "You are not going to effin' Wales or some northern effin' university, I can barely understand you now! They all speak funny up there and don't know a good chip if it was thrown in their face," Eddie said. Mac laughed at his friend's naivety and suspicion for places in northern England and outside his beloved Trevanston.

The next thing Eddie said was to come with him. It was no surprise to Mac. Eddie had been asking the same thing for the past three months. The next week Eddie was going to enlist in the British army. Although enlisting had just become mandatory, it was only for men eighteen or older but Eddie was convinced though he would be fine at seventeen. He was excited to join the army. Since breaking his leg, he had been looking for an adventure and he knew the army would cover medical expenses. He had delayed enlisting until after today, after the cup final, which was where they were heading to. Trevanston were playing Ashcoe for the Cup.

Eddie had regularly told Mac that he will single handedly kill Hitler, be a hero and then get a second chance to play football professionally. Mac, on the other hand, did not want to enlist. World War I had changed his dad and although Mac was not around to see him before the war, he knew he was a shell of himself. He'd been shot in the back towards the end of the war and was dragged from the trenches and as such had encouraged Mac not to enlist; if Mac's grades were good enough, he could go to university now or even maybe study abroad and avoid the war. Mac was torn. He wanted to serve his country and imagined some pride in doing so, but was a lot more realistic than Eddie in knowing that he could be signing his death sentence.

"Let's get today out of the way and then we can worry about tomorrow. Remember we're meeting Penny and her cousin tonight," Mac replied to Eddie. At that point, they met the rest of the team and their manager at the top of the village. To Mac's surprise, there were also about forty people from the village all ready to cheer them on. For a moment, Mac felt like a celebrity and he took in all of the moment before the manager shouted at them to get in the changing room. Twenty minutes later, they came out on to the pitch to a load roar of applause, as if all of Trevanston and Ashcoe were there.

Mac was extremely focused. In a state of intense concentration, his mind was working rapidly, going over repeatedly the reports on the opposition in the local paper about the opposition. Their goalkeeper was a lanky guy, taller than Mac. He knew the keeper always dived to the left. Mac even knew that he was superstitious. He was watching the weather, the grey clouds letting through a ray of sunlight onto the pitch. He suspected rain and maybe even sleet.

Eddie, on the other hand, was fooling around with a football and doing an impression of Hitler much to the roar of laughter from the team and the crowd. Mac called his friend aside and told him three important things:

1) If Trevanston won the coin toss, they needed to shoot to the left first, that way the wind would be in their favour the second half.

2) That rain or sleet was likely and Eddie would be able to do more sliding tackles, his preferred style.

3) If Eddie was to take a penalty, he should shoot to the right.

Eddie listened intently and thanked his friend before mocking him for being a bookworm and instead of studying wind he should look at beers and girls. They walked onto to the pitch; Eddie won the toss and chose to shoot exactly as his friend had advised him. The referee called Eddie over and said, "I will be watching you, don't do any nasty tackles." Eddie gave him a wink and with that the game was on.

Ninety minutes later, Mac was being hoisted by his team into the air after his run into the area had resulted in a penalty. Eddie had taken it and shot to the right, the game winner.

CHAPTER 2

Rose had barely slept the night before and yet at sunrise she was wide awake. The morning dew was still visible on the hills as the sun was rising above the valleys of Deerwich. Today was going to be a long day and it would undoubtedly be one that would change her life forever.

Rose was of average height with long brown hair. She was extremely shy and did not fully embrace herself; she rarely spoke with men, let alone date them. Her hair looked shiny and perfectly brushed as it touched her shoulders but it was not styled. She didn't wear any make up and her pale complexion was clear, highlighted by her rosy red cheeks. As a newborn, her cheeks lit up so much that her parents felt that no other name would suit her and she was named Rose. She loved her village but she just knew she needed to experience life outside of it. Today there was fear and excitement within her. Deerwich was a very small village in the Welsh valleys about twenty miles from Cardiff. It had one dusty road that led through it all. At the beginning of the village was a pub, a butcher, a baker and a part time post office. Then a stretch of residences, a primary school, and—finally— Rose's house at the end.

Miles and miles of lush green valleys lay beyond. Ensconced in them was a gunpowder factory. Since the mid 1800's, Rose's family ran it and every day Norman—her father—would walk the three miles to the factory. He would lead the men into dangerous conditions to create the gunpowder. For safety reasons, the factory was erected in the middle of the valley beside the river because if something were to go wrong, the unwelcomed explosion would only kill a handful of people. The demand for gunpowder had drastically increased due to the war and so once a week a series of trucks drove to the other side of the village and were met by Norman and his barrels of gunpowder. After careful loading, the trucks slowly wound their way to the docks of Swansea. From there, it was either dispatched across the army or to Cardiff. Now that the war was in full force, the factory had to be cautious in its handling and shipping. The fears of a German bombing were high ever since the formal war declaration in September of last year. However, Rose had only seen a German plane once in that whole time.

Rose was by her front door at six o'clock sharp and her father arrived exactly on time. At six foot three, Norman was extremely thin, with a long, wrinkled face. Norman and his wife Anne had three daughters, Rose being the oldest. They had tried for years with no luck and Rose's arrival had been nothing short of a miracle. Two years later, they were graced with Gwenn and finally Patty several years later.

On Rose's seventeenth birthday, she completed her school qualifications and five days later, she was leaving home. She had thought about working in Cardiff, which was an hour away from her house; she could have easily been a secretary but she felt an overwhelming urge to support her country and therefore had chosen to train to be a nurse. Most nurses had to be eighteen but Rose was given an exemption because of her academic qualifications. After numerous letters to hospitals, she had finally been accepted into Watford Hospital.

Watford was fifteen miles from London and she was meeting her cousin Penny at Paddington station later that day. Rose hugged her mum Anne, who also happened to be a at the local hospital and then she hugged Gwenn and Patty, now 14 and 11 respectively. Rose and Gwenn hugged and held on. When Rose opened her eyes, it was time for her to leave. Norman and Rose walked in silence as they quickly walked to the bus stop. Norman towered over Rose and his longer stride forced her to keep up. He carried Rose's suitcase with great ease.

Deerwich had no direct train line, but there was a bus stop about two miles from the nearest train station. The bus departed only once every three hours so they had hurried over. Norman was desperately upset about Rose going to London; he had avoided all wars and although his job was very dangerous, he always kept everything within his control. He was worried about Rose and did not want her to go, but he knew how headstrong she was and did not want to risk having a fight as their last conversation before she left.

They had five minutes to spare. He asked her to write. He tried to keep his emotions deep down, not to let any emotion into his voice but as the bus arrived there was a tear in his eye. He embraced Rose for what he hoped wasn't the last time. After the bus Rose had to catch two trains, the first was to Cardiff and the second on to London. On the train to Cardiff, Rose checked her things.

Norman had given her a lot of money, actually too much and she felt uncomfortable so she'd hidden most of it in her small brown briefcase. She was however appreciative that her father had paid for her train ticket in full to London and with ample time before her next train, Rose allowed herself a small cheese sandwich and with some water. The train was fairly busy but she still had a compartment to herself.

She exhaled deeply, letting out an impossibly long breath. As the second train left Cardiff, she realized there was no turning back now. Over the green valleys, low lying clouds hovered, grey, full, ready to rain down a storm.

CHAPTER 3

Unsurprisingly, Penny Jones was running late. She wasn't forgetful or even intentional about being late. Frankly, she hated it and hated that she was always late. Inevitably, something either happened to her or she'd say yes to something she should've said no to, which always made her late. Today was no different.

One of the machines had broken down and Penny had been desperately trying to get hold of an Engineer for its repair. Penny worked at a furniture factory as an apprentice, just outside of Wembley in North London. Built from red brick, the building was regarded by passersby as abandoned. The warehouse and storefront were more noticeable, mainly due to the open windows and signs. The shop was a small façade that preceded a fully-functioning factory, staffed by over one hundred employees with a variety of furniture offerings.

She was the fourth generation of her family to work there. Owain Jones, her dad, was currently the owner and manager but it was her mother's family who had started. Her mother also there worked part time as a receptionist. With her strong Scottish accent, her mum communicated with the staff, customers, and bankers, often to Penny's amusement.

Penny was really close to her dad; although he had originally wanted a son to carry on the business, Owain was confident that she would run the factory after him. The Jones's factory had been in business for over a century. Earls, Counts and politicians had all purchased their furniture from there.

Penny was tiny and not even five foot but yet she whipped round London like a hare at the dog track. She was curvy and plump, with curly brown hair and often wore red lipstick and a great deal of make-up. It covered her youth—she was only sixteen—and she told herself that people would take her seriously. Enamored with fashion, she always wore glamorous clothing, today being no exception wearing a white blouse and blue skirt and navy-blue jacket.

Penny grew up in London; she loved the city and knew it well. She was due to meet her cousin Rose at Paddington station at ten past noon. It was now noon and she had a long way to go. She knew that the underground was the quickest option but being a Saturday and the city all abuzz despite the war, she opted for weaving in and out of the side streets as fast as her legs would carry her.

Every summer Penny had gone down to Wales visit Rose and play in the waterfalls. They only saw each other once or twice a year but were close. The plan was to fetch Rose, then head to Trevanston to meet with Mac. They'd been dating since they were fourteen and she adored him. She had left school last year at fifteen, despite her father's disapproval; she felt that formal education wasn't for her. Mac continued with his and that left them only the weekends to see each other. He had spoken of moving away for university, but Penny loved London. She hated going to the countryside to see him and hoped he would move back so she wouldn't be forced to leave. For all of their differences, they complimented each other. They were a fantastic couple —Penny had no idea why he was so in love with her since she was shorter and fuller-figured than most whereas he was a brain with an athlete's body. Despite all that, Mac only had eyes for her.

Penny and Rose planned to meet at the end of Platform Four and she arrived just as the train pulled into the station. Her brow covered in sweat, Penny wiped it off with relief. The station was full of people, noise and steam as they found each other and embraced. "Welcome to London," Penny said with a broad grin. "It's so great to be here," Rose said. "What's the plan?"

Penny explained how she hoped Rose would join her to meet Mac and the football team tonight, then the next day take Rose to the hospital, and guide her around London. They would go to Penny's flat to freshen up. Her family owned it and let her stay there on the condition that she pay a proportion of the rent as well as visit them when she had time. It overlooked the Thames, was close to the factory, and offered a great view of the city.

Penny hadn't figured out a way to tell Rose that Mac would be spending the night. They changed and freshened up; Rose was surprised by the amount of makeup Penny had on while Penny was shocked at how little Rose wore. They headed out and onto the train to Trevanston. Exhausted from travelling but wanting to please Penny, Rose sat quietly wondering what this Mac fellow would be like.

CHAPTER 4

The entire football team was at the Kings Arms Pub. They had been in there since the early afternoon. As one of Eddie's brothers, Bill, was the barman there so the team had adopted this bar as their own. Bill now managed the Kings Arms because of a leg injury from the Great War. He was Eddie's age when he'd enlisted and now, he hobbled everywhere. Bill was in his forties and the oldest of Eddie's four siblings.

Many villagers were delighted with the team's Cup victory and purchased several rounds for all the players. Mac lived for this camaraderie, something he'd never found in London. He remembered their coach's words from halftime, "You win together, you lose together." This resonated deeply with Mac and Eddie and it showed in their play.

Eddie was in his element in this bar; he loved this town and was proud to be part of it. His whole family was here and he wanted to spend the rest of his life in Trevanston. He wanted to go fight in the war and come back a hero. Despite the bravado, he was well aware of the risks. His brother was a constant reminder. Bill had already warned Eddie of the risks of war but was also his biggest supporter. "Represent your country and make Trevanston proud," was all he said.

Eddie was at the front of the bar when he first noticed Penny and her friend walked in. He'd been with many girls , but there was something about this girl that kept his attention. He could tell she wasn't from Trevanston and that the bar was overwhelming her. His instinct to introduce himself and wow her was stopped by his gut which told him to wait. Mac came up from behind and grabbed him. "Listen, Penny is here with her cousin," Mac said.

"Her cousin?"

"I told you she'd be here with Penny. She's from Wales and looks to me a wee bit nervous. Come with me and hang out with them," Mac said. Eddie didn't need a second minute and walked over there with his usual swagger.

"Penny! Great to see you!" Eddie bellowed and gave her a big hug. "This is my brother's bar. Why don't we all sit round the back, it's a bit quieter there. Oh, and who is this beautiful lady?" She knew that she needed to get out from the bar. The noise, the crowd, the energy was too much. But she felt something else, something deeper. It grew stronger the more she looked at Eddie.

"My name is…Rose," she slowly replied.

"Well Rose, this is my small village. My whole family lives here and you are our guest tonight, so I want you to relax and enjoy yourself. Welcome!" With that, he grabbed her hand and kissed it, before walking her 'round the corner to the empty part of the bar.

Mac had walked up and grabbed Penny from behind, spun her, and then slowly kissed her. He had been so excited to see her and couldn't restrain himself anymore. He had imagined spending the evening kissing Penny by moonlight but knew he had to make Rose feel comfortable and welcome. He walked over to Eddie who was preoccupied assembling a chair and table. He left for drinks and returned with one for each.

Eddie sensed the nervousness in Rose. She was very quiet, visibly uncomfortable, and had not touched her drink. "It must be tough," he said to her breaking the silent tension. Rose looked up but didn't say anything. *What was tough? How could he possibly know what she was feeling?* She was tired, away from her family, and in a strange, rowdy pub with a bunch of random football players.

Worst of all—she hated football. Eddie hated having to work for a girl. He knew there were at least half a dozen girls in the bar that would love his company and he also loved spending the night with his team. So normally,

Eddie would walk away from this scenario. But, there was something about her; yes, she was pretty but it wasn't just that. He'd sat down with them as a favor for Mac but he stayed for Rose. He felt sorry for her. Eddie had known Trevanston all his life and even though he was enlisting in the morning, he strongly believed he would come back and spend his life in Trevanston. He admired Rose for her bravery to leave her home and sympathized with her.

"Hey, look this is a really small town, I know everyone here. I can imagine how tough it must be for you to leave Wales," Eddie said. She nodded and started to open up to him. She told him about her village and her family. Eddie listened and enjoyed it. He even wanted to travel there some day.

Penny and Mac joined them and the conversation went the war, to politicians, football, rations and more. Eddie was enjoying his time with Rose so much he had completely forgotten about his teammates. She was getting quiet again and looked distant. "Fancy a walk outside?" Eddie suddenly piped up in the middle of a conversation about British politics. Everyone looked at him and Eddie realized he invited everyone instead of just Rose. Amazingly, Rose instantly responded,

"Yes." Before Penny could say anything, Rose told her stay with Mac. Penny didn't object and they agreed to meet up at midnight at the station. Eddie wanted to show her Trevanston and make her feel more at home.

Eddie was telling her about his siblings as they walked down the high street. They stopped outside the butcher's shop and Eddie paused mid-step, deep in thought.

"You hungry Rose," Eddie asked.

"Well…yes. Actually, I'm starving!"

"Great, let's go inside," Eddie said.

"But it's closed."

Rose was so confused. The lights were turned off and the doors closed. Eddie simply strolled in and woke up the building. Lights on, windows open, and noise started from inside. Rose caught the faint smell of bacon. It was slowly overpowering and so good. She cautiously walked behind the counter, found the smell growing stronger along with a great chatter. Eddie shouted something from the back. It became more audible as Rose walked towards the back where she heard a bustle.

"Come in, come in!" Eddie continued to holler. Rose was shocked to five others sitting around a small kitchen table. "This is my brother Charlie and owner of this shop." With a big smile on his face, he handed her a bacon sandwich and motioned for her to eat. *Isn't meat rationed?* Charlie read her look and answered,

"Eat up dear, Eddie said you must be hungry. These are all the bad cuts so you needn't worry. Go ahead and enjoy!" Rose nodded in agreement and took a huge bite. From behind her, a voice said,

"Take extra bread, we baked it just before we shut the shop." Rose turned 'round and a bright blond girl appeared.

"My name's Catherine—I'm the baker here as well as Eddie's sister. Here, enjoy some of my bread."

The more Rose ate, the hungrier she realized she was. More introductions followed; there was Dorothy, their grey-haired mother, and Edith who was also a nurse and also worked at Watford Hospital. Rose let her excitement show and was astounded at the serendipity of it all. Eddie sat there contentedly. He'd made this girl feel welcome and forget her homesickness. Rose spent the next few hours learning about Trevanston, Eddie's precocious childhood, and his love of football. She thoroughly loved the evening and felt better. She was grateful for Eddie and everything he'd done.

Penny and Mac, meanwhile, had spent a couple of hours in the bar just holding hands and chatting. Mac had wanted to talk to Penny about enrolling, how it was on his mind, that the more he thought about it, the more he felt he was running away from something significant and he'd forever regret it. He was no fool though; enrolling was dangerous and the fact of the matter was that he could lose his life.

"Let's just run away together," he said to her.

"We can't do that! I have to learn how to manage the factory. It's what my dad wants. Look hun, I know what you are thinking, you want to serve your country and enlist with your team. Think about it, you are seventeen and the war has just started, maybe if you enlist now you can control your own destiny rather than be forced to enlist in a year." Mac knew she was right, but he didn't want to tell his parents he was going regardless. He was terrified of the prospect of war.

Eddie and Rose returned to the bar and after it closed the four of them walked out together. Eddie led the way through a few alleyways until they were in a farmer's field. Eddie and Rose were smiling and Mac was sure they were holding hands as well. He nudged Penny and she looked up at him and smiled. Suddenly, Eddie lay down in the middle of the field. It was a cold night and everyone stared at him. *What was he up to?*

"Everybody, join me," he said. Rose was unsure but joined while Penny and Mac followed suit. They huddled up together for warmth.

"This is why I love Trevanston, the stars are so bright here. My father told me once before he died that wherever you are in the world, look up at stars and know they shine the brightest over Trevanston. He would say they would guide you home." Eddie said.

They stayed there until the cold roused them to their feet. They walked back to the town. It was late and the girls had missed the last train out. They went to Mac's and his parents agreed that girls could stay but they'd be downstairs. Eddie had walked back with them and as he left Mac said,

"I'm enlisting with you next week." Eddie hugged his best friend with surprise and delight, then bid him goodnight.

CHAPTER 5

Sunday came and went. Eddie had spent the day with different parts of his family, before going on his traditional Sunday morning ten mile run. An English Duke owned much of the countryside but opened it to the public, so it was a combination of peace and beauty.

Eddie lived in a very small terrace house. It was a red brick Victorian with two bedrooms on the top floor and a bathroom, kitchen and living room downstairs. He lived there with his mother and one of his sisters. As the house was very cramped he often spent time at his brother's and sister's homes in town.

He would run from his house to the end of the road, turn right, and head to the Duke's fields. First, he would run past the horse farm and on occasion he would stop briefly to feed them with mints he had in his pocket. Next he would turn left and follow the cobbled road until he stop at his sister Edith's house. She was normally on shift at the hospital on Sunday and her husband was in the war so Eddie would pick up their dog Mugsy. He was a Border Collie and should have spent his days rounding up sheep. Eddie had a fondness for Mugsy and had trained him to run alongside. The two of them would set off down the alleyway behind Edith's house and just go for it.

This Sunday was a particularly muddy morning, it had rained over night and the mud splattered everywhere. Mugsy loved the puddles and made a point of jumping in every one. After about a mile on the alleyway, they ran over a bridge and through a wooden stile and would end up in a cow field. Eddie never knew if this was part of the Duke's estate or not, but no one had ever told him he couldn't run through it. After a second stile, he would run onto a steep grass hill and Eddie would always sprint down it. The momentum would then guide him up the full slope on the other side and by the time he got to the top he was exhausted.

It was seven o'clock and the sun was still rising over the valleys and through the mist. As Eddie caught his breath, he paused to admire the view. It really did look like a scenic painting. To think London was only thirty miles away. Eddie had occasionally heard planes overhead but for him, Trevanston felt a million miles from the war. Eddie appreciated this moment. Tomorrow, he would join the army and this might be the last time in a while that he would appreciate this view.

When Eddie finally carried on, he moved through the top of the hill, tucked left, went down another hill, and followed the canal, which looped round Trevanston and connected Birmingham to London. Eddie followed that for several miles before ending up on the high street. He stopped outside Charlie's butcher shop so he could get some cold water and clean off Mugsy before heading back up to Edith's house.

Every week, his whole family tried to get together over a roast dinner that his mother prepared. The talk normally involved news from the whole family and no one minded the tight conditions. This week, however, was all about Eddie and his enlistment. He was being given advice from everybody to the point it was overwhelming and so he changed the conversation to talking about lifting the Cup the day before and how significant that was for Trevanston.

Mac's Sunday was different. His mother and father sat down for breakfast with him. His dad, Roger, normally read the paper and his mum, Rebecca, finished the crossword and they sat in silence. Mac told his parents that he was going to enlist in the morning. Roger was disappointed and tried telling his only son that he was insane and he shouldn't go. Mac had spent most days either in London visiting Penny or his parents. Mac made it a point to tell them that he'd be called up eventually; at least now, it was his decision. Rebecca was heartbroken. The silence returned but this time there was an uncomfortable tension in the room. Mac thought about this all day and wondered if he had made a mistake.

Monday morning arrived and Mac and Eddie met early. Mac was surprised to see all the other players were also there. It appeared they had all waited until the season was over to join. The local enlisting location was in Ashcoe, which was a town about 16 miles away and the team they had played in the cup. Mac was instantly glad he'd made this decision; he didn't want to be the only team member not doing their part for Britain. Mac sat with Eddie and Malcom Smith, the goalkeeper.

When they arrived at Ashcoe, Eddie led the team off and down to the high street. As they rounded the corner, a line of over hundred men greeted them all ready to sign up and support the war effort. Eddie suddenly shouted, "This country needs winners lad's. Maybe you chaps should pick up the bins in London." Mac turned round and saw that the whole Ashcoe team was also there.

There was a natural respect and camaraderie for each other teams and Mac found himself chatting to the player he had marked on Saturday. The line slowly moved and eventually Mac was walking under the arch of the Town Hall's entrance with Eddie, Smithy, and an Ashcoe player.

When Mac got to the front of the line, there was an army officer in a wheelchair sitting at the desk. *Hardly encouraging,* Mac thought. "Where you heading to then lad," the officer said with a strong Birmingham accent." Mac said the Navy and was directed down the hall to a separate room. Eddie was heading to the main room so they agreed to meet at the pub next to the bus stop.

Eddie was in an out of the place in about an hour. He gave his details for the Army, took the medical, passed instantly, and was then told he would report for duty in North Yorkshire on Friday. *Yorkshire!* Eddie thought with disgust. They could have sent him to any of the training facilities but the Beds and Herts regiment was to train in Yorkshire. *Full of Northerners* Eddie thought. The good news for Eddie was that eleven of his team, including Smithy, and seven from Ashcoe were all in the same unit.

Mac didn't have any problems with the medical, but it was more complex with them testing him for seasickness and a battery of other mental tests.

Mac was told to report to Scotland on Friday with another player called Dylan. They were given instructions on what train to catch and what they would need. Mac was fully prepared by Tuesday morning while Eddie finally had things ready on Thursday night.

For most of the week Eddie spent time with his family, ensuring he visited all of them, getting free food along the way, and taking down everyone's address. He had also spent at least part of every day with Eddie and the team playing pick-up football and drinking at the Kings Arms.

On the Thursday night, Mac sat down with his mum and dad for dinner and suddenly Rebecca burst into tears.

"I'm so proud of you but I will miss you so much!" she said. Mac had tears in his face and even Roger embraced him.

"I will write every week and be back soon," he said.

On Friday morning they were all to catch the train to London. From there they'd head from King's Cross to Yorkshire and then Scotland. Mac and Eddie were on the same train although Eddie's journey was shorter than Mac's.

It seemed like all of the town's residents were at the station as the train arrived. Mac embraced his mum one last time, shook his dad's hand, and boarded. Eddie shook everyone's hand and jumped on the train just as the guardsmen blew his whistle.

CHAPTER 6

Penny loved London, she loved the vibe it had and how friendly everyone was. That had disappeared by the time the war started. Last May, London was bustling. Penny remembered the streets around Trafalgar Square and the National Art Gallery were packed with visitors from all over England. She remembered a newspaper had christened London the "party capital of the world." Families would travel from the North, spend a few days in the capital, then take the train down to Kent where they would work all summer on an apple farm and spend the last few days vacationing on the beach.

Some of the wealthiest would stay out in London hotels and visit a show. The poor would go walk around the city, tour the outside of Buckingham Palace, maybe ride the underground and enjoy a meal of bangers, mash, and jellied eel in one of London's many seedy cafes.Last summer, Penny would finish work and visit the bars by Bank and hang out with all the stockbrokers, traders and bankers. All of them would smoke and discuss trading and banking activities while sitting in a beer garden. Penny and her friends would have drinks bought for them all night. Penny, of course, always went home with Mac. He hated that she flirted with these men but it was all good fun for her.

But now, everything was different. The streets were empty, there were no tourists around. The conscription laws had changed and most men from twenty to twenty-two had to enlist meaning they were either at war or would be soon. The rations had drastically changed what people could and couldn't eat. Businesses, market stalls and cafes were becoming more and more empty.

She and her family were very middle class. Her grandfather and father were both very smart men and their acumen had helped their business survive for over sixty years. Her dad was raised in Wales and was set to join his brother and father in the gunpowder works but on chance met his future wife on a trip to London and took over their family business. The furniture they sold was designed for the very wealthy and as such when the big crash and recession hit in '29, their sales drastically dropped. However, the family had savings to fall back on and the business had pivoted into new markets.

With the economy bouncing back, the last few years had been great for them. Penny had started to work there as a result of the boom and had loved it. Penny was facing many battles with the business. One, she was a female and not many women worked, particularly in the manufacturing and engineering industries.

But Penny had earned respect by listening to everyone and quickly picking things up. She also struggled to earn respect because her dad ran the company, but she now felt that she'd earned the employees' respect through her hard work. She cared a lot for the employees and had even forced her dad to improve the working conditions for them. As Penny entered the office area, she knew something was instantly wrong.

It was Monday morning, Penny didn't even have a cup of tea in her hand, but her mum and dad were in the office chatting to two men, one in an army uniform and the other in a suit. Penny walked in and her mum nodded for her to sit in the chair in the corner. "You have to understand everyone needs to help the war effort." Owain, scratched his chin and eyed the blueprint. "It is not as easy as this indicates," and tapped his long finger on the paper.

"Also we need to consider finances; if this war ends tomorrow, you need businesses to boom to ensure our country survives. This plan does not indicate anything about payment," and he again tapped the paper. At this point the suited man presented a new document and Owain reviewed this for a few minutes. The silence was killing Penny and she wanted to say something, anything to break the tension. Owain put the paper down and stared off into the distance. He signed the document and looked both of the men in their eyes as he calmly said,

"We will make this work." After a few smiles and handshakes, the men were shown out and Owain calmly walked back into the room. He was tall, skinny, balding, and looked about sixty even though he was forty. He had a perennially calm demeanor and worked in methodical way.

He sat down at his desk and looked at Lorraine, Penny's mum, and Penny. "We have work to do" he said. He showed the blueprint to Penny and explained that the RAF needed their factory to help manufacture plane parts and weapons. It was deemed their factory was big enough to handle the production quotas and store then distribute it. Some of their machines would be engineered to make pilot seats and three new machines would be added to make weapons for the aircraft. They were still allowed to run their shop and make a limited amount of furniture but eighty percent of their output would be for the RAF.

The British government would pay them for the output and Owain would hire thirty employees, all British Army Engineers who would oversee the production. He was also to partner with his brother and ensure the weapons were loaded with gunpowder. Owain had looked at the proposal and knew instantly it was a smart business move. The factory's production had slowed and this war was not going to end. This deal guaranteed the survival of his business and was a sound business decision.

However he wanted to appear thoughtful with his business decision. He wanted to ensure he was in charge. The deal had also been arranged with his brother in Deerwich, Wales. He ran a gunpowder works and would be shipping his product to Owain, who had ensured his brother would also benefit from the deal.

Owain's biggest concern was that this was a secret operation. He knew it was only a matter of time before Germany tried to bomb London. If the cover was blown, his factory would become a primary target for the Germans. He had ensured that everything was undercover and any delivery was done in secret. All distribution was done through canal boats and trucks that would have furniture logos on the outside.

CHAPTER 7

It had been whirlwind few days for Rose. She was still getting used to her new surroundings and had enjoyed being somewhat of a tourist in London. The trip to Trevanston had also reminded her of home and made her more comfortable. Now she found herself in Watford. It was a large town, with a football team, a high street with shops, loads of industry. But it was only a fraction of the size of London and yet on London's doorstep. Rose arrived on Monday morning and went to the nurse's quarters. The quarters were a large block opposite the main hospital. When Rose arrived, she met two of her roommates, Rita and Evie both of whom were smoking cigarettes. Evie appeared a little timid. She was tiny, with short brown hair and a plump figure. She seemed genuinely friendly which put Rose at ease. Rita, on the other hand, sounded more like a dockworker than nurse. She swore constantly and talked about her night out with two sailors when Rose sat down and introduced herself. Rita was a redhead with a fiery personality but Rose found her amusing. Both of them helped her settle in and discussed what to expect at the Watford and hospital.

After Rose had settled in and been taught all about the best bars in Watford, she went to officially check in with the matron. Nurse Talbert was a stern woman who looked down at Rose. It made Rose wonder if her soul was showing. "You ever been a nurse?' she asked Rose aggressively.

"No," Rose mumbled.

"Well then, your first shift's tomorrow, from six 'o clock in the morning to eight o'clock in the evening. You'll be allocated a buddy and you'll be expected to study for your nursing qualifications while actively on duty. We run a tight ship here and you will have to pick up the pieces. Ensure that you help everybody out or *you will be out*. Report here at six tomorrow. Don't be late."

Rose returned to her dorm almost in tears. Her fear and terror of Nurse Talbert made her question her desire to be a nurse. The thought of hopping on a train back to Wales crossed her mind.

Evie noticed this and put her arm round her, "Talbert is a ball buster. She should be fighting with the boys on the frontline. But when you get to know her, you'll learn how amazing she is. Don't worry. Now, let's get you unpacked and get a few drinks down before you start tomorrow."

For the next few hours, Rose read her nursing and medical books alone in her dorm. She read at a torrid pace; she was gifted and her talent had shone in school. She tested out before her classmates, which was partially why she was here now. She was already through one of the books when two new faces entered. A bubbly young blonde introduced herself as Jenny. She pointed to her friend and said that was Lily aka Lil Jarvis. *How strange*, Rose thought. They would be staying with Rose for the foreseeable future. They would be working the day shift with Rose. She warned them about Nurse Talbert and told them about her first encounter. They nodded along, unsure what to think of this place.

Later that night, all five nurses wound up at The Whip and Collar, a popular pub. Rose sipped on lemonade while the others drank. She and Lily had started to connect almost immediately; the other nurses started to call them "The Bouquet of flowers" because of their names and how inseparable they were.

Lily had grown up in Wembley, not far from Watford. She had been raised by her mum and dad in a small apartment. Her dad ran a newsstand near Euston station and her mum worked in a launderette. Both were quiet, quite different from the other girls. Lily had also finished school early and was ambitious; she wanted to work in a large hospital in London. As the night passed, Rose grew more comfortable with her colleagues and enjoyed their company. When she walked in, she was shocked to see that Lily had beaten her and was ready for work. Lily smiled and winked, acknowledging Rose's surprise and motivating her to get ready, they couldn't be late.

When they arrived, Nurse Talbert had them doing rounds, asking them questions and giving them an endless amount of tasks. That night Rose slept as soon as she hit the bed, only to be woken up the next morning by Lil to start all over again.

Throughout the next few weeks, Jenny, Lil and Rose immersed themselves into the daily routine at Watford General. The nurses all supported each other and they enjoyed themselves on the wards. Rita was the social-life mastermind, ensuring the new recruits managed their work-life balance adequately. They'd even learnt how to work effectively with Nurse Talbert and many of the doctors.

Rose had written to her family every week and loved that it gave her time to reflect. One night Rose sat down to write to her parents about how Jenny had tripped while carrying a bedpan. She was horrified but everyone else, even some of the patients, had laughed about it. She missed her parents like mad, especially Gwenn. Her mind wandered to Penny, Mac and Eddie while she stared out her window. The stars were heavy and bright, bringing her back to that late night in Trevanston.

CHAPTER 8

Eddie had arrived at the base in Yorkshire. He, along with most of his team and another bunch of lads from Northampton, had come up by train for most of the day. The other two groups came from Manchester and its neighbor Bury. Once at the station, they had to walk several miles to the army base, making sure to stop off at a pub on the way. The locals seemed to like the new recruits; the pub's proximity afforded them the luxury of new customers every six weeks so they saw no reason to complain.

The army base seemed very simple and Eddie suspected that at one point in time it had been a farm. One hundred bunk beds were stationed in a large room with a single bathroom at the far end. For the next six weeks, this would be their home. The friendly banter on the train quickly became competitive. Two groups from Manchester were sorting out who would be the top brass. "Bloody Northerners thinking they're all that," Smithy said to Eddie as they were getting ready for bed. "Hope we're not in the war with them. They'll probably trip over their bloody laces!" Eddie laughed.

The next morning the whole room awoke to loud banging and lights flickering. Amidst the groaning, a single voice shouted at them, "I am Lieutenant Mercury. I have the unfortunate job of getting you all ready for war in the next six weeks. You look like a sorry lot, maybe the worst bunch I've ever seen!" Eddie rolled his eyes, convinced that this was the standard speech for every new recruit "It is 0430. There is a well up over the valley five miles away. The teams you arrived with will be your squadrons. In the army you work as a team, so the challenge for you is to run to the well and back. The first squadron with every single member back will win and be rewarded with breakfast. The last team will be on drill duty at midnight all this week. You have five minutes to get ready!" Eddie was confident in his ability to beat most of the people here. He was certainly the fastest on his team but he wondered about the others. He looked at the other southern team from Northampton and didn't think they were a threat. One of the Manchester teams looked very fit. Eddie knew some of his squadron were out of shape, especially the men from Ashcoe.

The key Eddie knew was that they had to get everyone across the line, so Eddie quickly gathered his team. "We stick together and help each other with the run. No man is to be left behind! This is a cup final; we have to give everything." The team locked eyes and nodded in unison. Huddled together, they lined up for the race.

The race started and every squadron sprinted off the line. With the adrenaline flowing and the bellies empty, Eddie wasn't surprised but worried his men might bolt. "Pace!" They all looked at him and slowed down in order to run as a unit. "This is a ten-mile run. With that kind of start, they'll be exhausted. We've got it in the bag!" Eddie's plan was spot on and soon, they were over taking others who had slowed to a walk or stopped with side-stitches. On the return, one of the men caught his foot in a rabbit hole and badly sprained his ankle. He screamed in agony and the whole team stopped. Their spirits fell and their victory was in doubt. Eddie walked up, surveyed the man's injury.

"Alright, men—let's grab a limb. We're going to carry him off. We have to finish together." With a man under each limb and Eddie taking up the man's torso, they lifted the player and slowly carried him back to the base.

They were overtaken by the Northerners and one of the other Southern squadrons. As the base came into their line of sight, their pace increased and their stomachs dropped. *I bloody well hope we're not last*, Eddie thought. Lieutenant Mercury strode up to them, assessed the injured, and waved over a medic. He turned and looked at each man before announcing, "You boys came third. Not great but I'm impressed with the teamwork." He then pointed to Eddie, "You're squad leader from here on out. Well done."

Eddie and his team were shocked and proud of their efforts. They'd stuck together and seen their mission through to the end. The Manchester unit was unimpressed with them. "Hmmph. Southerners, stick together like lovers and can't even handle a turned ankle." They laughed and walked off while the Trevanston squadron all squared off, ready for a fight.

Throughout Basic Training, the rivalry between the four units grew. Every drill seemed to be a competition and it was normally between Bury and Trevanston. It was a friendly rivalry and on nights off, all of them went to the pub together.

The day had a familiar routine: in the morning they would exercises and practice drills, eat oats for breakfast, followed by team drills and army tactics, weapons training with more drills, and finally, exercise before a stew dinner. This wasn't quite what Eddie had in mind but he grew to enjoy it. He loved the camaraderie but sometimes he found himself wondering, *How's Mac?*

CHAPTER 9

Within an hour of his arrival, Mac had determined that he disliked the navy. He had liked Dundee in Scotland and the people. Mac had met numerous Scottish people in his life—most notably Penny's mum Lorraine and his football coach and all had been friendly. This was the same since he arrived as a bunch of Scots had helped him disembark the train and gave him directions to the port. Only problem was that Mac couldn't understand a single word of theirs. Mac was out of his element and now he was feeling it.

Rain came down every day and whenever it stopped, a dense fog built up around the dock making it miserable. The training was split between a large industrial building in the dockyard and a decommissioned warship. All active naval vessels were either fighting in the war or docked in Plymouth, Southampton, or Liverpool. Every new naval recruit was sent to Dundee before being assigned their orders. Mac was one of about three hundred recruits stationed there.

Mac was socially distant from the rest of the recruits. Since his arrival, he'd gone out a handful of times with a few others but felt uncomfortable. Now, he spent most of his evenings reading in his bunk about the ship's functions, operations and procedures, and emergency information in case of attack. He'd also written four letters to Penny in eight days as well as to his parents. He missed home deeply and felt he'd made a mistake in joining the Navy. He told himself that his parents were right. He could have applied to some universities and could be spending the spring and summer working at Penny's parents' factory while drinking beer in the evenings. He still couldn't shake the sense of pride of preparing to fight for his country.

His daily schedule started with calisthenics, general ship rules, the operations and procedures of a warship, and finally naval strategy. Mac was fairly fit, but this physical training was wearing him down. Every day started with a run, followed by sit-ups, burpees and—Mac's new nemesis—rope climbs. For eight days straight, he tried and failed to climb to the top of the rope. His arms felt like jelly and his stomach sank with every attempt.

Mac enjoyed the naval strategy and ship drills though. They had covered Fire Safety and this week they were preparing for when the ship would be sunk by a torpedo. Depending on your section assignment, you would receive your own evacuation plan, even your own lifeboat designation. The navy even had timeframes to get on the lifeboat, otherwise they would assume you'd be dead so, they'd evacuate without you.

All the pamphlets and books were created before the war and therefore were written with the assumption that the ships were never going to be attacked. This was the British Navy after all. Mac read these intently and knew each plan down to the letter. All roles seemed safe when under attack, except for the ammunitions team. They held by far the most dangerous roles on ship. If the ship were attacked, they were to be locked down with the ammunition. This way, the impending explosion would only create a minimal loss.

Every drill needed to be signed-off as completed by the drill team lead, otherwise Mac would have to redo all of his training or be reassigned to the army. Today had been a particularly terrible day. Mac had been up all night because of it so he decided to write to Penny. It was the first day they had actually unanchored the ship. The metal coil ties needed to be unwound in order to take off.

The team had trained for this but the first group of lads were nervous and did it wrong. Before they realized it, the metal coil shot loose and in slow motion Mac and all of the other men saw it unwind and whip out at a recruit. It snapped like a snake and cut the man in half. "We aren't even at war, yet and we're losing men," Mac wrote with a tear streaming down his face. With that he put the paper down, and curled up in bed hoping it would all end sometime soon.

CHAPTER 10

The past weeks had flown by for Penny and her family. The factory administrators had met with the War Council and their production orders grew overnight. Owain was now supplying furniture to the Armed Services but was caught off-guard by the sheer demand. His fleet of trucks were not enough so he partnered with a trucking company to handle the demand. One fleet exclusively dealt with the Army while the second went to the Royal Air Force. On top of that, Owain had secured a deal with a train network to further extend their shipping.

He hopped on a train to Hampshire to determine how ammunition was loaded, the amount of time it took, and how much the train could carry. With these calculations, he would be able to create a more realistic and sustainable timetable for his production and shipping teams. "If you're going to do something, do it perfectly," he would often say to Penny.

Penny's job was to shadow her father and learn at his side. She planned to run this entire operation one day and was determined not to miss out on any opportunity. Owain and Lorraine approved of her ambition and supported her every step of the way. Right now, with the wartime effort, most businesses had no problem interacting with a woman. Who else could they do business with? All the men were gone! Penny knew that once the war ended, things would go back to the way they were and her life would become much harder. Now was her time to get ahead and secure her place as a woman of industry.

Every Tuesday, Owain and Penny spent the morning inspecting every machine, operation, and verifying the daily work and objectives. In the space of a month, they'd implemented all of their plans and were looking to further expand their operations. Owain peppered each employee with questions. *How were the machines holding up? Was the current manufacturing schedule sustainable? Could we eke out more production? How much more, you think?* Penny dutifully took notes during these colourful exchanges.

After the walkthrough, she'd type up all of her notes and add in her father's recommendations. However, today Owain was summoned to the War Council to meet with the Cabinet. He had to report on his progress and make further recommendations. His hand covered Penny's notes as he motioned to her coat and hat. "Come with me," Owain said (more demanded than asked).

Five minutes later, they were on a red London bus heading towards Westminster. Owain had previously been to the Cabinet once, but Penny had never been. From the outside it looked like any other historic building, with its combination of red brick and grey stone. The entrance to the building went down stone stairs into a basement. There, two military policemen standing watch greeted them and asked for identification. They were escorted through a dingy corridor into a meeting room.

The room was surprisingly big and well-lit for a basement. There was a giant oak table in the middle of the room and a drink cart on one end along with a bookshelf. "Recognise that table?" Owain winked at Penny. Their factory had made it a few years ago.

The men that had originally been in Owain's office were sitting on the far side of the table and rose when Owain and Penny entered. For the next hour, they discussed the progress with the operation. At first, they were reluctant to discuss anything in front of her but Owain dismissed them with a hand wave. Penny pulled out her notepad and listened to the men compliment and praise her father.

He'd done such a tremendous job with production and they wanted more expansion. He sat silently and his face betrayed no emotion; he didn't smile at their compliments and instead only offered a look of concentration as they spoke. As the meeting came to an end, Penny caught some movement out of the corner of her eye. Someone had shuffled out of the room and quickly down the corridor. From nowhere she saw the prime minister walk out. Penny merely caught a glimpse but she instantly sat up in rapt attention. There was an aura in the corridor and his presence demanded your attention. Something seemed off, though. Penny detected some stress in him.

Fixated on what was going on outside the room, she had not listened to anything said for the last few minutes. She was trying to move her chair to get a better view without looking uninterested. To her amazement the prime minister was heading straight to their meeting room. The door opened and there he was, in the flesh. "So, you're the fellow helping us build ammunition right here in London.

Doing a fine job I hear. The war effort really appreciates it." The prime minister shook Owain's hand while he spoke. Owain's stone face wore off and was replaced by shock. He's shaking the Prime Minister's hand! He then introduced Penny to him. "Young lady, you and your father are doing your country proud." Penny shook his hand furiously and beamed with pride.

That afternoon, they headed back on the bus. Normally they traveled in silence, but Owain was anything but. "That was one of the most surreal experiences of my life," he said. They broke into a fit of laughter and spent the whole evening talking it through with Lorraine, who couldn't hide her envy. *I can't wait to tell Mac about this,* Penny thought.

CHAPTER 11

The six weeks of Basic Training had passed. It was now June and the war had taken a new twist—France had fallen and pictures of the Nazi flag flying over the Eiffel Tower were spreading throughout Europe. France had boasted about the might and size of their army before the war but they had fallen in just six weeks. The full might of the Third Reich was evident and now Belgium and Holland were poised to be the next targets. The British were sending troops to bolster the Belgians and the Dutch. It was likely that England would be under attack soon. In the final two weeks of training, two additional units were added to Eddie's training post. He now sat in a tent surrounded by hundreds of other men ready for their marching orders. The men had stopped reading the papers and were no longer preoccupied with the French fall; they sat at attention while Lieutenant Mercury laid out all the full details. It was true; they would be deployed to Europe to support their Belgian and Dutch allies. Upon hearing that, a few men cheered loudly. Finally, a chance to test their mettle.

The sun was setting and their Captain took advantage of the dramatic setting. "Tonight, you'll rest. Tomorrow, you'll win!" The clapping and enthusiasm were high and palpable. They would leave the barracks tomorrow at noon towards Yarmouth on the Eastern coast of England. From there, they would board a ship to Belgium where they would land at dawn and march toward the front line.

Eddie felt more than ready and was excited to see action. The fun and games were over, now was the time to see what he was made of. They had conducted training raids across the Yorkshire Moors, practiced their marksmanship, and even covered hand-to-hand combat. The last one puzzled Eddie. Why bother learning how to punch, kick, and stab when we had rifles, bombs, and artillery?

Eddie had made a lot of friends throughout the training and was ready to lead these men into combat. The lads from Trevanston were forever grateful for their training; they'd become fitter and learned to work as a unit. More importantly, they developed deep ties to one another, to the point where they were more than just friends. Eddie didn't believe that calling them his brothers would be much of an understatement. Mac was one of only a couple missing from the team and Eddie longed for him to be with him as they entered into battle.

Lieutenant Mercury recommended the men stay for the night but hadn't ordered it. None of the units were about to do that and so all the men hit the town centre. The town was prepared for this, having seen a rapid influx of young men due to their proximity to the base. The town was more alive than ever and all the bars were packed.

All of the Trevanston boys had based themselves in Hales, a cramped Victorian style bar off the town centre. The ale was great and the boys all seemed to be in good spirits. A few started to sing war songs and the others responded them to. "King George commands and we obey!" rang throughout the pub and into the night. The bell for last call rang at eleven o'clock and all began to make for the door and back to the barracks. Eddie planned for a morning run and big breakfast before grabbing the coach and heading to the frontline. He'd had his fair share of rationing and wanted a tasty *bon voyage* meal before heading out.

Smithy, a fellow Trevanstonian, wobbled to the bar and bumped into the lanky Manchester goalkeeper. Despite knowing that they were going to war together tomorrow, the hostility between the units never waned during their training. He poked Smithy in the chest hard and moved him back a few inches. "You better have our backs when we go out tomorrow. We don't want no southern fairy running away at the first sign of a fight!" That insult brought all of Trevanston to their feet, ready to brawl. The rest of the Mancunians obliged them and were ready to start a war when Eddie jumped right into the center.

Although the goalkeeper was nearly a foot taller than him, Eddie rose onto the balls of his feet and looked him square in the face. "You Northerners are a joke. You can't play football, you're unfit, and we've bloody well carried you for six weeks now. It wouldn't surprise me one bit if we did the same thing on the battlefield, carrying the sorry lot of you off. You should be bloody ashamed!"

His men hollowed in approval while the Mancunians scowled harder and balled their fists tight. "Well, we're better than you part-timers at football," was all their captain responded with. After a bit of shoving, the barman came over and stopped the whole mess. He poured them all a shot of whiskey to calm their nerves and it all seemed finished until Eddie shouted,

"Prove you're better than us. Let's play a kick about tomorrow morning and the winner can have bragging rights.

"Let's make it interesting," the goalie said. "Losing team gives up their first rations. Put up or shut up, you pricks."

"Done. See you at 0800 on the field," Eddie shouted. The thought of consulting with his mates never crossed his mind.

The next morning Eddie woke his whole team at 0715. Some were groggier than others and so Eddie made loads of tea and brought it by the tray. He watched them all eat, making sure they'd be prepared for this important match. They walked the pitch while Eddie focused them on the task at hand. "Remember the rules, let's check bumps on the pitch and know how we play." They nodded in agreement and continued walking, readying themselves.

The other team arrived at 0750. They too looked groggy. The team arrived with a referee; it was the barman from the night before. Eddie had no objection with this and both teams warmed-up before their pre-game huddle. All eyes were on Eddie. What would he tell them? "Listen, we go to war today with these guys. They're our brothers in arms. However, that doesn't mean we play lightly and give them bragging rights over us throughout Europe. We're fitter than them. Let's play to our strengths, keep it simple, we'll beat them." The team roared and the game kicked off.

For a friendly game, the match started with an unexpected high intensity. Within a minute, Eddie was running across the pitch to pick up the ball. He placed a long pass thirty yards up the pitch but their goalkeeper easily picked it up. Eddie was soon in action again, sliding in, tackling one of their players before running past two others and passing the ball across the area for one of his teammates slammed it in the back of the net. The team cheered and Eddie knew he'd be dictating this game.

As the game went on the men from both units tired, and the hangovers hit them. The game became a stop start affair and the team from Manchester started to control possession. One of their players hit the ball outside of the area and it in thundered in the back of the net, breaking the net in the process.

Eddie did not want to lose, but saw his players tiring, so insisted they kept it simple. Eventually the referee blew the whistle and the game was a tie, all the men shook hands with one another. "Great game" Eddie said to one of the opposition. "I look forward to having you on my side when we are in battle together" the guy from Manchester responded and with that they were ready to leave.

CHAPTER 12

Eddie was on the first coach heading to Norfolk. From there, he would be piled onto a boat headed to France. The reality was setting in for him now. The football match had ended in a tie but the moment that encapsulated it was the camaraderie among the men. The bus was merry with singing and joke telling. Eddie joined but quietly. They pulled up to the port and saw a mammoth ship. Eddie strained his neck, looking at how big it was.

The squadron leaders—Eddie was one—were instructed to lead their men off the bus and jog onto the ship. Navy men were all around and Eddie instantly thought of Mac. *What is he up to?* He hadn't heard from him or anyone and wondered if he was ok.

All the men boarded and placed themselves in this large empty space. They all stood in formation and the Captain entered. His name was Captain Martin and he would be overseeing the men and the boat's operations from now on. The boat ride would be two hours and the time of departure would be 0300. Embarkation hadn't been long, so they had about eight hours to occupy before they started their voyage. Quickly, antics started and card games played. Whiskey bottles were also being passed round and a football had found its way on deck. Eddie had no idea how the men had smuggled in any of that but he enjoyed the moments.

He swigged on several whiskey bottles, smoked ten hand-rolled cigarettes and relaxed. It was like a party and though they were advised to get sleep, every man was still awake to the boat leave port. By the time the boat docked Eddie had vomited several times. He wasn't sure whether it was seasickness or nervousness about the impending assignment. He rolled out of his bunk and made his way up top. All of the soldiers had been summoned to the deck for their orders and waited for their Captain in the early light.

"Gather round men. Now that we are safely docked, I want to tell you about our mission. As I am sure you know, the Nazis have invaded France and their army has been engaged with our boys throughout Belgium and France. We are currently in the port town of Dunkirk and the government has ordered a retreat of the men. There are two hundred of you and over three hundred thousand men fighting here. Our mission is to ensure their safe arrival back home and as well as guard this town from any outside attackers. We will be the last ones here. Are you ready?"

The men had not stirred during his briefing. They stood at attention and yelled, "Yes Sir!"

Eddie and his men were to guard the outskirts of the city. He, his men, and the Manchester Unit would be stationed parallel to each other and form a funnel for the retreating English troops to walk through. They would be the safety net for these weary soldiers. At first, Eddie was confused as to why he and his men weren't sent to fight and why all the troops were being called back. He'd been a loud critic but admitted that strategy wasn't his strength so he preoccupied himself with managing his new duty.

The men marched off the ship and as Eddie looked over the dock, he noticed fishing boats and other small vessels heading their way. Eddie and his group positioned themselves in a barn eight miles from the city centre while the Mancunians were camped in a farm less than half a mile from Eddie.

Soon, a loud rumbling noise rose from the distance. Hundreds of men marched straight towards them. Eddie readied his gun but soon realized it was the British troops. Most of them looked to be in good spirits but others had injuries. One man had a bandage round his head and dried blood on his face. Another had his arm in a sling and as he walked past, Eddie could see he'd lost his hand. Out of empathy and sadness, Eddie reached for the man and offered a cigarette. The man smiled, shook his head no, and kept walking. Eddie's men were clapping and cheering for the weary. Eddie found himself shaking hands with many of the men. He was overcome with a sense of pride and respect. It could have been him had he had signed up a few months before.

The soldiers marched past all day and night. Eddie heard several gunshots and tank blasts in the distance but hadn't felt threatened at all. He was exhausted though; he hadn't slept for nearly two days and he'd eaten candy bar rations all day. At 2215, a messenger arrived with good news. Captain Martin had ordered them to be relieved tonight but they'd return to this post tomorrow.

After three days, all the men had been evacuated and they had a new mission, retrieve all the tents and equipment from the front line. This was the action he'd been waiting for and Eddie's adrenaline kicked in. They jogged up to the front line, but were amazed how quiet it was. It seemed like a war had been there but now an eerie silence prevailed.

They searched the area and the whole time, the hairs on Eddie's back rose. He expected an imminent attack but nothing happened. They drove back to the dock with all the gear, disappointed with their first sense of "action". If the war would be this easy, Eddie would gladly want to come face to face with the Germans.

The whole situation changed upon their return to the beach. Overhead, planes buzzed while Eddie searched for the ship. All he found were a bunch of fishing boats. They were all anchored off the coast. They abandoned the truck and half of the equipment. He ran through the surf with what they could carry and boarded the boats. A loud explosion came from the beach and the truck had been reduced to rubble.

Eddie helped all of his men onto a first ship quickly. Then he helped his mate John Lockton from Ashcoe on to a second boat and when it came time for him, he slipped in and fell. He screamed in pain and knew instantly he had done some serious damage to his wrist. His bone was poking through the skin and Eddie screamed at the sight.

After they set sail, Eddie sat in agony and frustration. After seeing all the injured men over the last week, Eddie felt ashamed he'd hurt himself climbing into a damn boat instead of fighting. Nearly all of his squadron along with all of the squadrons from training were in the lead boat while it was him, Locky, and a bunch of Frenchmen who didn't speak a lick of English in the second boat.

Eddie sat down and tried to concentrate on the journey home, while nursing his wrist. He heard planes overhead, which grabbed his attention. Then gunfire erupted followed by explosions. Eddie ducked down until the attack seemed to cease. He looked up in horror, the boat with all of his friends was on fire.

A German plane was rising into the sky after a successful bombing run while another was laying down burst of machine gun fire at both boats. Those who weren't on fire were torn apart by the bullets. In a fury, he grabbed his gun and started shooting at the plane but it was no use.

"We have to help them," Eddie screamed at the boat captain. "We can't," he replied apologetically. "We have seventy men on here. We're exceeding personnel capacity as it is. We can't turn around and risk their lives." Eddie continued making demands until a few French men grabbed him and pulled him back. They understood his pain, but also knew they could not turn back. Eddie watched all of his good friends die in the flames as the ship sink. Tears streamed down his face. He had lost nearly all of his friends from Trevanston and other men in his unit in a matter of minutes. He had played football with them all less than a week ago and now they were all gone.

CHAPTER 13

The grueling training had finally ended and the new recruits were going to be relocated to a new operation: submarine, warship, or even land duties. Mac hated the idea of a submarine specifically, and hated the Navy and the war in general. He'd made a huge mistake in signing up. He told himself he should have listened to his parents and avoided enlisting. The best he could hope for now was a position as an analyst for Naval Intelligence. Besides avoiding the subs, he would also have the benefit of being on land altogether.

Mac was sitting in a gigantic school hall that smelled of old wood and sweat of PE lessons past. The administrators would be allocating the recruits here. The room was filled with energy, excitement, and nervousness. Mac's leg bounced and shook as he waited to speak with the recruiter. Multiple recruits had walked in to meet with the recruiters. Some reemerged excited, others walked straight out. Mac didn't care for most of the men here but he had become good friends with a guy called Herbert Gilbert.

Herbert was from London and had been also been an apprentice at Penny's dad's factory. He was an east Peckham man, a wheeler and dealer, worked hard, and was extremely fit. Herbert was extremely loyal to Mac, especially after Mac helped him write letters to his wife. Herbert had dropped out of school early and struggled with writing and reading in general. Herbert was just a little older than Mac but had met his wife Doris when they were both sixteen. Doris was Catholic so they were married shortly before Herbie enlisted. They'd met in a corner shop while Doris was still a student. Herbert was buying his morning smokes before a construction gig over in

South London. Having no fixed job, Herbert took jobs wherever he could. He swore it was love at first sight and met her after school let out. They'd been dating since. Herbie loved her with all his heart but was also very passionate about his Britain, so he enlisted in the Navy.

Sitting together in the hall, Mac tried to hide his feelings about this miserable situation. Herbert, on the other hand, was excited but expressed how much he missed Doris. Mac's name was called. He took his time down the hallway. He could hear his footsteps and breathing. He was escorted into an office and took a seat. The room was filled by a small desk with a shabby red carpet. A tiny bald man sat the other side of the desk.

"Recruit Macpherson, after reviewing your file, it's clear to me you don't interact well with others and you're smart. It looks like you are keen to get started and be part of the war," the man said.

"No sir, I really want this war over," Mac replied.

"Unfortunately son, the war is happening. We need you. We wanted you to work as a member of a submarine crew. You have all the intelligence for it but you requested not to be part of that. So instead, you'll be a member of the ammunition squad."

It took a second for Mac to react to this news. Being in ammunitions was his worst nightmare. They called submarines "coffins under water" because there was no escape. The ammunitions squad on a ship was nearly as dangerous if not more. He remembered reading about it in all the reports from the beginning of training. You were in charge of all the weapon maintenance and ammo resupply on the ship.

In one, large room are all the missiles, mortars, bullets, and every other weapon you could think of. On top of that, the ammo room was a target for the Luftwaffe. Mac shuddered at the thought of dodging German bullets and payloads while also avoiding being blown up on his own ship.

"With all due respect sir, I think I would be better suited on the Captain's roster. I know how to navigate ships better than any of other recruits. I think I could work my way up to even being a captain, Sir."

"This is true kid but we're short of ammunitions experts. They play a crucial role and we can't be without them. Plus many men have started here and become Captains. You'll set sail for Gibraltar tomorrow evening from Southampton on the HMS Valiant. Pack your stuff and get on a train down to London this morning and be on at base by 0900 tomorrow."

Mac shook the recruiter's hand and left the room in anger and disbelief. Mac waited for Herbie. He wanted to know his assignment as well as tell him goodbye. Twenty minutes later, he got some good news. Herbie was also to be assigned to the Valiant but as gunner. At least he'd have a familiar face. They returned to the dorms, packed, and caught the train.

It was still early morning but the next train wasn't for an hour so they bought some beer, which they slowly drank while basking in the sun. Mac fell asleep early and when he woke up, London was outside his window Mac said goodbye to Herbie then Mac headed round to Wembley to surprise Penny at the factory. Instead, he'd found Owain. Penny was with Rose in Watford. Mac made two quick calls, thanked her father, and left.

CHAPTER 14

Mac rushed back to the station and jumped on a train as it pulled out. It was busy with men in suits, returning from the banks of London. Mac had forgotten he was in his navy uniform and so as he walked down the train, got a few nods of approval and even a few thank you's. Mac was surprised at how busy and full this train was. Most of the men were in their forties and fifties—well beyond enlistment age— but he wondered if they would also be called up to fight if the tide of the war changed.

Thirty minutes later the train pulled into Watford. Mac jumped off with his bag and then waited in the main entrance to the station. It was an early summer evening and the sun was still high above the ground. A new train pulled in and he became visibly excited. Both his parents disembarked. He ran over to them and gave his mum a huge hug. "We didn't think we would see you again so soon" his mum said grabbing him tight while tears ran down her cheeks. His dad—never one for emotion—shook his hand and then pulled him in for a hug.

Mac's first call had been to his parents at their school. He had explained the situation and the timeframe and without another word, they'd boarded the next train to Watford. They walked and eventually ended up in a park. His mum placed down her two bags and laid out a picnic in the park. They'd brought a beef stew in a couple of jam jars along with mash potatoes and vegetables. She beamed at her son as his eyes lit up. Mac wolfed down his meal while being careful not to stain his uniform. To him this was the best meal he had eaten for quite some time. For the next hour, the three of them sat and watched the sun begin its descent.Mac told them about his training, his friend Herbie, and how he was to set sail tomorrow morning from Southampton. He was talking faster as he spoke to them. At first it seemed to be nerves but he wondered if he also didn't detect a hint of excitement. *How surprising*, he thought.

His parents said that nothing changed in Trevanston. They had spoken to Eddie's family briefly when they collected their rations, they had not heard from him. Mac missed his friend, he had read the newspapers on the Dunkirk evacuation this week and wondered if his old team were involved. They walked back to the station and waited for their train to Trevanston. Mac's mother excused herself and while they were alone his dad said, "We miss you dearly but we are both so proud of what you are doing." Caught off guard by his father, Mac couldn't hold back the tears. Those words meant so much to him. They hugged before his mother returned. Mac watched his parents get on the train and go, waving hard as their hands stretched out the window. He turned and made his way towards downtown Watford.

Mac found himself in the Nag's Head pub. He looked around and spotted Rose. His face was beaming. He walked over and saw that Penny had her back to him. Rose saw him and he winked at her, holding his finger to his mouth. He crept up behind Penny, put his hands over her eyes and said, "Guess who?" Penny screamed and fell off her stool. Mac helped her up and she embraced him with long, hard kiss.

"How are you here? How did you know I'd be here?" Penny let out another scream, fast and high pitched. Mac explained that he'd called the hospital and asked where he could the find the nurses after hours and how it was a surprise since he'd be given a brief furlough.

After grabbing them some drinks, Mac met other nurses, including Lily and heard about Penny's meeting with the Prime Minister. Rose was happy for Penny but couldn't help but think about Eddie. He'd been on her mind a great deal ever since that evening in Trevanston.

Rose was now well into her nursing and She and Lil had become inseparable. She saw Edith a great deal which continued to foster her feelings for Eddie. Rose and Mac asked each other if they'd had any news about Eddie. Mac shook his head. Rose had had a letter from Eddie dated several weeks ago and she updated Mac about Eddie. He was promoted to squadron leader, which was no surprise to Mac.

It was late so Mac and Penny grabbed the last train to Wembley. He was relieved to hear about Eddie and catch up with Rose, but he was more eager to catch up with his dearest Penny. The train was empty and entire compartment was theirs. They kissed the whole time and when the train pulled into Wembley they said their goodbyes.

"Write me when you can" Penny shouted to him as she got off the train. "Every week. I love you so much," Mac shouted.

"I love you, too," she yelled as Mac pulled out of the station.

It was a short ride to Euston, where he would catch the bus to Waterloo. When got there, he was exhausted and fell asleep on a bench in the corner of the platform. He wound upon the 0420 "milk train" to Southampton. He looked over and saw crates upon crates of milk; this was the train that transported all the dairy to the ports for the sailor's breakfast. The train was packed with sailors and Mac noticed that a few of the men were wearing their hangovers so sat away from them in a quiet compartment. He was hoping to sleep again, however by some fate Herbie had found him and they spent the entirety of the ride talking about their nights.

CHAPTER 15

Eddie was out on a run in Trevanston with Mugsy. He'd been frustrated for the past six weeks since he'd broken his wrist. After initially being told he was heading back down south, the medic had informed him that it worse than he thought and had sent him to a hospital in Norwich, a large city about an hour from where he had docked. He was assessed further, operated on, and was told his wrist would actually function normally when healed.

For nearly a week, he'd sat there bored until they finally released him. He had a cast on the lower half of his right arm and was told it would not be removed for at least six weeks. He had then headed home to Trevanston via London and for the past few weeks he'd been there, working at the bar with his brother. His mind constantly replayed the torturous scene and he could not shake the memories. Every time he saw their families, he saw his friend's in his mind. Everyone was polite to him, but he struggled with the question—*Why did I live and they die?* He felt that others also thought this as well.

So on this cold September morning, he'd gone for a run with Mugsy. He was due to see a doctor today and then based on those results he was hoping he could at least be assigned home duty. Eddie knew nothing about what that entailed, but from what his brothers had told him, he felt it was going to be a waste of time. *Send me out to Belgium with the rest of them, I could hold a gun in my other hand. I'd be more useful there,* he thought.

His whole family was busy with their own lives. This wasn't any different from before his enlistment but then, he was busy working construction, playing football, and having fun with his mates in the pubs.

Apart from Mugsy, he was alone now. Eddie had brought a ball with him and once they stopped running, he threw the ball to Mugsy. He had lovingly returned the ball every time until he saw sheep in the distance and had chased after them. Mugsy had returned and let Eddie know it was time to head back.

They strolled back to the butcher shop and bakery where Eddie spent another hour with his brother, sister and mum before leaving Mugsy.

Eddie had his check up in Watford and so after a cheeky beer with Bill, he got on the train and arrived at Watford hospital. He had hoped to see his sister Edith there but was directed into a ward where he waited for the doctor. Finally, a doctor and nurse walked in. It was Rose! He winked at her, but didn't say a thing. The doctor ripped off his cast and examined it. "You need this on for two more months. Nurse recast him," he said. Eddie was devastated that this was the news but was distracted by Rose.

"How are you, treacle?" he asked Rose. Before she could respond he hugged her. He winced as he did because it hurt his wrist. Rose smiled and carefully sat him down.

She worked on his wrist slowly. Rose was still shy, especially around Eddie, but they chatted about each other's training and about the war in general. Eddie could not stop staring at Rose and her dark brown eyes. She was really beautiful and completely different than all the other girls he knew. After about an hour, she eventually finished. Her nerves making her restart multiple times. "When does your shift finish," he asked.

"In about two hours, Eddie" she said.

"Great! I'll meet you over by the main entrance."

"That's great, but I can't. I have to study for an exam next week."

"Yes, you can," he responded. "Spend a couple of hours with me, I beg of you."

Rose looked deeply into his eyes, smiled, and said she would. She finished her rounds, quickly changed in her dorm, and found Eddie outside waiting on a bench. He grabbed her arm and they walked down the road to a local café where they had a simple dinner. It was mostly vegetables as the government was advising people to grow their own food for the war and "dig for victory". Eddie felt incredibly comfortable with Rose and loved how their conversation flowed.

"I have one more plan for tonight. Can you spare a bit more time," Eddie asked. "Yes," Rose whispered. They strolled hand in hand to the Palace Theatre, a tall Victorian with bold pillars and carvings as well as eccentric artwork.

Eddie purchased two tickets and they walked into the illustrious theatre. It could host 600 people and that evening, it was awash with people. They were a little under dressed, Eddie in his ripped trousers and Rose in her nurse's outfit.

"Never been here, but Catherine says its good fun," Eddie whispered to Rose. Truth was that the only place he had ever sat down to watch anything was a football stadium and he hoped this place would be good as the tickets had cost him.

The curtain opened and for the next hour they were entertained by the variety show. The best by far was a stand-up comedian who made the whole audience roared with laughter at his impressions of Hitler.

Eddie walked Rose back to the hospital and kissed her. They lingered in each other's embrace.

"Not sure when I will see you again, if ever," Eddie said.

"You will" Rose said. "I just know it."

"Stay safe," he said.

"You too."

With that they departed and Eddie headed back to the train, fighting the urge to skip. He had never been in love, never felt anything for girls but this one was just different. Rose returned to the dorm and was greeted by all of the other nurses who eagerly awaited the details. Rose embarrassingly told them of the evening and the kiss, blushing the whole time. "You like him don't you," Lil asked. "I can't. We're at war, and it won't last," Rose responded "but yes, I think do."

CHAPTER 16

HMS Valiant was an older ship by British Naval standards. It was commissioned over thirty years ago and had seen action In World War I. There was rust in many of the corners, drips and leaks everywhere, especially down the metal corridors, and a damp smell was easily detected in the sleeping quarters.

The men worked in shifts. When they weren't in battle, they took turns sleeping or relaxing. Mac was in his metal bunk writing letters to his parents and Penny. There was a postal unit on the ship but Mac had no idea how his letters got back to England, or if they even did for that matter. He still wrote the letters in hopes that his loved ones received them. The activity of writing down his thoughts helped him feel a connection to them, a lifeline he sorely needed now at sea and in the future to come.

When he finished, he walked to the mess hall, stuffed his letters into the mailbag, and ate dinner. He took a seat next to Herbie, who was part of a larger squad of sailors. He'd become close with one of the men in the group. Jeremy Cockton, or Jezza as he was more commonly known, had become close to Mac since he was running one of the main guns on the boat.

He fired large mortars so he and Mac ran the practice tests together. Mac had to run from the ammunition room with a trolley full of large mortars, each sixty pounds and the size of a dog, to Jezza who then loaded them as quickly as possible. Jezza was also from just outside London. They'd bonded over that and football—he was a good football player as well. It was lunchtime and the three of them were due to start their shift again at 1800.

In their downtime, they played dominos while Herbie played the harmonica and sang songs to make the others laugh. They all sat around the table generally chatting when there was announcement. "Attention, attention. This is Captain Cunningham; all men are to report on deck for battle instructions! This is not a drill! I repeat: report to the deck for battle instructions NOW!"

The boat had been sailing for several weeks, briefly docking in Gibraltar before heading towards the Mediterranean. No one knew exactly what their mission was but with Italy recently entering the war and France effectively taken over, there were rumblings amongst the crew that they were about to attack an Italian fleet.

When all men assembled on the deck, Mac could sense a large operation was in the works. He saw land in the distance with at least three other battle ships in front of it. Mac assumed they were also British vessels. Despite her age, the Valiant was still a formidable battle cruiser in the British fleet. She had eight large guns, torpedoes, and fourteen smaller machine guns positioned throughout the ship. The whole crew was informed that they were part of a mission against the French fleet docked in the Algerian town of Mers El Kebib. The mission was called "Operation Catapult". With the French effectively defeated by Germany, they had ships docked with highly sensitive data and they had a fleet of navy men who were now essentially fighting under no command.

It was a highly complex situation and the men were informed that the British had been trying to work out an arrangement with this fleet of ships but communications had deteriorated. They had posed an ultimatum to the French fleet. They could either sail back to England with the British ships, dock themselves in a neutral area such as Portugal or—if they failed to accept either one—the British would attack them.

The gasps from the man during the briefing were loud. No one had expected they'd be attacking their ally. Despite this shock, the British sailors were fully trained and prepared to carry out their mission. From 1500 and onwards, all men were busy preparing the ship for potential skirmish. Mac was now part of a team of ten preparing every gun nest and gunner with the appropriate ammunition as well as maintaining the ammunition depot.

At 1725, the Captain made the announcement. "Fleet, the orders have been received. Prepare for our attack. The target is the French fleet." Silence abounded as the bottoms fell out of the men's stomachs. Of all the battles to engage, this seemed the most absurd and yet here they were, running final checks and preparing to sink the French.

Mac was standing, taking in the absurdity of it all. The battle sirens startled him from his reverie. Since they were locked in the depot for the safety of the ship, Mac looked out of the small port window for a clear view. They were not to leave unless the guns needed more ammunition. If so, they were to await a radio transmission from the gunner in need of ordinances and the team would load a trolley. One man would hurry it, quickly load, and return to the depot.

Suddenly, Mac heard loud explosions and he could make out a flame in the distance. For the next hour, booms shook the ship but it seemed the other vessels were unloading most of the munitions. The radio chirped with alarm, "Gunner, Port Side 2 needs more ammunition." Mac would be the runner for this one. Once loaded, Mac pushed the trolley as fast as he could through the corridor and then up the lift to the deck. He had done this hundreds of times in training but this was real and the sweat on his face wouldn't stop dripping. If he dropped these, he ran the risk of exposing the vessel to a dire explosion.

As soon as Mac set foot on the deck, he'd be a target for the enemies. He breathed in big gulps as slowly as he could as the lift doors closed and the slow, thirty second journey to the deck started. If a nest were destroyed, the ship would still be operational and maintain a fighting chance. But if the trolley were to explode on the deck or on a connecting ramp in the middle of the boat, the gaping hole resulting from the explosion would render the ship useless.

This is it, Mac, he thought. He pushed out onto the deck and tried not to watch the missiles being launched. Mac couldn't help but think of Roman Candles as they streaked through the wine dark sky. The flames danced round him as he moved methodically through the deck and towards the port side nest. He tried to ignore the shouting and all the other noise.

When Mac arrived, he could see Jezza was at the helm. "Load me up, pal" was all Jezza said. Once done, Jezza winked at him as a thank you and took charge of the gun. He turned it forty-five degrees and launched three large missiles in quick succession. All three were a direct hit. The ship began to flounder and it was then that Mac first saw the ugliness of war.

In the distance, several French ships burned and sank. He made out several sailors who jumped into the water, many without lifejackets. Mac stood still, not remembering to move, unsure if he even knew how to. A part of him wanted badly to help them. Despite being the summer in the Mediterranean, the water was still freezing and men were flailing for their lives. The image of the burning ships and the Frenchmen dying in front of him was forever etched in his brain. He turned around and jogged back to the elevator and to the ammunition chamber.

The next morning an "All Clear" order was issued. All available sailors began the clean-up detail. The mission had been a success and the fleet had been sunk. There were rumours that over one thousand Frenchmen had died. Mac felt like he had blood on his hands.

That evening, he, Herbie, and Jezza were again sitting together in the mess hall. Jezza and Herbie were reenacting what they had seen. They were smiling and excited to share their stories. Mac remained troubled and sat mostly in silence, telling them he hadn't felt well. He did not sleep that night. The images of those men jumping to their icy deaths was on repeat, a mental loop that haunted him without remorse or end.

chapter ten text here. Insert chapter ten text here. Insert chapter ten text here. Insert chapter ten text here. Insert chapter ten text here. Insert chapter ten text here. Insert chapter ten text here. Insert chapter ten text here. Insert chapter ten text here. Insert chapter ten text here. Insert chapter ten text here.

CHAPTER 17

Eddie and Mugsy were on another run. Instead of lovely Trevanston, Bromley in Kent was the new background. Kent was called "the Garden of England", but Eddie hadn't seen what all the fuss was about. He was assigned to a home guard squadron based near the RAF Biggin Hill base and given that he had very little to do, he had decided to bring Mugsy down with him. Today's run was the fourth this week. They were currently in an apple orchard, which he guessed was about three miles away from the base. He stopped and picked a couple of apples off the nearby tree. He was sure this was a private farm but with the rations and the war effort redirecting the food, he didn't feel too bad about plucking some low-hanging fruit. *Surely the farmer won't mind a few missing apples,* he thought. Eddie chewed on one and fed Mugsy a bit of it before pocketing a couple more. They promptly turned around to run back.

The home guard squadron, except for Eddie, was mostly comprised of older men. Some of them had fought in the First World War and others were a hodge podge of men from all over the place. There was a former banker, a few older men that had worked in a newspaper printing factory, and a former teacher, who in Eddie's opinion was more of a shape than in shape. The Captain of the squadron was a sixty year-old, WWI veteran who spent his days sitting on a chair smoking. He didn't even run any practice duties, so Eddie spent his days running and keeping himself amused.

Eddie knew if the Germans did invade and made it to the base, the squadron would be smashed to bits. The most the squadron had done since he had been there was to take down all the road signs.Eddie jogged back and stopped at the top of a hill to overlook the airbase. He caught a glimpse of a line of Spitfires preparing to take off. They all took off in quick succession and Eddie was amazed at how they could fly. He swore one of the pilots waved at him.

Once back at the base, Eddie and several others from the squadron did a weapons check for the umpteenth time and then Eddie organized a few light drills to eliminate some of the boredom. He felt they appreciated shooting practice and learning how to load a weapon. Then after a few rounds of cards and multiple cigarettes, the men got into their bunks for some shuteye while two men patrolled the perimeter. Eddie had often volunteered to do the night shift to keep himself amused, but tonight it was the others job so Eddie snuck off the grounds with Mugsy and walked a mile to the air base and the pub next door. There he met with an RAF squadron from Bristol. They were good lads and Eddie was quickly won over by their football talk.

Just as Eddie was guzzling his fifth beer and feeling slightly merry, the siren went off to signal another imminent bomb attack. *Damn,* Eddie thought. He said his goodbyes to the RAF squadron and then went searching for Mugsy. He found him in the kitchen enjoying some scraps from the staff. It was pitch black so Eddie resigned himself to following Mugsy. *I hope he knows where he's going,* Eddie thought. He ducked into an air raid shelter situated in the middle of a field by the base. It was cold, damp, and crammed with his whole unit.

"Where you've been lad," asked the overweight Captain.

"I was with the RAF. They asked me for a favour," Eddie replied.

The Captain stared at him but didn't want to reprimand him so he ignored him. Eddie sat down in the corner of the shelter and tried to sleep. Eddie thought he heard a few planes but there was no action. After waiting in the dark and not hearing any blasts, Eddie felt it safe enough to walk out and relieve himself behind a tree. This was the second time in a week Eddie had spent the night in there and he suspected this wouldn't be his last.

The next morning when the "All Clear" was signaled, Eddie wasn't given any tasks for the day so he and Mugsy walked up to the airstrip and met with some the lads from the pub the night before. Given his wrist was still in a cast, he couldn't do much but the pilots introduced him to the mechanics. Eddie occupied himself with the airplane's mechanics; he had some knowledge of car mechanics from a side job he had once had and was able to pick up the mechanics of the airplane. Seeing as how nothing else would be assigned to him in the near future, this kept him amused and more importantly gave him some purpose.

CHAPTER 18

The city of London had installed war sirens as soon as the war had started in'39. The first time Penny could remember hearing the sirens was September last year. It was late at night and she and Mac were in her bedroom when it sounded. They descended to the garden level and spent the evening in their homemade tin shelter with her parents while she wore a gas mask. All parties were equally embarrassed to be sitting there in the pajamas, but made the best of it and spent the night playing cards.

It was called an Anderson shelter and the government had sent them out and instructed people to construct them. Owain with his engineering background had constructed it with mud on top and he welded the corrugated tin. Since then the sirens had gone off three times and Penny had noted each occasion. Two of which were tests, and one was a false alarm. If Penny was at her parents home, she'd be instructed to go to her shelter. Penny felt it was pointless as it was made of tin and would be blown up in the blink of an eye. If she was at work then she was to head down to the Wembley tube station and if she was in her apartment, she was to go down to Willesden Junction tube.

But an attack on London was inevitable. For several weeks, the Luftwaffe had been flying over the coast and bombing British coastal towns and the aircraft bases. The news reported of German planes shot down on a daily basis and Owain had warned Penny that London would soon be attacked. It was September 7th and things had been very busy. Penny knew the date, as it was her 17th birthday tomorrow. The factory was churning out weapons at an astounding rate and there were constant talks that they would expand operations. Penny was famished. She had not eaten lunch and so she decided to head home for dinner.

Lorraine had already cooked a meal for them and her dad had had a meeting today so Penny was alone in the factory. She packed up and locked up the whole factory before heading out. The walk home was about fifteen minutes and it was a surprisingly grey night with a tint of rain and mist in the air. As soon as she walked down the road, the sudden loud roar of the air raid siren startled her. *Damn,* Penny thought. *Should I head home and risk being exposed or head for the nearest shelter and stay put for Lord knows how long,* she wondered. She fretted over the time she was losing. Her decision was soon made for her as a number of people were walking out the local pub and heading underground.

"You coming love? Radio said they seen German planes in Kent," the passerby said. This was no false alarm, they were actually being attacked, and the war had finally come to London.

She followed the crowd of twenty people to the underground station. As she walked down, she noticed that there were still people on the streets and very few authorities leading them to safety. Penny was anxious as she waited. She cursed herself for not leaving the factory earlier. Her parents were probably worried sick. *Would this underground station be safe enough for her? How long would she have to be down here?*

When the siren roared, Lorraine and Owain quickly headed down to their garden and entered their shelter. Lorraine was pacing up and down, crying hysterically because their fears were becoming reality and they had no idea where Penny was. "She'll be fine," Owain said repeatedly. Lorraine kept pacing back and forth; eventually, Owain wrapped his arm around her and fell into lockstep. They had a portable radio with them and some food. They knew this threat was real and hoped all they had to do was wait for the next few hours. Owain had an engineer's mind and his worry grew as they waited. He had always known this was going to happen, but knowing a problem and experiencing it were worlds apart.

He was very uncomfortable with the shelter and if what he had learnt from the ministry of defense was true. He was naturally very worried about

Penny, but knew that she was smart and he was sure she would be safely underground in one of the tube stations. The factory was a big concern of his. He doubted the Germans knew of his operation but if a bomb hit the factory, he knew the resulting explosion could destroy Wembley and injure its residents.

Penny sat down on the cold floor and put her gasmask on. She had originally sat on the far side of the platform and had counted the rats on the tracks, but a bunch of rowdy guys from the bar had sat down next to them and she decided to move before punching them.

Instead she found herself between two families, both of which had young children. One boy was very scared so Penny sat down next to him. She started to chat, hoping her nonchalant body language would calm him down. She suggested they play a game of "eye spy." Penny checked her watch and wondered how much longer she'd be down here. An hour had passed and the sirens could still be heard. Soon after she checked her watch, there was a loud bang above ground, followed by screams from the station. Penny had no idea what that was but now feared for her life. Throughout the next few hours there was a constant sound of bangs, most seemed very distant except for one.

Owain and Lorraine had sat in silence wearing their metal helmets for the past three hours. Lorraine was very upset with everything and sat motionless. Owain was listening intently, keeping count of the number of planes and bombs dropped. Wembley was the north of London and he had not heard many drop near him. He guessed they were flying in from the coast near Kent and up the Thames to South London, dropping their payloads and then turning around for a resupply. He was fairly sure that only one bomb was dropped nearby.

Penny and the little boy had fallen asleep on the platform. Her coat was folded up as a makeshift pillow underneath her head while he nestled on her arm. She could not remember when she'd fallen asleep but was awoken by shouts of "All Clear." At the call, everyone rose and walked back to the surface, unsure of the aftermath.

The wreckage near the station wasn't as bad as she had imagined. There were a few broken windows and rubble that had fallen off due to the shockwaves of the blast. As she made her way to her parent's home, she noticed one wall from a lemonade factory had fallen. At their home, she walked in and was promptly greeted by her mum. Lorraine ran over quickly and hugged her tightly. "I was so worried," she said. The hug was hard and heavy. Penny could hardly breath. Owain was relieved to see her as well but had a focused look. "Penny, use the bath, get some food down, and come to the factory. We have work to do. Oh and happy birthday"

CHAPTER 19

For the past few weeks, Eddie witnessed the air battles over Kent. Over beers one night, the pilots told him that about their system of radio signals all across the coast. They told him about how as soon as they detected a German plane, an alarm would go off and the pilots would sprint to their planes, which had been prepped by the ground crew, and launch as quickly as possible to intercept the German planes before any damage could occur. Eddie was seriously impressed how organized they were and of all the new technology.

There were bases all over Kent and South East England. All instructions, however, for every unit came from London. They were organizing tactics for every RAF unit across the country. The air-to-air combats or "dog fights" happened on a near daily basis but somehow the planes were flight-ready within hours. The problem was the lack of pilots, not aircraft. Every couple of days, Eddie ran into a new batch of pilots in the pub. Eddie had briefly thought about changing his terms of service and becoming a pilot but he realized how smart they were with the number calculations they had to in the air and he could hardly add or subtract so he quickly squashed that fantasy.

On this Sunday morning, Eddie was at the airbase refueling the planes and fine-tuning the engines. Most of the pilots were in the local chapel along with Eddie's unit. Eddie and a few others were the only ones left. This wasn't Eddie's task but he enjoyed it. Eddie's brother Bill had visited him earlier in the week. He'd taken Mugsy back with him so the RAF was now the only source of entertainment for Eddie. The siren blared while Eddie finished refueling the planes. Within an instant, he saw all the pilots running out of the chapel. Eddie stayed nearby, helping a couple of the pilots into the cockpit and then stepped back as the planes lined up on the runway. At the drop of the runway technician's green flag, the planes shot up into the air.

"Eddie," one of the ground crew shouted as the last plane took off. "Round your men up and get them on the guns. This is going to be one huge battle." Eddie sprinted back and told his Captain the news. Eddie was worried the Captain would argue with him, or order him to stand down but he didn't. The Captain saw the fear and terror on Eddie's face and in his voice so he issued the order.

Eddie heard loud noises from above and spied several Luftwaffe heading towards the base. They were quickly followed by a Spitfire. The Luftwaffe's machine guns laid an offensive volley at the base. The Spitfire had started to wheeze heavy black smoke. The smoke became a roaring fire and as the plane quickly nosedived, the rushing air fed the fire until all you could see was a fireball the size of a Jaguar.

Miraculously, the pilot made a controlled landing just off the airfield. Eddie made a perfect dash towards the plane with a fire extinguisher in hand. As he got to the aircraft, he quenched the flames and was shocked to see that the pilot only had a facial cut and gash on his leg. " Can you get out" Eddie yelled above the noise. In the background, his unit was firing at another plane. "I need to get back up there ASAP! There are hundreds of them up there." Eddie looked at the plane.

The plane was covered in foam but the fuselage was intact. Still Eddie was having a hard time believing this plane would fly again today. But he wanted to do what the pilot asked for and so he and the pilot got behind each wing and pushed it towards the hangar. The mechanics ran out and started working feverishly on the plane while the pilot went back to the building. To Eddie's amazement, the pilot was back up in the air within thirty minutes.

Eddie was busy refueling a plane while keeping an eye for an incoming attack. No sooner had the engine started than there was a loud crash. One of the German planes had crashed. A message came through from RAF command that they needed to capture that plane as it had some important intelligence about the Nazis.

Eddie grabbed two men and they dashed to the crash site. The German pilot was dead. Eddie dragged the body out and gently placed them him under a tree. The plane had hit another tree on impact but looked in good condition. The engine would not start at first but they managed to get it going and then Eddie drove it back with the two others running behind.

When they got back to the base, there were pilots seated everywhere on the ground, drinking water and eating chocolate bars while the ground crew refueled. Overhead there were still swarms of German planes and Eddie had to move out of the way for an onslaught of machine gun fire.

Eddie helped refuel the planes and watched them all take off again. This process reoccurred all morning. The planes went up, fought the Luftwaffe, and landed for fuel, water, and food before returning to the dogfight. Meanwhile, Eddie and his unit managed the guns. Eddie was sure he'd hit a German plane but it did not come down near them.

Just after 1400, all the pilots were on the ground and had been for over an hour. Command felt that the skirmish was over. They'd lost ten planes and the mechanics were working like mad to get them all back up. A new truck had arrived with parts and supplies and Eddie wondered if it might be from Penny's factory as it had previously had a logo similar to theirs on the side. By 1600, the planes were nearly ready to go. Several new planes had even been delivered. The siren went off again and the pilots went straight up again for another battle. Eddie resumed his gunnery post and almost immediately, the battle was right over his head.

This time, the Germans were lucky, nailing the last plane on the runway along with the main hanger building. There was a loud explosion and the men sprinted out from there.

The battle continued until about 2000 when the sirens stopped. Smoke still filled the hangar and many of the planes were damaged. Eddie was exhausted, drenched in sweat, and the pilots all looked injured and exhausted. As they sat round on the floor drinking beer, they talked about their lost comrades. Three had been shot down and declared KIA. Then there were the additional casualties. His wrist ached in his cast but he ignored it. *This was nothing in comparison to everyone else's injuries,* Eddie thought. His unit had performed admirably. All of the men had battled today and Eddie had celebrated with them. At 2200 the siren went off again.

Eddie's unit was order to retreat to the air raid shelter but they all looked at each other and went straight back to the air base where they manned the guns and went to battle once more.

CHAPTER 20

Penny, Owain and the whole team at the factory were swamped. The production line ran non-stop and the factory was now open six days a week, twelve hours a day. Owain was immensely proud of his and his team's efforts. In the few months since they'd started, they had converted the factory, doubled their expected outflow, and the government was so happy with their efforts that they asked Owain for advice on a near daily basis for their other production operations. Owain was doing so well he was now in negotiations to buy other factories and get them working as well. He truly despised the war and had a difficulty justifying weapons production. They could and would kill people. But the war was happening with or without his help and he was profiting from it.

He suspected the war would continue another year and if things continued as they did, he would make a small fortune from it and be able to retire early. He sat at his desk thinking of retiring to Wales, being a landowner with some good books to read. He would also love knowing that Penny and her future children would be taken care of for the rest of her life.

It was a cold damp Wednesday morning and Owain was in the factory alone. He enjoyed this time to go through mail, the news, and other paperwork before all of the distractions of the day started. This had been a tradition for him but now he found these moments less frequently. Penny was normally the next in and she knew to leave him alone. Lately, things needed fixing right away.

Owain glanced over a government report on his desk. Since the bombings had started in London and across the UK, British planes were going down at an alarming rate. For every squadron of eighteen that went up, only five returned. He was spearheading the domestic operations for all plane equipment manufacturing. He had to ensure that every squadron in the UK had all of the necessary equipment to keep their numbers up. His factory now provided many parts of the Spitfire and sent them to RAF bases throughout London and the South Coast.

Owain was initially concerned with the demand on his factory. *Can we produce everything on time and on budget? My team is overworked*, he thought. He knew this was unsustainable. But Owain had answers for this. First, he pitched to the government the idea of simplification. The Germans spent a fortune building planes but his idea was that the RAF would only have a handful of models. It would be easier and faster to maintain the fleet and keep production high. Second, with Penny, he could recruit local women to work for him.

He figured since Lorraine and Penny were performing well, how hard would it be to find other women who would work as well? Within a week of the pitch, recruitment posters were all over London and now he had women queuing up to work at the factory and do their part for Britain. London was now bombed on a near daily basis. Owain was very fond of the local community and he had promised them that his factory could help out them out. Every time the air raid siren went off, Penny escorted people underground and cleared the streets as a warden. This made him immensely proud and he promised to do the same. Now when the air raid siren sounded, Lorraine would travel to the factory's small kitchen to cook large portions of rations. When everyone was underground, she came down with food and hot drinks.

With the operation in full swing, the risks increased and he was worried that he was endangering the lives of others. Last week, one of his trucks was blown up by a German airplane. The government said the truck was on an airbase and therefore part of that attack, but Owain was still cautious. The moment his operation was known to the Germans was the moment he and everyone he loved were in great danger. They had started to change protocols to ensure the safety of the drivers but they were still in immense danger. They had changed the distribution to include the canals and local boats as well. They had even started to use trains. They were currently re-enforcing the ceiling of the building with more concrete and they had also started to build equipment underground.

Currently Owain's factory was number one in the entire southeast of England but the government released figures stating that other factories in the area were providing more output. The theory was that if the Germans somehow infiltrated the UK government, they would target factories smaller than Owain's. Penny's entrance into the factory stirred him from his thoughts. Penny was exhausted. She had slept underground again and patrolled the streets before that.

She had just popped back to her apartment, bathed, and returned to the factory. Her dad came down the stairs and smiled at her, which made her feel better. Owain gave Penny some coffee and told her to sit with him. Penny thought she was going to get some new instructions or details of a new operation. However, they sat together this morning and talked. They talked about Owain's plan to retire, visiting America, football, and Mac.

Later, the other workers walked into the factory and so Owain hugged Penny hard and then walked back to his office while Penny headed to her post. Both smiled for a long time that day. That hour together had meant so much.

CHAPTER 21 -1941

It was hard to believe that Rose had moved away and been a nurse for nearly a year ago. She had just spent Christmas in London with all of her family. Penny organized it and Rose loved every moment. Her mum, dad, and sisters had all traveled to London to have a nice feast on the 27th because Rose was working so many shifts. Everyone was busy. Penny, Owain, and her dad Norman had been working in the factory and the bombings had hampered plans a little. They had now gone back to Wales and Rose was back in Watford working shifts.

The good thing was that Rose had Lil. They had become inseparable over the last year, so much so that the doctors and even the other nurses called them Lil Rose or the two flowers because of the fact they were so close. Rose had friends in Wales but never felt really connected to most of them, with Lil it was different there was already a special bond.

With Lil she had met a true friend, someone she hoped would be part of her life for a long time. They were not exactly the same, but they were both super smart and were excelling above the other trainee nurses. When Rose had met Lil she had been timid like her, but now she had become a bad influence on Rose and had taken her out drinking often. It was a Tuesday morning and both were walking around the park before their shift started. Both were smoking.

Rose had never smoked a cigarette before she had moved to Watford but all the other nurses smoked and she had found it actually helped relieve her stress and control her hunger. Yesterday, they had taken their nursing examinations and today they were to find out if they had passed and if so would they be re-located. Watford was a teaching hospital for doctors and nurses. They were used to a high turnover, what with their talented staff being poached by other hospitals. Rose was hoping she wouldn't be relocated.

She liked Watford and she liked Trevanston, which was near by. She and Lil had now been there a couple of times drinking in the Kings Arms and saying hi to the Hartley clan.   Rose felt she was just settling in to her surroundings.

As they walked back towards the hospital, Lil started worrying about the results. "I really think I've failed," she said for the fourth time that morning. Rose re-assured her that she hadn't. Rose was fairly confident that she had passed. She answered all the questions and the revising had paid off. She had revised with Lil every night for the past two weeks with the exception of Christmas and was sure that Lil had also passed unless she'd totally screwed things up.

They walked into the hospital and headed to the main ward. There was a chalkboard with every nurse's assignment. Rose was assigned to the children's ward, which she loved, and Lil was assigned to Ward B, which was next to the children's ward, and normally had patients with broken bones. They headed up there together and set about on their morning duties.

At half past eleven, Lil and Rose met up and headed down for another cigarette. They'd planned this and started to talk about their mornings when Nurse Talbert cornered them.

"A word with both of you please," was all she said. Lil and Rose looked at each other nervously and slowly walked into Nurse Talbert's office.

"I am sure you're wondering about the results of your nursing qualifications. As you know twenty nurses took the exam yesterday, several failed including your friend Jenny. They will be staying here to re-take it or consider a new career." Rose instantly felt sad for Jenny. She was lovely but had not revised with her or Lil often. Rose knew she was not as qualified as them but it was still sad to hear.

"You two, however, passed with flying colors. Lil, you had the highest score of everyone." Lil and Rose were shocked and when the color returned to their faces, they beamed and hugged each other.

"Yes, congratulations. I'm very proud of you both," Nurse Talbert continued.

CHAPTER 22

News of the Battle of Britain, as it was now called, spread across all of England and the papers the world over. Against all odds, the RAF and the Spitfire planes had fought gallantly for the past few months and Hitler had now halted operations to attack Britain until the winter was over.

That had not completely stopped the nearly nightly bombings but the main battle was now over. Penny, like all Londoners, was excited by this news. They were not beaten and they were going to win this war. The factory operation had also kept up with demand with over two hundred women now in the Wembley factory. They had plans to expand further and needed to assess where they would expand to and that meant a trip to Wales. Penny was excited about this, as she had not been to Wales for a few years. She was looking forward to seeing her aunt, uncle and cousins and to be spending time with her mum and dad outside of London.

Her dad had mentioned on several occasions that this was a work trip but she was delighted to be able to get out and take in some different scenery nonetheless. They were to catch the ten o'clock train from Paddington to Cardiff and then another train to Swansea. Once there, they were to inspect the docks and another factory.

They'd head back to Cardiff to catch another train into the valleys, have dinner with her family, and explore the gunpowder works before heading home. As usual Penny was sprinting to be on time. She hoped her dad had bought tickets already, as there was no way she was going to have time to buy any. Her dad had told her to meet him and her mum at Platform Five.

Penny was late and she nearly knocked a man off his feet as she dashed through the streets. Finally, she got to station and ran through to see her dad holding his watch while rolling his eyes.

"Sorry," Penny said while trying to catch her breath. Lorraine hugged her while Owain walked ahead with his dark hat, long coat, and briefcase. He looked like an accountant. To Penny's surprise, they entered the first class coach. "Courtesy of the Ministry," he winked. Penny had never ridden in first class before. This was nice; they had their own compartment and although the seats seemed similar, they were much more comfy. The train set off and Penny fell fast asleep before they had left London. She was awoken by her mum in Cardiff.

They grabbed a tea and scone in Cardiff before heading down to Swansea, which was a Welsh dock town. As they got off the train, a gentleman and developer named Huw Jenkins met them. Huw had a car and drove them down to the ocean and docks. It smelled very much of fish and the streets were littered with grease and mess from ships. However, they arrived at a building that looked more like a ghost house than a factory. Huw warned them to mind their step. There was broken glass all over the floor. "Used to be toy factory this place and the toys shipped to Ireland," Huw explained. Penny thought it should have been knocked down but Owain looked around, carefully taking notes, and pulling out his measuring tape.

After about thirty minutes, they stopped and started to chat. Finally, Owain said loudly, "My calculations indicate we can have this place operational by the end of February. Can you ensure we have enough employees by then?" "I'm sure. We have a number of women here and old navy dogs," Huw replied and they both shook hands eagerly. Huw took them back to the station and talked with Owain about rugby the whole time.

The three of them departed for Cardiff again and Owain informed them that they were expanding operations and opening that factory to provide more supplies to the RAF. This operation would prepare equipment for foreign RAF missions and the docks would use existing Navy ships to send them.

After a long journey, they arrived and met their family. There were lots of hugs and kisses. Both Norman and Owain were quite reserved but they were genuinely delighted at seeing each other. The brothers embraced for a long time. They ate a hearty meal made with vegetables from the farm and meat supplied to them from others in the village. It was amazing to Penny that unlike London that was heavily bombed this place was just as she remembered it before the war. They were getting on with life as normal.

"Have you heard that Rose moved to Carshalton?" Her aunt asked with sudden worry across her eyes.

"I had a letter to say she was settling in there," Penny said. "I did, too," her aunt replied.

"I wish she had stayed in Watford or even better, gone to a quieter hospital."

There was obvious distress in her voice and her uncle put his arm round her. After the silence, Penny chimed in and said, "I'll check in on her when I get back but she is doing amazingly."

The rest of the evening Penny spent with her younger cousins Gwenn and Patty and she told them everything she'd experienced. They were awestruck with what was happening in London and kept asking questions. Gwenn had already declared she would be following in her sister's footsteps as soon as she could. The next morning Penny got up and found toast, marmalade, eggs, and bacon all ready for her. Her aunt informed her that they had walked up through the valley to the gunpowder works.

Penny felt a little sad that her dad had not taken her with him, but that was quickly forgotten over the tasty breakfast. Later that afternoon, Owain returned and he called Penny into the lounge with him and Norman. He wanted her to learn from the process and understand what they were doing. Essentially making gunpowder was very dangerous but transporting it to London had become even more dangerous. "The train is less than a mile away from the works, so we are going to have gunpowder travel by train more frequently now," Owain said.

By the time they'd said their goodbyes and boarded the train back to London, Penny had nearly forgotten all of the distress she was returning to. That feeling was short lived as she pulled into Paddington station that evening to the loud air raid sirens blaring overhead. She spent another cold winter night underground.

CHAPTER 23

Eddie finally had some meaningful work to do. The Battle of Britain had engrossed his life for the past few months. He had been at the air base every day, helped fix the planes, and even shot a German plane down with his squadron's gun above the air raid shelter.

He had managed one trip back to Trevanston but had been so busy he had spent Christmas on the air base. He was currently sitting in a field watching the flames consume the wood he was burning. The ground was wet and icy and it had not helped with lighting the fire but he was now enjoying it. He was due to report to the air base in thirty minutes.

He could see it from the top of the hill so he took in the peace and quiet of the Kent countryside. He closed his eyes and still had images of the boat being blown up last year. He wasn't sure if he was religious but someone had definitely looked out for him that day and put him on the other boat.

At the same time, he thought about the recent attacks and action at the airbase. He didn't know many of the airmen well, but yesterday the squadron had lost their third casualty in two weeks. Eddie had known that pilot through the pub. The saddest thing was that he had a baby back home. Most of the air crew at RAF Biggin Hill had survived attack after attack, some had been hit and crash landed, some had injuries but most had survived and then yesterday all it took was a hit to the wing and the plane crashed, exploded on impact and other lives lost.

Eddie stared at the flames licking the wood and pondered. He wondered how Mac was getting on and the few others from Trevanston not on that boat. He wondered how his family were and wondered about others like Penny and Rose. Was everyone he knew going to die in this war? He got up and jogged back to the air base as today he had an important job to do. Was everyone he knew going to die in this war? He got up and jogged back to the air base as today he had an important job to do.

The RAF squadron had shot down five German planes. Eddie and another soldier from his unit were to escort them back to a location in London. Eddie was fortunate that he could drive because it meant he was assigned this task and gave him a day away from the normal routine.

He arrived at the base and headed over to where the German prisoners were being held. None of them had spoken a word since their capture and were kept in a small wooden shed. Eddie was handed keys to the truck and given directions of where to go. He was joined by Elliot Cahill. Elliot was in his late thirties and had been a print worker before the war in nearby Maidstone.

He had signed up to fight but they had deemed him too old. On top of that, he had a limp and was assigned home duty. Elliott and Eddie walked over to the shed and opened it up. Eddie had been thinking he might just kill them all with his bare hands. In his mind one of them probably shot the ship his friends were on was what he told himself, however as he opened the door he was taken back at just how normal and scared they looked. The five airmen all huddled together and looked up at Eddie. "Anyone speak English?" Eddie asked. The tall pilot in the back nervously raised his hand. "Tell your friends we are taking you to a prison in Trent Park in London." The tall pilot then softly spoke in German.

Eddie was amazed these guys were as young as him and he tried to put himself in their shoes. They were doing what they were told, same as him, and if he was in their shoes, he'd probably be scared too. For the first time, he had sympathy for his enemy. They loaded the truck with Elliot and the prisoners in the back. Eddie and Mugsy were in the front. Mugsy had returned just after Christmas with Bill who had again come to visit and felt

Eddie needed the company. After a couple of minutes, Eddie unexpectedly pulled over. Elliott shouted, "Do we have engine problems?" Eddie said no and got out of the truck. The Germans were all staring at Elliott who cursed his colleague, abandoning him with five enemy prisoners but less than a minute later Eddie returned with his hands full with apples.

He passed an apple to each of the prisoners, who were at first skeptical but after seeing Eddie eat one they all quickly ate them.

The rest of the journey was uneventful and apart from Eddie getting lost they arrived at Trent Park several hours later. The only other thing that had happened was that Mugsy had made friends with the prisoners as he had quickly hopped into the back of the truck. As they pulled in, Eddie glanced at his rear mirror to see the German men rubbing his belly and letting him jump all over them.

Eddie pulled up to a nice house and checked his paperwork into the Army guard posted at the entrance. Eddie had seen large houses and estates before such as the Duke's estate in Trevanston, but this place was on another level.

Eddie was supposed to unload the prisoners and head back, but he was one of eight trucks carrying prisoners and they all arrived at the same time. Eddie therefore volunteered to take the prisoners into the building himself. They walked into the great hall where the German prisoners were to receive food. "Thank you. You have a great dog," the tall German said to Eddie as they parted. There was a moment of mutual respect there. Eddie had fed and looked after them when he could have been more malicious.

Eddie and Elliot were invited for tea before they left and they sat with one of the soldiers in command there. He told them that they wanted the prisoners to feel comfortable here in order to gather some intelligence about the enemy's plans. They had no idea that the British were listening in the whole time and taking notes.

Insert chapter ten text here. Insert chapter ten text here. Insert chapter ten text here. Insert chapter ten text here. Insert chapter ten text here. Insert chapter ten text here. Insert chapter ten text here. Insert chapter ten text

CHAPTER 24

Mac had hated this war before enlisting and now a year after training and the action he had seen, he despised it. Adolf Hitler and the Nazi army were quickly conquering Europe and this was a huge danger. Mac had read articles in the newspapers since as early as 1936 about their rise and the atrocities they had conducted.

Mac clearly remembered his parents sitting down with him and explaining what had happened after Kristallnacht where Jewish businesses were ransacked and vandalized. That memory had stayed with Mac and he was upset whenever he read stories about the way they killed and abused Jewish people along with their discrimination of black, disabled, and homosexual people had struck Mac's nerves. He despised any sort of discrimination and this was a big part of why he'd signed up. Right now, he despised everything about the war and he seriously regretted signing up. He thought the men around him were mostly idiots, they had no idea why they were fighting Germany, and just fought because Britain needed them. All of the newspapers and most advertisements now were full of propaganda so Mac had no idea what was true and false. He didn't know why he was fighting and to top things off, he had recently seen firsthand a French ship blown up and hundreds of French sailors suffer and die. He had seen the eyes of some of them as they drowned in front of his ship or rolled around in flames screaming for their lives. To top it all off, Mac was also tired from sleep deprivation and hunger.

Since the battle of Mers El Kebib, Mac's ship had stayed in the area for the last few months to monitor the situation. He spent Christmas day running drills and laughing with Jezza and Herbie. The ship had been there, cleaning the water of debris and bodies. They were also on guard against future attacks. Mac was mostly confined to the ammunitions chamber but every time he did go on deck, there was a retched smell of death.

They had now set sail for Gibraltar where they were to pick up some passengers and return to England. Mac was spending some down time in his bunk. He had eaten with Jezza, Herbie, and a few other men but now wanted some time to himself. He came in, sat on his bunk, and wrote to both Penny and his mum and dad. He knew full well from the mailmen that no mail was being picked up as they were due to dock in Southampton in a few days. It was pointless to write as he was hoping he could get off the boat and see them, but writing calmed him and gave him time on his own.

Right now, he couldn't write because of his overwhelming anger towards the war. He should have listened to his parents. He could have gone to study at a university, maybe in America, and never had to have be near the war. Mac had four hours of rest and he finally dozed off for a few more before being awoken by some of the crew. He reported back to duty and spent the day on general tasks before arriving in Gibraltar that evening. They were only there for twenty-four hours and then were headed back to Southampton.

They took on two thousand five hundred passengers consisting of French refugees soldiers and air service men from Czechoslovakia and other countries. There were also French families boarding the ships and tensions were very high. Based on the fact they had limited space, they had to tell families to leave many of their possessions behind and Mac was asked to be at the frontline because he could speak basic French. Mac had just been spat at and accused of murdering a father when all hell broke loose and people tried to rush onto the ship. All of the sailors suddenly had their guns pointed at the families and it was the men from Czechoslovakia who calmed everything. Eventually with the ship over max capacity, they set sail for England. Mac felt sorry for the immigrants but at the same time he was trying to help them from certain death and they should see this.

He spent the next twenty-four hours in the ammunition chamber out of the everyone's way and then they eventually docked in Southampton. Mac was again asked to guide people off the boat. The tensions had calmed and some even offered their thanks.

Mac was half expecting that when the boat was empty they would send him on his way and that would be the end of the war for him. However this was not the case and the tannoy announced that all staff to be in their formal outfits by 1400. Again, Mac assumed this was to be an end of mission formality where the captain spoke to all of the crew on deck. Instead, they were informed a special guest was boarding the ship.

All men stood at attention and uniformed men walked on-board in unison followed by the prime minister himself. He was taller than Mac imagined and had an aura about him. He addressed the whole crew, congratulated them on their success, and the importance of the navy over the coming months. He walked around and met all of the sailors.

Mac waited patiently for his turn and then finally the Prime Minister approached him. He had a strong handshake. With his cigar in his non-dominant hand he shook Mac's hand and congratulated him on his service. Mac thought about smacking him in the head and saying killing French ships was a disgrace, but politely took the handshake.

CHAPTER 25

It was hard to believe of how much time had passed. The escape from Dunkirk was months ago and Eddie had now spent nearly a year in Kent. Eddie had actually grown fond of his squadron, deep down they were all good men. The RAF pilots and the mechanics were great and he enjoyed spending time with them.

Today he was heading into London to see a doctor to diagnose his wrist. It seemed fine and after the recent attacks on the Air Base, he felt he could do anything. He had taken the train back to Trevanston the night before to spend the evening with his family. He left in the morning after saying goodbye to Mugsy, his dear friend and with a sore head after spending the whole night drinking with Bill.

Spring was arriving in England and the sun glistened off the dew. Eddie enjoyed the train ride into London. He could see lambs bobbing in the countryside and farmers out in their fields. Eventually, London materialized through the engine's steam. He had passed through the city several times in the last few months but had not stopped. This time he clearly saw buildings on fire or collapsing. A fire grew in his belly and he was keen to get back out and fight, to punish those who had destroyed his beloved city.

For some reason the army insisted he had to see a doctor in London to give him the all clear. He was in a building outside of Marble Arch where he was in a waiting room with about thirty other men.

Eddie assumed they were all there for the same reason. The wait was excruciating, Eddie had tried to strike up conversation with a few in the room with the usual talk of football, but it was to no avail, so he sat there in silence. Finally, they called out "Hartley" and he went through a large solid oak door and was greeted by a nurse. Eddie instantly remembered Rose. He wondered where she was now and wished he had asked his sister that last night. The nurse took his vitals and then put him in a room.

The doctor then walked in and immediately got to the wrist, he removed the cast and carefully examined the wrist. Eddie had to do a series of tests including lifting up his arm and holding a wooden gun.

Eventually, the doctor cleared him. He was to report back to duty. Given Eddie had already completed the basic training and his original unit had disbanded because most of the men were dead or injured, he was to report to the Wembley army base as that was now the nearest to his home of Trevanston.

Eddie walked through London back to Euston station and was amazed at the damage London had endured. There were bricks and rubble all over the ground. Policemen were busy cleaning up the streets and yet there was a sense of normalcy returning. People were busy their daily business. Eddie noticed a lot more women than men in London and they all seemed to be working and supporting the effort. Eddie found the Army base and had to sit in another waiting room. Finally, a captain came in and Eddie saluted him. "I'm Captain Bond. You must be the brave one from Trevanston, right?" The captain spoke again, "Wait, I actually know you as well. You play football, right?" he continued.

"Yes, sir," Eddie replied.

"Welcome to the Royal Fusiliers, son. We're a good squadron, good lads. We already did a tour in France but we are heading out to Africa tomorrow. We're experts in going in to the battle early, think you can handle that?"

Eddie nodded and was informed of all the details by the new Captain, whom he instantly liked. He seemed to be an expert in war and had the scars to prove it. Plus, he loved football. The Captain had said to report back tomorrow morning, which meant he had the evening off. Given how near Eddie was, he decided after the briefing to head to Penny's factory on the off chance that she was there. Eddie liked Penny and had been fond of her ever since his mate Mac had started dating her. She wasn't like other girls and could hold her own; besides, she was good for Mac. Eddie walked in the front door, which was as he remembered a retail shop for furniture. He had been there several times before with Mac.

He was not sure where to go or what to do next, so he just followed the alleyway that led to the back and followed the noise. The noise became deafening and he walked in to see over one hundred women on a factory line moving metal objects and welding things together.

Eddie stood still and took it all in. It was really impressive. Suddenly, he heard his name being screamed and from the far side of the room, he saw a small figure dashing towards him. It was Penny! "What on earth are you doing here?" She hugged him and Eddie told her of his story.

Eddie went upstairs and met Owain. He vaguely remembered him from once before but he seemed to be a great guy. Penny grabbed her coat and they went to a local bar. Penny told him that she often came here to take a break. Eddie loved it especially the home cooked food. By the time they had finished chatting, the sun was setting. They had spoken for hours on what they had both endured.

Eddie was amazed at her operation and was sure she was part of the reason why the Air Base he'd been on was fully loaded. Eddie had gone through his experiences and Penny wept as he described that trip back from Dunkirk because she knew some of the players from when she watched the team while supporting Mac.

They also spoke about Mac and Rose and Penny could see a glint in Eddie's eye when he asked about her. Eddie was going to go home but the sirens went off and so he ended up sleeping with Penny underground. He was so glad he had gone and found her and spent time with her today

CHAPTER 26

The U-boats had been causing all kinds of problems and headaches for the British Navy. They had a way of creeping up on boats and sinking them with devastating effects. Mac and all of the men on his boat were well aware of the stories of whole ships being sunk with the crew mostly perishing.

The most notorious of all of these U-boats was the Bismarck. Mac was on a boat that was believed to have seen the Bismarck and was now hunting it down. The captain had been ordered to get this boat at all costs as it would be a huge morale boast for the country. Mac wasn't so happy about this plan as he felt they were hunting a ghost. In his opinion it was like fighting in a boxing ring while you are blindfolded and your opponent isn't.

Mac's ship was up in Scandinavia and it was a beautiful day. Mac was on the deck with the gun crew watching the pine trees. The landscape was breathtaking. Birds of prey swooped silently around the trees, there was an elegance to how they hunted, and Mac again thought of Bismarck. For all the hatred he had towards the enemy, Mac couldn't help but respect this boat.

There were men all over the deck with binoculars trying to spy the Bismarck and suddenly on the port side, someone spotted a U-boat breaking the surface. It was about a mile away on their left. It was amazing how quickly the communication reached all levels of the ship and almost instantly the ship maneuvered and started firing all its weapons guns. Mac heaved a shell into the gun and saw it fly out and hit the water next to the submarine. "I think we got him," Herbie shouted at Mac, but they couldn't see. There was no explosion and they looked out for the next five minutes but it was not reemerging. There were raw, unrestrained emotions going on around the ship as the day passed. Some of the men were angry that they failed to sink the ship. Some people had low morale, thinking they let Britain down. Others just didn't like the pressure of hunting the Bismarck. There was certainly a feeling that the whole of Britain was watching everything they did.

Emotions changed about 2200 that evening when a British aircraft carrier had spotted the Bismarck again. It seemed to be heading towards Brest, France. That made sense to Mac. He knew from his studying that Brest was where U-boats were repaired. The captain had ordered the gun nests to be fully stocked for war, so Mac was busy running up and down on the deck with a trolley of ammunitions. Mac wanted to be on the deck so badly and watch the battle but instead he had to make do with a small circular window from the ammunition depot. For someone who hated the war, he found himself excited with the battle.

He could see an aircraft carrier and then he looked out of the window and saw the Spitfire planes flying low overhead and the guns firing. The pitch-black sky lit up with bullet arcs. He imagined that if dragons had existed, it would have been a similar scene.

Suddenly, Mac saw what they were firing at. The Bismarck was there in the ocean and seemed to be struggling. Mac could tell instantly that the ship's rudder was broken, based on how it was maneuvering. From what Mac could see it seemed to go under again. Maybe it was capable of getting to Brest, which was less than 20 miles away.

The ship jolted twice and alarms went off. They'd been hit. Mac could do nothing apart from load the guns in the middle of ship and also load the trollies when needed. Several of the shelves around him fell and he was desperately trying to clean things up when he was knocked off his feet as the ship jolted again. *Wow* Mac thought *we really are under attack*. He had a small cut on his head from the shelves crashing onto him but he was ok and he hoped the ship was ok, too. The planes were flying in low and firing down again now on two German ships. Again, Mac saw the dark sky light up with flames.

There was an explosion to the left and Mac looked out. The aircraft did another run and a Spitfire went down but a German ship was clearly hit and smoke poured through the skies. There was a knock on the door. Mac opened it and loaded a trolley. "How's it going," he asked? "We got two of the buggas and the Bismarck is out there," a man responded.

Mac went back to the window and screamed as he saw the Bismarck turning, he could see it under the water like what he imagined a humpback whale would look like under water. Luckily, others had seen it as well and Mac's ship just let loose on the Bismarck. . Within a couple of minutes, flames lit up the sky and the Bismarck was hit well and it started to sink.

Mac suddenly felt sadness as he knew most of the men on the ship were going to die they were probably the same age as him. It could have easily been him. *War was unforgiving* he thought. The sirens continued for a while and when they eventually stopped. Mac was desperate to get out of the confined space so he dashed up to the deck. There was chaos around him and a mixture of emotions. The front of the ship had been hit fairly badly from what he could tell and smoke rose from one corner. There was a doctor running around to the injured men, but there was also a lot of cheering. They had sunk the Bismarck.

Mac walked around and noticed a man being covered up with a sheet. He looked underneath and it was Jezza. Mac stood frozen, seeing his good friend dead in front of him. Herbie walked up and put his arm around him. Apparently, an explosion had hit Jezza. Mac knelt down and said his goodbye to his friend. He went back to the dormitory and tried to sleep but couldn't. His good friend had died and he was traumatized with what he had seen.

About thirty hours later, their ship headed back to Southampton for repairs. Their fuel tank was damaged and they hobbled into the port. They arrived at the dock with a crowd cheering and wildly celebrating. All the men waved on the deck and there was lots of hugging and smiles. Mac fell into the moment and it felt like the cup final win the year before. He felt guilty cheering and celebrating after his friend had just died, but human emotions lean towards good. The press jumped on and took pictures of the whole crew. It was a strange feeling for Mac but he loved every moment.

Several days later, Rose was doing her rounds and happened to stumble across a newspaper, the headline read "Bismarck Sunk" and there staring at her was Mac! When Penny arrived in the factory that morning Owain had thrown the newspaper at her, "Seems your boy is doing ok," he winked at her. Penny had a huge proud smile on her face.

CHAPTER 27

Most people in England had been overwhelmed with the war. It had been going on for over a year now and with the Dunkirk evacuations and the Battle of Britain, the feeling was that they were losing. Hitler's speeches and actions had dominated British news and propaganda. Now Italy had joined forces with Germany and were now heavily involved in this war. Mussolini had focused Italy's arrival in the war with operations in Northern Africa. British and Commonwealth troops had already been engaged with battles against Italian forces. Mac and his boat were about to ship hundreds of British troops to Egypt to stop the Italian forces from entering there.

Mac had had a week off to see family and Penny but was now back in the full swing of Navy life. Mac's captain told the whole crew about this mission and they were now preparing the ship for the troops to arrive. At the dock, Mac and his team were also equipping the ship with as much of an arsenal as possible. His leader had informed him separately that the Suez Canal was of strategic importance for the British in the war and they were therefore to expect hostile activities.

Mac was busy loading ammunitions, weapons, and anything else. It was the first week of June and he was sweating immensely from carrying everything. One thing he could say about the war was that in the last few months his body had transformed itself. He had lost weight and gained muscle; his stomach was now like a washboard. Penny had been impressed when she had seen him last week.

Eddie instantly liked his new unit. He had arrived in the morning and saw his new unit starting out on a jog. They jogged around Wembley stadium, which was surreal for Eddie. He had dreamed since he was young to play football there. Captain Bond jogged next to him and Eddie noticed more scars on his face than the day before. "We have a tight unit here, we train harder than most, we stick together and we get the job done," was all Bond said.

Once he returned to the base, the unit showered. Eddie left the shower to find all of his clothes had disappeared. Another transfer named Aiden Doyle was also missing his clothes. Aiden had been a great laugh and really supportive to Eddie. He had moved from Cork to England two years ago just before the war and he had also escaped Dunkirk. He had been stretchered out with two broken legs, recovered and had joined Captain Bond several days before Eddie. This unit lead by Captain Bond had lost many men in Dunkirk and so had needed recruits. Aiden had bright red hair and freckles, the typical Irish appearance.. He was a stocky five foot seven and was a little overweight. The rest of the unit was laughing. "Newbies!" shouted Ben Paxman, one of the men. "It's initiation time. All new recruits have to sing a song to the unit or have their body shaved!"

Aiden instantly piped up with the Irish national anthem and his clothes were thrown back at him. They booed and chanted at him to sing "God Save the King". He smiled and quickly put on his uniform. Eddie was taken aback by all this but also had a smirk on his face. There was no way another man was coming at him with a razor and so he needed to sing. But at that moment he couldn't think of a song apart from one that his niece had sang to him the other week. Eddie started to sing, "I'm a Little Teapot." They told him to sing louder.

"I'M A LITTLE TEAPOT, SHORT AND STOUT, HERE IS MY HANDLE AND HERE IS MY SPROUT," Eddie shouted. "That'll do sunshine," Aiden shouted and Ben threw his uniform back to Eddie. For his "fearlessness", Eddie was instantly accepted. By the time he had boarded the truck to head to the south coast, he had a new nickname: Teapot!

The journey down to the docks took several hours and Captain Bond had snuck on several large bottles of whiskey for his men. By the time they boarded the ship, they were all singing. There were other units on the boat and all of the Sailors all looked to Fusiliers. They were put in a hold and told that they were headed to Cairo. The trip would take five days and nights. Just as the ship was about to set sail, there were rumblings around all of the units to head to the deck and Eddie duly followed the other men. They all crammed onto the deck and someone shouted, "There she is." Eddie squeezed his way to the edge and saw a stage set up.

Mac was on Herbie's gun and could clearly see the stage. Out walked Sarah Sharples to the loud cheers and wolf whistles from all the men. Mac couldn't believe that she was here singing to them. Sarah Sharples was one of the most famous celebrities Britain had and every military man loved her. She was the voice of the nation. She started singing and the cheers were deafening. As the ship cleared the port and the men headed back to the hold they were all still singing. This day had been great, Eddie thought and the men played cards and drank all night.

Mac tried to avoid the deck during the day and stayed in the ammunition hold as long as he could. He didn't want to be around a bunch of over excited squaddies. But on day three of the trip, Herbie came down to the hold and told him that there were some boxing matches and plenty of bets going on. Mac thought this would be fun.

As he climbed up, he looked down and saw that a make shift ring had been created and bets were going round. The next fight was to be with someone from Wembley called "Teapot" and someone from Newcastle called "The Northern Nail." Mac thought of Penny when Wembley was mentioned. He looked down and could not believe what he saw. His best friend Eddie was walking into the ring ready to fight. *No way* he thought. But it was Eddie.

Mac dashed down and pushed his way to the front of the ring. Mac got there just as the bell rang. Eddie circled the ring, looking confident until his opponent smashed him square in the face. Eddie continued to get pounded in both the gut and the head but he stayed on his feet. Mac could hardly watch. Eddie ducked a punch and then moved in quickly to land an upper cut on his opponent who quickly fell to the floor. There were loud cheers around the boat and Eddie was hoisted onto the shoulders of others. Money and cigarettes were exchanging hands all around Mac. He tried to shout to Eddie but was blocked out by the noise of the cheering men.

He had boxed with his brothers for years so was confident in his ability but this was still a real high. He was on the shoulders of Aiden and others looking around, out of the corner of his eye, he saw Mac. "Put me down, put me down," Eddie said. He pushed his way through the crowd and jumped on Mac. "What the hell!" Men all around were confused. Was this another fight? Mac and Eddie hugged for what seemed like ages. Eddie shouted to all the men around him, "This is my best friend from home!" All the sailors and army men cheered. They knew what they saw was rare.

Mac showed Eddie around the ship and they spent the whole of the day chatting and catching up. Eddie introduced Mac to his unit and he drank with them, even though he was on duty. It was the most rebellious he'd probably ever been. The best moment for Mac was hearing that Eddie had seen Penny several days before. Mac wanted to cry but couldn't in front of his best friend. Eddie and Mac were thousands of miles away from England but they felt right at home as they docked.

Eddie went to find Mac before disembarking from the ship and they hugged one last time.

CHAPTER 28

Apart from the two weeks in Dunkirk, Eddie had never been abroad and when he stepped off the boat in Egypt he was glad he hadn't. It was so hot that by the time they had got to the base, his shirt was drenched in sweat and all he could see was sand. He had sand in his eyes, on his arms, legs, and everywhere else. He instantly hated this place; however, the chances were he'd be here for a long time.

All of Eddie's unit as well as the other units on the ship were joined by Australians and South Africans. It had been a football stadium and now had hundreds of tents as well as a medical office, Command HQ, and the other facilities of a typical base. Eddie, Aiden, and Ben shared a tent and settled in for the next few hours. All of them drank water and Eddie didn't move from the tent. Even in the shade, the sun pounded down on them. There were no clouds to protect them and the base was very open.

As the sun went down the weather became cooler and they subsequently sat around a fire, chatting and drinking. Captain Bond came over to tell them that their unit was to be joined by a unit from Australia. They were to spearhead a military operation called "Operation Catapult". The Italian forces were based in Libya and were trying to attack Egypt. They were to hold the line until the bombers could provide air support and take out the Italians. They were to head out to the new location with a tank brigade tomorrow evening.

The next morning, they set out to the Libyan and Egyptian boarders. Captain Bond had explained to the men that they were outnumbered 3:1

but they had to capture and hold down this fort at all costs. Otherwise, the Italian forces would embark onto the port and that would mean the British would lose their supply route through the Suez Canal. The men travelled up in trucks before the tank brigade. The tanks would strategically place themselves around the fort, start the attack to the West of the fort and then the men would come in from the East and surround them.

This would give the Italians the impression there were more of them than was actually the case. Once Eddie and his unit were in from the East, the tanks would advance in and air support would finish off the job. There were jokes going round in the trucks but mostly from the Australians. Eddie was quiet and nervous.

He could tell that others in his unit were feeling the same, although they were always trained to put the serious face on during battles in war. For Eddie, this was going to be his first real action and even though he had expected it before, this time he knew he'd be facing real danger.

They arrived at their location and dug themselves in on the sand. It was mid afternoon and it was hot. They were waiting for the go and just sat there in silence. Eddie could see the fort up ahead. It looked like a palace in the desert and as the wind howled, it picked up and sprayed the fort with sand. It was about half a mile from where they were stationed and on the signal, they were to sprint to the fort and get in by any means. The distance was just half a mile but running through sand was going to make it feel longer and they'd be completely exposed.

The wait seemed forever and Eddie became more and more nervous as darkness fell and the silence grew. The sweat that had soaked his shirt sent shivers down his spine. He could hear the tanks rolling in on this fort and their loud guns ripped open the fort. Tanks from Italian forces fired back almost immediately and the only noise now was the sound of the tanks. Then, almost without warning, the Captain screamed "Go," and all the men jumped to their feet and ran as fast as they could towards the fort. Eddie was one of the fastest runners and was up ahead.

As Eddie started running, bullets whistled past his head. One Australian who was running next to Eddie was shot straight in the head. Eddie was sick at the sight but the adrenaline kept him running forward. They reached the wall and a back entrance. Some other Australians came up with explosives and blew open the doors. Slowly the men entered the fort and gunfire rained down. Aiden pulled Eddie to the ground and hid behind an old carriage. They realized they were under serious attack and could not move.

When the Italian with the machine gun stopped to reload, Aiden led Eddie into a small building. The machine gun started again and Eddie saw other men being mowed down. He realized the machine gun was coming from a building 200 yards to his left and he knew if they were to seize this fort, that gunman had to be stopped. Aiden had the same idea so they devised a plan. When he stopped to reload again, several others would provide cover and the two of them would sprint to the location and dispose of the gunman. Two minutes later the gunner stopped. Eddie and Aiden sprinted toward the location. They heard background gun cover but Eddie also saw several Italian men coming towards them. Aiden shot at and killed all of them. Eddie ran forward and dove into the machine gun nest.

He turned around to see an Italian man about to reload the machine gun, without thinking Eddie fired his gun and the man slumped over his gun. Eddie and Aiden used the machine gun to fire onto the other Italians and provided cover for their men who were now taking other positions in the fort. After an hour, there were loud rumblings from overhead and Eddie peered out of his little cubbyhole to see planes dropping bombs. The British tanks rolled in four hours later and the men had rounded up the Italian and Libyan soldiers as prisoners.

Eddie and his unit held the Italians at gunpoint and marched them back to their new base. Eddie was exhausted from the battle. He could barely see where he was but he walked silently back with the Italian soldiers standing next to him with their hands on their heads. They reached the base and there, Eddie realized what he had done. He was a killer. The thought of this made him physically sick and he dashed off to vomit. He had just killed several men in cold blood and he had not even hesitated. *They could've had families,* he thought. *Either them or me.* After several deep breathes, he regained his composure and re-joined the men.

There were a few cheers as they had taken the fort and the mission was successful. Aiden was sitting down near the medical tent and he walked over to see that Ben had an arm injury. "The git shot me in the arm," Ben said. Eddie was just relieved to see that Ben was ok.

The men stayed up all night. The whole night, Eddie kept seeing the image of the man he had shot hanging over the machine gun.

CHAPTER 29

Mac had felt a whole mix of emotions in the past couple of months. At one point, he'd been fascinated by human psychology and had read several of Freud's books. Now, he had to think that Freud and others in that field would be perplexed by him. He had gone from hating the war to feeling a sense of excitement with the battles, to the euphoria of seeing Eddie to feeling an overwhelming sadness and loneliness. Eddie had left the ship nearly several weeks ago and since then, Mac had felt lonely. He kept himself busy with daily tasks and such as cleaning the ammunitions but he kept thinking of Eddie, his parents, but most of all, Penny. He wondered everyday what they were doing and also wondered if he would ever see them again. He felt despair and fear. This war could be the end of him. Ships were being sunk all over the world and Mac and his crew could be next.

Right now, they were situated several miles off an Egyptian port. In the eyes of the enemy, they were there solely to strike fear into them. But, they'd been given specific instructions that the port was to be attacked and hopefully captured by Australian soldiers in the next few days. They were to provide air support with planes taking off from their aircraft carrier.

In its current state, the ship was vulnerable and the sailors were worried the enemy would strike soon. On three occasions, the alarms had gone off and they'd entered battle mode. Italian fighter planes shot at them but they only caused minimal damage. Mac's ship had actually shot down an Italian plane, which had crashed into the ocean.

Mac was on shift duty again. He started at midnight and he had slept a few hours during the day and was now just finishing his hundredth game of cards with some of the men before heading down to the ammunition depot to start his shift. As he walked down the long metal corridor, he noticed that there were several men at the door of the unit.

It was the Captain and he shook his hand and greeted him. The Captain waited until the other shift workers were in place. He explained that the Australians were to capture the port tonight at 0500. They were to ensure the guns were loaded at all times and would have to run under the cover of night. This was Mac's worst nightmare.

Mac waited patiently and frantically checked his clock every ten minutes until 0500. He checked the phone line to make sure it was working. 0500 came and went but nothing happened. Mac thought the operation had been called off but at 0540 the phone finally rang. The Op was a go. Gun One needed reloading soon after the mission had started and Mac's colleague Mike did the first run. Mike returned ten minutes later and as soon as he returned the phone rang again. Gun Six needed reloading. Mac grabbed the trolley of heavy mortars and sprinted out of the room towards the elevator to the deck. Gun Six was on the port side of the ship and Mac ran through to the gunner and automatically started to load all the mortars into the gun. When he was done he looked up to see the port in flames.

Mac was running back to the elevator when he clearly heard the sound of engine above him. There was a huge explosion at the front of the ship and it was covered in flames. Mac fell to the floor and saw a large bomber plane flying overhead.

He dashed to the front of the ship grabbing an extinguisher on the way. When he got there, over fifty men were already tackling the blaze. There wasn't much he could do to help. There was damage to the ship but nothing dramatic.

Mac returned to the ammunition unit and told the ten other men what had happened. It was obvious that the ship prioritized the fire since no more calls were made to reload the guns. At 0700, the phone rang again. "Understood," the Ammunitions Leader said before hanging up the phone. The ammunition leader was Gregory Thomas and he was a tiny man. At five foot four, he was built like an athlete. He was selected as a sprinter for the UK National team and had trained for the 1936 Olympics.

He gathered all the men including Mac in a huddle and relayed the message to them. "The ship is sinking. The hit has made the ship slowly gather water from the front. We are to immediately return to the UK. Hopefully, we will make it, but we are too heavy at the moment, so the Captain has asked us to dump all ammunition off the boat and then help dismantle the guns. Everything is getting dropped in the ocean." There were gasps around the room. Mac had a horrid feeling this was his last night. The journey to the UK would be several days at best. If they were slowly sinking, would they even make it? Even if they could make it for at least three days, they'd be sitting ducks during day, sitting in the ocean like a rubber duck in a bath. Mac didn't argue, however; he trusted the Captain and knew this was the best chance they had. The team got to work and each grabbed trolleys of weapons, ran to the deck and then proceeded to throw them overboard. After Mac emptied his first trolley, he saw some men dismantle one of the smaller guns and throw it into the ocean.

By daybreak, the ship looked more like a cruise liner than a warship. Most of the kitchen, including the ovens had also been thrown into the ocean. They'd even thrown chairs and tables. All men were strategically placed in the hull of the ship to level the weight as well as be undercover, so no one would be exposed on the deck.

For five days the men ate nothing, sat in silence for the most part, and prayed that they'd make it. Every jolt, every stutter brought fear into their hearts. They were worried they'd sink. The battle signal went off several times and Mac heard gunfire near them twice. On the morning of the 6th day, there was a shout on the tannoy. They had finally made it to British waters.

Mac stepped onto the deck to see two tugboats pulling them in. The extent of the damage was clear; there was a hole on the starboard side of the boat the size of a small car. The front of the ship was almost under water. They arrived at the dock to huge relief.

CHAPTER 30

The good news about Mac's ship being hit meant that he had a week back home before he shipped off again from Liverpool. It was exactly what Mac needed so he could realign his mind and focus on the nicer things in life as opposed to the tragedy and misery he had endured the last few weeks. A week off was not a complete vacation. Mac had three days of leave before he had to return to the base for training. He therefore did not want to waste a single minute.

It was 0700 and Mac ran off the boat with his belongings with him. Herbie and another sailor named Teddy had all been assigned to the same boat. Mac was still struggling with Jezza's death but support from others like Herbie had been invaluable.

The three of them caught the train from Southampton to London and said their goodbyes outside Waterloo station. Teddy went with Mac to Euston. Mac contemplated going back to Trevanston but decided last minute to get off the train at Wembley and walked round to the factory. As he walked down the street, he noticed where the bombs had struck and the damaged buildings. There were men mending the roof of several terrace houses that waved at him. Mac had forgotten he still had his Navy uniform. There was a universal appreciation for everyone fighting.

Mac knew the factory well but was surprised it had changed since the last time he had been there. He was surrounded by the loud metal screeching and pounding of machines. Mac was amazed by the many women working at the factory. They mostly ignored him as he walked by, several stopped to stare at him, but none questioned why he was there. He walked through the whole factory stopping several times to see the ammunition being made and then walked up the metal staircase to the offices.

"Oh my God," Penny screamed as she looked up from her desk and saw. She stumbled off her chair and almost tripped over her wooden desk as she dashed to the door and jumped on Mac. They kissed until Penny became too heavy for Mac to hold.

"Why are you here? How are you here?" she gasped. Mac explained how he had sailed down to Africa, saw Eddie, been shot at, and how the barely made it back to the dock. He was interrupted by Owain coming in. He thought he'd heard a familiar voice. He shook his hand vigorously and Mac repeated his story. Owain felt like he'd just seen the son he'd never had. On the front page of the paper sitting on his desk was a photo of Mac. It was around lunchtime and Mac planned to go for a walk with Penny before going back to see his parents that evening.

Owain insisted Penny take the day off and spend the day with him. Penny excused herself and Mac found himself with her dad. Mac was nervous but he'd hoped for this.

"You're like a second father to me" Mac started, mumbling. Owain listened intently but his face didn't move. "Being near death has cleared my mind. I've thought my future with Penny and with your permission sir, I would like to marry Penny." Mac was sweating. Owain stared at him and didn't say a thing. Eventually, he walked over and hugged Mac. Owain was not a hugger but felt this was the right thing to do. Besides, he'd love to call Mac his son.

Penny walked back in the room, eager for the walk and afternoon with him before Mac jumped on the train to Trevanston. After leaving Penny, he headed home. He walked the long way to his house and knocked on the door, it was the end of the school day so Mac wasn't sure if his parents would be home yet.

The door opened, his mum saw him, and burst into tears. They hugged for some time before his dad came to the door and shook his hand with the tightest grip possible. That feeling of love was what kept him going.

Mac enjoyed a great evening with his family and the next morning headed back to meet Penny. She kissed him at the station and said, "I have a plan for you today." Mac followed her onto a train that headed into central London. After a fifteen-minute train ride followed by a twenty-minute bus ride, they arrived at their destination.

Mac initially had no idea where they were, but soon realized they were outside the Victoria & Albert museum. It looked vastly different to what Mac had remembered when he last visited five years ago. It had a large hole in the roof, where smoke wafted through. They walked in and found that their feet were soaked. The staff had attempted to put the flames out to prevent the fire from damaging the artifacts but they'd caused flooding. The curator was excited to see guests and led a private tour for them. He explained how many of the artifacts had been moved to the British countryside, but there were still some fascinating collections.

After that, they walked around Chelsea and West London for the day. Finally they sat down in a café and had a nice bacon sandwich for dinner. They walked back to the bus hand in hand and returned to Wembley. Mac didn't want this moment to end and they kissed for hours.

The loud air raid sirens interrupted them unfortunately. Penny led Mac to the now familiar underground station and they sat there as the bombs came down. Penny fell asleep in Mac's arms and he felt extremely happy. The next morning he could not bear to go back to war. He wanted to run away with Penny and they actually joked about it. They heard the sound of the train and the steam came into view.

Mac got on the train and then had tears down his face as his head was out the window. Penny was bawling and blew him a kiss. "I love you and I'm going to marry you," he shouted, although he wasn't sure she'd heard him over the sound of the engine and equipment. While home, he grabbed his uniform, said his goodbyes to his parents, and headed up to Liverpool.

CHAPTER 31

It was Halloween and the crisp chill had hit Carshalton. Rose and Lil had been working for several months at the new hospital. Each day was new, dynamic, and challenging and yet they had quickly fallen into a typical routine. However, for tonight they'd got lucky, both of them had the night off. Rose had roped in Lil to help her with bobbing apples and chocolate for the children on the ward. She assured her seeing the smiles on their faces would be priceless.

Lil had then in-turn persuaded Rose to go out on the town. Rose had been working sixty to seventy hours a week recently and had wanted to go back to the dorm, write her family some letters, and sleep. However, she promised Lil they would go. Although Rose did not like to drink, she was determined to have a good time. The hospital warden had warned all nurses not to go out tonight or any time this week given the dangers of the airport constantly being targeted for bombing raids. That said, other nurses had been out this week and told Rose they would be fine.

Lil and Rose were getting ready in their quarters. Rose had a nice dress that she'd purchased in Watford with her first pay check. She'd borrowed red lipstick from another nurse and several other nurses had helped with her make up. One of the nurses wolf-whistled at them as they left. They had to sneak out the back exit and walk round the premises to a side alley.

It was bitterly cold outside and Rose could see her breath. They immediately realized there was problem with their plan —the buses were not running so they decided to walk the one and half miles to the centre of

Carshalton. They hoped the walk would warm them, but Rose was not so sure as a gust of wind hit her knees. Rose had not been to the town before. It was a clear evening and the stars were bright in the sky. Rose looked up and remembered that evening with Eddie in Trevanston and wondered about him. It had been a long time since she'd seen him.

She rarely saw Edith so she couldn't keep up with Eddie. She hoped he was ok and they'd see each other again. It was eerily silent, no cars, buses, people, or air raid sirens. They could hear every click of their heels.

When they got into the town centre, there were soldiers, sailors, and civilians. Despite being classified as part of London, Carshalton was on the outskirts of the city and therefore had the look and feel of its own small town. Rose made a note of a quaint park she passed that she should return to on her next day off. As they walked up the high street, they came across the Fisherman Arms, a large, popular pub. It was a white, curved building and seemed to have some life in it so they walked in. It was much larger on the inside and there were fifty people in it. Rose remembered the warden had issued an eleven o'clock curfew for all non-working staff. Rose checked her watch—it was ten to eight so they had a good few hours. Rose had never drunk alcohol before leaving Wales but since then was fast becoming an expert.

She decided to have a Gin and Tonic and Lil had a glass of white wine. They sat down in the corner of the pub and just started talking. The two of them had become best friends, chatting every day. They decided to talk about the other nurses and the doctors. Lil told Rose about a crush she had on one of the doctors. Rose agreed that he was attractive but given he had a reputation for being a selfish pig, Rose did not share the enthusiasm.

Just as they were finishing their third round of drinks, the air raid siren startled everyone. They all got up and started to evacuate. Rose was upset their night had to come to an end. Having not wanting to go out, she had found herself enjoying herself. They couldn't afford to miss the curfew. Therefore, instead of going to the nearest shelter, they both decided to walk briskly back up the country hill towards the hospital. When they stepped outside it was even colder than before and the alcohol was the only thing keeping them warm. They walked arm in arm to fend off the cold.

They had walked no less than ten minutes when they both heard the loud engines from planes overhead. The planes were camouflaged by the night sky. Suddenly, less than a half mile ahead of them, a bomb detonated and leveled the trees. They were alone on this road right in the middle of a bombing run. Rose panicked. *What are we going to do? Should we run to the hospital and risk it? Can we even make it back to town? Either way, we're sitting ducks,* she thought.

From the darkness they heard a voice, "You idiots! Get in here!" They looked around and saw an old man at the front of his house screaming at them. They ran towards him. "What are you doing out, can't you see the bombings!?" Lil explained that the two of them were nurses heading to the hospital. "It doesn't matter if you're nurses! It's far too dangerous for you to go up there now. Let me phone the hospital and tell them you're safe with me," the man said. Rose was grateful for the old man but feared the reprimand they'd get from the warden. The man sensed Rose's discomfort and said "Young lady, don't worry. I worked at that hospital for twenty years. I'll make sure you're ok and you can go up at day break."

Rose was calmer. With that, the old man hobbled to the phone and phoned the hospital telling them he had both Rose and Lil. He instructed them into his basement where he offered them cakes and a cup of tea. Rose did not realize how hungry she was until she ate three cakes.

The three of them spent the whole evening down there. The old man introduced himself as John Wessex or Dr. Wessex as he was formally known. He was a widower, his wife having passed three years ago. He'd also fought in the First World War. He was a retired surgeon and went into details of how he had created procedures that they both knew today. Both were fascinated by him. John was now a frail old man and the struggle in his face was obvious. He was obviously in pain and he winced every time he got up. His breaths were labored and shallow. At some point, he struggled to get the kettle so Rose told him to sit while she fixed the next cups.

He had a son but he now lived in northern England near Newcastle. They rarely saw each other. He had three grandchildren, but had not seen them in several years. The corner of his right eye teared up when he mentioned this.

John eventually fell asleep and Lil placed a blanket on him as he gently snored. Rose grew very fond of him and when daybreak arrived, she promised to come back and visit him on her next shift. They walked back to the hospital and crashed on their beds at about seven o'clock.

True to their words, Rose and Lil started to visit John every opportunity possible. He was a true gentleman and constantly made cakes for them. It was obvious to anyone that he loved their company. Rose wondered if it weren't for the war, would she have ever met Dr. Wessex?

CHAPTER 32

Eddie had now been in North Africa for what seemed like forever and he despised the place. He was sure he had lost weight through the sweating and every time he sat down he brushed all the sand off himself. One time he removed his boots and poured enough sand to build a sandcastle.

Since the attack on that first fort, Eddie's unit had been involved in battles for two other forts. Every time his unit had gone in first under the protection of gun and mortar fire from tanks. Eddie had personally shot four men dead and killed another in hand-to-hand combat. He knocked the Italian unconscious, breaking his jaw, and stabbing him with a bayonet. Eddie's unit joked that after the first kill you become numb to it and that was exactly what had happened to Eddie. He didn't see the faces of his kills, didn't wake up with sweats, he simply got on with it.

His unit had now formally combined with the Australians who also had a reputation for being elite soldiers. His unit had been nicknamed "The Desert Rats" and so far they had satisfied every goal set with minimal injuries. Eddie had a cut on his arm and blisters on his feet but he was in more pain from the wind pilling sand into his face. For the past few days they had camped out in a base they'd taken over. It had been a nice relief for Eddie. He was inside a little concrete building and out of the sun. He was on watch duty with two Australians, Shane and Clarence. They were to keep watch in case any Italians came over the dunes to attack but in three days the only thing they had seen was a local with three camels. The three of them took shifts to keep watch and the other two slept or relaxed a bit. There had been some banter of course. Eddie had called them both criminals and they in turn called him a stuck up Pomme. The next day, they were to leave that post and march down to a port called Tobruk. This was a strategic port that helped supply the whole British operation. They had been due to head out and attack this port three days before but a sandstorm had prevented this.

Morning arrived and they marched mostly in silence led by Captain Bond. When they were about a thousand feet from the city walls, the Australians cut the barbed-wire to get them through safely. They then dug trenches and waited. It was early in the morning and when the sun rose they found themselves under attack from several machine gun posts. Captain Bond had told them to remain down and not to fire back. The Italians had the higher ground so Bond wanted to limit the unit's exposure. They waited behind cover until they heard the rumbling of an aircraft. The British plane swooped in and dropped all off its bombs on the city. Eddie didn't look up but heard loud explosions and the screams of the injured carried by the wind.

The radio controller listened carefully for when the aircraft had made its final approach on the port. There had been other explosions as well. Eddie guessed they were coming from the British Navy outside the port. The radio controller confirmed that they should no longer be under enemy fire. Captain Bond took out his binoculars to further assess. The coast was clear so they continued to march. Eddie rose and ran in unison with his men. He was fully expecting another bloody battle but by the time he got to the city there were white flags all over.

Captain Bond ordered that no prisoner was to be hurt so Eddie, Aiden, and Ben rounded the men into the middle of the port. The Italian men looked tired, hungry, and defeated. Eddie felt sorry for them.

By the time the sun had fully broken on the port, the whole town had been captured and other British units along with the Australians and South Africans had been celebrating in the streets. None of the units had a Union Jack and so Eddie, with Captain Bond's approval, allowed the Australians to raise a flag. They had after all been part of the battle. Some of the men drank whiskey but Eddie, Aiden, Ben, Clarence, and Shane all just drank water from a local fountain. Feeling emboldened by his comrades' celebrations, Clarence jumped in the fountain and they all followed. Later that day, Captain Bond rounded up his men. "Great execution boys. We're four for four here in Africa. Good work. Keep it up." "Hoorah," the men shouted.

They broke out in their regiment chant, followed by "God Save the King." They'd now been ordered to board one of the Naval ships at the dock. "We're heading to Greece," Bond said. The war had now affected those islands and because of their regiment's sterling reputation, they'd be leading the British front. The only thing Eddie knew about Greece was that it was part of Europe.

Most of the Australian men were to stay behind. They all shook hands and said their goodbyes. Clarence was the only one to join them due of his skills with explosives. Eddie looked out at the African sunset one final time as the ship set sail. That night he could clearly see the stars and he slept alone on the deck thinking of Trevanston and of that night with Penny, Mac, and, of course, Rose.

CHAPTER 33

Ever since Halloween, Lil and Rose had tried to visit John on every occasion possible. They had tried to swap shifts as best they could so they could visit him together and had been to see him at least twice a week. Both Rose and Lil adored him. He had an old man's humour. He moaned and complained about everyone and everything, not caring a dot what others thought. Rose and Lil often found themselves laughing out loud. John had loved their company as well since he had been very lonely for a long time now.

Another advantage of their visits was that Rose and Lil would bake cupcakes. John somehow had an infinite supply of flour and sugar, despite the rations and his next-door neighbour had chickens so he always had eggs. "I hope you are better nurses than cooks," John had joked on several occasions. John hadn't just been a doctor at the hospital—he had been THE doctor. After the First World War, he'd been one of the top pediatricians in the country. He had worked out of both Harley St and the hospital in Carshalton when it opened. He'd even been the doctor who oversaw the birth of the royal children. He had agreed with Rose that children's care was the better career path. "They are nicer than adults and don't think they know it all," he constantly reminded Lil.

That morning they'd gone down to see John in the early morning and they had left his house by 8 o'clock. It had been a shorter visit than normal and the reason was that today the hospital was to have a very special guest. John was also to join them and he had shooed them out so he could get ready in peace. They both dashed off up the hill and got back to their quarters by a quarter past eight. There was a queue for the baths today so they waited nearly thirty minutes to get a bathtub and even then, had very little time or water to fully bathe. There was also a queue for the laundry area and nurses were even pushing each other to ensure their uniforms were pressed and presentable.

Rose had a shift starting at noon and so was unsure if she was even going to meet the special guest, but wanted to look her best just in case. She started her rounds at twelve on the dot and there had been no sign of the guest. Lil and the others who were not on shift were to wait until called and then meet outside. Rose had completed her rounds by one o'clock and looked out the window to see people gathering. She was going to miss the opportunity to meet the guest.

Disappointed, she decided to continue with her tasks and went to administer the medicine to the children. There were several kids that were very ill so she spent extra time with all of them and spent time talking about football or at least pretending to listen. Rose knew that Preston North End was one of the top teams but wasn't sure who else was and had no clue about football. However, it kept the children happy.

At about 1.30pm, the ward matron came running down the ward and informed everyone to stand in line, as the special guest was soon to arrive. Rose was beyond excited that she was going to actually meet the guest and about a minute later she saw a large group of men walking down towards them and several flashes from the camera. Then she heard the clicking of the cane and saw the prime minister walking towards her. Everyone was staring at him. He stopped by to check in on several children. The kids were fascinated by him. Finally, he approached Rose and the other nurses and he shook all of their hands. They all bowed to him and he stopped to talk with them all. When he got to Rose, he asked for her name and she replied.

"You are not from around here," he bellowed to her. Nervously Rose replied that she was from Wales originally.

"I love Wales, great walks there," he again bellowed and then he joked about how much the Welsh loved their rugby. Before Rose could even take in what was happening, the photographer who accompanied the prime minister suggested a photo of the two of them. Without even moving, he put his huge arm around Rose and they both smiled. Rose was beaming while the prime minister faked a smile to perfection—he knew a propaganda opportunity when he had a chance. With that finished, he carried on down the hall and eventually turned out of the ward. The matron ordered all the nurses back to work and Rose had such a long and exhausting day that by the time she hit her bed later that night she had nearly forgotten what had happened. Lil jumped on her bed "So did you meet him". Rose told her she had. Lil was super jealous as she'd barely even shaken his hand.

The next day they went back to visit John and he had a smirk on his face as he opened the door. "Here was me thinking I was the only famous surgeon and celebrity in this group and then I see this." he said and winked at Rose before handing her the daily paper. She could not believe it but there on the front page were two pictures: one of John and the prime minister, and the other of a smiling Rose with him. Despite the smile, she looked petrified in the photo and they all laughed at her.

CHAPTER 34

Mac arrived to see Liverpool in smoke. He'd now seen several times the damage that London had endured but until now he'd only read in the newspapers that other cities had also been hit but now as he left the train, he deduced the amount of damage from the nimbus of smoke. There was rubble and partly destroyed buildings as soon as he left the station.

Mac had been to Liverpool a few times but was still green. He strolled down to the docks by asking locals for directions. There were many men in Navy uniforms and Mac simply followed them. Eventually, he made it to the Mersey docks and in front of him were four docked ships. Mac was looking around when he bumped into someone. "Sorry," he said but as he turned around, he realized it was Herbie. They hugged each other and started walking together down the dock until they eventually found their ship at the end.

They walked up the gangway and at the top there was a man with a pen and a clipboard. "Name," he asked each man before looking through the sheets of paper for their bunk and reporting assignment. Déjà vu—Herbie was on a gun and Mac was on ammunition. They got to bunk with each other and so they walked down the thin metallic corridors to the dorms. Each dorm housed about twelve men in six bunks so Mac and Herbie introduced themselves to the rest.

This was a larger battle ship; it housed more guns than most others but also was not an aircraft carrier so planes did not take off from there. Given the smell of paint and newly cut metal all around him, it was clear that this was a newer ship. The sheets on the dorms were clean and new. If he was going to be stuck on this ship, at least it'd be a clean one. Mac had to report the ammunition deck later that afternoon so he and Herbie toured the perimeter before their report. Every British ship had a similar layout with some variations. They found the mess hall, located Herbie's gun and all of the other guns in case they were switched to different positions.

They found the elevator down to the ammunition hold and they even found the quiet toilet. The first ship Mac was on had limited toilets and you were meant to do your business over the side of the ship. This was much better. Mac went to report to his ammunition unit in the afternoon. He was the first of twelve men to arrive and was greeted by the head of ammunitions, Lieutenant Matthew Kelly. Lieutenant Kelly was nice, friendly, down-to-earth, and looked about the same age as Mac. He was actually in his late twenties. He had blonde hair and baby-faced features. He reminded Mac of Eddie. Before this boat, he'd been on a ship that sank and he was rescued, so he was seen as an expert amongst all.

The rest of the men slowly arrived in the ammunition unit and the last to arrive was Teddy, who greeted Mac with a huge hug. He introduced everyone and that included two brand new recruits who had to do a push up challenge as part of their initiation. This had the team roaring with laughter and instantly there was a good spirit, much more than Mac had experienced on the other boats. Mac felt more and more at home and they hadn't even set sail yet. Lieutenant Kelly then explained the operation and it was essentially everyone help each other out. He said that he would give orders but only if he had to and the more they helped each other the better it was for all of them.

At 1700, all the men were escorted to the deck and stood on parade. The captain came to the front and with a microphone attached to the tannoy.

"Welcome onboard. I am Captain Baxter," the captain bellowed. He explained that their next mission was to travel to New York. It was a six-day journey and they were to be part of an escort for American supply ships returning home. Upon arrival, they were to refuel and escort supply ships back to the UK. The captain explained how crucial this was to the war effort. At the present moment, Britain was starving. He explained the risks of the Atlantic and the risks of running into a U-Boat were high; four ships in the past week had been hit. They were to be on alert at all times.

There were cheers from the men as they looked over the decks and watched as people waved them off. They all headed back to their respective units as the ship set sail into the sunset. Mac saw Herbie wink at him and shout "Here we go again." As they left the port the sirens were heard overhead and, in the distance, bombs were clearly heard being dropped over Liverpool.

They arrived about midnight in Belfast where they docked briefly to pick up supplies. Mac and his team loaded some weapons onto the ship in the meantime. It was a clear night so he looked up at the stars and started thinking of Penny and Eddie. Mac stayed up all night and with a few other men watched the sunrise as the ship set off towards America.

Insert chapter ten text here. Insert chapter ten text here. Insert chapter ten text here. Insert chapter ten text here. Insert chapter ten text here. Insert chapter ten text here. Insert chapter ten text here. Insert chapter ten text here. Insert chapter ten text here. Insert chapter ten text here. Insert chapter ten text here. Insert chapter ten text here. Insert chapter ten text here. Insert chapter ten text here. Insert chapter ten text here. Insert chapter ten text here.

CHAPTER 35

The ship had been sailing for less than twenty-four hours when the plans changed. The Americans were building up a naval fleet and needed British naval men to help train them; it would be a two-week period on an island called Hawaii. Mac had never heard of it. The ship was to now briefly dock in Canada and then head round the Artic Ocean before docking again in Seattle. From there, the whole crew would be flown to Hawaii while their ship stayed in Seattle. As opposed to a six-day trip, it was now a twenty-five day trip. Their arrival date in Hawaii would be December 1st and they would be back in Seattle with enough time to head back to England for Christmas.

The crossing through the Atlantic had been uneventful, but the trip round the Artic Ocean had been brutal in November. It was so cold the men could not even stay outside for more than a minute. Multiple men were stricken with frostbite and rumours ran riot around the ship after two men lost fingers from prolonged exposure to the cold.

Mac had been out on watch for a few hours and was still shivering an hour after being inside. The other problem was maneuvering around icebergs. There had been creaks and bangs constantly. Mac thought of the Titanic which had sunk thirty years earlier and he prayed they would not end up the same way. Eventually, they made it to Seattle and even though they had not fired one gun, the whole crew was excited to be docking in a safe town. They spent the night in downtown Seattle where the men were given the night off and mostly went to local bars.

The Americans loved the British accents and their company and were disappointed when they went back to the ship. The next morning snow had started to fall; it was early December after all and they reported to duty on the ship. They were taken via buses to the airstrip where the American planes were waiting. Mac had never seen a plane that big. *How in the world would that behemoth even take off?* To his surprise and pleasure, it did and nine hours later they landed in Hawaii. They had their own base with nearly three hundred British men.

"This is the life," Herbie said to Mac after a morning run along the beaches. They'd been in Hawaii several days now. This place was heaven. They woke up every morning, ran drills with the U.S. Navy and Mac had found himself in the best shape of his life. His day consisted of working on a US Navy ship training new recruits about the ammunition department. Every night since he'd arrived he spent in a bar with Herbie, Teddy, and even Lieutenant Kelly and the mood between the British men and their US counterparts had been positive. There was a feeling from the US men that they would never have to see combat and they would let the rest of the world attack each other.

The US men were in peak physical condition, full of energy, and passion, which was infectious to everyone. The US men had been willing to learn from the British but Mac found himself learning from them. Herbie and Mac stopped jogging on a beach and sat down, out of breath and sweating. He stared out at the sea and thought about excuses for him to stay here and away from the war.

"How do we get this gig full time?" He half joked with Herbie who completely agreed. Unfortunately he knew it was never going to happen. After half an hour of staring out and daydreaming, both men slowly walked back to the mess quarters so they could get breakfast and be ready for the day. Breakfast included fruit and local food like purple sweet potato that was sweet and delicious and nothing like anything Mac had ever eaten at home. He ate like a king since there were no rations and the portions were huge. After shaving and showering in lavish quarters, they dressed in their uniform and were ready for the day.

Mac and Herbie boarded a bus that would take them to the dock where they were to go train again. Ten minutes into the drive, the air raid sirens started blaring. This was apparently a typical Sunday routine. Teddy joked,

"These bloody Yanks don't understand Sunday is for rest and nursing hangovers." The whole bus laughed. But the sound of aircraft shut them up immediately. Before they realized what was going on, hundreds of planes were flying overhead and low.

There were loud explosions all around them and the bus veered off the road, crashed into a tree, and turned on its side. Mac was dazed; he had no idea what had happened, but suddenly Teddy was standing above him and screaming at him. Mac slowly grabbed his hand and was pulled to the top of the bus.

All around him he saw chaos. The bus was on fire at the front and smoke billowed from the engine. Mac quickly came to his senses and helped Teddy pull out Matthew Kelly and five more men. Together the men jumped off the bus and ran back towards the base. Their bus exploded and all of the men were thrown to the ground. Mac's ears were filled by a buzzing noise and he was dazed. He looked around and did a quick head count. There were only ten of them and suddenly realized that some of his comrades had just died in the bus explosion.

"We must go back and help the rest," Herbie yelled, but several men held him back.

"They're gone!" Lieutenant Kelly screamed. Mac felt like he was frozen in time but everything was still moving around him. He felt something wet on his head and after examining his scalp, his hand came back sticky with blood. *That will have to wait,* he thought.

Mac looked up and saw planes flying overhead. From where he stood, it looked like one of the tails had a Japanese flag. *Weird,* he thought. *Since when had the Japanese entered the war?* Lieutenant Kelly had taken charge of the remaining men. He was a natural leader and reminded Mac of Eddie more and more. He was checking all the men for any wounds and injuries. Most seemed fine and mostly although Mac noticed that a sailor had a huge gash in his leg.

"We need to get back to the base and take him to the medical infirmary. With these planes overhead, we need to be careful," Lieutenant Kelly said. They all jogged in unison carrying the man and ducking in between the trees and foliage for cover. It took them fifteen minutes to get back to the base and the men at the gate let them in. They all grabbed water and went to the infirmary. Loud explosions continued all around them and the base was fully under attack. Mac and his men were the only ones in the infirmary but the nurses knew that casualties would be coming in soon, so they tried to help the British men as quickly as they could. Mac put some gauze on his head and thanked the nurse. The group of ten left the infirmary together with the exception of the injured man and as they walked out American naval men began to pour in, Mac recognized one.

"What happened," he asked. "The God damn Japanese attacked us," was all he said as he walked inside. When they walked outside, the attack was still in full force. Mac and the men could see the damage. There were several ships on fire and one was sinking in front of their eyes. The USS Arizona, which they'd been on the day before, was covered in smoke and, even with the noise of the aircraft around them, Mac swore he could see sailors screaming and he thought he saw men jumping from the ship into the ocean. Several American military men sprinted past Mac and his crew.

"You fit and able," one screamed as they ran past. "We're loading the guns."

It didn't take Mac and the other Brits a second to join them in a full-on sprint across the naval base and toward the airstrip. The planes overhead kept coming and the now fifteen or so men were a clear target. One plane came in low and Mac ducked his head on instinct. A second later another plane made a dive and this time started firing towards them. They should have taken cover but adrenaline took over and all the men the US and the British kept on running. One American soldier was clipped on the shoulder by a stray bullet but it didn't hamper them.

They turned a corner and went past the quarters of the naval men and saw the airstrip being attacked. Multiple planes were on fire. To the left of the strip were three heavy-duty machine guns and they all seemed intact. The American who shouted at them before took the lead and ordered the men to split up in groups of three. Mac shouted at him, "Where is the ammunition held?" The man pointed at a hangar behind the guns, about three hundred feet in total.

Mac and Teddy took off toward the hanger and the others followed. They were used to ammunition runs like this .The hangar was locked. Mac didn't have time to look for a key. Therefore Mac hoped the door would open if he put some force into it. He ran at it and luckily it opened enough for him to squeeze in and then pull the door open from inside.

Like on the ships, the ammunition was well organized and Mac found the bullets for the three guns. He loaded as many belts of ammunition as he could over his shoulders and headed for the door. Others followed suit. Lieutenant Kelly and Mac worked in unison organizing the men for ammo runs timing them so when a plane had passed them, they sprinted with the munitions over them. Mac got to the first gun which the Americans were operating and dumped the bullets. He then headed to the second and did the same and returned to the ammunition area. As he ran back, another plane was coming in very low and Mac knew the plane had guns armed so he dived for the cover just as bullets sprayed the whole area.

After thirty minutes of constant loading of the guns, the planes seemed to disappear. The men that Mac had armed had actually shot a plane down and cheers briefly erupted. After Mac did his final run, he paused to take in the scene. There were flames, smoke, and the stench of death everywhere. Mac sat down for a moment, drank some water, and threw up.

Mac and the British men who were not gravely injured helped their American colleagues for the rest of the day, carrying the injured to the hospital, giving blood, putting out fires, and doing whatever else was needed. That night, the British were quickly flown back out to Seattle. Mac was exhausted.

The next day, he boarded the ship and caught a glimpse of an American newspaper headline. In big, bold font, the front page simply said, "Japan Attacks, America Enters the War." This was a global war now.

CHAPTER 36 -1942

Eddie's trip from Africa had not gone to plan and the men had been on the boat for what seemed like a lifetime. They'd left Egypt but soon turned around because of a mechanical failure. They had been told that it would be best if they didn't leave the ship, so they sat docked in Cairo for two days, sitting on the boat playing dice and cards. Eventually, they sailed up the Suez Canal, through the Mediterranean, and onto Palestine. The ship needed to refuel and so they were stuck for another week. The ship had become their base and even though they disembarked, there was very little for them to do at this port. Christmas was so different. Eddie and the men played cards, drank warm beer, and shared a loaf of bread and olives from the locals in Palestine. Eventually after what seemed an eternity, they set sail for Greece.

Eddie had never been much for geography so besides from learning where Greece actually was in the world, he also discovered that Greece had a mainland and as well as an archipelago. As they pulled into the docks, Eddie could see the beaches and thought to himself what a great place this would be for a vacation. Shame the Nazis were currently destroying it he thought. Eddie vaguely remembered learning about the Greeks at school but nothing in particular was recalled. *Didn't the Greeks rule the world for years and create the first Olympics? What did it matter,* he asked himself.

It was New Year's Day and Captain Bond had rounded his men up and explained the situation to them. Italy had essentially entered the war in the last year. The Brits were well aware of them based on their battles in Africa but now the Italians and Nazis had been knocking on Greece's door. Hitler knew that the ports of Greece were important as it gave the Italians and Germans access to the Mediterranean. It was clear that the endgame was to blockade the Allies' supply routes from Asia. Initially, the Greek army had refused help from the British but now had reconsidered the offer. Eddie's unit was chosen to provide support.

There were a number of British troops that had arrived or were arriving. The problem was that they had no set plan and the terrain was diverse and treacherous. As far as Captain Bond knew, his men were to head up the mountains and try to mount an attack against the Germans coming over the mountains. After that, there was the tank division that needed to be dealt with. After the ship finally docked, the men dashed off the boat. Eddie could not believe Mac wanted to be in the Navy; he had hated being confined into that floating metal coffin.

The Greek army was meant to take the lead and so they arrived several miles from Athens with orders to report at a base just outside the city. For three days, they stayed in a make shift base while plans were continually discussed between British and Greek leaders. The rough terrain and weather were brutal on the men and, even in January, the weather was intense. Captain Bond was quickly becoming frustrated, as there were no maps, bad roads, and poor infrastructure. They had no idea where they were going. Eventually, the unit discovered a route and marched for another three days to their new base.

It was hot and humid and the terrain was rough on the men's feet, Eddies were cut to shreds. He was exhausted, he had a headache from dehydration and his lips were bleeding because they were so dry. So the new base was a welcome relief. They spent several days at the new base recuperating. Despite being filled with Brits, Greeks, and even some Czechoslovakians, there were two things they all had in common: a dislike of the Italians and Germans, and a love of football.

Rumours spread that German and Italian troops were just round the corner, but then again there were rumours going around that they had retreated. The food supplies were low and the unit had to rely on cooking wild hares over a fire to ensure they were fed. After several days of this, Captain Bond rallied the troops together. "I'm sick and tired of the poor communication," he exclaimed. "British HQ told us to advance north and the Greeks are sitting around telling us to wait for the enemy to attack us here. I've made a decision, tomorrow, we are heading up the mountain and once we're over the other side, we are going to attack the advancing German forces."

The men cheered and they set off at dawn the next morning without the Greeks. After several hours of walking over rocky roads, they reached the bottom of Mount Atlas and almost immediately were under gunfire as they started to climb the mountain. This wasn't part of the plan and they had no idea where it was coming from. The unit took cover under rocks and randomly fired up at where the gunshots seemed to be coming from.

After an hour of bombardment, Captain Bond told them to fall back. They had passed a town earlier in the day and Captain Bond was keen to ensure the women and children of that town were protected as well as the army base they had left earlier in the day. They ran down the mountain as safely as they could and found themselves on farmland. There were only about one hundred men and they quickly realized they were out-numbered by two thousand German soldiers. What was worse was the rumblings of Panzer tanks coming down the road.

Eddie thought this was going to be his death and he briefly thought of his family and friends. He felt ashamed of such thoughts and quickly changed his focus to the job at hand. The squad spread out and started firing as the Germans came down the road. The battle became very fierce very quickly. Ben was shot in the shoulder but he kept fighting and as the time passed Eddie thought that they might actually survive this.

They had easily killed two hundred Germans and had blown up a German tank. However, the Germans kept coming. Eddie went to check on Ben and several other men. One man was dead and the other had his hand blown off. Eddie had no idea where the medic was so he tore his shirt off and wrapped a part of it round the man's arm. As he gave Ben some water, there was a hissing noise and Eddie realized he had been shot. Suddenly, there was a burning pain in his upper arm and he looked to his left to see blood all over him. Luckily, he was still able to hold a gun, so he ducked down and fired back.

Eddie crawled to safety and kept firing. Explosions and gunshots were going off everywhere and German tanks were on the horizon. The men kept going and were determined not to let these tanks down the hill. Eddie saw Captain Bond sprint up the mountain with Clarence and put explosives on the ground. Eddie and several men provided cover fire for them. Clarence hit the button and the tank went up in smoke. Rocks were loosened and fell all around them, hitting and stopping the tank. Through the gunfire, there were even a few cheers.

The battle continued for five hours Eddie and the majority of his men had held off the German advances, but most were injured now and all were exhausted. Night was setting in and every time the wind blew, Eddie felt excruciating pain from the bullet wound on top of his arm. All day the men had constantly moved and changed location to survive without advancing much on the mountain, but the Germans had not been passed. Eddie was standing next to a man and they were reloading when a mortar was fired at them from a tank. Eddie was sprayed with blood as his comrade was hit. He was dead and Eddie now had a burning sensation on his hip and realized he had a deep cut there.

He hobbled over to another cove in the mountain. Next to him was Aiden, who had blood pouring down his face as well as what appeared to be a bullet wound in his leg. "Great knowing you pal," was all he said, winking at him while the tank reloaded. They lit cigarettes and smoked for a few minutes while the rumbling of tanks drew nearer and nearer. *This was it,* Eddie thought. Their hiding place would be discovered any minute and they were toast as soon as the tank saw them.

Eddie closed his eyes and prayed. At that point though, he couldn't believe what he heard. The mechanical noises were overhead and when he opened his eyes, he saw several RAF planes swoop in and shoot down a bunch of Germans. After that, there were loud roars and Eddie saw, despite his weakened vision, the Greek army finally approaching. He knew they were going to make it, let out a big sigh of relief, and headed back up the mountain.

CHAPTER 37

For months, Penny had fallen into a routine. She would get up in the morning, bathe, walk through the destruction of London, get to the factory, work there for the day, and finally head to the underground station when the sirens went off. There she'd spend the evening, maybe sleep a little, head back to her flat when the all clear was sounded, and sleep there for a little before the next day. She would even warden the streets occasionally and get even less sleep. People fall into routines and so it had almost seemed weird to her that for the past two nights she and her dad had stayed late at the factory. She'd had dinner with her parents and spent the whole night at their house. There had been no sirens and no air raids. This was nice.

Everyone had ration cards and once a week, you picked up your rations. Penny was fortunate that her family had some money and so she occasionally bought additional food from a cafe. On this morning she passed a café that had a wonderful smell coming from inside. She inquired inside and found it was homemade vegetable soup with fresh bread. It reminded her of Eddie's family who had a bakery in Trevanston. She loved the fresh bread so she got out her purse and purchased a loaf and two mugs of soup. She walked through the streets of London careful not to spill any and walked into the factory, straight into her dad's office.

"I got you a treat," she shouted over the factory noise. She wore a broad smile for her dad. He jokingly chastised her, that she'd be better off spending her money on herself or others who needed it but gladly accepted the soup and for the next half hour, they enjoyed the makeshift breakfast. They were very close and so they discussed several things throughout the morning, but one topic that kept coming up was Mac.

Owain told Penny about his request for her hand in marriage and she had been gleaming since. Owain was not a wedding planner but enjoyed listening to Penny's plan, although he kept joking he would have to open more factories to pay for them. After their impromptu meeting, Owain left the office and headed out for the morning. Penny cracked on with the work. He returned later that afternoon and called Penny into his office. "Fancy a walk," he briefly said. Owain often wanted to walk outside for a brief half-hour; it helped him clear his head and gather his thoughts.

Penny often accompanied him and sometimes they chatted, sometimes they walked in silence. Today was one of those days where Owain wanted to walk and talk but he surprised Penny by asking her a question about Lorraine. "Your mum and I have been married 20 years." Penny had no idea where this had come from or where it was going. "With the war and the factory, I don't often show how much she means to me so I bought her something today," and he pulled out a box from his pocket. Inside it was a beautiful opal necklace. "Wow Dad, it's gorgeous," Penny stammered. He then reached in his pocket. "You also mean the world to me," and handed Penny another box. She stopped walking. In the box lay a matching opal necklace. Penny had tears in her eyes and she hugged her dad. They headed around the neighbourhood in silence. When they went back to the office, they worked for the rest of the afternoon but Penny was constantly smiling.

It was five o'clock and it was just still light outside. It was early February and cold outside, but it had been a mild week. Penny was just about done for the day and was heading home when the air raid siren blared. Typically, the warning meant they had thirty minutes until the bombs actually starting falling. Penny could go to the underground station near her apartment or the one near the factory.

She went to see if her dad was around and he was.

"I just phoned the house. Your mum said she would head down to the underground so let's go meet her." He picked up the opal necklace and walked out. They left the office and headed down the stairs. The staff had left already and so they turned the lights off and locked up. They walked out of the factory and headed down the back roads to the main high street.

Most of the houses were dark and there was a slow flutter of people all heading in silence to the underground. There was a real local feel and Penny nodded to several people she recognized. Just as they got to the top of the stairs for the underground, planes were heard overhead and a loud explosion dropped near by. Panic set in for everyone around them and suddenly everyone was rushing to get down the stairs and underground. Owain stood to one side and created order by carefully organizing the people. There was a loud scream from a woman near Penny and Owain. She worked in the factory. "What's wrong," Penny asked her.

"My daughter, I lost my daughter," the woman screamed. While hysterical, she explained that she thought her daughter was with her mother but the grandmother said she thought the granddaughter was with her. Owain remained calm and spoke clearly to the lady and asked where her house was. It was just down the road so Owain told Penny to go and meet Lorraine.

He would run to the house, pick up the kid, and head back. Penny stayed at the top of the stairs with the mum and saw Owain sprint down the road. A loud explosion happened near by and smoke started to rise. Owain found the address and kicked the door down. He told himself that it could be fixed later.

"Jane! Jane! Jane!" Owain shouted out. No response. He ran through the downstairs as another loud explosion rang out, this time closer than the first. Owain thought the house shook a little. He went upstairs and checked every room and still nothing. Owain was about to give up when he heard some movement under the bed. He looked down and saw a tiny girl in her school uniform—grey shorts, white shirt, and plimsolls.

"Hey, buddy," Owain said calmly. "You want to go and find your mum?" The girl was petrified and slowly nodded.

"Are you a Nazi," the little girl asked Owain. "No, I'm a friend of your mum. She works for me." With that, the girl put her arms around Owain and they headed out the house. The run back to the underground was short but the streets were now deserted and there were bombs dropping nearby. Jane started to cry with the loud bangs and Owain put his hand on her head, reassuring her while sprinting to the underground.

They reached the underground and started down the stairs when a loud explosion blew Owain off his feet and down the stairs. In an instance, Owain turned in mid-air so that the child would fall on him. He fell over thirty steps and he heard a loud crunch as he landed. The girl landed on him and then bricks fell all around them.

Owain was trapped. He was bleeding from his head and he could taste blood in his mouth. He felt stickiness on his shirt and was sure he was bleeding on his chest. The little girl was lying next to him. "Hey Jane," he gasped. Jane moved and Owain knew that was enough, that she was ok. Owain was in so much pain but tried as long as he could to keep his eyes open. Eventually though, he was forced to close them. *It'll be just a second, and then I'll be fine. Just a quick blink.*

Penny met her mum and they sat down on the platform. Penny was sure her dad was caught up with the human traffic and so they sat there and tried to relax. There was a loud explosion right above the underground and there were some noise down the platform as a few bricks fell in. Lorraine fell asleep on Penny and then Penny fell asleep, too.

They awoke at five o'clock the next morning as a bunch of people were walking past because the all clear had been given. They got up and went to find Owain. As they got to the entrance, there was a crowd of people all helping remove bricks and then Penny saw it. Little Jane was being carried out from the rubble. Penny's heart sank, she knew something was wrong. She pushed her way to the front, her small frame easily fitting in between the gawkers and onlookers in front. She broke down on the floor as she saw the image. A pile of bricks covered her dad. Penny scrambled to get the bricks free so that she could see his face. Men all around her were helping remove the bricks and as the final brick was removed there was an extremely loud howl. Lorraine had arrived on the scene and became hysterical. Owain mustered a breath and he slowly whispered to Penny as she knelt down next to him.

"I love you and your mum so much." His hand opened, revealing Lorraine's opal necklace. He drew one last breath and died. Penny and Lorraine were both in hysterics. Penny could not move and felt it was a dream—no, a nightmare. He was going to wake up soon. He didn't. Penny and Lorraine both laid next to him crying until a police officer had to drag them away.

"I'm sorry, but he's dead."

CHAPTER 38

Rose had gone down to see John on her own one morning. She and Lil had been on different shifts and it had been hard to co-ordinate for both of them to visit him together. Rose had picked up milk and the morning newspaper for him." Survived another week," he said with a wry grin. John was in a great mood as he slowly moved into the kitchen where he started to boil water for tea. It was before seven am and Rose had a shift starting at eight o'clock so she puttered around the kitchen, found some mugs, and made the tea. They sat down and went through the news together.

"London was hit hard last night," Rose mentioned to him and John nodded in agreement.

"Have you gotten to use penicillin yet," John asked her.

Rose had not and he therefore discussed how penicillin worked and that it would change the future of medicine. Rose was fascinated with his knowledge and how he kept up with it all. As she got up to leave, John did something he had never done for Rose before. His face was overcome with emotion. "I've loved spending time with you and Lil. Thank you," he whispered. Rose was shocked. He'd never spoken like that. He always had a dry wit and humour. "Are you ok," she asked.

"Yes, yes, of course. I just felt you needed to know I care about you. Now go to work and make sure you bring cakes tomorrow." With that Rose left and headed back to work.

Her day was a busy one. They had nearly one hundred kids in the hospital at the moment and not enough beds. Over twenty new kids had come in overnight from the blitz. Rose was one of only two nurses caring for all of them, so she tried to split her day equally.

However, she had spent a good three hours with an eight-year-old girl named Gemma who had severe burns on her back. Every time Rose tried to clean the wound the girl screamed in agony and it broke her heart.

Rose was meant to end her shift at six that evening but was doing her final rounds and it was already nearly eight. She'd even started reading bedtime stories to several kids whose parents were not around after fulfilling her medical duties. She had not eaten all day and went down to the cafeteria. The nights were still long and so it was dark outside as she walked there. She managed to buy some food which she devoured quickly on her way back to the nurse's quarters when the air raid siren went off.

The hospital had a large basement and all the nurses and staff were to evacuate there. Rose started to head down to the basement and bumped into several doctors she knew on the way. As they walked down the stairs, Rose noticed that the porters for the patients looked overwhelmed. The doctors noticed it as well and so they all ran to help transport the patients. It seemed like the whole hospital was in motion helping patients into cover and Rose kept running up the stairs to help bring the scared children down into safety. She was up in the ward and was helping a couple of kids down the stairs when suddenly she heard a humming noise. It became a loud explosion and suddenly there was glass everywhere. Instinctively Rose covered the kids and ducked down onto the stairs.

On the floor above them, bricks fell down everywhere. Rose calmed both of the children who were crying hysterically. Rose tried to get them to walk down the stairs but another explosion rocked the building. She was thrown off her feet as the stairs around her collapsed. Her face was cut and she realized they were trapped. She moved bricks out of the way to sit and pray.

After an hour the children had fallen asleep and Rose was starting to succumb to fatigue as well.

"Anyone out there?" *Where did that voice come from?*

"Here," Rose screamed.

"We're on the other side of the rubble. We'll get you out when we can," the voice said. This reassured Rose as she gradually fell asleep.

When she awoke there was loud clanging, like metal banging and scratching against rocks and Rose could see a hand. People were digging her out. She started to help from the other side and eventually grabbed a doctor's hand. He spoke to her, telling her that she would be free soon, just hang in there. Rose felt a huge relief. After a while, she squeezed through the debris, helped pull the children through, and they entered the basement.

She looked around and it was a total war scene. Nurses and doctors were helping patients and also helping each other. Everywhere she looked people were injured or being covered in white sheets. Rose aimlessly walked around. She felt like it was all a bad dream. "Rose." She looked around to see Lil standing ten feet away. Lil's face was bandaged heavily on one side. They hugged tightly, both quietly crying but grateful to have the other.

"Rose, the explosion knocked out all the glass in the nurse's quarters. I couldn't get out of the way," was all she could say. The glass had sprayed her face and she explained how she could now see through her right eye only. Rose wanted to cry and she did when she looked across the room to see the girl with the burns being covered. Rose had never seen a dead body of a child and didn't want to start now.

The all clear was given and people headed back up the stairs. It was morning and the sun shone down on the hospital. Rose walked round the grounds and noticed that the entire east wing had been destroyed. There were smoking buildings all around. Rose suddenly had a fear about John. She told Lil and they both dashed down the hill towards his house.

The front of the house had collapsed and bricks were everywhere. She hoped John made it into the basement. "John," they both screamed. He didn't answer, so they entered the house by climbing over bricks. Eventually Lil tapped Rose on the shoulder and she looked over and saw John's body on his sofa. Rose went and checked on him but he was cold and his eyes were rolled back. Rose and Lil just stood there and cried.

CHAPTER 39

Eddie awoke with sweat pouring down his face. He opened his eyes and it was pitch black. Fear struck as he didn't recognize his surroundings. He instinctively reached around to his side for his gun. It was there, unlocked and ready to fire. He realized he was on a bed and as his eyes adjusted to the surroundings, his vision opened up to the inside of a tent. He could now see the entrance and slowly he sat up. His head throbbed and his hip hurt. He looked around as he sat up and noticed there was someone else asleep next to him, Eddie pointed the gun at him. As his eyes further adjusted, he knew it was one of the men from his unit Daniel Thatcher. Eddie vaguely remembered the gunfight and he thought he had dragged Daniel into safety but it was all a blur. He made the decision to slowly step out of the tent, gun first. "Stop pointing that at me! You'll get us both killed!" The voice was familiar so Eddie's finger hesitated off the trigger. Aiden looked down at him and winked. It was the middle of the night and the ground was rough. Eddie thought he heard the ocean waves cracking against rocks and it was still remarkably hot.

As Eddie's eyes adjusted further, he could see there was a whole row of tents and Aiden explained that they had retreated to the sea front. Apparently, Eddie had been shot in the arm, cut his hip, but he and Aiden had carried four men back to the village before falling on his head and going out cold when the planes came.

That was twelve hours ago, which explained the headache. Eddie remembered the shot in his arm, and slowly examined the bandage; his hip actually hurt more but he had now officially been shot. At that point,

Captain Bond came over and shook Eddie's hand.

"Stern effort, son. You saved Daniel's life." Captain Bond then filled Eddie in on details of the mission and how the German forces had advanced with fierce strength over the mountains. The Brits had to retreat when the Greeks and the Air Force came in. Bond mentioned that they had lost multiple men and most had injuries, including himself and Aiden who both large gashes.

Bond went on to explain that in three hours, they would be shipping out to Crete and their unit will be based out there for the foreseeable future. Aiden offered him a cigarette and as Eddie smoked, Aiden filled him in on all the men. Aiden was on parole duty until dawn, and Eddie felt strong enough to join him. After several cigarettes and a whole ton of local chickpea-based food, they headed back to Bond who was talking to another Captain.

"Eddie Hartley, Aiden Doyle, my name is Major Wheaton. You two are both hero's as well as everyone from Captain Bond's unit. You were outnumbered five to one and you held the Nazis at bay for six hours. "

"Err, thanks" said Aiden. Major Wheaton then looped them in on the conversation he was having Captain Bond.

"Before we continue, all my men need to hear this," Captain Bond interrupted. Aiden and Eddie went through the tents, waking the men.

After about ten minutes, nearly all of the hundred men were gathered round. Most had bandages or visible wounds but not one man mentioned them. They all embraced each other and were just glad they were alive. Major Wheaton was a tall muscular man, Eddie suspected early forties and he had a dark beard. He was very assertive with the way he spoke, it was clear what he said was the law and Eddie found himself mesmerized by his every word.

Major Wheaton explained to all the men that tomorrow they would head home for a couple of weeks to recover. To refocus on their enemy and why they were fighting. Then they would meet at Folkstone in Kent and head out to the small island of Malta. They would train as elite soldiers and then head out to India under his company going forward. He only wanted the best British soldiers and they were it. Wheaton was in charge of protecting India, especially its borders with neighbouring countries like Burma. Now that Japan had entered the war, he was convinced they would move towards India to cut off the British supplies. Eddie was not really sure where India was, but had heard of it. He felt going there was a waste. Captain Bond's "Desert Rats", as they were now notoriously called, had battled in France before Eddie joined, then Africa, and now Greece.

Going to India to protect something that had not happened yet seemed crazy when they could be sent to the front line. Eddie was not the only one with these thoughts. The next day they shipped out on a six-day boat ride back home. The temperature in England was much colder. He felt the chill as soon as they landed in Dover but it was great to be home.

CHAPTER 40

Penny still couldn't believe what had happened. Four days had passed since her dad's fatal accident, she still expected him to walk in the office at any moment. Penny by default had taken charge of the factory and had to deal with the fact that sixteen of her staff were missing. Authorities presumed them dead and the rest just did not want to work.

The entrance to the canal from the factory had been damaged so she had men from the factory and some local school kids rebuilding the wall. Today, she had to travel to the war ministry and talk to the war cabinet about her factory's efforts and she was in way over her head. Owain would normally do all of this.

Her mum was inconsolable. She had been with Owain since they were sixteen and she had been little help. Penny had spoken several times to her uncle in Wales for advice, but she needed someone else, so her first executive decision had been to promote Albert Monk to help her run the company. Albert had worked at the factory for years and knew the ins and outs well, but he would also be respected by the war cabinet and the factory employees because he was a World War I survivor.

Penny and Albert walked into the war cabinet meeting room in silence. Albert hobbled in because of an old war injury. He looked every bit of sixty years old with grey hair and weary eyes. Penny had briefly spoken to him before about what to expect and he had seemed excited but they had no plan. Right now, this was the last thing she wanted to do. The image of her dad lying dead at the bottom of the subway still haunted her. She had mixed emotions from despair to anger. *Why were they still at war? Why didn't the government do more?* She knew deep down that the government and everyone in England was doing more but she was hurting.

The government ministers all shook Penny's and Albert's hand and expressed their deepest sympathy for Owain. They explained how Owain had been advising them on how to move forward and had helped transform over one hundred factories in the UK. Albert had no idea about this and seemed amazed. Penny just felt pride. The government still needed help making their factory as well as the others in London and the UK more operational.

At this point Albert chimed in, he had suggested ideas on how to work longer hours and he guaranteed the factory would be fully operational by next week. Penny admired his enthusiasm but at the same time rolled her eyes at him. *He was out of his depth.* However, Albert spoke for twenty minutes and cut Penny off every time she interjected. This went unnoticed by most but eventually one man acknowledged Penny.

There was a sense of gratitude from Penny. She was sure Albert hadn't meant to exclude her from his thoughts. He was treating her the way he'd always seen women be treated. Weren't women inferior and therefore, should be excluded whenever possible. She inhaled deeply and with tears in her eyes she said, " We have to increase the number of women in the factories and to do that, we have to make them proud of the war effort." Penny went on to explain that many women felt like her and were resentful of the war effort because they had lost loved ones. They need to do their part more with pride. Penny continued with ideas for posters, radio campaigns, and promised to help the government set this up.

She also spoke of the women in her factory, how she needed to make it a fun environment so she would set up counseling and support. Finally, she needed a team of builders to fix her factory and others in London. This was a project Albert could oversee.

The government officials took copious notes and agreed with everything Penny had said. Penny had fallen into her father's shoes perfectly and she hoped he was proud. She stared at a startled room of men, many of whom smoked their pipes and said nothing. She was clearly right but no one wanted to accept that. Eventually one man said "Right, let's get started."

With that, they agreed to have regular meetings with Penny. As they left the meeting, Albert stumbled on what to say but then apologized to Penny for his behavior and told her how much he admired her. "For 18 years old, you are a very unique breed. You are a running and advising the government on how to run factories. Your dad would be very proud." At that comment, Penny could not hold it in any longer and tears ran down her face.

She decided to walk back to the factory which was over eight miles away and Albert left her to head back on the train. He sensed she needed time alone and she was grateful for this. As Penny walked through London, she had tears in her eyes constantly and all she saw was despair. She walked past Buckingham Palace and there were fire fighters putting out a flame in the corner of the building. She walked along Oxford Street where the shops and theatres had been thriving less than a year before. Now nearly every building was rubble or damaged. The worst though was the smell of death. It was everywhere and even if you could not smell it, you could sense it.

Dead bodies were being hauled out of the rubble. Young children were desperately crying in the street and everywhere she went there were cloths covering the dead. What she had said to the ministry was true, but she was not sure she could handle this responsibility, as she could not guarantee that this war effort would seal victory. She stopped and sat down in St James' Park under a tree and thought of Mac. She missed him so much and needed him right now. She wrote him a letter and told him about Owain's death and cried until she could not shed another tear.

CHAPTER 41

Eddie was back on British soil for the first time in a while and it felt great. He had two weeks off to recover before being declared fit to go to Wheaton's unit in Malta and India. Eddie's unit all had the same time off, so they split up to see their family and friends.

Aiden had travelled to Liverpool, Captain Bond to Berkshire, and the others had gone to other locations. Being Australian Clarence had promised them that he was going to drink in every bar he could find in London, which they had all laughed at before departing.

Eddie was still recovering from injuries and given that the hospitals were brimming with injured men and women, he had been discharged very quickly. That was fine by him, and he headed straight to Trevanston.

He walked into the Kings Arms and was instantly given a hero's welcome. His brother jumped over the bar and hugged him. As a result of the age difference between them, they had never been that close growing up but now they were hugging like best friends. "So good to have you back brother, let's get you a beer."

Eddie knew everyone in Trevanston, or he liked to think so. But it was weird being back as there was a void in the town because so many of his friends were not there. Eddie spent the whole afternoon in the pub talking to parents of others on the football team or classmates. For the most part, everyone was glad to see him and continuously bought him beer while thanking him for his service. He found himself repeating his stories of Dunkirk, Africa, and the battles in Greece. However, there were a few who had a shown a little resentment because Eddie returned from war and their kids had not. Eddie understood that.

After a few hours in the pub, Eddie staggered to his mum's and sister's shops. Dorothy broke down in tears and wailed out loud seeing Eddie walk in. Catherine heard the noise from next door and also broke down when she saw him too. Eddie was a little drunk so this was very overwhelming, but he sat down in the kitchen at the back of the shops and his mum quickly rustled up some food. Then he heard scampering and opened the door to see Mugsy jump on him.

That night Eddie was with his whole family and for the first time ever, he really appreciated this. His mum, two sisters, two brothers, an aunt, and uncle all came over for dinner. It was a great time and, apart from sharing his stories, he had forgotten the war zone.

The next day happened to be a Saturday and Eddie had someone he really wanted to see. He got up and ran with Mugsy throughout the downs. He was still injured and therefore struggled to run due to his hip but he wanted to get out and see the Trevanston countryside. He had missed this—it felt so good being back. He headed round the streets of Trevanston to a street near the canal and walked up to the green door. He breathed and then knocked. Mac's parents answered the door. There was a moment of awkwardness as they had not been expecting Eddie and then the ice was broken when Roger said "Well stone me, Eddie nice to see you. come in"

Eddie had been worried about seeing them. He influenced Mac to sign up for the Navy and Mac's parents had always thought of Eddie as a bad influence. Rebecca boiled some water and made some tea. Mugsy quickly made himself comfortable in front of the fire. Another awkward moment passed and the conversation started about his story and why he was back in Trevanston. Eddie told them about randomly seeing Mac on the ship and his boxing match. That had been the last time he had seen Mac.

Mac's parents said they had received several letters and that he had recently been in the States. They told Eddie he was there when Pearl Harbor happened. Rebecca also broke the news of Penny's dad's death. She had written to them and informed them of the funeral.

Eddie's head was spinning with everything he heard and suddenly had a moment of fear, as he would never forgive himself if anything happened to Mac. Roger must have read Eddie's mind as he ended the conversation by saying "You guys would have had to have gone to war anyway. You are his best friend, so don't have any regrets for taking him to sign up". That meant more to Eddie than anything.

Eddie spent a few days in Trevanston and had recuperated well, so he decided to head down to London. He had been to Penny's factory only a couple of times but was able to find it. He walked up and gave Penny a big hug. She was shocked to see him and surprised at the hug. "I'm so sorry for your loss," was all he said. Penny was glad to see a friend. They sat down in the office and ate Digestive biscuits. Penny was glad to vent her frustrations and pain with Eddie. He was his typical self—a joker but at the same time, a thoughtful listener for his friends.

Penny had opened a bottle of whiskey and the two of them drank most of the bottle by the time they decided to call it a night. They walked down the stairs and the factory was pitch black, so they fumbled around until they found the light switch. Just as they were heading out, the sirens started. Eddie decided to take Penny to the underground station. Penny felt very uncomfortable being at the same place where Owain had died so Eddie stayed with her all night. Unsurprisingly, Eddie was the life and soul of the station—singing with some, smoking, drinking and generally having fun. He knew Penny was suffering but this was the only way he dealt with death and sadness.

Eddie awoke the next morning with a slightly sore head. He left Penny sleeping in the underground, thinking that she would be fine. He had one more person to see and he had no idea how he was going to do that.

He caught the milk train up to Carshalton, asked directions to the hospital, and there he asked a handful of nurses if any of them knew Rose. Eventually one nurse was able to help and through sheer luck, Rose walked out to the front of the hospital with a huge smile.

"I'm on shift, can I see you later," she quickly asked, feeling guilty from being away from the wards.

"I ship back out tonight," he responded sadly. Without thinking, Eddie grabbed Rose and kissed her.

"Thanks for keeping me alive; it's worth fighting when I know there are people like you back home." Rose gave in to the kiss and slowly stroked Eddie's arm. The meeting was brief and they said their goodbyes, even though Rose was desperate to spend more time with him.

Eddie then caught the train back to Trevanston, went to the baker's, picked up Mugsy, and ran along the Trevanston park one last time. Had a cheeky beer with his brother, said his goodbyes to his family, and then departed in the train to London. He stared out the window the whole time wondering if this was going to be the last time, would he ever see this country again.

He was joining an even more unique and dangerous Army regiment, going to unknown lands. Eddie met with Aiden and a few other men and boarded the ship. They settled in the quarters for the long boat ride ahead.

CHAPTER 42

Rose had received a letter from her aunt several days earlier informing her of Uncle Owain's death. She fell to the floor devastated by the news. By now she was used to death, but this one hit her hard as it was a loved one and more so, he was a great man.

Lorraine informed her that his body was to travel back to Wales, that the government had made an exception for him due to his contribution to the war and he was to get a full funeral service. This was rare because all government employees were extremely busy during the war. Last week, Rose and Lil had buried John before their shift and it was a quick burial with only twenty people from the hospital.

Rose had a couple of days leave acquired and swapped a few shifts with other nurses so she could have four days to travel and spend time with her family. Owain's death was a tragedy but it did allow her to spend time with the ones she loved and she was excited to head home, especially after the bombing of the hospital and John's death. It had been a trying time and seeing her sisters and parents lifted her spirits in this horrid situation.

Rose headed into London, crossed over to Paddington station before taking the train down to Wales. The journey took several hours and during that time Rose wrote letters, did some knitting, and let her mind take in the English countryside.

Once she arrived in Cardiff, she waited an hour to get the bus and then took that for before being dropped off three miles from her village. She knew the journey well and had done it multiple times, but she was exhausted by the time she arrived at her family home. Her mum met her at the door and hugged her hard. She embraced her sisters, her mum, and her dad all at the door and was ushered into the house with gleaming smiles. It had been over a year since she had seen them and she could not believe that her little sisters were growing up so fast.

The next day Lorraine, Penny, and the body of Owain arrived in the family area and the mood changed. Rose and Penny hugged for a long period of time when they saw each other. But the mood was one of deep sadness. All of their family had a burial spot at the end of the village and both had been to their granddad's funeral several years before. But today was different; Owain was so young.

The village all turned out and crammed themselves into the tiny old church at the centre of the village. Everyone knew Owain and like many other small villages in the UK, they all looked after each other. It was almost one big family. The church was from the 14th century, its walls built with old grey stone. Given it was a cold February morning, the walls were also a little damp and had a smell of old mold. The wind howled throughout and several candles blew out. The village sang hymns and the body was escorted to the burial plot and laid to rest. It was only then that Rose noticed her dad crying. Norman was such a hard man; he never ever showed emotions to Rose but today it was clear how affected he was by the loss of his brother. Rose was briefly introduced to Mac's parents, who had traveled from Trevanston and they had discussed Mac and Eddie. Penny was really touched that they had come.

The next morning, they all ate fresh chicken eggs and meat from the local farm and butcher's while reminiscing about Owain. Norman actually opened up the most and told stories of how the two of them had played rugby together and practiced for hours up in the Welsh valleys. Something neither Penny nor Rose knew anything about. Another time, they stole some gunpowder from the factory their granddad ran and used it to fashion makeshift grenades that they threw into rabbit holes.

Later that day, Rose and Penny decided to go for a walk together and brought along Gwenn and Patty. Rose and Penny had always been close growing up, typically seeing each other several times a year. Since the war, they had become closer and developed a deeper relationship. Gwenn and Patty were now old enough to join them although mostly stayed quiet. They walked for several miles without anybody really talking and then they spoke about Mac and Eddie.

Penny mentioned that she had written to Mac several times but had not heard from him since their surprise date night a few months ago. She hoped he was ok. Both spoke of their recent engagements with Eddie. Rose beamed as she did and her two sisters giggled. The Welsh countryside really was beautiful; it was so peaceful compared to the torment of London. They walked under a waterfall, past several others, and had a picnic overseeing a sheep field.

Eventually they headed back to the house for dinner and Penny and Lorraine left. Rose spent the extra day catching up with her family. It was great to be back but by day three she was ready to hit the wards again. She had learnt so much about being a nurse for the last year and she realized how much she loved what she was doing. She stocked up on soap and food that was rationed and headed back to Carshalton.

CHAPTER 43

Eddie was back on duty and ready to fight but he still ached from the recent firefight in Greece. Lifting his gun put stress on his shoulders and he constantly felt as if he had completed a marathon. He had travelled to Malta and been in training for a couple of weeks. He knew he was not fully recovered but hid it as best he could.

As he stared into the mirror one morning, he could see in his cheeks how much he'd aged. He now had stubble, his eyes looked drained, and scars ran all over his body. General Wheaton had recruited Captain Bond and his men including Aiden, Ben, Clarence, and Eddie for missions in Burma, so they had been training in the warm climate of Malta. Wheaton was all for pushing the men to their limits, so they had done mountain sprint training, wilderness survival, and war games where they practiced flanking enemy lines. They had been running drills late at night purely to acclimase them to the darkness. Captain Bond took some pride in getting his men into the best shape possible. "We are the Commandos now," he bellowed one morning. "We are the best of the best in the British Army and I expect you to be perfect soldiers."

Malta was similar to Greece in terms of climate and the training was going to help them prepare for the jungle climate in Burma. Eddie wasn't even sure where Burma was. They told near him it was near India but he wasn't sure where that was either. He much preferred the English climate but was becoming accustomed to the heat. The unit was well run and they had all become weapons and explosives experts.

That evening, they all sat in a make shift movie theatre watching an American film and newsreel. The men were bonding and drank beer. Bond had made it clear that they were there for each other. Eddie could feel that with this group of men. He had always remembered what his old football coach had said, "You don't have to be the best players, you just have to be the best team. If you help and support each other and all want to win for each other, you will win." He'd been right. That year, the team—including Mac who at the time had been the worst player—were not that talented but had won the county cup due to their mutual belief in each other.

Hitler had appeared on the newsreel and he started spouting off, jumping around, and orating in German. The room was filled with boos and shouting. The British commentary on the reel said, "Hitler has promised Britain that wherever they land in Europe, the Germans will be ready for you."

"Bring it on," someone shouted and the crowd laughed.

Unbeknownst to the men, Wheaton had received a new mission earlier that night and so at the end of the movie, he stood up in front of the company.

"Gentlemen." The whole room instantly stood to attention, beer bottles fell to the floor and no one spoke. "As you all know, we were due to ship out to Burma in a few weeks and have been preparing for it with explosives and stealth missions for several weeks now. However, the government has a brand new mission for us first. It will be a great experience for us to practice what we have trained for. Afterwards, we'll ship out to Burma. Who's in?"

"YES SIR," the whole room responded.

The next morning Captain Bond rounded his men and told them of their mission. They would be heading to Norway to blow up some factories. There were going to be four units total. Two would land, infiltrate, and set the explosives while the other two would function as support. Of course, Eddie and Aiden were going to be the ones landing. In reality, they were selected to be first on the floor. Eddie had rolled a cigarette and smoked it while listening intently to the instructions, each drag helping him concentrate on the plan.

Captain Bond, through Wheaton, had acquired intelligence on the port and using beer bottles, matchboxes, and paper, the men had constructed a model of the port. They discussed their strategy and then practiced it over the next few days. Eddie loved that he could add influence and it reminded him of talking tactics with Mac although he was paying attention this time. The men eventually boarded a ship in silence and set sail.

The boat they were on took them to the French town of Bordeaux and the journey lasted several days. They were travelling with the Navy but at Bond's request, he told them not to mingle with others and so they stayed at the bottom of the ship, eating and laughing between themselves and going over the mission.

At Bordeaux, they were to take passenger train disguised as a cargo train. They sat in carriages which were meant to be carrying coal. It was uncomfortable for a day, but no one cared. Eddie was getting excited to be in battle. There was something about mentally going into a battle and Eddie was ready for the action. There was a hint of anxiousness around the men and Eddie felt nerves in his stomach, but no one shared these thoughts. They kept saying, "Let's give it to Hitler." Once they got to the tip of Holland, they boarded several fishing boats and set sail for the Norwegian port. 'So far, so good," Bond whispered as they hid in the boat.

The men had learned how to blend in with camouflage and had mud all over their faces. No one smiled, no one spoke. They were disciplined soldiers and, as Bond kept reminding them, Britain's elite. They had set sail at midnight. When they started to arrive in Norway, the sun was rising, but there was an eerie fog so they could not see the port clearly. It was also deadly silent. Eddie imagined this was like the boat to hell.

They couldn't get into the port as planned so they got as close as possible, jumped into ocean and quickly disbanded into small groups, splashing through the ocean and then climbing up into the port. It was only about 0600 and they were told there would no one in the town but the factory may be occupied. As soon as they came onto the tiny beach, the town came into view and they instantly spotted an old couple. Aiden moved his fingers to his lips to indicate silence and several of the men rounded them up.

There were two factories being taken and they walked through the streets with barely any noise. The men saw two guards at the front gate of the first factory, came up behind them, and quickly put guns to their heads. The guards fell to their knees without resistance and again Commandos at the back rounded them up as prisoners.

Aiden cut the fences and the men circled the building. Eddie gave the signal and they entered the factory. "Get down, get down," the men shouted. "Geh runter, geh runter," was repeated in German so they understood. A handful of workers came to a sudden stop. Everyone seemed scared and there was no resistance. In total, Eddie estimated there were about fifty men and most seemed Norwegian and almost wanted to be rescued.

They were told before the operation to try and not kill innocent people. This was a new division of the Army and they wanted to publicize how good they were. So the men rounded the prisoners and sent them back to the other units. One prisoner simply said "I want to fight for you."

They placed the explosives, set the ignitions, and sprinted out. Eddie heard loud bangs and turned around to see smoke billowing from the building. *One down*, he thought. The second unit met them in the town centre and Eddie soon saw smoke from the second factory. Gunfire suddenly broke the silence and Eddie and his men ran down the tiny streets to where it appeared. They rounded a corner and found the men from the other unit crouched down behind some dustbins. Apparently a few local Norwegians had resisted arrest. This was a quick battle and Eddie circled behind the Norwegians to trap them.

Eventually, all the prisoners were marched out of the city. Eddie estimated about one hundred in total. There had been no casualties and the mission had been completed with ease. Captain Bond met Eddie, Aiden, and the men on the port and took control of the prisoners. Then Bond pointed down the dock, which was now more visible as the fog had transpired. Bond indicated that they were to board a boat and take control of it before setting explosives.

They only had a few explosives left and this wasn't part of the original mission, but no one questioned it. They simply moved in unison and surrounded the boat from all angles.

Aiden, Clarence and a few others boarded the ship. Eddie could hear the shouting from the distance but he didn't hear one gun shot. He could see the crew being marched off hands above their heads and Aiden worked with Clarence, to set bombs. The ship was blown asunder a few minutes later and the men watched it sink.

Once the mission was completed, all the men sat drinking water, smoking, and eating a local fish dish from an old man who had thanked them for freeing their town. Aiden piped up "Hitler and his claims of 'We will be waiting for you'—what a joke! Where is he?" The men roared with laughter, even Wheaton and Bond laughed. Eddie had an idea now and he found a note pad and pen. He started writing, "Dear Mr. Hitler, you said you were going to be there wherever we land. Well, we are here in Norway and we don't see you." Eddie grabbed an envelope and marked it "A. Hitler, Berlin".

The men roared. One of them had a small camera to film their operation and he shouted, "People of Britain, see this? We attacked Norway, we got this German coding machine from a German boat, blew up two factories, rounded over one hundred prisoners—who by the way want to fight for us—and we had no casualties. We are going to win this war! Where are you Hitler?"

The men headed back to their new base in Malta and several days later, the video was on every newsreel in England. The Prime Minister had ordered the commando group and it had been a huge success. Penny had seen it with some girls from the factory. She laughed at her friend Eddie when his face was on the screen. Mac had seen it on Port and was boasting to everyone that was his best friend up there.

CHAPTER 44

Penny had been instrumental in helping the government for the past four months and had gone from being the girl at the back of the room to leading the government efforts on female recruitment into the war effort. She had presented facts about her factory role to all of the top ministers, advised them on how to hire new women, and demonstrated that women could do the role typically designed for men. She was never the assertive type and never wanted to be a business leader, yet she had fallen into this role. She still thought of her dad every day, though. He had brought her to that first meeting and had been the one asking for her opinion. It still frustrated her that she was often speaking and the men in the room spoke over her, ignored her suggestions, and—when they didn't ignore her—took her suggestions for themselves, but she did feel she was making progress and she felt that she was doing her father proud.

What was even more frustrating was the fact she still had a business to run, which was rapidly expanding and the government constantly requested her attendance at meetings, typically at the last minute. So here she was, helping unload a delivery of gunpowder and audit how much she needed to order from her uncle, and then getting a phone call where she dropped everything and dashed round to central London to meet with the War Ministers, despite not knowing who she was meeting.

The bus journey always gave Penny time to reflect. She closed her eyes and relaxed for a moment. She was beyond exhausted and just rallied on a day by day basis. It was a warm spring day and the sun beamed down through the window she was leaning on. Her bushy brown hair made her hot and she could feel beads of sweat forming on her forehead. If she wasn't helping the government, she was at her factory or one of the partner factories every day. She was down in Wales at least once a month, ensuring that ammunition and supplies were travelling to the right location, and then every evening she was still walking the streets making sure people were safe. Penny longed for this war to be over. She would daydream of her and Mac raising kids, Mac running the factory, and them watching football all weekend.

After the current daydream of Mac, she thought about her mum. Lorraine had been engrossed with London projects—helping homeless children and families so Penny rarely got to see her but she was excited to spend time with her later. When the bus arrived at Marble Arch, there was the usual smell of London smog and stench of death was vibrant. Penny decided to walk to the government building, which was about ten minutes away. She took in the sights of London, but she saw more smoke and pain instead. She hated seeing this beautiful city in dire straits, especially as she remembered how beautiful it was several years ago. This was a city on its knees and she longed for the war to end.

When she arrived at the ministry building, she was immediately taken aback because there were more military personal surrounding the building than ever before. Normally she just walked in the building, but today she was stopped at the door and asked for identification. She scrambled through her purse until she found her rations card and, although crinkled, this sufficed and she was escorted in. Instead of the usual boardroom, she was ushered away downstairs to the basement. There she stopped in her tracks cold with her mouth open. In front of her was the King of England, his wife the Queen, and a young girl who Penny was unfamiliar with.

Penny did a curtsy for the king and queen, hoping that was correct. The king opened up a cigarette box, lit one, and then offered Penny one, which she politely accepted. She was awestruck and had no idea what was happening. She felt the sweat trickling down her face and she wanted to speak but started to stammer, so just looked down to the floor.

The queen spoke first, "My daughter, Princess Elizabeth, turns sixteen next week and she has requested to enroll and help the war effort. The King and I are concerned about this but at the same time know she is a head driven woman and that this is going to happen. I would like you to sit down with her and help her to understand how she can best assist." Penny was in absolute shock and couldn't say anything.

"Umm, thank you," she finally whispered and then she turned to the princess standing there who had been shy and silent the whole time. The princess was a few years younger than Penny but she looked so much younger.

"Shall we take a seat," Penny asked and the girl nodded and followed her to a little room. Penny got tea for both of them and they sat down.

"Have you thought about what you want to do," Penny started.

"I would like to do something that can really help and I do not want to be protected by my royal status."

Penny and her majesty spoke about different career options for the next hour or so. Penny liked her. She partly wanted her to work in the factory with Penny but deep down she knew this was not a viable option.

The location of the factory wasn't ideal for the princess to commute to and because of its assignment as a plane and ammunitions manufacturer. The risk of becoming a casualty due to a bombing run was too high. Eventually, they discovered a great role for her maintaining cars and trucks in Surrey.

Two security guards broke it up but the king waved them away, indicating it was ok. The family left and the princess took Penny's information with the promise to stay in touch.

Penny left the building after signing a secrecy document declaring she was never to talk about the meeting and disclose the location of the princess. She met her mum for tea and was desperate to tell her everything. She figured that her mum wouldn't tell anyone and she was so excited about her day. They sat in their garden that night eating canned corned beef and her mum was completely shocked. "I wonder if she can loan me a few pounds to fix the roof," Lorraine said and they started to laugh.

CHAPTER 45

The port in Malta was awash with green. There were soldiers everywhere Eddie looked. Eddie stood at attention with his unit at the top of hill overlooking the port and all he could see were green uniforms, bags, and—occasionally—cars driving onto one of the three boats ready for deployment.

They were not the standard Navy ships Eddie was used to. Instead, they looked more like cruise liners. *No dinner suits on that rig,* Eddie thought. He chuckled as he thought of himself in black tie regalia—that would never happen.

Despite being home and cleared for duty, Eddie's injuries from the recent firefight were still fresh. They hurt while standing at attention. His muscles tensed and burned. He longed to just put his gun down on the floor. Eventually, Captain Bond gave them a nod and the men followed until they were in line with the other units. Eddie caught Wheaton leading the men and they all boarded the ship. This boat was designed for leisure and numerous guests; had many sleeping quarters and bunk beds, so to say it was over crowded was an understatement. There were men everywhere.

Aiden, Eddie, Clarence, Ben, and several other men from Bond's unit decided that they wanted a bit more space, so they spent an hour walking the ship before finding a large open space on the back deck. It was partially covered and they set up base there. It wasn't long before the whiskey started flowing. They had become experts in smuggling alcohol onto boats and the men started to sing. The engines of the ship roared to life, the funnel started pouring smoke, and they set sail. Eddie looked out onto the island of Malta as the sun set above them, closed his eyes briefly, and let the sun hit his face one last time. Eddie had been joined by all of Bond's unit, Bond included, and they all continued to drink whiskey and tell stories of about home. When it came to Eddie he looked up and told them all about Trevanston, his family, and that last night in the pub while the stars were out in full force. When he was done and it came to the next man, Eddie got up to pee over the edge of the deck, and he realized he had tears running down his face. He thought of everyone he cared about. It was the first time he had really truly missed anybody and at that moment he also realized he may not see them again.

The boat ride would take a week and by the end of the second day, the men were all hungry, bored, and tired. Sleeping under the stars had lost its appeal with the choppy waters and the occasional wave coming over and soaking them all. Eddie felt nauseated for most of the trip. This was not helped by the fact that the food quarters were always over run by soldiers and meal portions were rationed. To take his mind off things, Eddie had decided to find a quiet area to sit down and write. He gave up three cigarettes for the pen and paper.

The ship's porters had promised men that any letters would be delivered once the ship returned. Eddie had just seen everyone at home but writing was a good distraction. He first wrote to his mum and told her of where he was, that he was safe and—for her sake—everything was great. She did not need to know about the several near-death experiences he'd had or the dangers he faced.

After her letter, he wrote to Mac, although he didn't have an address for him. He cursed over the wasted paper. He decided that Penny might know of Mac's whereabouts and she'd also been in London so he wrote to her but addressed to them both.

He had one piece of paper left and he knew instantly whom that letter would go to. Eddie had been with numerous women and yet he had never felt like this before. He longed to be with Rose, even just to be in her company, to hear her voice, even see her grin. He felt a connection with her even though they were opposites. He remembered her stories of Wales and he wanted to go there. He flashbacked to the night in Trevanston when he took her to meet his whole family. He'd never done that before.

He started to write and the words just flowed. He asked what she had been doing, he told her where he was going, and before he realized it, both sides of the paper were covered. He ended it with "Miss you, Eddie" and sealed it. He wasn't sure of the three addresses and hoped they'd get there. He walked round the whole ship and found the postal area where he gave them the three letters. He slowly walked back and he found himself staring into the vast ocean. For the second time in a few days, he found tears streaming down his face. This time though, they were unstoppable. *How had he ended up here in the middle of nowhere? Will I ever return home?*

The ship was so crowded that he rarely had moments like this to himself. These few minutes felt like a lifetime. He went back as the dusk approached and made up some excuse that the seawater made his eyes red. With that, he went back to being one of the lads. They played cards, drank more whiskey, and smoked a carton of cigarettes. Despite all that, Eddie didn't sleep. Instead, he stared all night at the stars.

CHAPTER 46

Rose was exhausted. She was so tired that her eyes struggled to stay open. The thought of sleeping for a year straight didn't seem unreasonable. It sounded great. She sat on a bench at the train station, waiting for her train to arrive. The warmth from the setting sun behind her made this spot as good as any for some rest.

It had been a long time since she was in Trevanston. She thought about that first night in Trevanston and meeting Eddie, Mac, and the football team. She still daydreamed of that brief encounter with him several months ago. Much had changed for her since then and as she reminisced, she wondered how Mac and Eddie—especially him—were doing and where they even were. Eddie had written her a letter dated over month ago saying he was on a ship to India and then Burma, maybe. Rose thought was quite exciting but the tone of the letter seemed sad and she was guessing he was also going through his own living hell.

For Rose, going back to Wales for her uncle's burial and to see her family seemed like distant memories now. She had been working non-stop. The hospital was short on nurses for a number of reasons, not least of which was that they kept getting bombed and nurses were either injured or, worse, dying. Rose heard that at least one of the nurses in Watford was no longer around. One of the best things about the war was her friendship with Lil who was accompanying Rose to Trevanston now.

As a result of the shortages and the increase in patients, especially the children, Rose was typically up by five o'clock each morning and worked until seven or eight that evening. Technically, there were shifts and a maximum number of hours you were meant to work but these rules were thrown out of the window like paper airplanes. It was an all-hands on deck scenario and everyone had to get on with it. No one ever complained though and as Rose sat there thinking of Mac and Eddie, she fully accepted how lucky she was compared to others.

Tonight was different. It was the start of August and the sun glared down on them as evening approached. Rose checked her pocket watch—it was five minutes to six; the train was late. Most trains were these days and people just waited patiently. The good thing about tonight was, apart from going back to Trevanston which Rose adored, she also had a good meal and a well-deserved night off.

Eddie's family had stayed in touch as promised for over a year now and Rose and Lil had both managed to take a night off. Eddie's mum Dorothy had also promised them a bed for the night, knowing they would likely miss curfew with the unreliable train times. With some shift swapping, they were in for food and rest.

The loud hoot of the steam engine woke Rose from her daze and they got to their feet. It was a Tuesday evening and the train was half empty. They found a compartment, bought their tickets, and set off. Forty minutes later, the conductor informed them that the train was now at Trevanston. The station had steep stairs up from the platform to the street and they slowly walked up on their heels.

They strolled down the street and watched the leaves fall. Trevanston station was located on a country lane which was shaded by the trees.Eventually, they got to the baker shop and saw the light on at the back. Catherine and Dorothy both gave Rose a huge hug after she peered through the door and walked.

Lil had never been there but was also given a great reception. There were eight people in the room: Eddie's mum, brothers, sister-in-law's and two cousins that Rose had never met but was soon introduced to them. Dorothy seemed to have aged more than the calendar year. Rose guessed she was at least sixty and she moved a little slower. For a moment she reminded her of John, and she thought fondly of him. She thought briefly about how John and Dorothy would have been a great pair together.

As the chatter faded, they sat down to what appeared to be the biggest meal Rose had ever seen. Eddie's brother, Charlie, had caught a pheasant that morning, which was now laid out in front of them. Several other family members had brought their homegrown vegetables and there was even a pound cake for desert. Rose ate everything including the vegetables which she was not so keen on. They chatted for several hours. Rose and Lil were asked about their jobs, how crazy London was, and the hospital. Lil, with three ales down her, was now telling them all the funny stories of the patients, including an eight-year-old boy who had put his mum's dress on and then was hit by a bomb so he'd to come to the hospital wearing a dress. There were roars of laughter all around.

Catherine revealed that she was pregnant, her husband had come back from the war in Europe, and it had happened by accident. Rose had guessed as much due to the complexion on her face and how her mousy blonde hair looked a little greasier. She was worried that her husband would not come back, a fear many women shared, and Rose felt really sorry for her. Eventually they spoke about Eddie. Rose told them all about her letter and they were surprised as he was so cheerful in his letters to Dorothy. Eddie's brother had mentioned that more than half of Eddie's friends from that football team were now dead; Trevanston in total was half the population that it was a year ago.

The evening ended and Dorothy showed Rose and Lil Eddie's room where they could stay for the night. Rose had had a few glasses of wine so was glad for the bed, but it felt weird sleeping in Eddie's room and she could not sleep easily. Lil on the other hand had passed out snoring within about five minutes of being there. Dorothy woke them in the morning with a cup of tea and bacon sandwiches. Then before they headed out Charlie grabbed them and gave them some cut meat, he said it would go to waste and for them to share it with the nurses. They hugged everyone and set off.

Rose boarded the train and Trevanston receded into the horizon. It was as distant and real as that first night. She had loved last night and had fallen in love with Trevanston.

CHAPTER 47

School had ended and that previously meant joy for Roger and Rebecca. They got to enjoy six weeks of time off and they would often go on holiday with Mac somewhere in England. Plus, they would have time to be together.

Roger had fought in World War I as a seventeen year old and he married Rebecca as soon as it was over. Roger adored Rebecca, worshiped the floor she walked on, and smiled every day when she came down the stairs. His tough persona melted around her and holidays were a great time to spend with her and Mac. However, for the past couple of summers, the six-week vacation had been something to dread. Roger and Rebecca were both in agreement and as they left the school for the last time, both had very little to say.

There were a few reasons for this despair. The first was that school, especially Trevanston's, was a safe place. The classroom was the same throughout the year, but during holidays the kids were in danger. Five students did not return after their summer break last year due to the bombings. Add to the fact that Mac was now away which meant this was the worst time of year. The lack of family time together was often too much.

They walked out together in silence, actually longing to walk back into the school building, when out of no where a man in a suit called their name. It was as if he had appeared from a locker—he was a small man, maybe five foot five, with strawberry blonde hair, a little stubble, and wire frame glasses."Mr. and Mrs. MacPherson, I've been looking for you."

"I'm sorry, who are you," Roger replied.

"My name is Mr. Smith. I work for a certain government department and I was hoping we could chat somewhere in private." Both their hearts sunk.

"Is it our son," Rebecca stammered. Mr. Smith abruptly shook his head, so they went into a classroom and sat on the wooden desks."

"I will get straight to the point. I work for a government agency just up the road in a place called Bletchley House.

We are using cutting edge technology and need mathematicians; I have looked at both your backgrounds and feel you could really help us. I'm curious though— why are both of you here?" Roger didn't like him. He didn't have a clue who he was and his invasive questions did nothing to endear him.

"Why Trevanston? Because I was sick of the city and I like the peace and quiet," Roger replied abruptly.

"No—sorry, I should explain myself better. I am curious how two graduates from Cambridge ended up teaching school kids. Rebecca, you graduated with honors—impressive."

Roger and Rebecca had never told Mac that they had graduated from Cambridge. It wasn't that they were ashamed, it was more they had chosen a different path. Rebecca had wanted to help others and did not like that she was being pushed down a path of motherhood or being in a back office with no say.

She had always wanted to teach. She met Roger at university and he was in a bad place. He had gone to war and seen some terrible things. He was naturally a very smart person but had left the war angry. He met Rebecca and she helped him to use his skills for good. Since she was set on being a teacher, it only felt natural for him to follow her. They grew up and were married in London but Roger hated the bustle of the city and seeing men who had fought in the war try to go about their daily business, so they moved to Trevanston to be in a peaceful place. Mac hated the move originally but the football team and in particular Eddie had helped him and the town had helped Roger. Roger was about to answer but he was surprised that Rebecca spoke up here.

"Mr. Smith, I was top of my class in applied mathematics, statistics, and linear equations. I wrote papers on coal efficiency for the government which I know will save our country millions of pounds and yet it was rejected by government officials. I even had a lecturer tell me he was not sure why I was there when my job would be to raise my children. I now find it ironic that the government is coming to me. That said, if our son has decided to put his life in danger because of his beliefs in this country, then I am sure my husband and I will listen to you and what you need."

Both men seemed to be in shock and it took Mr. Smith a minute to gather his thoughts. He fumbled his papers and wiped sweat from his large brow before recomposing himself. "Right now, I cannot tell you anything apart from this being top secret. Would you come to Bletchley House and meet some others?"

They agreed and the next day found themselves cycling along the countryside to the address given. Neither of them had ever heard of this house, but for a manor house it was amazing how tight the security was for them to enter.

They both walked in hand in hand, staring around at the gardens and the large red brick building. They entered through the large wooden doors and into a huge hallway with wooden floors, a majestic staircases, and artwork around. It had that historic, musty smell and Roger was only sure they were in the right place because of the security.

They were told that they would be meeting people separately. Then throughout the day, they met with a bunch of Army and Navy commanders, other leading mathematicians, some of whom they both knew and had studied with, and government officials. They had signed three secret documents and had been informed that the purpose of this place was to crack something called the Enigma code. It was the communication the German Navy was using to position U-boats and other naval vessels.

Rebecca was sitting in a room, waiting for an another official. She was bored of this whole process. She wanted to be part of this team, she wanted to help this program so that she could potentially protect Mac. She finally felt she could use her knowledge. But it had been a long day and right now more than anything, she wanted to reconnect with Roger and wanted to go home tonight to a good cup of tea. An Army officer walked in.

"Mrs. MacPherson, I am Field Marshal Brown. We have decided that you would be an ideal recruit for this program and would love for you to start. You will work for me, of course. How do you feel about that?" Field Marshal Brown said in a strong voice." Great, my husband and I will be here tomorrow." There was a long pause and Brown glared with his piercing brown eyes and then calmly spoke.

"Your husband will not be joining us. We are too worried about his mental state after his war efforts." Rebecca didn't blink. She calmly got up and said "Well then, thank you for the offer but I decline." "What!" "Field Marshal, you want the best mathematicians in the country. I am one of the best; I scored higher on the tests than at least half that room, but it's a package deal. My husband is also one of the best and we work as a team. It's either both of us or neither of us." Two days later, the couple were cycling to their new work. Upon arriving, they were sworn to such secrecy that they couldn't even inform Mac of their new work.

CHAPTER 48

Penny had kept herself busy ever since Owain's death. This was partly due to the amount of extra work she actually had to do, and also because she felt anger towards the Germans growing larger and larger. It was so strong that her mood was often in flux; whenever she stopped, she found herself crying.

Her mum had put on a brave face and tried to get on with things as normal, but Penny knew that she was hurting badly. Lorraine had been doing a lot of work with the homeless shelters and young widows. Her parents met when they were sixteen and they'd been best friends ever since. It was the little things Owain did, like buy her flowers or kiss her head. Because both were trying to be strong and brave for the other, it was almost awkward being together. And that is exactly what they felt on this cold October night, underground in the tube station, both sitting around their space with a silence and a cup of Bovril in hand. Penny was on warden duties and had slept very little. Her mum was exhausted and was reclining up against a wall with two blankets over her, her head nodding up and down into a half sleep. She stared down at her mum and saw the opal necklace round her neck. Penny grabbed hers and for the umpteenth time that day, fought back the tears.

People would say to her that you have to move on from death after six months but Penny could not fathom that, she still went through the emotions every day, from anger, to hurt and pain talking to her dad in her own way. Penny would take her nap after the next check. At exactly eleven o'clock, she headed up the stairs, passing the hundreds of children and families asleep all over the station and, as quietly as possible, opened the entrance door with a gas mask in hand. Her job was to guide everyone to safety but also to check the streets at certain times to make sure there was no one on the streets, at risk from the bombings. A few weeks earlier, she'd helped rescue two children from the rubble of a building. She felt the danger was worth being able to save lives. She remembered the night Owain died, he was trying to save that little girl Jane and she often thought he would be out there, doing the same thing.

There were several other volunteers doing the same thing and Penny had her set route. She would head out, turn left, and walk along the pitch-black road until the primary school.

There, she'd turn left along the alley way, turn left again, and loop back along the main street. Most nights, the sound of the sirens wailed and Penny could hear the sounds of the planes overhead, but tonight it was eerily silent. The freezing cold temperatures became more of a constant thought.

Penny cursed, having forgotten her handmade gloves, so she dug her hands in her pockets for warmth. Her heals echoed in the silence and her bones ached. The walk was uneventful and Penny headed back down the underground and found her mum along with the others still asleep. Penny leaned next to her and kissed her forehead like her dad would've and fell asleep next to her. The next morning, they both awoke early and headed back to the house. For convenience, Penny now only went back to her flat once a week and spent most of the time underground, taking baths at her parents' house.

Again, they walked in silence, changed, and bathed with very little said. Today, they were to spend the whole day together, so Penny forced conversation with her mum. She suggested that they go grab a cup of tea before their meeting. They sat and spoke about Mac and how he hadn't written to her in a while but Eddie had although the letter was dated several months earlier. They spoke about Rose, the cousins, and what they'd been doing. Penny had been running the factory with some of the most senior men.

The factory and her growing empire had become a huge success that was now manufacturing a whole host of things, including seats for most of the planes in the RAF. Owain had influenced the RAF's decision in keeping production simple and only used a handful of supplies and planes. Penny's factory had been so successful, she'd actually been able to purchase several others in South London from the owners' widowers.

Today, they were due to meet a government official about a new project they had both been asked to work on. They arrived at the big white building and after debating which door to enter, they walked in and found themselves with twenty other girls. They checked in with an official and were told to wait.

After thirty minutes, both were called into a room. They were briefed that the government wanted more posters of women contributing to the war effort. They loved their story of a mother and daughter operating key factories on the home front. They were then moved into another room with makeup and clothes to wear and their hair was done nicer than Penny could ever remember. Finally, they were taken into a large room and a photographer started giving them instructions. At first, he didn't like what he was seeing. They weren't smiling. He had them make awkward faces and hold unusual expressions while staring at each other.

The discomfort of it made them buckle and break into tears of laughter. It had been the best remedy for them after months of internal suffering. That night, they went to a pub and drank shots of whiskey, Owain's favourite. They reminisced about him and shared stories. Afterwards, they headed down to the underground when the sirens rang and fell asleep together.

CHAPTER 49

The journey to India had been hell. Eddie spent several weeks feeling sick, eating poor food and generally living in terrible conditions. When they finally landed, India wasn't much better. As soon as he'd walked off the boat, the humidity and heat hit him and he instantly began to sweat. There was a foul odor at the docks that Eddie could only imagine was a combination of human waste and decay. They stood in formation and were given a large meal at a small base about a mile from the dock. Eddie had heard of rice but had never eaten it before. That didn't stop him from devouring it as quickly as he could.

The next morning the men, led by Wheaton, got into their trucks and drove for several hours until they reached the border—their new home. They were the first men to occupy this makeshift base as it had been newly erected by the locals. The complex was imposing, with big dorms and showers. It even had an attempt at a football pitch although the dry heat had dried out parts of it.

The men settled in well and after a month, they'd established a clear routine. The mornings were for exercises as a unit. These varied daily, from tactical to fighting to general fitness. Captain Bond was determined that his unit would be the best of the ten units at the facilities.

Every morning at 0500, they'd wake and run for seven miles. They lapped around the facilities, then around the villages. They were often joined by the local men and boys from the neighbouring areas. The local men were keen to help in any way possible and the boys just wanted to run with the white men. The amazing thing was that there were also men from neighbouring Thailand and Nepal who had hiked many miles just to be able to fight the Japanese. After the run, the men would do sit-ups, push-ups, and other exercises before they started training with the other units. Given that the base had a kitchen, Eddie found himself eating regularly. Coupled with all the exercise, his body had become pure muscle. He looked in the mirror one day and thought about his boxing days on the boat to Africa the last time he saw Mac. He thought he could beat anyone now.

Wheaton was very organized when it came to his training sessions. They would do fighting sessions with wooden knives and bayonets, in case of hand-to-hand combat. He did sessions on jungle training, even going over walking through the rough foliage as quietly as possible. He did multiple sessions on the gliders and how they would fly in silent and then jump out of the plane. He even did sessions on first aid—how to handle bullet wounds and snake bites for example.

Wheaton kept his cards close to his chest when it came to mission intel and logistics. He was close to the men but only trusted a few with mission information. Eddie had noticed that Bond and the other Captains were spending a lot of time with Wheaton. That meant only one thing—they were talking strategy.

The afternoons were typically free for the men, so Eddie, his men, and the other units found a number of things to do. One of the soldiers, Clive Oaks, had organized a football tournament between the different units. Naturally, they named it "the Wheaton World Cup". Oaks was a former referee from Sheffield, so he officiated all the games and even had the chalkboard score board up. Along with the ten units, there were also six local teams from villages—even one compiled of the Nepalese men.

Oaks had organized it well. There were two matches every day with four groups of four teams each playing each other. The top two teams would advance. Eddie's unit had played two and won them both, but were up against a unit from Liverpool. They had the same record so it was a winner-take-all. Despite Eddie's men being fitter, the Liverpool players were remarkably good and their star player, a fellow named Bradborne, played lights out on Eddie and his defense, scoring two goals and assisting with another. Eddie's unit had only scored one in reply. Eddie's team would advance to the quarterfinals but play a tougher team. Eddie loved this whole concept, as he felt almost at home playing football and enjoying the banter with the others. Clarence, Ben and Aiden were like brothers to Eddie. Aiden and him were inseparable but he was fond of all of them. Ben was from London and he really reminded Eddie of Mac, with his thoughtful personality, Clarence constantly had Eddie laughing and Aiden was someone he just knew he would be friends with for life. Between them, they had all spent a lot of downtime together.

They explored their local surroundings, going on long treks from the base together. Apart from the heat, Eddie had quickly fallen in love with the country and area. He was also fond of the locals. At first, there was a cautiousness towards them but he found himself spending more and more time with the locals, learning their ways. He visited temples and small villages where he was greeted as a king. He and the men had also gone back with presents of footballs and British newspapers, that were from the ship and several months old but the locals adored them.

It was amazing to Eddie how quickly he'd become accustomed to life and he looked forward to his quarterfinal match like the days of cup matches in England. The bubble was broken three days before Christmas when Wheaton ordered all the men together. There were now nearly a thousand men under his command and Wheaton entered the stage more like an entertainer than an army officer. The men cheered and then were brought to silence. With his every word, they were captivated. Eddie sat fascinated.

"You are all here today because you've been picked for this kind of warfare. On a map our country may be tiny, but our empire and dominance in this world is renowned and well known. India has been of British significance for over a century. Every time you think of a cup of tea, you think of India. This country is the porthole for our operations in Asia and Australia and we are proud that India is part of our empire." He paused while a few heads nodded in unanimous silence. "Earlier this year, I got the ear of the Prime Minister and I told him that with Japan entering the war, they would look to attack India. He disagreed with me until they went and conquered Singapore. Now he has asked me to defend this country from them and I have picked all of you to do the job."

There were a few cheers now. "To the west of us lies a country called Burma. It's roughly the size of France and there are jungles, rivers, and unknowns out there. The Japanese have been working for months now, trying to maneuver through Burma. The training and exercises you've completed have given us the best chance of success. If we stick to the plans and work smart, we will destroy their communications and destroy their access to India. We will deploy soon. And just remember—I believe in every last one of you." With that, he jumped off the stage and started shaking hands with everyone. There were loads of cheers and Wheaton was almost like a celebrity. Suddenly he came up to Eddie and asked, "How's the body after Greece, son?" "Ready to kick some Japanese arses, sir."

Wheaton smiled and walked on. Eddie was impressed that he'd been remembered.

CHAPTER 50-1943

The last couple of months had been a whirlwind for Penny and Lorraine. It had been nearly a year since Owain's death and after the initial awkwardness of their grieving, both were now closer than ever, despite being busier than ever before. Their influence in the government continued to grow. They were regularly attending and leading meetings on increasing female participation on the home front for the war.

Lorraine had been instrumental in developing poster campaigns and had visited women around London in order to raise awareness about their roles and abilities. Just after Christmas, Lorraine was asked to attend a government meeting where she presented her efforts and results to American politicians.

The Americans instantly felt Lorraine's passion. After her presentation, they turned to each other and spoke in whispers. After all their heads nodded in agreement, the middle American spoke up.

"Lorraine, how would you feel about coming to America and recreate this campaign for us there?" Had she heard them correctly? *Me—come to America?* Lorraine felt honored and scared. Wouldn't she be out of her league?

She'd also never been abroad. Whether it was fear or shock, Lorraine didn't know why but she said that Penny had been the catalyst for all of this, not her. The Americans took her word. So, Penny awoke to banging on the door and a man yelling for her to get ready. There was a car waiting for her.

"Pack your suitcase! You and Lorraine are going to the nearest airbase!"

Penny could not believe that men had seen her in a nightie and without any make up. Lorraine stepped into the flat and whispered an apology while Penny was digesting everything that had happened in the last fifteen minutes. Lorraine put the kettle on while Penny went upstairs to get ready, she found a suitcase and quickly threw clothes in, not knowing where they were going or what to wear. She sat down at her vanity and started with make-up. The best she could do for her hair was to get the knots out. Eventually, Penny was ready and took the tea from her mum. With a disapproving look, Penny said, "What on earth did you get me into?" They headed out and sat in the car in silence. They were put on a bomber plane, strapped in like a parcel, and breathing into gas marks for several hours during their flight. Penny had never been in a plane before and after this, she never wanted to do so again. The flight lasted for seven hours and Penny was desperate for a bathroom.

A gentleman in a suit held a sign with their name on the tarmac. They were driven to downtown Boston. It was so different from London. There was no rubble, no smoke from explosions, and tons of cars. It seemed like the city was enjoying life and not in the middle of the war. As they drove around, Penny looked up at a sign hanging above them which read "Loose Lips Sink Ships." This brought a smile to Penny's face, as Owain had been fond of that saying. She suspected an American government official had copied this from him.

They settled in at a hotel, which seemed unreal to Penny. There were very few hotels in London anymore. It became crazier when they were taken to see a game of baseball, which Penny likened to cricket but had no idea of the rules. *Why did Boston have a team named after socks?* They ate like queens as rationing rarely occurred in America. Penny enjoyed her first beef burger with cheese and a huge portion of chips which they called fries.

After becoming accustomed to the American way, they met with US officials. They wanted to know how to inspire their female population to work. Like England, they needed a massive marketing campaign and it had to focus on the average American woman. "How is America typified? Where are the factories helping the war effort?" The men pondered and then suggested that maybe Chicago and the Mid-West would be good examples. Penny had never heard of Chicago, but Lorraine had remembered it was in the news when Penny was a baby. Chicago was frequently associated with gang crimes and drinking prohibitions. She did not like the idea they were heading there, but said nothing.

They boarded a train to Chicago, which was a two-day trip. Flipping through an atlas, Penny could not believe it that America was so big! *No wonder it's going to take two days to get* there, she thought, *this place is the size of bloody Europe!*

They arrived in Chicago and were taken to another hotel. As they started to unpack, Penny found a radio and turned it on. A song was playing about a girl named Rosie who was heading to work. It was a catchy song and Penny found herself bobbing to the beat, almost dancing even. *That's it!* Rosie was going to be the American girl and this song was going to help. Penny was so desperate to hear the song again she asked her escorts to find and play it for them. They didn't know where to start so they waited and listened to the rest of the radio broadcast. Eventually, the song came back on later that evening. Penny jumped up, grabbed her mum, and they sat and eagerly listened. By the time they went to visit the first factory, they were singing along to the song.

There were a great amount of factories around the Chicago area and Penny and Lorraine visited many of them over a few days. Like the UK factories, women mostly operated them but typically men were dominating the leadership roles. Penny encountered a few sexist remarks and one man from a factory in a nearby town refused to meet with Penny, stating he would learn nothing from a British woman. When Penny heard that, she had wanted to throttle him, but decided against it. She did not fancy time in an American jail. Many of the women, though, were inspired to talk with Penny and Lorraine, and one woman even said she was going to work harder. "To help our friends over the pond," she said with a smile.

Penny felt that the factories were operating well and the women she spoke to were all fantastic but she had still not found her Rosie. They were frustrated. They decided to cut their trip in Chicago short and went next door to a state called Michigan. It was famous for Detroit and being the birthplace of the car industry but there was actually a lot more to the state than Penny ever knew. She visited a factory that was really similar to hers in London in that it now built airplanes for the war effort. Penny was fascinated with some of their processes and was busy taking notes. Then out of nowhere she heard this loud American with a southern American accent above everyone else in the floor. Penny turned around and saw this girl bursting with personality, talking to everyone, smiling and busy riveting parts to a plane.

Penny wanted to meet her, so they headed over. "Well, hiya little'n," the girl boomed while putting down her tools.

"Hello," Penny replied and introduced herself and her mum. She explained that they were looking to learn from American factories.

"The name's Rosie, let me show you around!" Penny and Lorraine looked at each other and Penny stammered, "Sorry, what was your name again?"

"Rose Sara O'Grady, but you can call me Rosie."

"Well I'll be damned," Penny said, "Any chance you know the Riveter song?"

"No, should I," Rosie replied.

"I think you'll like it. Let me play it for you," Penny said. Rosie showed them around, almost skipping through the factory floor with energy and talking to all the men and women. She showed them the machines and the work. Penny loved how involved she was.

That night Penny, Lorraine, some of the American government officials, and Rosie were at steak house brainstorming ideas on how she could be "the American Girl". She was the embodiment of Rosie the Riveter and she was the poster girl Penny was looking for, that America needed, no less. Penny loved Rosie.

Originally from Kentucky, she moved to work in factories. She hated the chauvinistic pigs that bullied women and she was passionate about the war effort. Penny could see them going out in London and being good friends.

Penny and Lorraine headed back to Boston several days later and caught a plane back to England. She'd enjoyed America, particularly Rosie and the large portions of food. Several weeks later, the American government launched a series of posters with Rosie. Penny hoped it would be successful.

CHAPTER 51

Wheaton's speech was over a month ago and now the men were anxious to actually get into the action. The tension followed like a shadow. After Wheaton's speech to the men, they'd been confronted by and frustrated with the delays of their deployment. First, there'd been a series of monsoons and storms. The airstrip where the gliders were to be deployed from had been flooded. Then there'd been a delay with the food supplies due to the sinking of a couple of ships.

Finally, the intelligence was that the Japanese were building the train lines in a completely different location to where they had originally thought and this had meant that the whole plan needed to be scrapped. During this time, the Japanese had continued to advance into neighboring Thailand, occupying certain cities at an alarming pace.

Eddie and all the men had tried to keep their spirits up as best they could. They continued their football tournaments and camaraderie continued to build but there was no doubt that they were anxious to carry out their mission. The men from Nepal had finally been deployed several days ago. They were marching in with mules and would prepare a landing area for the men.

Finally, Eddie's unit, led by Captain Bond, and a unit from Liverpool were to be the first men deployed with Major Wheaton leading the pack. They checked their bags, supplies, and parachutes in silence, then drove over in the black of night to the airstrip. It was still warm, even in the middle of the night, and Eddie wondered how cold it must be in England. He could not believe it was February over here with the heat. No one said anything during the journey, but nearly all the men smoked and most had checked that their dog tags were fastened tight around their neck. Several men had written letters to loved ones and had placed them in their boots. Eddie didn't bother with that as it was far too superstitious for him. He felt confident that the mission would be a success. They could only carry so much personal food and other supplies but Eddie's bag had a small bottle of whiskey, three tins of cigarettes, and some bread. The extra weight was fine as he knew he'd need these.

They arrived at the airstrips at 2300 local time and took off several minutes afterwards. The men were deployed in these large gliders and they would be released from the planes, landing behind enemy lines undetected then they would parachute out and hopefully meet with the Nepalese men. As soon as the gliders deployed from the plane, Eddie knew there was a problem. They were in a nosedive and heading taking too fast toward the ground.

Wheaton screamed for all men to deploy and they all hastily jumped out of the plane. Eddie had been one of the first out, so he landed with a bump and quickly packed his parachute before holding the position. While Eddie's eyes adjusted, he saw outlines of men all around him. He heard a crash followed by a loud crunch. Eddie went to the landing site and saw a soldier from Liverpool wincing in pain and holding his ankle.

Wheaton—to Eddie's amazement—pulled a knife and cut the guy's throat. Wheaton returned to Eddie and said calmly "We couldn't carry him." Eddie, shocked at what'd happened, automatically took the guy's dog tags. The glider crashed into the jungle a mile or so ahead and was met with a loud bang and then gunshots. The Japanese were there for sure. The men grouped together in silence and using as little light as possible, they tried to determine their location.

All around Eddie and the men were noises. The jungle was alive with a whole host of creatures who had not liked being disturbed by strangers in the night. It was decided that they would move East and Eddie obeyed. The jungle was very overgrown, so the men in front had to cut down the foliage. Eddie being in the middle of the pack could only hear the hacking of the blades as they cut through overgrown trees and foliage. He stayed close to all the men around him and just followed the feet in front. Eventually, they walked into a large clearing and instantly there was noise around them.

All the men were armed, ready to fight but to the relief of many it was the Nepalese men who had successfully walked in behind the enemy lines and had made a clearing for all the men. Eddie looked over at the mules and was amazed that they were not making any noise with the all of the commotion but as he got closer, he realized their voice boxes had been removed. *How sad,* Eddie thought, he was a huge animal lover and could not imagine anyone cutting Mugsy's voice box.

The men silently spread out over the clearing and were instructed to try and sleep. The Nepalese men had indicated through hand signals that they needed to be silent and make little movement as the Japanese were in the trees around them.

Eddie settled down next to a few men, among them the referee Clive Oaks. Eddie knew he wouldn't be sleeping tonight; he felt movement all around him. The two of them were in an area with only a few other men and out of nowhere, a voice appeared. "Tommy, you got a light?" Eddie didn't recognize the voice and something bothered him about it but it was too late. Oaks replied but it was muffled by a shot from Japanese soldier hiding in the tree line. Oaks went down, his blood all over Eddie.

Eddie had his gun ready to shoot back, but Captain Bond jumped in and signaled for the men to stand down. Eddie knew he was right; a gunfight with men in trees in the pitch black was suicide. Instead, Eddie spent the whole night immobilized next to the corpse of Oaks next to him, the blood drying on his face.

Sunrise came and Eddie suddenly, instantly focused. If they could shoot someone in the middle of the night, they could certainly get them in day. Flooded with the soft morning light, Eddie could see everything. Oaks's body lay on the ground. Eddie noticed there were two other dead bodies on the ground. One had been shot and the other man had been poisoned. Eddie stared wide-eyed at his purple skin. "Snake got him," Clarence whispered to him. Eddie hated snakes and shuddered at the thought. Eddie stared into the tree line and as his eyes adjusted, he saw two Japanese soldiers were lying dead, their uniforms torn from the volley of British bullets. Eddie suspected they were the snipers that got Oaks. The men quickly dug a shallow grave and buried all the bodies, including the Japanese. At first, Eddie wondered why they even bothered. Clarence reminded him between shovelfuls of dirt that two dead comrades would raise more alarms they would want to deal with it.

The men marched all day through the thick jungle. Eddie wondered if they were on the right path but he trusted Wheaton and the men leading the pack. The heat and humidity would have done in a lesser trained soldier but Eddie was more than up to the challenge. He remembered from his training in Africa to preserve his water, so he just took deep breaths and sipped when he could. Eventually, the jungle stopped at the high grass. Eddie could at last see the sun setting.

Wheaton got all of the men into a huddle and finally detailed the rest of the plan. Half a mile ahead lay a bridge with a train track, crucial supply line for the Japanese supplies. They were to blow up the tracks in order to put a hole in the Japanese supply chain. They were to detonate explosives on both sides of the bridge and further up the tracks. He handed out the explosives and split the men into groups.

They continued walking all day. Wheaton's half a mile felt longer and took all day since there was no clear path. With the sun setting fast, they took camp for the evening near the target. Eddie was exhausted and quickly ate some bread before settling in for the night. He managed to sleep for about an hour or two but a growing paranoia meant he was tossing and turning, sitting up at every noise he heard in the darkness.

The next morning, they could see the bridge and spent the whole day gathering intelligence. It seemed finished but only two trains passed over the tracks. The good news was that the bridge went over a river, a key for their escape. The men built a temporary base in order to observe and plan the operation. They observed the trains, the Japanese men who patrolled the area, even the tide and flow of the river. After using up all of his bread and whiskey, he'd become seriously hungry and tired, but—like all the men—just carried on. Wheaton had devised a plan and the men all knew exactly what was required of them. They were to strike just before the next day's sunrise. The goal was to blow the bridge and then escape down the river before the tide got too high. No man slept that night. Eddie was hungry and craved tobacco but wanted his tins to last him, so he didn't give into temptation. Wheaton ordered the attack and the men started their plan. In the darkness, the men waded through the river to the bottom the struts where they placed the explosives.

Wheaton lowered his hand and all the men lit the fuses at the same time. Eddie was one of the support men and he started running through the river behind the others. Their splashing footsteps were the main sound until the explosions brought the bridge down.

That's when everything went wrong. The men were not a safe distance from the explosion and the percussion knocked them off their feet. As they gathered their bearings, gunfire erupted all around them and Eddie quickly took cover behind a rock in the river as an impromptu battle started.

CHAPTER 52

The bullet whizzed passed Eddie's head before he fully realized what was going on. Engulfed in chaos, he sat alone behind a rock in the middle of the river. He breathed slowly and took in his surroundings. The water was shallow but still moving rapidly. He was getting soaked behind this rock and knew that people looking down from the valley would have the advantage so he had to move.

The bridge was behind him and as he glanced around the wet rock he could see the smoke and flames. The explosives worked, so the primary objective was accomplished. The bridge was beyond repair and parts of it were slowly yet menacingly falling into the river.

To his left were gunshots, so he glanced around but did not see any Japanese troops. He could see several of his colleagues lying on the ground and assumed they were all dead. Eddie knew he had to move, but where to go was the question. There were several hundred British soldiers and they had decided beforehand to follow the river downstream for ten miles to a rendezvous point the Nepalese soldiers had created. Eddie, however, was not confident about this as it forced the soldiers through open ground where they'd be vulnerable to enemy fire.

Some of the men were to the left on the river bank firing back at the Japanese and Eddie's instinct was to go help them. However, before he moved Captain Bond and several others from the original unit slid in next to him. With blood pouring down his arm, Bond ordered the men to retreat. "If we can get back to the rendezvous point, we can send in the others," Captain Bond said to the men in between frantic, shallow breathes. They all looked at each other and agreed. "Cover fire," Bond shouted. He jumped up and aimed his machine gun toward the trees. The rest of the men jumped to their feet and sprinted down the river. They made it three hundred yards before they found a ditch in the riverbank and ducked in together. They returned the cover fire so Bond could make a break for it. Several others had joined him including Wheaton.

There were now fifty men at the bottom of the ravine shooting up at the Japanese on the other side. They were ankle deep in mud, but could clearly see the enemies. Eddie got his bearings and was relieved to see Clarence and Aiden together and ok, thirty yards from his position.

Because of Wheaton's tactical prowess, the men spent three hours fighting the Japanese and trying to get as many of the British to the bottom of the ravine so they could escape as a group. It was a fierce battle and Eddie's mind was solely focused on survival. He had seen several British men get gunned down trying to reach the ravine, some had been injured but most seemed to be ok. Eventually, Wheaton gave the order and they all started running down the river en-masse. This strategy worked for two miles and the gunfire eased. All of the men hoped that they had outrun the Japanese soldiers and the rest of the journey would be easy. They all caught their breath and drank water. When they started strolling down the river, the gunfire started again.

Eddie sighed and started running with the rest of the men. It was unbearably hot and his uniform was drenched with sweat and river water. He had leeches all over his body and was covered in mud making it harder to run and on top of all of that, he had a stitch.

The Japanese seemed to be getting nearer from one area so all the men focused their fire over there. Eddie could see a squadron of twenty men coming towards him. He didn't have to squint to see the lines in their faces, the determination in their eyes. He fired at them wildly and hit one in the head. It was another kill for him but there was no time or mental energy to process it. His only goal was survival.

Several of the men from Liverpool had grenades in their packs. They pulled the pins and lobbed them at the Japanese. There were loud bangs and explosions followed by screams. The grenades had worked and given them the opportunity to run down-river again. The gunshots were behind them now and there was no telling where to grab cover due to the thick smoke. One man got shot in the back and fell dead. Wheaton ordered the men to grab the injured if possible but leave the dead.

Deep down Eddie could see the compassion in Wheaton and admired that from him. Eddie ran up to the dead body and saw that it was Ben. Eddie was devastated as his friend lay motionless on the side of the river. Eddie grabbed the dog tags, took a deep breath, and continued running. The fatigue, shock, and adrenaline gave Eddie tunnel vision so bad that he didn't notice the rocks in front. His boot caught the side of one and down he fell. His ankle burned hot with pain as he yelled and cursed. He tied his boots tighter and pulled on the laces until he couldn't feel his foot. Despite the injury, he was faster than most men anyway and he just pushed through the pain so that he could survive.

The bullets returned and continued to whiz past them. Eddie heard the scream first then cursing. "Son of a bitch," Captain Bond said. Eddie couldn't stop staring at the red blot growing steadily larger on Bond's chest. "I'm fine, keep going," was all he said. Eventually, the river turned a tight corner and the current grew more rapid. The men knew that was a sign they were near the clearing. However, the map did not show them the small waterfall on the river that the men now needed to plunge down. Eddie jumped and landed awkwardly. He'd heard a loud crack and knew that was a bone. He looked around and saw someone else had his bone sticking out through his leg. Instinctively, Eddie grabbed him and started to support the lad while they hobbled on. All the men stuck together, the camaraderie was unreal, despite the exhaustion and their weariness. Five tanks were waiting for them on the riverbed, surrounded by British and Nepalese forces.

The injured were taken away and tended to first. Eddie was given a blanket by some of the Gurka Nepalese men. He took it along with some tea. A medic was busy treating all the men, including Captain Bond who looked in a bad way, but seemed to be OK smoking a cigarette. Slowly, Eddie wiped the mud from his face and started to slow down his breathing. Aiden and Clarence came over to where he was sitting and they all embraced. Eddie had put bandages and a support on his ankle but he was. Aiden had a bloodstain on his thigh and a cut on his face and Clarence had an arm injury but all seemed fine.

By nightfall, they had determined the final count; out of two hundred sixty men, one hundred twelve had made it back. Eddie felt lucky to be one of them.

After several days of recuperating, they were ready to evacuate. The men split into units and Captain Bond, Clarence, Aiden, and Eddie were all one unit. The idea was that being split up into smaller groups and taking different routes would mean that the men could travel quicker and go undetected. They had mapped out their escape back to India and it was estimated that the march would take eleven days. They'd had a food drop with rations of cheese, bread, olives, and tea but that would only last them two to three days. They expected another drop on the way but still needed to ration. They marched for several days, mostly in silence. The men just wanted to get to the base. In the evenings, they marched as well to save time. They all lit cigarettes so they could follow the light. The food drop didn't arrive and so by day four, they were running out of food, yet still they marched.

By day nine, they were completely out of food. Eddie could not go on and was at the brink of collapsing when the men came to a clearing and saw the other British troops. They ran over and helped them onto the trucks. They'd somehow made it back to the Indian border and were heading to the base. Eddie looked up at the sky and the stars and thanked whoever was out there that he'd made it back.

CHAPTER 53

Rose had been working a number of shifts, so many in fact that she'd been ordered by the matron to take a night off. This gave her the motivation she needed to finally head into central London to see her cousin Penny.

The journey from Carshalton to London was quick but the trains ran infrequent due to the bombings. Never the less, she packed her handbag and set off for the station. She bought a return ticket and waited in the little waiting room for the next train to arrive. It was a weird-looking evening. To the West, the sun was setting, painting the skies a beautiful pink but to the left was a huge dark cloud accompanied by thunderstorms heading towards London. Spring was arriving and the temperature was increasing every day. It felt good to get out of those stuffy layers.

Eventually, the train pulled into the station, the horn bellowing across the platform. Since it was a weekday evening and heading towards London, it was empty. The guard actually sat with her for the majority of the trip and they talked about their experiences. This guard had been running the rails for over forty years and now in his seventies, had hoped to retire but couldn't because of the war. He described his experiences from thirty years prior during the First World War and he mentioned how the smell of those trenches still haunted him today.

It was the first time in a while that Rose had thought about Eddie. She had gone to see his family nearly six months ago now and she had not heard from him in a long time. She wasn't even sure where he was in the world. She knew that the army was not great at sending back news. Lil's brother had died in combat and it had taken several months for the news to reach her. She hoped Eddie was still alive somewhere.

The train pulled into London Waterloo and the station was eerily quiet. She had been here several times before but this time it was quieter than normal. A few people in suits moved around. Rose guessed the bankers were going home to families in Surrey. She saw several Navy men, then a few families but it was quiet enough for her to hear her footsteps and the stone floors. She was not sure if the underground was working, so instead she hopped on a bus and stared out the window as the rain started and turned the sky into total darkness very quickly.

She knew she had to get to safety quickly as darkness normally meant attacks, although she wondered if today would be one of those days. Rainy days had typically been safer as flying became more difficult and so they had fewer bombs.

Rose found herself near the factory after about 2 hours of travelling. She had quite liked the bus as it had given her a great tour of London, all for a shilling. Now however she was lost and confused. The factory seemed shut and as the rain poured down and she did not know where to go. Surprising Penny had perhaps not been the best plan after all.

She walked towards the nearest underground and thought she would dry off there when the sirens went off. She picked up the pace and hoped to find the entrance to the underground, but she was lost, she was wet and she was starting to panic.

"Rose—what are you doing here?" It was her Aunt Lorraine.

"I came to see you and Penny."

"Well let's get you into safety" her aunt said.

"Very dangerous out there tonight." Rose followed her aunt into the underground and was amazed how many people were down there and how much of a community was down there. People had bought bunk beds down, people were playing cards, people had their washing out to dry. It was like a little underground town.

Lorraine explained that Penny was on warden duty and would come down later. That later was actually sooner than expected and Penny bounced down the platform to Rose embracing her and giving her a huge hug. "Crazy for you to come down just to see us," she said. Penny and Lorraine's little corner now had blankets and food. They made Rose a spam sandwich and sat down to chat.

Penny looked tired, borderline exhausted. She explained that the factory ran itself and she was also now working with the government to ensure women did her part and then Lorraine told her of their American adventure a couple of months ago. Lorraine then lectured Rose to start growing vegetables of which Rose suddenly felt very guilty.

Then they talked about how the rations were hitting them. "Can you believe the no stocking until winter" rule Penny gasped at one moment. This was the rule which meant that stockings had been rationed until next winter hit in about nine months and in between then they were not allowed to wear stockings or had to rewash the ones they had. Penny had said that her legs were constantly filthy walking around London with high heels. Rose had actually bought a gift of chocolate that was from one of her patients and Lorraine and Penny were thrilled with this as chocolate had also been on low supply.

The women chatted throughout the night and Rose found herself sleeping underground for the first time. It was really fascinating to see all the women work and she actually joined in on the production line for an hour. Penny discussed how Norman, Rose's dad, had been working closely with Penny and they were now operating over one hundred factories. Penny even owned several. Rose rarely spoke with her parents, but still wrote them every week. She was very proud of her dad and had no idea how involved he was.

Penny decided to take the morning off to show Rose some parts of London. She forgot she had only been there a few times. Rose loved every minute. Penny had a camera the government had lent her and so they took a picture in Trafalgar square, outside Buckingham Palace and the Houses of Parliament. Rose was tired and needed a good night's sleep.

She headed back to the nursing quarters and fell asleep at four o'clock that day. It had been a fun trip. Several weeks later, she received a letter from Penny and it contained all the photos they had taken. Rose pinned them in her dorm and smiled.

CHAPTER 54

Mac had been sailing for the Navy for three years now. He couldn't believe what he'd seen and that the battles in the sea had no end in sight. They were setting sail from western coast town of Plymouth for another Atlantic mission. Every time they set sail, Mac looked to the sky and hoped for a safe passage. Even before the war, for centuries the Atlantic had been a graveyard for dead sailors.

Mac often thought it should be crimson with the blood it had absorbed over the years. They were literally sailing through hell now. They had to avoid the mines dropped in the ocean, German vessels on alert, and of course the dreaded U-boats. Mac had been part of the crew that had sunk the deadliest of them in Bismarck but there were still hundreds of ships and U-boats out there. In recent weeks however, the tides had turned and as Mac and his crew set sail, there was a sense of euphoria in the ranks. In the last week, the British Navy had sunk three ships, so their confidence was high.

It was dawn but despite a warm May morning, the sun was nowhere to be seen. Mac was always amazed that come rain or shine, there was a crowd coming to cheer them off. Mac even recognized some of the faces now. One old man apparently had seen off every ship in Plymouth.The engines roared and Mac could see the tugboats pulling them off to the sea. Mac and his team were on ammunition duty and so that whole day was spent preparing the guns and testing the new depth charges and sonar scanners.

By nightfall, Britain was behind them and the alarms were starting. The crews had seen a U-boat emerge just ahead. The men armed the guns and fired in its direction. They would be able to hit the U-boat as long as it had not gone too far under. All of this was eerily reminiscent. As a child, he'd gone hunting but never was fond of it,. Mac also despised fox hunting, which was only for the wealthy and he was grateful his family never participated in it.

That was only for the wealthy, plus he hated the idea of hunting innocent foxes. It struck him now that he had simply traded foxes and small prey for German ships and the sad thing was he actually enjoyed the hunt now.

Mac reloaded several of the guns but was startled by the explosions coming up from the water. The crash of the waves against the hull were followed by scattered cheers from the sailors huddled across the deck. The smoke in the distance meant that they'd hit the U-Boat. Instructions were to try and board the U-boats in capture to reclaim and salvage their equipment, but this boat was sinking fast. The ship just kept sinking and Mac knew he had blood on his hands again. He remembered their first encounter against the U-boats. When did surviving become a guilty endeavor? As the U-boat sunk in front of him, all he felt was a cool numbness and the wet foam splattered across his uniform.

The rest of the night was quiet, but early the next day the alarm rang and the men jumped to action. Mac had been dozing but like all the others, jumped up and ran to the deck. Over on the port side was a German cruiser ship. Its guns were aimed squarely at them. The energy of the moment made Mac's instincts take over, just like when he played football back home. Mac sprinted to all the guns, took a mental note of which ammunition was needed, and sprinted down to the ammunition room with several others in tow. Mac loaded up the carts and then sent people dashing up after them. The man in charge of ammunitions was lazy and slow. Mac had no time for this so after the runners left, he locked the doors to keep the boat safe and started preparing more carts.

From the middle of the ship, he could hear the booms of the guns. He hoped that this was a gunfight his ship could win. When he had glanced at the deck, the German ship looked smaller but ready to fire. For an hour, Mac and the head of ammunitions were locked in the room, unaware of what was transpiring. Mac had broken the silence and asked about the man's backstory. The man's name was Smith and was a recent graduate from the Naval Leadership program. He'd come out as a lieutenant and this was his first ship. The British Navy and Army still held the tradition of taking university degree holders and enrolling them in training program to be captains and leaders of ships, despite their lack of experience.

Smith had graduated from Leeds University in '42, had not been enlisted, and was allowed to finish his education prior to his enrollment at the Naval Academy. He seemed to be a nice guy. They made other small talk, had spoken about America, and where Mac had been, but Smith was scared and so Mac knew it was up to him to take control of the ammunitions.

They'd heard booms and Mac was sure some of them were near their ship. But he and Smith had to hope the others could fend off the Germans. If their ship were hit, Mac would be doomed—such is the fate of locking yourself in the ammunition department.

Eventually, someone banged on the door and Smith answered. Two runners were standing there. Mac had done such a good job organizing the munitions that they were up and running straight away. "What's happening," Mac asked. "We got one. There's smoke coming out of it and I think we're going to board it. Another one is on the horizon," he said before leaving.

Mac and Smith were both stunned. "I've never been in three battles in the space of twenty-four hours," Mac said. Smith seemed to appreciate that and they spent the next hour or so talking through Mac's experiences and battles. Smith was clearly scared but at the same time, the battles fascinated him and Mac grew fond of the guy as he started talking about ship calculations and what was needed.

Eventually the alarms stopped. Mac was starving; he'd not eaten for over a day, so when the doors opened, they got food and reported to be relieved of duty. Mac waited for what seemed like an eternity and then dashed to eat the last bits of chicken and potatoes. The crossing to America typically took five days, depending on weather and the number of battles engaged. Mac discovered the next morning that they had taken some damage but had sunk three ships and now had fifty German sailors being held prisoner. The whole ship was in euphoria.

There was a sense of disappointment though, when they were told they'd have to head back to London with the prisoners. But the tricky part was that one can't just turn around in the Atlantic. Plus, they still had a job to do of providing support for four American supply ships that had just left New York. This all meant they were to wait in the middle of the Atlantic for these ships to arrive. So the excitement evaporated and the fear had consumed the boat. All the men knew that sitting still in the Atlantic made them prime targets for any other German vessels out there.

At 0200, the alarms rang again. Mac was hoping that the American ships had gotten within range and along with another ship they could guide home. Instead, a U-boat had been spotted on the sonar. Mac was ordered to be on watch and with several other men, he was again at the front of the ship in the middle of the night looking for a hidden ship. But Mac saw it first. "1 o'clock," he screamed, and the whole ship behind him stepped into action. The loud guns bellowed in his ears and water came up all over him as he ran back to help the gunners. It seemed every man on the ship was right there on deck.

Mac had amazing eyes and from the distance, he saw something in white. He asked a lieutenant next to him for the binoculars. He could see a German officer on top of U-boat waving a white flag. They were surrendering. Mac told the lieutenant who sprinted up to the deck and the captain immediately ordered the cease-fire. A boarding crew was dispatched and the men loaded small boats. Half an hour later, they returned with close to one hundred more Germans. These men looked scared and starved; Mac felt sorry for them. They had no space to hold them so the captain ordered Mac to use them as laborers in the ammunition department.

Mac did the humane thing and went down to the kitchen for a tray of hot Bovril and offered it around. At first there was hesitation—they must have been thinking it was poisoned but several took it and they all eventually drank. Mac was impressed that Smith had been able to speak fluent German and so they had made their prisoners feel comfortable talking—of course—about football. Smith had grown up as tennis player and had no real interest in football but had explained to Mac that he was by default a Norwich fan as that was where he grew up.

The Germans spoke little English but the teams of Dortmund, Freiberg Dusseldorf were clearly mentioned. Mac had actually enjoyed his twenty-four hours as a prison guard and it seemed the men were in decent spirits. Chaos began again just as they were heading into the Port of Belfast, which was their new destination. The alarms started and Mac, who had not slept at all, realized they were heading into another battle.

The German men were escorted to a corner of the ammunitions department and Mac hastily put a make shift fence around them. Then they loaded the ammunitions and started the trolley runs. There was a small German vessel off the port side which in some cases they might have ignored, but it had taken aim, so they were now in attack mode.

Mac was confident, especially after the four battles they'd been through. Mac knew they could take down the ship but hoped they'd surrender, just like the last one. Having bonded with the Germans, his thrill of hunting had disappeared and his hatred for the war had returned.

In the lull of battle preparations, Mac's mind wandered. He imagined a hunter sitting in the bush waiting for the perfect shot, only to be interrupted by the deer himself. *'Ello—it wasn't me you was waiting for, was it?* Surely, the hunter would realize the deer was more than a deer and that this whole hunting business should be reconsidered—wouldn't he? The guns boomed and within minutes a fire had erupted on the other ship. Smoke filled the air and men were seen jumping into the waters. The alarms stopped and Mac was back to guarding the prisoners. He now dreaded going to see them. When he returned, one man simply asked "Gone?" Mac simply nodded his head and he could see a mix of emotions in the prisoners' eyes. Some clearly felt lucky to be alive, others felt sad that their brothers in arms were lost to the sea, while others felt anger towards Mac and the rest of the crew.

The German men were remarkably upbeat for the last few hours of the trip; they respected that being POW's was simply a part of war and they would probably have done the same to the British. It was a strange kind of mutual respect. Mac was saddened by their departure off the ship. As much as he hated this war, it continued to broaden his perspective.

That night he sat on the ship watching the sunset, looking up at the stars, amazed at what had transpired these last few days. For the rest of May, Mac was based in Belfast. The papers made his crew national heroes of the British Navy. The press called it Black May because forty-one German ships had been sunk. Mac wasn't proud of this but thought he would love to tell Eddie and Penny about it one day.

CHAPTER 55

London was on its knees. The bombing had persisted for over two years. The loss of life and now the shortage of supplies meant that the heart of England was struggling. As a result, the government ordered a mass evacuation of the children of London to the more rural (and safer) places within the UK. The newspapers and newsreels ran daily images of mothers and fathers saying goodbye to their children at train stations as they set off while the parents stayed to help with the war.

A notice had gone up in the nurses' quarters asking for volunteers to be evacuated along with the current sick children and stay in the small, northern country town of Hemmington in Yorkshire. There, more focus could be placed on the children's recovery without fear of being blown to bits. Rose had been torn on whether or not to volunteer. On the one hand, she'd loved working with children, she enjoyed healing children and seeing their passion for life. Because of them, she'd decided to continue this path when (if) the war (ever) ended. On the other hand, she moved away from a rural village to be part of the hustle, so that she could really feel she contributed to the war.

At first, she decided she would rather stay, but after several weeks of Lil's constant persuasion, she decided to put her name in the hat. Lil had always been unhappy in London and every time she visited Trevanston she loved it, so was desperate for this transfer.

More than half the nurses put their name in the hat and there were only six slots, so Rose felt confident she wouldn't be chosen. The matron came round on the Monday morning with every nurse, including those on duty, lingering in anticipation of the result. Both Lil's and Rose's name were called out. Rose suspected it was rigged as Lil had a way of getting what she wanted. Most of the nurses went back to work and Rose instantly felt despised by her colleagues. She overheard some of them whispering, "She didn't even want it!"

Rose and Lil had no time to say goodbye as they were asked to pack up their belongings and then all of the children's things and to prepare to leave at four o'clock that evening. Rose didn't have much so she spent the time writing to her parents and Penny to inform them of the change, then went around packing up the kids. There were twenty-two children in total who could make the trip, most of whom had broken bones. They ranged from the youngest, four-year old Holly to the oldest Michael, who was twelve. Rose had a fondness for Holly as her mum was also a nurse on a local air base and her dad was a pilot. Every shift Rose was on, Holly always asked her if they could have tea party, which always made Rose smile.

Several of the kids had broken legs and so the porters helped them on the train and eventually, the train departed up north. Rose tried to sleep, unfortunately the noise of Lil flirting with a doctor and the children partying or crying meant there was very little peace. Rose instead looked out the window and watched the English countryside go by. The smoke that bellowed out of the front engine created the false sense of fog in her picturesque view. England really was a beautiful country, she thought as the sun set.

Grassy green fields, sheep, cows all resting, quaint little villages that looked untouched by the war. As the sun set, it was a clear night and she could see the stars. She thought of that night in Trevanston, every time she looked at the stars she went back there in her mind. She had not heard from Penny since her trip to London earlier in the year and had no idea on Eddie or Mac's whereabouts. It made her sad. She wondered if the four of them would ever be in the same room again—she doubted it.

The train jolted to a stop at a little after eight o'clock that evening. Rose and Lil were both starving but had to get all the kids and their belongings off the train and onto the three buses waiting for them. From there, they drove in the pitch black on country roads to the hospital and finally had to make sure all the kids were in bed. Plenty of tears, laughter, and even some vomit had to be dealt with but eventually all the kids were in their ward, safe and sound. Rose finally got to meet some of the staff. They were mostly all local and seemed friendly.

Rose, Lil and the other four nurses had no idea where they were staying so for that night, they slept in a hospital wing, a local doctor had found them a small, unused room. They both fell asleep exhausted and famished. It had not hit Rose yet that her whole routine and life had just drastically changed.

CHAPTER 56

Penny's relationship with the government had certainly helped her company financially. They were now one of the leading manufacturers for the RAF throughout the UK. The British RAF had decided, based on Owain's recommendation, to keep things simple and only develop a few types of planes. This meant it would easier to build and maintain them.

Given they were now three years into the project, Penny and her firm were well trusted and as such, she had been asked to consult and train other manufacturing firms. Penny had been shrewd like Owain and had seen several business opportunities here for the present and the future if the war ended. She had been able to invest in or acquire multiple factories from others, mainly from older men who had lost sons to the war and had no one to hand the over to. On this particular day, she was traveling back on an early train to London from an English town called Stockport, outside of Manchester. She had a grin on her face because the evening prior, she had acquired a new factory. It had previously been a hat making factory and she had bought it from the owner who was happy to retire and she planned to turn it into an operation to make more seats for the planes. The easiest part was that there was enough space to add more machinery into the floor and not remove anything additional. She also had about thirty employees there and the condition of the purchase was that all current employees stayed and she would enlist other local women. When or if the war ended, it would return as a hat factory, which Penny would run.

Penny was to go back to London and meet with some of the government officials about a new project she knew little about. She was on the four am train and the terrible watered-down tea she had purchased before her journey had not done anything for her fatigue. As she got into London, she purchased a coffee, something that was new thanks to the Americans but she was getting used to the taste and it certainly gave her a kick.

She walked through London to the government buildings near Westminster. As always, there were firemen putting out building flames and there was a mixed smell of burning wood and death. It was amazing how many people in London got on with their lives as normal, the bombing had been going on for years now and the London spirit was still there. One government official had previously said to Penny that London had been attacked for two thousand years and it always bounced back.

Penny entered the building and sat in a large boardroom at a table her father would have been proud of. In fact, she knew he was proud of this as she recognized it as one her factory had made before the war. It was maple wood, well polished and looked as good as new. She gave a wry smile and thought of her dad. This was short lived and her thoughts were interrupted by a bunch of men entering the room.

Penny knew most of them now, from the head of RAF to the war ministers and a few other companies similar to Penny. They were all chatting together, with several smoking cigars. Penny was definitely the minority of the room but she was used to this now.

The meeting lasted several hours. Penny explained that in the last three months, she had increased productivity by twenty percent. Finally, the crux of the meeting arrived. The RAF were planning a daring mission to destroy dams in Europe with a large new bomber plane and a new type of bomb. Penny and the other factory owners were each given instructions on the parts they needed to build and given only a couple of weeks to complete the order. Penny felt this could be achieved if everything went to plan and also knew it was best to shut up and agree with this order as opposed to try and fight the status quo.

Penny went back to her office and started putting the plans in order to make the seats for the plane and also more importantly the bomb. She'd been entrusted to help replicate and build it on a mass scale. It required them to build a brand-new machine and she had fifty men working on this for four days straight until everyone was happy with the machine and the outcome. Penny had made bombs in her factory in the past, but this one was special so she had been allocated engineers who recently graduated from university and had designed the bomb, helping her team with every step.

Penny had also called her uncle in Wales to help with the gunpowder and he had been in the factory with her for the last couple of weeks. Eventually, the bomb was built and now it was time to test it. Norman and Penny drove with RAF officials to a test site in Sussex. It was a base on the sea next to the town of Brighton. Penny sat in anticipation in a little bunker, hardly able to look out of the window because of her height. They started to talk about Rose; both had received a letter that she was now in Yorkshire, having been evacuated and there was clear relief in Norman's eyes, although Penny thought she would dislike being back in the countryside.

Suddenly there was a loud noise and the glasses on the table started shaking. Overhead, a huge plane—the biggest Penny had ever seen—flew in and it seemed to be just above ground. Penny felt excitement as the plane went overhead and then continued out to sea for several miles before dropping the bomb. There was clearly a loud explosion but had it worked? After a few moments, there were cheers in the bunker as the bomb had worked as intended. It was designed to bounce over water and it had done just that. One of the RAF men who was nicer than most, came over to Penny hugged her and thanked her. "We did it," he said.

The next week all of the same men were back in the office building sitting around the same table all with tense faces. On this evening, the bombs were being delivered to dams across Europe. No one spoke for hours. They were waiting to hear if the mission had been a success. Finally, a radio crackled. "Requesting to land, mission accomplished." Huge roars erupted around the room and Penny, her mum, and her uncle were all there celebrating. The newsreel the next day read "Dambusters and Bouncing Bombs Kick it to the Nazi's." Penny was proud and told everyone in the factory they should all be proud of what they've achieved.

CHAPTER 57

Mac stood onboard the deck of a new ship and was ready, in line with the other sailors to hear new orders. As the sun glared down on his face, he had time to think. He had been on numerous ships already and this was another ship with another mission. By now, he was three years into his Navy experience and, therefore, a senior. Unlike other naval men who had spent their whole career on one ship, Mac had somehow ended up working on different ships, been in different battles, travelled to different countries, and had more experience than some Navy men with a ten-year career.

After Black May, he had been asked to join a new ship as they needed experienced staff. Mac had travelled to a British town of Weymouth and joined the crew, which had set sail almost immediately. They had docked in a smaller dock in New Jersey, USA, refueled and reloaded, and were now heading straight back.

Mac missed home and was glad to be heading back to the UK; he was allowed leave when he returned and he could not wait. The Captain had just announced on the tannoy that the supplies in the UK were really low, so this ship and two others were to provide support for five American freight ships that were bringing essential supplies to the people of the UK. Mac was more excited about this trip than many others as he could taste the time off. He had not spoken to anyone from the UK in a long time and desperately wanted to see his parents and Penny. He already had plans on who to go see first and what to do when he arrived in England. His good mood carried with him when the ships engines started and set sail. Mac passionately reminded his team how vital this mission was because their loved ones would finally get some food. Mac was still on the ammunition duty but this time he was in charge of the ammunitions so they locked him in the room as soon as they set sail from New Jersey. Mac had been locked in before but not for such a long time and he wanted to be out on the deck waiting for a glimpse of England. However, he was not to see daylight for five days and so he sat on his own hammock ready to deploy weapons at a moment's notice.

Mac was so organized that he had already set up loading trolleys and ensured everything was ready to go before they had really left the port. The runners, who he had been part of, came and went and other crew members were around but being in charge of the ammunition meant you really were not to leave to hold.

After about three hours, Mac realized that this job could actually be the death of him, not because of the danger he faced but because of boredom. He had already done two audits of the weapons and completed all the tasks. The room was spotless and he was now waiting for the runners to run and get him dinner. It was like prison. He didn't even have anything to read so had read all the manufacturers labels on the weapons.

The first twenty-four hours of the journey went by very slowly, but then chaos occurred during the second evening. At 1900, the alarms triggered throughout the ship and they were to prepare for battle. Mac and his crew were all ready, the runners were set up to provide the ammunition and Mac was ready to co-ordinate. There had been a loud explosion to the west and Mac had been informed that a submarine had hit one of the supply ships. It was now smoking and sinking.

The mission had been to protect those ships and with one supply ship down, the Captain announced over the tannoy that they had to protect the other supply ships at all costs. The runners quickly sprinted up to the deck with weapons to the gunners and Mac loaded the guns from below with several others. It was nonstop action and explosions all around. Mac had been taught to keep a disciplined unit and so he jumped into barking orders at the men a to ensure the whole ship was armed. After several hours of continued action, it seemed to be dying down. Mac was drenched with sweat; he had been carrying weapons and his muscles ached.

Apparently, they had been in a battle with two German ships and it appears they had won. The alarm settled and Mac sat down for several minutes, drinking water copiously. He needed to replenish the stock count but he also needed a little rest. Mac had barely closed his eyes when a deafening, loud bang erupted around him. Mac was flung across the room, smashed into a metal shelf and fell to the floor. The whole room was spinning and his ears were ringing. *What the hell just happened?* As he came to his senses, he tried to get to his feet and felt an excruciating pain in his leg. He looked down and nearly vomited. His leg had a huge gash down it with a piece of metal shelf sticking through it.

He couldn't move and fear came over him. At that point, the phone from the Captain's deck rang which indicated they needed weapons again. Then the ship's battle alarm went off again. Mac crawled toward the phone. Slowly using all of his arm strength, he eventually managed to get to the phone. He whispered into the receiver, "Mayday, Mayday, Mayday. I'm injured and weapons cannot be distributed!" He dropped the phone and fell to the floor. There was a warm feeling around him and he thought to himself this was it. His last image was of Penny before he passed out on the floor, blood from his leg creating a puddle underneath him.

CHAPTER 58

For the first few nights in Yorkshire, Rose spent them in the hospital but it was cramped and not exactly a home. They hadn't been able to unpack and her brown, tattered suitcase lay unopened against the bed. It was decided that the nurses and doctors from London would reside on local farms. As well as Rose's hospital, several others had sent doctors and nurses and so on this warm morning Rose, Lil and the rest walked up a stone path past a field of cows to a concrete hut.

They were looking at Rose's and Lil's new home. The summer weather was there but there was a fog descending onto the Yorkshire dales, reducing the visibility. However, from what she could see there were miles and miles of countryside and beautiful green valleys. This was about as far as she could get from London and the war.

There were about fifteen huts, all of which were previously farm enclosures for the animals and their food. They'd hastily been converted into housing in the last few weeks. Rose walked in to see a tiny kitchen, a bathroom, and a room with two beds. The walk from the hospital had been a good thirty minutes. Rose's blood was pumping and her body felt hot. It was only once they stopped and sat on the beds that it dawned on both of them just how cold this shelter was, even in summer.

Lil went to fetch some branches and lit the stove in the corner of the room. They huddled around it for an hour. After they unpacked, they realized that this home was far from ideal. They had a limited trickle of water into the house that was freezing cold. To have a bath, they had to fill and boil their cast iron kettle four times just for enough warm water.

In the past, the hospital provided them with food and shelter but now they had to walk to Hemmington to pick up a few supplies. The walk was a good fifty minutes in the opposite direction from the hospital, so they set off through farmland. They passed the pigs, sheep, and cows that looked at them in a frustrated "what are you doing here" way. The fog had risen slightly as they walked towards the town and Rose could now clearly see the beautiful countryside.

It reminded her of home back in Wales. The silence was difficult for her to get used to again. She had forgotten just how quiet the world could be and as they walked down into the town, all they could hear were their shoes on the gravel and the occasional bird overhead. Rose actually missed the hustle, bustle, and noise of a busy hospital.

They eventually made it to town and found themselves around a small market. It was still only about eleven o'clock, so the market was in full force. Between them they wandered through the vendors and decided to buy themselves a loaf of bread, some marmalade and jam and some local cheese. Most of the vendors were old men and were appreciative of new customers.

The ration cards were shown, but one man told them, "It's a little easier here as everyone grows or makes everything." They got to the end of the market and found an old man selling apples. Lil joked, "An apple a day keeps the doctors away." Something they often joked about in the old hospital was the fact the doctors were notorious for constantly harassing the nurses and trying to court them. Lil secretly loved it.

Rose dropped her purse and bent down to pick it up, but found that someone else's hand was on it as she was on the ground. "Here you go, ma'am," the gentleman said with a strange accent. Rose looked up and stared into his eyes. She did not recognize the uniform. "You keep hold of that, now." The gentleman spoke again. The man was incredibly tall, easily over six foot three and had short brown hair cut in typical military style along with deep brown eyes and a stubble across his face. He was a very handsome man.

"Name's Adams, Clint Adams," he told her. "We are part of the US Airforce based around here. And you beautiful ladies are?"

Rose was lost for words, so Lil interjected. "Rose and Lil, nurses for the children's ward. We just moved here from London. Another gentleman who until that moment Rose had not even noticed raised a hand an introduced himself. "Arthur Bryant, pleasure is all ours."

After the initial awkwardness, the men insisted on taking them both for coffee although Rose was much happier with tea. The men knew of a tiny café and Rose got her ration card ready, but it wasn't needed. The café only had tea and coffee—no food—which was novel for Rose. Clint and Arthur ordered coffee and tea for them and all. They informed them that the US Airforce had a base just south of the city and they flew missions to help the Allies from there. The Americans had been in Hemmington for about three months now. Both men seemed charming and Lil was instantly fascinated with Arthur.

The men informed them that there was a dance downtown tonight and that they should come and bring others. Lil was sold and spent the whole walk back convincing Rose that they should go. Rose wanted nothing more than an early night but felt Lil would not relent and so she agreed. They both got ready and Rose rounded up the other doctors and nurses so that twenty of them set off in the evening for the dance.

CHAPTER 59

Mac had passed out and he had no idea for how long. He remembered pulling the alarm and had no other memory. He slowly opened his eyes and saw a bright light. *Is this heaven?*

It took several minutes for his eyes to adjust to the light. First, he saw a couple of shadows and then, actual figures. He tried to sit up but instantly felt pain in his stomach and leg, then he sat back down. "Woah there, fella," a voice said. The guy sounded like he was underwater and he remembered the loud noise before. Mac closed his eyes and breathed slowly, trying to calm himself.

He was obviously still alive and as he looked around, he was fairly sure he was in the medical quarters of the ship. The room itself was large but Mac remembered from his training that the medical room had limited supplies. With his eyes still shut, he focused purely on listening. "Where am I and what happened?"

There were two voices. The first one Mac recognized as one of his crewmen. He explained that the enemy's submarine had fired directly at their ship and had hit the ammunition room, causing a large explosion. Mac was extremely lucky; the munitions had not detonated and therefore, the blast was restricted. Locking himself into the room had saved the whole ship. Once the crew had found him, they carefully defused the missile and came to his rescue. The ship was damaged but was able to continue on home.

The second man was the ship's medic and he slowly went through the list of Mac's injuries. It was like listening to someone list a whole football roster. "Let's start with the skull. You have a concussion from hitting your head on the shelving, your eyes are damaged from the bright explosion and you will never have full visibility again. You probably have a perforated eardrum as well due to the proximity of the blast. You have cuts all over your arm and chest from shrapnel, a gash on your stomach, a large cut down your whole leg, and some shrapnel that we removed. You really are lucky to be here with us," he said. Mac didn't feel so lucky though.

He found himself awake for an hour or so, but then went back to sleep. He continued to toss and turn until most of the pain had subsided. He slowly shifted and sat up. The doctor came in and helped him up while Mac slowly asked for food. He asked for the time. It was 0600. Mac was informed that despite the ship's damage, it was still operating slowly, and they were about twenty-four hours away from Liverpool.

After eating some bread and relieving himself in a bedpan, Mac started to inspect his body and the extent of the damage. The morphine had started to wear off and the pain was becoming more intense. He spent the rest of the morning with visitors. Most of the others, especially ammunition crew, came by to check in on him. Even the Captain had come by, shaking his hand and telling him that the ship was lucky to have him.

Captain Pollack was a sea veteran. He had been a Captain even before the war had broken out and to the crew he was typically known as a ball buster, a no excuses type of guy. He had survived two wars and despite numerous attacks on his ships, he'd never been sunk. He was an old man with white hair and a white beard. He was originally from Sheffield and had a strong Yorkshire accent. His voice boomed with every word and it was clear he was in charge. He had a scar across his face that fascinated Mac. He wanted to know how Captain Pollack had gotten it but the timing wasn't right. The Captain ended their conversation with the best compliment for a sailor, "Get yourself better boy—we'll have you on the next ship."

By the afternoon, Mac was feeling more and more comfortable and ready to get back to work. He couldn't really move but he felt stronger. He had written to Penny and the fact he was bound to be given medical leave actually excited him because he would have time to see her. The doctor started to sweat and kept fumbling around on the wound on his stomach.

Finally, Mac said "What is it doc? I'm not pregnant I hope," he said, trying to be funny. The doctor looked him straight in the eye. Mac couldn't help but notice the fear.

"The wound is infected and we don't have the medical equipment to treat it." "Ok—so I will get it cleared up in twelve hours, right?"

"I'm sorry sailor, you probably won't make it through the night." Tears streamed down Mac's face; he didn't want to die. It took Mac several minutes to realize what he'd just been told. He sat there unable to move, staring at the metal ceiling with its condensation dripping onto the piping around him. *What now? Do I just sit here until it happens?* He called one of the junior men to bring him some paper and a pen. First, he wrote to Penny. He scrapped his earlier letter and wrote a new note.

"I am so sorry, I let you down. I wanted to come back to you. I want to spend the rest of my life with you but it seems fate may have other plans." He knew the address of the factory by heart and so, he addressed the letter there. Then he wrote to his parents. He adored them and had an immediate wave of guilt over him. He should have listened to them.

He could have gone to university, he could have gone to university in America and he would have been safe, but he listened to Eddie and the team and ended up here. With that, he wrote a final letter to Eddie. He had not heard from him in years and hoped he was safe. "You are the best, most loyal friend anyone can ask for. See you on the other side." He addressed it simply – Eddie Hartley, Trevanston. Knowing that would be enough to get it to his family at least.

Mac shut his eyes, ready for the inevitable. However, his brain refused to turn off and his body could not rest. Every time he opened his eyes he saw the metal coffin of the ship and it drove him crazy. So, when the doctor came back, he had a plan. "Doc, if I am going to die, I want to die on the deck looking up at the stars." The doctor looked at him, confused for a second as no one had ever made a request like this before. The doctor went away and returned minutes later with a stretcher and four other men. They carefully placed Mac on the stretcher and carried him through the galleys of the ship to the deck. Mac heard applause and was surprised that there were men all around applauding him. Several men leaned over the stretcher and whispered "Thank you" to Mac, in return he smiled.

The crew had created a hammock for him and slowly the men placed him in it. A few more pats on the shoulder and then Mac was left alone. It was cold but they had given him blankets. As he looked at the stars, swinging slowly in the hammock, he felt peace with the world.

CHAPTER 60

Lil was in her element now. She was already on her third glass of wine and as the music picked up, she loved having conversations with the American airmen. She longed for a man to whisk her off her feet, marry her, and start a family with her. If he happened to be rich on top of that, she wouldn't be opposed to that either. The idea of someone taking care of and looking after her, now that sounded great.

Lil danced between several men and was a little flirtatious with them. Although she'd been out with Lil and other nurses at the pubs on many a night, Rose, on the other hand, felt like she was in the middle of a nightmare. She had never been to a dance before. She didn't know how to dance nor did she want to learn. She had slowly started drinking and smoking. It seemed like everybody was smoking and drinking now. She didn't really like either and she was still painfully shy. She was socially awkward when talking to others and she felt nervous all the time.

The other nurses' bags kept her company while she took heavy drags on her cigarette. She contemplated going home but wandering aimlessly through the countryside at night back home didn't appeal to her either, so she sat there thinking about the world. She took a sip on a Gin and Tonic and mindlessly sucked on the ice cube. Occasionally, Lil and the nurses would sit down and chat with her. They even tried goading her onto the dance floor.

"Come on Rose move those hips," they said. Rose consistently declined.

In the smoke-filled dance hall, the smell was of people dancing and their alcohol mixed with the aged wooden floors. She was amazed that everyone acted like they weren't in the middle of a war. Everyone in that room knew someone that had been injured or died.

Everyone knew someone that was fighting overseas and yet no one seemed to be thinking about them. Lil put it to her differently. "This might be our last night, so I am going to live like it is!". Rose knew she was right. But her thoughts wandered to her uncle getting killed in London, to the attack at the hospital where she lost some good friends, and then—finally—Mac and Eddie. She fondly remembered that night in Trevanston where Eddie had made her so welcome. He knew how shy she was and yet, he'd made her feel right at home there. She imagined that if he were here now, he'd be singing and dancing with everyone and yet somehow still making her feel ok. She just simply was not having fun. She hadn't heard from Eddie in a long time. Same for Mac as well but apparently Penny heard from him a few months ago. Eddie's family had been kind enough to invite her and Lil to Trevanston, but a few months had passed since she had written to them and remorse suddenly came over her.

She left the bar for some fresh air, maybe try and find the hospital to go and check in on the children. *Maybe that'll cheer me up.* She remembered that most of them were from London and had left their parents behind, not all of them understood why and most missed them. She picked up her bag, looked around the room at everyone dancing, and walked out without saying goodbye.

As she stepped out into the fresh night air, the coldness hit her hard and she instantly regretted the move. "Hey there little lady," said a voice from the darkness. Rose tightened up in fear, clutching her bag to her shoulder. However, from the darkness came a lit cigarette and then a man in uniform appeared. It was only when he was in front of her did she realize it was Clint.

"Oh, hi Clint," she mumbled. Clint noticed that she was shivering and wrapped his jacket around her.

"Where are you going," he asked.

"I was going to check on the children in the hospital. That dance wasn't my scene," Rose replied, still mumbling but a little clearer this time.

"Mind if I join you?"

"Really not my scene either," he said. Rose was surprised that someone else didn't like the scene, so she allowed him to follow along. After walking through the market in the darkness and silence, Clint spoke again.

"Probably a good thing I found you because you're heading in the wrong direction," he laughed. Rose smiled.

Clint started to lead them, walking Rose through the town and holding her hand. They started to talk about each other's journey to Hemmington. He signed up for the Air Force the day after America was attacked at Pearl Harbor. He had enlisted with his three brothers, two of which were in another airbase in Asia and the other was fighting with the Army in Africa but was due to come to Europe soon.

Rose told her story of Wales to Watford to London to Hemmington. They spoke about their shared love for anything sweet and Rose smiled when Clint called biscuits cookies. Clint told her that she had to go to the cinema to see the latest Charlie Chaplin film. It seemed like they had been chatting for hours, but it had actually only been twenty minutes before they arrived at the hospital. Rose walked into the ward and noticed all the kids were deeply asleep. It gave her great relief and after checking all of their notes and chatting with a few of the night nurses she walked back out and Clint was still there. "Thought you would get lost walking back," he said with a grin. Rose smiled again.

They walked for the next forty minutes in the pitch black hand in hand through the town and countryside and eventually made it to the concrete building Rose would now call home. "Well good night, Ms. Rose," Clint said with a smile and without knowing what happened, he pulled her in close and kissed her. It felt so great and Rose wanted to just fly away with the moment. They embraced for what seemed like a lifetime and Rose actually pulled him close when he started to move away, something she'd never done. "Good night," she mumbled and she walked inside. He walked back down the valley and into the darkness. She fell asleep smiling.

CHAPTER 61

Mac was awoken by an unbearable horn. The sun shone down on him. This is it—his entrance to heaven. He assumed so until he heard the noise of many men all around him on the deck. "By George, he made it!" "Mac's alive!"

Men that Mac had never even met suddenly surrounded him. Many were shaking his hand and Mac could hear them say, "He is definitely a good luck charm. I want him on my ship!" Somebody had grabbed the doctor and he came running towards Mac. "How you feeling," he quickly asked.

"Cold," was Mac's response as he shivered. "Your body is going into shock. But we're thirty minutes from docking. You can make it!"

Mac had one thought on his mind, his family. *I'm so close to seeing my family and Penny gain. I'm going to make it. I have to make it!* He remembered the letters he had written the night before and found them in his pocket. He ripped them up, letting the scraps fly into ocean. "I'm going to make it," he continued whisper to himself. The next thirty minutes moved so slowly for Mac. It was as if he was watching life go past him in slow motion. Men from all over the ship came to shake his hand. He'd been a beacon of hope for the men. Even the Captain came over to shake his hand. "Get yourself better and then write me—I want you on my next ship," Captain Pollack reiterated.

Mac felt a mixture of emotion. He had no idea why everyone was so happy to see him alive. He had seen men die on ships and he'd never seen this.

He was also feeling cold, exhausted, and his eyes kept closing. He forced himself to re-open them and watch the port get slowly closer. The sun glistened down on the city and its rays cut through the smoke that remained from the previous night's fires.

It seemed to take forever to actually dock in the Albert Docks. Mac felt immobilized as people shuffled around him, he tried to move but the pain in his stomach was unbearable, so he gritted his teeth and waited. The medic jogged over with two others and a stretcher. Mac closed his eyes again as they carted him off to the waiting ambulance. He didn't remember anything else.

Mac awoke because of a strange rumbling and forgot where he was. He was in a big room. *Is this a hospital ward?* The rumbling was another man's snoring in the bed next to him. There were twenty men in total, scattered around the room. It was dark outside, which made looking around for his watch and other possessions all the more difficult. It was 0500. He'd been in bed for at least a day, perhaps longer. Mac looked down at him stomach and noticed the bandages wrapped around most of his body. More sensations flooded his body, especially the sudden urge to pee. *Can I even walk to the toilet?* He noticed that the bed pan near his bed, but he'd no intention of using that again.

He slowly moved and felt a burning pain in his leg. His stomach felt sore, as if he was back in basic training. He wasn't sure if he could put pressure on his leg but he wanted to try. He was more worried about the fact that he would wake the others in the room. Eventually, he built up the courage and planted his feet on the floor. As soon as he did, he felt excruciating the pain rise up his leg. He wanted to scream but he couldn't as he would wake others. He found a pencil on his bedside and bit down hard as he walked to the end of the room. The pain subsided as Mac moved around the ward. He observed was not the most badly injured person in the room; some poor guy had no legs and another looked like he'd been burned at the stake.

Mac walked through the room and quickly found the loo. After relieving himself, he wanted to find a nurse and figure out what had happened to him. He walked down the hallway and caught a glimpse of the nurse. She was slouched over her chair, asleep naturally. She seemed eerily familiar. *Penny?!?* He hobbled up to her quickly, bent down, and kissed her. She stirred and her eyes fluttered open quickly. She pulled back at the sight of one of the patients violating her space and let out a shriek.

What nerve! He's going to wish he'd died by the time I'm through with him! As she sprung to her to let him have one, she suddenly stopped and realized what she was looking at—a gaunt and weary Mac standing there in a hospital gown. She grinned and embraced him before whispering, "I nearly popped you one right in the kisser! Oh my lord, you need to be resting in bed." He politely refused and just sat there with her.

Mac had been in the hospital for two days, unconscious the whole time. The doctors had cleaned both wounds and then had used a new drug called penicillin to fight the infection and leeches to disinfect and treat the wound.

It had worked and twelve hours after Mac had arrived the wound seemed to be healing quite nicely. Meanwhile, Penny had been in Altringham purchasing a factory, which was twenty miles from Liverpool. She'd received a telegram that had been forwarded from her factory in London. It was from a Captain Pollack; Mac was recovering nearby and talking constantly about her. Pollock said that he had inspired many men and that everyone wanted Mac to pull through. Penny headed immediately to the hospital to see him and had been there ever since. As Mac heard the story, he could not believe his luck.

Mac was never one to stay still, even as a kid he had run around the streets of London every day. Even though the doctors recommended lots of rest, he found himself getting up and around every day. Penny had been with him as much as possible and many of his fellow shipmates had come to visit him. Captain Pollack had been past twice, and Mac found himself growing really fond of him. They talked Naval tactics and of home—probably the most exciting conversations Mac had had since joining the Navy. Several weeks after entering the hospital, Mac was ready to leave the hospital.

Many people were surprised with his rapid recovery and urged him to stay longer, just to be safe. He had been resting well and had become bored rather quickly. He now had two huge scars on his leg and abdomen but felt recuperated and had walked around Liverpool with Penny for the last few days. They both enjoyed this city; he promised her that they'd return once the war ended. The only problem was that he saw no end to the war. He truly believed that this could go on for years; a decade of war and skirmishes didn't seem to be outside the realm of possibility. *Is this ever going to change? What happens if I get injured again? Will I be this lucky?*

Despite his dark brooding and introspection, Penny had enjoyed the time with Mac. It was a necessary break but she had to return to London for a meeting with government officials. She'd been with Mac often but had also used it as an excuse to visit factories in neighboring towns. Her industrial empire had drastically grown in the last few months.

Mac and Penny took the train from Liverpool to London together and said their goodbyes. Mac had tears in his eyes as he said goodbye. He watched her weave her way through the crowd and then she was gone. Penny hid her emotions from him but when she rounded a corner, she did a U turn and hid out of sight from Mac. She was able to watch him compose himself and walk off, still slowly and cautiously. She started crying uncontrollably on a bench as passersby watched but did not comment.

Mac was still on medical leave so he used to trip to go back home and see his parents. He had written them but he hadn't seen them in some time. He walked down his local street in Trevanston and walked into his house via the backdoor. His dad was sitting at the breakfast table. He looked up in shock and disbelief, then embraced Mac with the biggest hug possible. His mum came down and almost fainted; the three of them hugged for what seemed like an eternity.

Mac's parents had not been able to visit him in hospital due to the recent start of the school year. Truth be told, they could not take time away from Bletchley. They loved having Mac home and Rebecca was hoping that he would not be fit enough to return to the service. Mac spent a whole week in Trevanston while his parents were teaching. It was September but it seemed to him that his parents were working longer hours than he had ever remembered. He spent the days around Trevanston visiting Eddie's family and the Kings Arms. He was amazed to see how little had changed—the village, the buildings, shops, and pubs remained unchanged, frozen in time. But it was now a ghost town. Every family had sons and husbands at war. Mac spent every night with Eddie's brother in the pub and dearly missed him.

At the beginning of October, Mac went to the naval hospital in Reading and was given the all clear. He was assigned a ship. Captain Pollack had kept his promise and requested him. Mac said his goodbyes and headed back to Liverpool.

CHAPTER 62

Wheaton's units had dramatically increased its size and the base now resembled small town with an estimated eight thousand personnel. It was even bigger than Trevanston. Major Wheaton was still around but when Eddie had joined this command unit, Wheaton was often out with the men, laughing and joking. Now he was much more behind the scenes. Many of the new men often asked questions about Wheaton with rumors that his missions were too erratic and dangerous. The training had also grown more intense and many of the men were exhausted.

Eddie ignored the comments from the new men. Wheaton had trained them well and that training had saved them in the first mission. More importantly, he had been fighting alongside them—he wasn't a leader who hid from danger and Eddie respected that. Eddie ignored the comments from the new men. Wheaton had trained them well and that training had saved them in the first mission. More importantly, he had been fighting alongside them—he wasn't a leader who hid from danger and Eddie respected that.

It was hard to believe that he'd been in this place for nearly a year. He was used to the heat and humidity now, the food and the way of life. On a daily basis, he woke up sweating and felt drained before the day even started. Major Wheaton had promoted Eddie to Captain. He now had a unit of men under him and was the squadron leader during drills and exercises. Wheaton was big on preparation and so every day all the units would do different drills. Eddie's men had just completed a two-day mission in the jungle. They marched day and night, through the pitch black and had experienced no sleep. It was therefore a welcome relief to be back at the base and having to deal with light exercises. Eddie was astute enough to know that a huge mission was on the horizon given the harsh preparations everyone was subjected to.

The base was very diverse. There were multiple men from Liverpool, some from Hertfordshire, men from Kent, some Australians, and some Nepalese locals. Eddie had bonded with a couple of lads from Liverpool, Hastings and Jenkins. Both were also Captains and had been there from the beginning. Most importantly they also had a love for football. Jenkins had played for Tranmere Rovers before the war. Eddie was still very close with Aiden and Clarence and even Lieutenant Bond, who had also been promoted and oversaw several units including Eddie's. There were very few of them left from the original few thousand. Some had died on missions, some had been injured, others could not accept the conditions and requested to be moved. There was therefore by default a camaraderie with those men who had stayed on. Wheaton's men had been nicknamed the "Chindits" which was a Nepalese for "lion". They had become famous in England with reporters from most newspapers diligently reporting their daring missions and this boosted morale back in England.

The problem was that the missions they ran were insanely dangerous. The morale in the camp had actually fallen because of the high number of deaths and injuries. That was fuel to the already growing fire of men who were unhappy with the training schedule. Eddie and the other leaders had their work cut out for sure. After recuperating from the latest training exercise, Eddie looked in the mirror for a moment. He could hardly recognize the man staring back. When he left for the war, he'd been clean-shaven with wavy blonde hair. Now, most of those blonde waves were shorn off and he had a short scruffy beard. His shoulders were heavily scarred due to the action in Greece and his eyes looked like an old man's. He stopped staring, put his shirt on, and found Aiden playing dice with some of the men. Aiden had a much more visible scar than Eddie's. It ran down the side of his face. A Japanese soldier had slashed him with a machete during his first mission. All the men knew how lucky they were to be alive. Eddie remembered meeting his unit at Wembley; most of them were now dead.

That evening, the men sat around drinking beer. The subject of fallen comrades had caused a deep silence. "Rumor has it there will be a massive operation going down soon," Clarence the Australian said, breaking the silence. Bond, who knew more than most, just sipped his beer and slowly nodded. That was enough for the rest of them to understand his meaning—*let's not talk about this*. All of them had heard the rumors and the exercises indicated they were going to do something big real soon. Eddie actually preferred a big assault; it increased one's chances of survival since it was strength by numbers as opposed to a few on a suicide mission.

"So, let's all get injured and go home," Aiden joked.

"What will you do if you get out of here," Clarence asked the group.

"See my wife, take our son, and go live somewhere away from everyone" Bond answered first.

"Go down to my local pub and drink until I pass out at the bar," Aiden responded. They all laughed. "I like that, I'm going to paint Melbourne red." Hastings had promised to go watch Tranmere play every week and the banter moved to how terrible they were. Then they looked next to Eddie.

Eddie pondered a minute and sipped his beer. He thought of returning home, hug his mum and brothers and sisters, then see his friends. He smiled and thought of the football team, of Mac, Rose, and Penny. He wondered if any of them were even alive now. He had not heard from anyone in months, partly because the mail service was terrible but also because everyone was fighting their own war. He simply responded "make sure my brother opens his bar all day and has decent beer". The crowd again laughed.

They finished their beers and went back to the housing with their respective units. Eddie decided it was time to write some letters and he spent the next few hours writing to Penny, Rose, Mac, and his mum. He didn't even know if they had a mailbox here, so he just stored them in his bag. Just as he fell asleep the lights went back on and Eddie was instructed to lead his men out to stand to attention. Flood lights lit up the base and the noise of insects filled the area. Eddie was so used to bug bites now that they didn't bother him. During the middle of the night, they were everywhere. Major Wheaton stood on a podium with Bond next to him and Eddie instantly knew they were heading out. "The Japs have a base we have uncovered and it also looks like a prison with some of our men there, we need to overcome this base."

Wheaton then went on to explain that Eddie, Aiden, Clarence, Hastings, and Jenkins were all to go in, led by Lieutenant Bond, and march straight through the jungle. While they attacked from the front, other units would parachute in and attack from behind.

"Kill the enemy, get our brothers home, send a signal that we own this jungle," were Wheaton's parting words. Eddie looked at to Bond and he knew from the grim look that this was indeed a suicide mission.

CHAPTER 63

Life in the countryside moved too slowly for Rose. In Carshalton, there was a constant buzz in the hospital, even if that buzz was due to a new bomb attack or people injured from fighting. Even though Rose never wanted that, she did miss the energy. Yorkshire reminded her of Wales and—more importantly—the reason she had left. It was too quiet there. Everyone knew everyone else in the village. What do you do when there's nothing left to be done?

Lil, on the other hand, was positively loving life right now. There was no curfew and her day was so easy. The nurses still worked in shifts and they were getting more children in from London or Coventry, both of which were heavily bombed. Rose and Lil could complete their rounds in a couple of hours and then find themselves with little else to do. In London, they would work twelve hours and still not be done with all their tasks. Carshalton was also a main hospital, so if other departments were short then the nurses would pitch in and help each other out. Rose had worked several shifts in the burn ward, the emergency department, and—her favourite—the orthopedic department where she cast broken bones.

Hemmington on the other hand was a small hospital and ninety percent of the patients were children who'd been sent here for their safety. Half the children that had come up with them had now been placed in homes around the area.

The town itself was desolate. Most of the men from the area were enlisted, so the whole town consisted of older men and women telling stories of the first war while the young women were anxious to hear if their husband, brother, or son had been another casualty.

Lil had been out with the American Air Force most nights and had developed a reputation for being fun. Rose had gone out several times, but had spent most evenings at the hut reading and writing. She was disturbed to hear in one letter from her mother that her younger sister had gone to be a nurse in France. No, maybe it was jealousy she felt. She had been reading a lot on nursing and was ready to take further qualifications. The war tended to halt any official career progress but she was keen to get as many nurse's badges as possible.

On this particular night however, she did have plans and she was excited but a little apprehensive. Clint had been flying a lot of night missions and so they had not really seen each other, but he had popped round the other day with flowers and asked for her company this evening. It was amazing to Rose that it was now nearly November and she had first met Clint in July. Time flies she thought as she prepared herself.

Clint was very attractive but she was not sure how she felt about him. She just didn't feel the warm buzz she'd had with Eddie. She had written to his family recently and his brother had replied to say Trevanston was the same, the Hartley's still dominated the town. No one had heard from Eddie in months, but they blamed the mail service. International service was notorious for being unreliable. Bill said that Mac had recently been home and had been injured, but recuperated well and had now gone back to the Navy. Clint had asked for Rose to meet him at the station and said he would organize the evening. She met him promptly at five o'clock and he was standing waiting for her. There was a kind of awkwardness as he went to hug her and they didn't kiss. "I thought we would explore somewhere else tonight," he said while winking at her. After a couple of minutes, the train pulled into the station.

For the next hour on the train, it was really quiet. They spoke about the English countryside; Clint mentioned that he grew up in a city and so before being deployed here, he'd had never seen so much greenery. They arrived at Sheffield. Rose knew it was an historically important city because of its steel manufacturing but not much else. The station was built of yellow stone and looked like your typical Victorian station. They found a small café and grabbed a spot. Rose enjoyed a good cup of tea while Clint drank beer. It was a Wednesday night and the café was mostly empty. They were relieved they could easily hear each other, which was a welcome change from all the noisy pubs they'd been to.

Rose talked about her family, how her two sisters were doing. One was still in Wales while the other, Gwenn was now in France. She talked about her dad's contribution to the war and how he worked with her cousin Penny now after her uncle had died. After dinner they explored the city. Like every other city in Britain, it had many derelict buildings and sirens ran over all the streets. But tonight, with a brisk wind attacking them, the streets and the sirens stayed silent. There were a few revelers coming in and out of pubs but the streets were empty otherwise.

Rose saw a tram and since neither of them had ever been on one before, they hopped on and headed towards the football ground of Sheffield Wednesday before returning back to the city. The conversation flowed and took a turn towards Clint and his family. He had three brothers, two of which were fighting in the Pacific and the last was now in Norfolk. Clint hoped to see him soon, his excitement very evident. His dad was a banker and they had lived a comfortable life. He had played American football and explained that he had been the star player—a quarterback—but he lost Rose in the middle of explaining the rules.

Clint had enrolled straight after Pearl Harbor, along with his brothers and thousands of others. He did basic training and was sent to the UK for his first deployment. He was an airplane gunner. Most of his missions were bombing runs over Germany. The idea of dropping a bomb on people left Rose uneasy. She knew very well what that scene looked like. Clint caught the look in her eyes and downplayed the missions, that he and his crew mainly bombed factories and industrial areas, places where there wouldn't be many people or civilians.

They ended back at Sheffield station and the conversation started to fizzle out. They spoke about their plans for the next few weeks. Rose was on shift permanently for the foreseeable future while Clint had to fly some missions. The train pulled into the station and Clint held the carriage door for Rose. It was a third-class cabin so it didn't have any lighting. The only illumination came way of wayward moonlight that bounced off the low night clouds. Occasionally a star would peak out from behind the curtain. Rose looked at the stars and thought of that evening in Trevanston several years ago. That was her first day away from Wales.

She'd been alone, she had never met Eddie or Mac, she wasn't even that close to Penny, and yet that night was a magical night. For some reason, the four of them in that field felt like it was meant to be. She had not heard from Penny in a while but her parents would tell her if they had heard anything. She had not heard from Eddie or Mac in a long time now, she could hardly even remember when. This war had taken so many lives, all she could do was hope they were ok.

Her thoughts were interrupted by Clint. They'd just pulled into the station. They walked up the hill to her hut in silence; when he went to say goodnight, they kissed. This time the kiss just didn't feel the same. "Clint," she said as he headed back down the hill. "I loved tonight. I enjoy your company but I'm not feeling a spark. I'm sorry, I know that sounds daft but something's not there."

"Thank God you said that," he replied, which took Rose by surprise. "Rose you are amazing but this whole time, I haven't been able to stop thinking about this girl back home. I'm the one who's sorry." They both laughed at the situation and instantly the heavy awkwardness was lifted. "Let's be friends," they both said at the same time. They laughed some more and that left Rose smiling the rest of the night.

Throughout the next few weeks, they spent their free time together. Everyone joked that they were a couple. The truth was Rose loved his company. He was a good friend and she saw him more like a brother than anything else. He had opened up about the girl back home. Her name was Jill and how she had gone to prom with him, which sounded very American. She told him about Eddie and even though she had only met him a few times, she spoke about him often and how she had butterflies in her stomach at the thought of him. She couldn't believe he had gone to see her quickly at Carshalton. They had become great friends and it had made the cold November in a lonely countryside more bearable and less harsh.

CHAPTER 64

For Penny, being an only child had meant that Christmas was normally a small occasion where the 3 of them sat, had a nice meal, played cards, and played records on before falling asleep. Before the war, Penny had spent time with Mac's family as well her own. It was nice and reminded her of what she'd always had with her family.

Last Christmas had been completely different, just her mum and Penny sitting in a cold underground station giving out soup to the children and ignoring the cheers before they both headed out to warden. This year, Penny needed something different. She needed a break from London and her work. Lorraine also needed a break as well; it was about time they both smiled, so she'd written to Mac's parents about spending Christmas together and they had loved the idea of spending Christmas, all of them together. Penny was hopeful she could turn it into a fun day.

The trains didn't run on Christmas day, so Penny had booked the two of them into the only hotel in Trevanston called The Staffordshire from Christmas Eve to Boxing Day. The Staffordshire was a luxurious Tudor building in the middle of the town centre. As dignitaries passed from Birmingham to London, they often stayed there. It was truly luxurious. Penny had never stayed there but had often walked past it. She figured why not phone them and see what was available and was able to get two rooms. So far, this holiday was off to a great start.

They met at Euston station and it was eerily silent. Christmas had almost been forgotten and the sound of the wind whistling through the station echoed. You could almost see the wind and Lorraine commented that it was the dead souls trying to get home for Christmas. *How creepy,* Penny thought.

The train ride was also quiet, and it gave Penny and Lorraine time to catch up. Penny spoke about the last few months at the factories. This year had been a complete roller coaster. Since Owain's death nearly two years ago, Penny had been busy negotiating and had purchased many similar factories from retiring owners. Now she leased them back to men wanting to work, but she owned most of the properties and was due a cut of any profit now and after the war. In total, she had built an empire and had forty-six factories in her name. As men now returned from war, she had relinquished control of most of these, sat back, and watched the revenue trickle in. *Who said women can't run a business* she thought.

Her mum discussed how she'd been helping other widows and single mothers to survive. Although lots of the children had been evacuated from London, many were still around and most schools had been closed. So, Lorraine helped organize school classes for children and support groups for mothers. They pulled into Trevanston station. The temperature had drastically dropped, so they scuttled down Trevanston road for about a mile in the darkness. By the time they got to The Staffordshire, Penny's lips were blue.

Lorraine said she wanted a bath in her room and to relax for the evening so they said their goodbyes and promised to meet tomorrow morning. "Merry Christmas dear, love you," her mum whispered in her ear. They hugged and kissed each other on the cheek. Lorraine stepped back and took it all in with wide eyes. "Such a lovely hotel, thank you." Penny went into her room and sat down to read, but couldn't. So, she decided she would head down the road to the Kings Arms pub, get herself a sherry, and fall asleep. She walked in and the nostalgia hit her; the last time she was there was the night she Rose, Mac, and Eddie were there.

That was Rose's first night in London and Mac and Eddie's last week before they signed up. She felt bad—she had promised to look after Rose but had not spoken to her in months since she moved to Yorkshire. She wondered about Eddie and Mac, of course. She still hoped that both of them would end up happily married, maybe even in Trevanston but she had seen so much heartbreak that her faith was waning. All of the factories were staffed almost entirely by women and every week there was notification that a husband or boyfriend had died.

"Well blow me, Penny is that you?" Penny looked up and Eddie's brother, Bill, was running over to her.

"How've you been?"

"Come in, come in," he said, grabbing and putting her on a bar stool. "What would you like?" he asked. Penny was taken aback but ordered a sherry and he came back with it. "On the house," he said. "Lads, you remember Mac? This was his beau, Penny." A few other guys nodded and welcomed Penny. "Nearly all the football team is gone, but these are the brothers, fathers, and uncles who were left behind," Bill explained. They talked and got into why Penny was back, how she needed a break, how the loss of her dad and the lack of hope in London made her bring Lorraine to Trevanston. "Say no more. You, your mum, and Mac's folks all come here and we'll be having a knees up anyway." Penny gladly accepted the offer.

The next day she met her mum for breakfast at the hotel. There were only a few other guests staying there, so they had a white glove service for breakfast even with the rations in place. There was the awkward moment of having to show her ration card before being served. Penny nursed the tea she had while telling her mum about the evening. She insisted that they all go to the pub today for lunch, but Lorraine wasn't so sure. Penny was not taking no for an answer, however. When she met with Mac's parents, she embraced them and led them to the pub.

Mac's parents were very reserved. Mac's father never drank alcohol and they preferred small groups of people to large crowds. Mac had been an only child from a young age and they had not been able to have other children, so this war had aged them. They had always liked Penny but she was very different to them. She was the life and soul of any party. She had taken Mac to dances and concerts in London and that was not them at all. But then again, Mac had fallen head over heels for Penny and Roger and Rebecca knew Penny was likely to be their daughter if Mac survived the war.

Today was Christmas, a time for celebration after all, so Roger drank lemonade while Rebecca had brandy as they sat with Lorraine. The best thing for them was that several young men, Bill included, had been taught by Mac's parents and so came up to them and told them how much they loved Mac, how he was a great teammate and member of the community.

Bill spent time with them, telling stories about Mac, such as him trying for hours to get a training regime in place for the team only for Eddie to turn up and tell everyone to go to the pub or the time Mac had got the cane at school because Eddie had booted a ball on the roof and they both climbed up there. They laughed and smiled; it was so nice to hear these stories, even if he wasn't as well behaved as they had been led to believe.

Lorraine spent most of her time chatting with locals from the pub, a nice change for her as opposed to the same stories she'd hear while in the underground. All of the Hartley's arrived in the afternoon and Penny welcomed them all. She thought Dorothy looked frail, but she still sat there with a sherry in hand. Bill had a piano in the corner of the bar and, after a few drinks, Catherine started playing the piano and singing. It wasn't long until the whole bar joined in. Roger, Rebecca, and Lorraine all seemed to be having fun. Penny kept grinning. It had been a fantastic Christmas for the whole village and Penny had realized how important life, not work, was.

Penny loved Trevanston and, although she loved London, she now felt more at home here. At the end of the night the last orders were ran and people started to go home. Roger gave Penny a huge hug. He whispered into her ear, "Thank you so, so much. You've made me smile again." For a brief moment, everyone was a happy family.

CHAPTER 65

It was cold up in the Yorkshire Dales; a frost lay on the ground and while it was not snowing there was no sun and just pure grey clouds filling the skyline. The wind howled at Rose's lodging and the whole room was freezing. She had a glass of water next to her bed and it had started to ice over. Happy Christmas she thought. Many of the nurses had left to go home for Christmas and there were only a couple of them around meaning Rose had to do multiple shifts. At least the hospital was warm she thought.

Rose stretched and put her feet on the concrete ground, it was unbelievably cold so she hopped to the bathroom, cleaned her teeth and then got ready for the morning. As she was leaving another nurse, Elaine was also leaving her living area and so both of them walked briskly to the hospital. Rose had a knitted hat on thanks to her mum who had sent it to her and that helped with the wind, but it was still cold. Elaine was originally from Leeds and so she was a local to the area, she like Rose, had volunteered as soon as possible and had been located at St Thomas' hospital in central London but had also been evacuated and had actually loved it as it meant she was near her family.

Rose liked her, she liked most of the nurses but Elaine was engaged to her fiancé who was fighting in Europe and was like Rose in the sense that she didn't want to go out drinking and partying every night. They walked into the hospital and got to work in an organized way. More and more children continued to be evacuated and then when they were better they were placed into foster homes throughout the English countryside. Currently this hospital had about 80 children. Rose saw where she was assigned and quickly started to make her rounds. She went into the first room a boy called Daniel was sitting in bed, he was an 11 year old boy, full of energy but had burns all over the left side of his body from a bomb and was drastically scarred. What was worse was that his mum had been killed in the blast and his dad was off fighting. Still Daniel was really happy to see Rose and started talking to Rose about football while Rose checked his vitals.

Then Rose moved on to Samantha. Samantha had a broken leg, again from a bomb blast. Her mum had written to her everyday and was hoping to have her back in Birmingham with her, but she had to work at the factory on Christmas. Samantha spoke to Rose about her love of Cadbury chocolate and how she could smell the factory from her home.

Rose continued her rounds for the next couple of hours and it was a similar pattern, the kids were all in great spirits talking about a lot of things including Santa, Christmas presents and other things to excite them. But there were only 3 parents in her ward, because many couldn't make it. She caught Elaine who had been doing her own rounds and she reported a similar situation and after a further investigation out of the 80 children only 7 had parents there at Christmas. These children didn't ask for the war, they were innocent and they deserved a nice Christmas Rose thought, but what could she do. Between the nurses they hatched a plan, Elaine was to go down to the hospital kitchen and bake treats and Rose and Lil were in charge of rounding up visitors.

Rose and Lil knew instantly where they were going, they wrapped up warm and headed to the US air base. At the entrance to the base two uniformed men stood at the checkpoint. They were obviously cold and bored and so stopped Lil and Rose in their tracks. They were in no mood to let them into the air base and so they were stuck and the plan had failed. Rose felt heartbroken.

Just then a truck was leaving the airbase, it stopped next to Rose and Lil standing on the side of the base and from the back of the truck two men got out. "You ladies need a lift" and Rose seized her opportunity "I need to talk to Clint". "He is at the base, they are flying tonight so he was sleeping when we left". Lil jumped in and explained the situation to the two men. "It's Christmas day and there are a bunch of children without presents and they need some cheer" Lil pleaded to the men, some of whom she knew and she used this to her advantage. Suddenly there were murmurs from the truck and other men jumped out. After a few whispers Arthur Bryant, the guy who had met Rose and Lil that first day with Clint spoke for all the men "We are in agreement, these kids need a good Christmas, hell we all need a good Christmas" we will be there this afternoon with gifts.

Lil reached over and hugged them all and Rose politely shook hands and thanked them. They gave them both a lift to the hospital and promised to be back about 2pm. The rest of that morning all the nurses, the few parents and even some local villagers were preparing a feast and also decorating the hospital. Other patients not children were also getting involved and there was a feel good atmosphere around the hospital.

Everyone ate lunch and shared stories. Rose felt this was the best day she had had in Yorkshire and she was enjoying the local spirit. but she was getting anxious, constantly looking over at the clock, the American airforce men had yet to arrive as the clock struck 2pm then 2.30pm, perhaps they were not coming.

Then at 2.40pm a loud commotion appeared at the entrance to the hospital, Lil looked at Rose and said "they are here" with a wink. Rose looked over to see Santa walking down the corridor, "ho ho ho" he bellowed in a deep American accent. "sorry we are all late, but we wanted to make sure we had gifts for the kids". As all the men walked in you could see the effort they had put in. The men came with presents including US airforce badges, model planes and cans of soda. They had even baked fresh biscuits although insisted on calling them cookies. Santa had gone to every child and their faces had been a delight, Samantha had the biggest smile ever as she got to meet Santa while eating an American biscuit.

Rose had kind of hoped to see Clint, but understood that if he had to fly he was probably preparing with his crew. Finally when Santa had visited all the kids he came to Rose, "I think you have also been a good girl this year" he whispered and Rose realized that Clint was in fact Santa. She pulled down his beard and he smiled at her. She hugged him and thanked him for this. He then gave her some American chocolate with peanut butter, very weird but still a nice gesture. They spent a good hour chatting about Christmas' and their families and then he really did have to leave. He was such a close friend to her and almost like a brother. She thanked him and then went back to the hospital to clean up. That night she fell asleep as soon as she got home, it had been a special day.

CHAPTER 66 -1944

The new mission had been outlined and rehearsed three days before Christmas, but they had been delayed by the weather for several weeks. They eventually departed, but this time using lightweight planes to put them behind enemy lines. From there, they would march up to the base. This time, they'd sent in another unit to build a make shift airstrip for them to land. They planted trucks in a strategic location for an easier exit. Wheaton was frustrated last time with the number of men left behind because of injuries, so he sought to make amends. The landing had more smoothly than expected. Eddie and his unit had been out here for over a year, behind the enemy lines constantly training and so the missions could go as smoothly as possible. One of Eddie's men, Johnson, had been trained in orienteering and had currently led the men for two days. Since he was the only one that knew how to read maps, they had no other choice. Eddie was however becoming frustrated with the whole thing, he could swear that they had walked in circles.

They had entered Burma and were heading East towards the Japanese line. They had estimated it would take two days to reach the enemy encampment and they were coming up close to that. This whole mission relied heavily on timing and proper execution—a delicate balancing act that left no margin for error. If they got there too early, they wouldn't have backup for the assault. Get there too late, the support unit would be exposed and their escape would have be compromised. Bond checked his watch as the sun set.

"We should see their base any minute now, assuming we're still on schedule," he whispered to Eddie. With one quick hand signal, all the men braced themselves ready for attack. Any noise would give them away and they knew Japanese snipers would strike quickly and mercilessly. They were in a field of tall grass, climbing a steep hill with the sun setting on their backs.

Eddie suspected that once they got to the top, the base would be at the bottom on the other side. It was still humid but their strict training and rationing had trained them to sip water and make it last. The ground was wet and muddy from a heavy rainfall and Eddie looked up to the sky. *A storm coming in as well,* he thought. *How ominous.*

Johnson checked the map again and whispered to them, "We should see the base by the now." He looked angrily at himself. Bond reassured him that the bottom of valley was nearby, that they'd see it soon. Sure enough, as they crested the hill, they saw a dark grey concrete building with razor wire on top in front of them at the bottom of the valley. Bond, Eddie, Clarence and Aiden all took out binoculars as the rest of the men duck down to take cover.

Aiden gasped and clenched his fist as he was looking to the left of the building. Eddie and Bond both looked in his direction and they saw men hanging from rafters and trees with British uniforms on. Along the ground, they saw a large pit full of dead bodies. They'd definitely found the right place and were staring at their fallen comrades. Eddie wanted go down there now but knew he couldn't. Anger ran over him; it was one thing to kill a man in a battle, another to kill a prisoner. These men had indirectly reported to Wheaton but had been located in a different area of the country and had apparently been ambushed several weeks ago.

Between the men, they hashed out a plan of attack. Eddie and his men would provide cover and throw grenades down as the other men would charge down into what looked like a side gate near where the bodies of the British soldiers were. There was a small, one-windowed building and that was likely where the rest of the prisoners were. That was now their new target. Bond tried to get in touch with HQ so that the attack could be coordinated but he couldn't. They had hoped the other men would fulfill their part. The plan had called for a night attack so they waited, ate their rations and geared up for the attack.

At nine o'clock, the men were getting ready when they heard a loud bang from behind the base. That was their cue—the other men had arrived and started the attack. Eddie and his men took cover from their vantage point all with machine guns ready, lying on the muddy ground while insects and other creatures crawled all around and bats were let loose from the tree line, startled by the gunfire and war cries. Bond coordinated the attack with Eddie, Aiden, Clarence, and the other unit. They gave each other a brief nod, shared a few hugs and said "God be with you," before marching down the valley and into battle.

There were gun blasts everywhere while Eddie tried to focus on enemies and shoot but he couldn't see anything. From the bottom of the valley, right next to the base, a huge orange flame appeared and all of Eddie's men were blown off their feet from the percussion and the heat. Eddie was disoriented for a minute but quickly got up and gathered all of his men. They all seemed unhurt but the gunfire was still flying around them. It was very hard for Eddie to concentrate and figure out if all of his unit were there. Yells came from behind them and as Eddie turned around, he saw men scrambling up the hill. They were British soldiers. Lying all over like carelessly thrown toys, the men were covered by the night while Eddie and his men ran to help them. They were in distress and Eddie felt around for a man's arm, found one and lead by example carrying him to the top of valley and tried figure out what happened.

"There was bloody oil on the ground and they lit us all up," the man whispered. Eddie nearly vomited at the thought. He was one of the leaders here and he needed to make a decision on what to do, but without more information, he couldn't justify having his men rush off and wind up worse than these troops. He just stood there with bangs and shouting all around him. He felt like a coward for not doing anything.

Someone grabbed him and dragged him into the fight; it was Aiden. Eddie squinted his eyes and could see Aiden had burn marks but otherwise, looked ok. "We need to get out of here," he said breathlessly.

"Where's Bond?"

"I'm here," he said. "Clarence's unit is all dead, as are Jenkins's unit. They walked in and were all lit up. I watched them all burn."

There was silence amongst them all now. Bond spoke up again and roused them from their trance. "Ok, gather round." He started to speak and all the men huddled in together and ducked down away from immediate fire. "Clarence's unit and Jenkins's unit are both dead, the whole entrance was lit up and they retreated back inside." "All my men are still in play," Eddie said softly, still in shock. "That includes Johnson," Bond asked.

"Yep, I'm here."

"Good. Johnson, get that map out and start looking at options."

"I have several injured and two gone," Aiden chimed in. "We were behind Clarence so they took the brunt." Aiden told them that Thatcher, the guy Eddie had rescued in Greece, had been shot in the head and another died from his burns.

"Sounds like the other units are still fighting and we still have the prisoners," Bond said, his statement sounding more like a thought. "How many grenades do we have," he asked in between wheezes. They had twenty-four between them. "So, here's the plan. Eddie, you and your men go round the back and help your comrades.

You are to get into that building, get the prisoners out, and sprint up the other hill with the men from the other unit. Johnson, you need to find the easiest way out from that side and get us back to the strip. Aiden, you and the rest of the men are going to get all the grenades and walk back down there. When I give the nod, throw the grenades in the fire, create a bunch of fireworks, and distract them enough for Eddie to get in, then we run round the side and everyone will leave as one unit." It sounded like an impossible task, but Bond was the leader and his plans always saved lives.

"Sir," a young lad named Clark spoke up. "I know where the trucks will be waiting for the men on the other side. It's a small village in the jungle. My brother is one of the truck drivers."

"You stay with Johnson and work that out on the map."

"Guys we can all be heroes tonight or we can die trying to save our brothers," Bond whispered with authority. With that, the men exchanged goodbyes for the second time in ah hour and started the plan. Eddie hugged Aiden and said, "See you on the other side." The two of them had hugged before every battle and it had become a superstitious ritual that they both felt it served them well.

Eddie's thought that if they stayed at the top of the hill, walking around it, he would eventually get to the other side. He had no idea what he was walking on and no idea if he would encounter the enemy but they kept walking. Eddie guessed this was like a valley in Trevanston which he used to run around so he thought it would take fifteen minutes to get around at his current pace.

After about ten minutes, a man in the unit started choking and fell to the ground. "Must be a snake bite or some insect," another man said. There was nothing they could do to save him. Eddie had to just leave him, although his heart winced. That boy had a mother and the unit had left him for dead. When the fight was over, they would grab the dog tags of the fallen in order to return them to the family of the fallen. Eddie heard a noise up ahead and then voices—English voices. "Who goes there?" Eddie asked them the same question back and a man said, " Third brigade." It was one of the units from Liverpool, led by Captain Hastings. They were accompanied by some Nepalese men.

Eddie counted thirty additional men in all who had retreated up the valley. He knew that if he went down the valley now, he would get to the back entrance. Eddie slowly peeked down the valley and could see the bright orange glow in the background. He told the other men of the plan and then they all crept down the valley. Gunshots had stopped and the attack on the base had stopped, but the Japanese knew they were still out there. The men got within a couple of hundred feet from the base in silence before someone shouted in a foreign language and gunfire erupted. Out of nowhere, the Japanese rushed and attacked them, it seemed liked they were standing next to Eddie. Instinct took over and he shot the first man running at him, before using his bayonet to stab a second. The man lay on the ground and Eddie slit his throat for good measure.

The gunfire was enough for Aiden to do his part and loud bangs came from the other side of the ravine. Eddie knew that was the diversionary explosion and the men charged. Eddie just fired in front of him, shooting two and running over their bodies. The men got to the gate and opened it, charging the compound, and shooting everywhere.

They found the prison and opened it. Eddie had no idea how many men he had left with, let alone how many were inside, but as he opened the door the stench of rotting flesh was everywhere. There was no light but Eddie could vaguely see men in just their underwear. They looked so skinny, they hardly looked like men at all. Eddie was sick with what he saw. Slowly, they ambled out and Eddie asked the last prisoner if there were any more.

He ordered all the men back up the valley and with guns firing everywhere, they made it to the top with Bond and Aiden waiting there. "Let's get the hell out of here!" All the men started running away from the base as fast as they could, but many of the prisoners could not walk so the men each carried one of them over their shoulders.

CHAPTER 67

Eddie's stomach ached, his legs spasmed—he was flat-out exhausted. They ran and stumbled as fast in the pitch-black jungle for over an hour. The prisoners who had escaped had been starved and tortured so Eddie and the remaining men had to carry their fellow comrades. Eddie was unsure how he could go on. He wanted to vomit, felt the acid rise into his throat. Starvation was overwhelming his senses and his jellied legs were due to give out soon but he had to find these trucks and get out of here. He was really hoping that Clark and Johnson knew where they were going. *Where are those bloody trucks?!?*

Eddie had some injuries—the worst seemed be a burn on his arm—but compared to the other men, he was one of the lucky ones. A mile or so back they had made the decision to leave a fellow soldier behind. He'd caught a bullet in his leg and couldn't move well any longer. He knew how much of liability he'd become if they tried to bring him back. *Left to die in a jungle*, Eddie thought. *What hell.* Eddie made sure to grab his dog-tags, something his family could remember him by.

Eddie thought of his mum in that moment, thought about when he had signed up he was the youngest in the family and conscription wasn't fully implemented. He wondered how many other family members had died and if his mum was even still alive.

One soldier told Eddie that since the beginning of time, war was needed to keep the world's population down. Therefore, according to him, this war was ensuring the survival of humanity. All Eddie knew at this moment was that he didn't care about saving others, nonetheless the bloody human race. He despised this war and wanted to get as far away as possible from it.

They kept going until Aiden indicated for them to get down. The next thing Eddie heard was the whizzing of bullets. Aiden crawled back down the line to talk with Eddie while under heavy fire.

"Two towers up ahead, big problem," he told Eddie. "If we sit and stay here, we'll be fine. It's so dark that they can't help but shoot blindly at us but in the morning we'll be sitting ducks. We can't shoot back yet. Maybe we can get them in the morning, but it'll be an all-out gunfight. We have no idea who or how many we are up against. The other option is that we can shuffle now on hands and knees and try to get away," Aiden said.

Eddie didn't like the options and the men were joined by Bond. "I think we have a better chance going through the long grass right now than in the morning," Bond said. They all agreed. The gun shots had stopped, and Johnson came to meet them. He was sure that they were guarding the boarder, so they wouldn't be looking in their direction. That also gave Eddie hope because if the enemy line ended a mile down the road, that meant the trucks and the British territory was almost at hand. The men got down on their hands and knees and crawled through the mud at a slow pace, trying not to be seen by the two towers. After about five minutes Aiden stopped them again. *What now*, Eddie thought. The long grass was waning and there were small huts appearing in front of them, probably less than a quarter of a mile from the towers. If this were an enemy base, they were screwed but as Eddie peered out, he couldn't see any guards, wiring, or anything resembling an encampment. *Strange,* he thought.

A lot of shuffling happened at the front of the unit but Eddie was at the rear of the unit with the prisoners now.For the meantime, he ordered everybody down. The prisoners were weak and were shivering on the damp ground. He was not sure what was happening on ahead, but they had to do something and get out of there.

Everybody lay in silence as two men walked over from the huts and stood at the front of the line. If these were Japanese soldiers, they would be game over. The men were waving them over frantically. *What in the bloody hell?* It took Eddie a minute to realize these men were locals and this was their village. Aiden glanced back at Eddie and he could read his mind; *they seem friendly but act with caution.* Slowly the men followed the villagers as they were taken down a hill. Every fifty yards, they'd bring their fingers to their lips, indicating for them to be quiet. In a ravine behind the towers was a cave. The two villagers indicated for them to stay. After they had exited, the men were worried they'd been had by the enemy, that this was a massive trap. The villagers returned with bread and water. They could not speak any English but it was clear they were trying to help. Eddie took a bowl of water, sipped some, and shared the rest with the prisoners. The meager nourishment was enough to bring them back to life.

Eddie gathered with Aiden, Bond, Johnson, and the two villagers. They were trying to explain something but all the men were having a hard time understanding it, so they started pointing down the cave. Aiden pulled out a pencil and piece of paper from one his pockets and the men drew out what they were trying to say.

The cave was a tunnel and it would lead them to the front of the towers. Just before they started to leave there was noise above, shouting then gunfire. The Japanese had entered the village. "We've got to go," Eddie shouted. Bond looked at him and shook his head in disagreement. He pointed his finger towards the celling, made a circle, then pointed at the two villagers. *The village. We can't leave without trying to save the village.* Eddie went to the end of the cave and could see the whole village. It was being spot lit. Through the rocks and up the ravine, he counted ten Japanese soldiers.

The villagers were huddled together in the center, all of them on their knees and with their hands on their heads. The women and children looked on with wide eyes as one of the villagers cried and pleaded with a Japanese soldier. He had the barrel of the soldier's rifle pointed at his temple. Eddie crawled along the ground to get a better look. The man was one of the two guides from earlier. The Japanese commander was shouting at him while the other kept the barrel pointed squarely at him. The commander pointed his finger and kept shouting. Eddie didn't understand a lick of Japanese, but he did catch one word he knew: *gaijin.* That was their pet word for the Brits. The commander was losing his temper and resorted to slapping and kicking the villager. Despite the abuse, he did not say a thing about the cave or their position. Eddie jumped down from the rocks and gave Aiden and Bond a situational report. "Gather the best men and prep for a firefight. I'll take the seriously injured and start walking them out. Lay the cover fire fast and quick. I don't want us to be exposed any longer than we have to," Bond said in between wheezes. Eddie was sure he had a problem with his lung, but he didn't bring it up. Eddie and Aiden rounded up half a dozen men and they all went back out.

"I really hope that after all this village is worth it," Aiden joked in a hushed whisper. The commander was laying into the villager mercilessly now. Fully enraged, he turned to one of his soldiers, barked an order, and pointed to a small boy in the group. He couldn't have been older than six. His cries grew louder as the soldier dragged him closer to the commander. The villager went from stoic to hysterical, pulling his hair and yelling at the commander. One of the women stood up and made a mad dash to boy but one of the soldiers hit her in the gut, dropping her on the spot. The villager ran to her, but the commander dragged him by the collar to the ground. The man cried for the woman, the boy lunging and crying for both. *This isn't good,* Eddie thought. He guessed the boy was their child and that the man was going to cave sooner rather than later.

The Japanese soldier held a gun to the boy's head now. Eddie, Aiden, and the rest drew their rifles and waited for the right moment. The soldier's eyes had a look of anxiety and confusion. Could he really pull the trigger? On the count of three, the British soldiers appeared from the rocks and started firing. The soldier flung the boy to ground and started running. Eddie took aim and clipped him in the shoulder. Gunfire ensued for a couple of minutes but the element of surprise had worked. The men were able to get the villagers down the ravine and into the tunnel. Eddie was the last man down and just as he thought he was in the clear, a bullet bit him in the butt.

Eddie fell and turned over to see a Japanese solider standing over him, readying to fire. Instinctively, Eddie grabbed his bayonet to stab the man, but a gunshot had gone off. Eddie winced and waited for the pain. Instead, the soldier fell. Behind him, the young boy was standing with a pistol in hand. "Thank you," Eddie winced. He grabbed the boy and hobbled as fast as he could through the tunnels. He followed the noise of the other men.

The men in front were running as fast as they could and after a moment, Eddie saw the trucks. After cramming all the villagers and prisoners into the trucks, Eddie scrambled onto the roof along with the boy and his father. He lay down, closed his eyes, and laughed. The laughter turned to tears as the events of the past twenty-four hours ran through his mind. He told himself he was safe now. An hour later, they were at the make shift airstrip waiting to be evacuated.

CHAPTER 68

Mac had been deployed as part of a new crew with Captain Pollack. He had departed just before Christmas; it was now the first week of March and he was currently travelling through the whole of America on train. He had boarded in New York several days ago and was now travelling through Iowa. He had no idea where Iowa was, what was there, but was fairly confident he would never return. It seemed beautiful, filled with vast fields and farmland. It was a tranquil view with the sun rising and defrosting the ice on the ground. Still, he missed England and wanted the war over with so he could return home.

Mac was travelling to Portland, Oregon with several other crewmen. He carried only a small bag and spent most of his time on the train reading about the typical American life as documented by *Life* and some newspapers he bought earlier. He read an article on school life in America. It reminded him of a time back in Trevanston when Eddie undid the screws of his desk in class. He sat there with a big grin as his desk fell apart like a wet box. He pictured the classroom and wondered how many of the boys from then are still alive. Mac's smile disappeared as he stared out the window. When they arrived at the Port of Portland, they quickly disembarked and reported for their mission. The wartime government struck an agreement with the US so that they could take some of their decommissioned ships. Mac and his men were going to guide this fleet back to England and get them ready.

As Mac walked around with the crew, he couldn't help thinking that this ship was a dump. The hull was rusted, some rivets needed to be replaced, and you had to throw yourself into some of the doors to get them to budge. She needed some love and care, but they were assured that she would sail. and Mac had no choice but to make her his new home.

It was only when Mac got back to the deck, did he realize the biggest problem. He pulled Captain Pollack aside.

"Sir, where are the guns?" Pollack looked around and laughed.

"Well, I'll be buggered."

There were empty patches where the artillery nests should have been. Pressed for time and a solution, Mac inquired about the location of the closest Army base. He and his men struck a deal with the local staff, loading a Jeep with machine guns, bazookas, and grenades. This was not going to be anything if they came up against a German battleship, but it will have to do. Mac had also found some broken anti-air guns and had even been creative with some gutters that he shaped into a gun, the idea being if they were spotted from a distance, others will at least think they were heavily armed.

That evening they set sail, travelling down to Central America, across the Atlantic around the Horn of Africa, and back up the Suez Canal. Mac had no idea why this route had been chosen or why he'd been given these orders. Sometimes, he wished the British Naval HQ were a bit more transparent and logical when it came to creating and dispensing orders. Was that too much to ask?

For the first few days, they travelled down the Pacific Coast. It was peaceful and picturesque; they saw dolphins and whales in a sea that glistened under the sun. Mac remembered being in Hawaii and thought of taking Penny to see this side of the world.

Plans changed on the fourth day. Instead of cutting across Central America, they were going to sail around South America due some intelligence determining this to be the safer route. What they didn't account for was the food. The supplies were meant to last for eight days; the revised itinerary made the journey at least twenty days. The mood on the ship became gloomy and the morale slowly slipped.

Mac tried to remain positive, but it was difficult knowing that a ship could be attacked at any minute whilst out in the Atlantic. This mission was a whole other level of anxiety in fear. They had no guns, no rations, barely enough water, and would be traveling into unknown waters to boot. But all was well. No U-boats or enemy crafts to speak of. The weather held and the ship was chugging along. The men rounded South America and headed towards Africa with no worries. For five days, the men sat around playing dominos, cards, telling stories, drinking, reading, writing letters home, and sleeping. They had refueled in Brazil and there US Naval men met them. The Yanks had snuck them a few extra supplies which boosted the crew's morale. While at the docks, he saw some Brazilians playing with a football and keeping it up; their skills were scarily good.

Watching them reminded Mac of the World Cup in 1938 where Brazil had finished third and not one to skimp on international relations, Mac and several others went and joined them for a bit. Mac hadn't kicked a ball in years and his leg was still not perfect from the injury before, but it was great fun.

On the fourteenth day, the trouble really began. To get home, they were to go through the Suez Canal, which was a vital supply route to Africa for both the Allies and Axis powers. The idea was that this would be quicker and there were enough of the British ships around that they should be safe. Mac was not so confident though. He still remembered being attacked several years ago and hobbling into port. It was nighttime when they entered the Canal, and everyone was on guard. The cold wind whipped at their faces. It was a cloudy night and the visibility was next to nothing. Mac could only hear the water lapping onto the side of the ship. In total, this leg would run eight hours, assuming no surprises. Every man acted as if they were holding their breath, compulsively checking their watches. After several hours, one of the men leaned over and whispered to Mac "Ya think we made it?" Mac nodded in approval before the ship barely skirted a depth charger. A geyser shot out from the water and held the men in rapt attention.

The ship was met with a barrage of gunfire and all the men took cover. All Mac could hear were the bullets as they whizzed around him. Then the roar of the anti-air guns started with splashes all around them and finally, the noise of a mortar directly hitting the back of their ship. Mac was thrown to the floor by the explosion and reverberation. He found his footing and scurried over to assess the damage. They'd been lucky—the mortar strike was not a direct hit. The Captain tried to turn and out maneuver the enemy, but they could still only guess where they were.

Another huge explosion hit on Mac's side. It sent water flying everywhere and all the men were doused. He was going to die here, this was it. He had just recovered from nearly being killed and he was now near death—again. Just as he closed his eyes, he heard the buzz of propellers and a squadron of RAF planes flying overhead. Lots of gunfire and explosions followed and finally a loud explosion in the distance with a small yellow flame. The enemy had been hit and they were saved.

The men stayed in position as the sun rose. Most of the men were covered in water and Mac was starting to suffer with hypothermia but no one moved in case of another attack. It was only when the sun fully rose, that they exited the canal and could see the full extent of the damage. They had lost two men who had been thrown overboard by the attack, Mac was saddened by this, thinking back to how they'd played dominoes the day before. But his mind wandered to the biggest problem now was the hole in the back of the ship due to the mortar strike. They were taking in water.

The day progressed and the men dried off. The ship was still moving forward but slowly sinking. The Captain ordered the crew to abandon all dead weight. So all the men started throwing chairs, tables, the fake guns, and anything else that was heavy overboard. The mayday message went out. The ship was slowing down and taking in more water now. That evening, several Russian ships had come to the rescue, tugging them into the port of Nice.

Mac spent a week in Nice while they repaired the ship before they disembarked for the Mediterranean. Again unarmed, the ship was making good time now. The spring weather helped and with luck on their side, they were able to travel round France and home to Portsmouth. The men all hugged each other after the mission and Mac even shared a cigarette with them. He could not believe he had survived another scare in the same stretch of water. He decided then and there he'd never ever go down the Suez Canal again.

CHAPTER 69

It had been two weeks since Eddie's last battle, but he was still haunted by what he'd seen. When he closed his eyes, all he saw were his comrades burning, him stabbing a soldier to death, the prisoners with no tongue, and the villagers helping him and his crew through the jungle. His mind played it on an infinite reel. He'd now been fighting for several years and had gone from wanting to fight for his country to loathing everything about this war. He kept telling himself that if he were lucky enough to have children, he would do everything within his power to prevent them from experiencing the same thing.

Although still technically on duty, he was recovering from his injuries. He and the other men were currently overseeing the construction of a bridge across the river in the Burmese jungle. Given the local Nepalese and Burmese Gurka men wanted to do most of the work, it meant he spent most of his time sitting on the riverbanks drinking beer and playing with elephants. These creatures amazed him with their friendliness and intelligence. Some of the elephants would be loaded up and carry large wooden panels while others would help lift the panels into place with their trunks. Eddie had been particularly fond of one, which one of the locals had guessed was about two years old. Eddie had called him Mugsy II. He would splash and shoot water at Eddie if he wasn't giving him enough attention.

Compared to others, like Bond who had multiple serious injuries, Eddie's injuries were not even a second thought, but still enough of an issue for him to be out of commission for a good couple of weeks. The lack of purpose, activity, and stimulation made Eddie's mind wander and he struggled to sleep this past couple of weeks. Some nights he would wake up sweating and panicking, recalling the battles he'd been in.

Last night he couldn't sleep and found himself crying the whole night. He still vividly remembered where he was when the war started. He was building a home and carrying bricks in a wheelbarrow when one of the other laborers heard the news and shouted to them, "We are at war again, lads." Eddie wanted to sign up immediately and go to fight. He wanted excitement in his life but never anticipated getting more than he bargained for. He remembered how he'd spent weeks trying to convince Mac to enlist. Reflecting on it now, he realized Mac and his parents were right to try and talk them out of it. "Let's finish the season and the school year together," Mac said. Eddie remembered the Cup final and that moment with Penny, Mac, and Rose, all of them staring at the stars. He had never felt anything for any woman, yet he had instantly cared about Rose. It was more than attraction—it was a connection that pulled him to her. He remembered the whole football team enlisting and he cried as he remembered their faces. Most of them had died in front of him. Now several years later he had travelled the world, been in multiple battles, killed men who were probably his age, and had seen easily one hundred men die around him.

The saddest thing for him though was that he did not know if he had anything back home to fight for. He hadn't received any mail in months. There wasn't exactly a mailman in the jungle either. He had no idea how his mum was or how his brothers and sisters were. Mac's whereabouts were unknown. To make matters worse, Eddie slowly began to realize that Rose had probably met someone else. He kept thinking over and over that he was in a no-win situation, that the odds of him getting out of this country were remote, and if he did get out, what would be left for him at home?

Eddie knew that it was on the mind of nearly every other soldier around him but none of them spoke about it. It was a hidden taboo and no one wanted to cry or show emotions in front of others. However, Mugsy II understood him. He constantly snuggled him and made him feel ok. Every day, the same elephant had come over and given him love and attention. Eddie wished he could take him back to England.

No one around him had signed up for this. The new recruits were not told of the conditions they were coming into and those like Eddie who had been in the war for a while now were ready to face the Germans and Adolf Hitler. Eddie knew very little about why Japan was even in this war. Technically Eddie, Aiden and Bond all had injuries that would warrant them a medical discharge but Wheaton had laughed off plans to send men home. He was still intent on continuing these missions and securing Burma. So, after several weeks the men were physically recuperated and sent to a base to train new recruits coming in.

Every day Eddie found himself lying to these young kids to motivate them to fight. He didn't believe in the cause; he didn't believe in the war and was half tempted to tell the kids to run away from this hell than stay and fight. But he wanted to get home now and that was his only focus. Getting arrested for abandonment or failure to do his job would be stupid.

Apart from the elephants, the only other thing that cheered him up was the fact that he was based in a small town in Burma instead of middle of nowhere India. More importantly, this town had a pub. The pub had been built before the war for the locals and for the British military unit who had been based here. It was run by a British man from Lincoln. He stocked bottled beer as well as spirits and a piano. Eddie felt like he was back at the Kings Arms. Eddie would spend every night there now drinking with Aiden. Captain Bond would join them on occasion. He had softened as a leader and was more a friend now, partly because they were the only three left from the original unit in Wembley. He'd also become disillusioned with the war which made going to the pub a no brainer. Bond was a good piano player so he frequently would play and sing. Aiden and Eddie would drink whiskey and generally talk football or anything that frustrated them. The local women all flung themselves at them daily and Eddie but he was not interested in talking to them. He secretly hoped that Rose was still alive. He dreamed of meeting her again and taking her for a date. He remembered her description of her family in Wales and imagined going to meet them, taking her to a football game, and going around London. That's what kept him going.

After several months of the same routine, Captain Bond called him aside one morning to tell him that there was a massive operation being planned. All the men, including Eddie's unit, will be going back in. "It's called Operation Thursday," he said. "Wheaton told the leaders about it this morning. Nine thousand men will be going in over several weeks." Eddie immediately started to focus again. His men needed to be ready—that was his goal. After everything he'd been through, he was committed to making it out alive and return to his normal life.

CHAPTER 70

A lot had happened to Penny in the last six months, let alone the last few years. She was sitting on a hill in front of St. Paul's Cathedral overlooking the Thames. She had always loved London, but her New Year's resolution had been to explore more of London so she had spent most of her afternoon walking along the Thames towards the banking district. She had crossed London Bridge, walked around the Tower of London, and found herself outside the cathedral. It was a beautiful March afternoon. It was perfect weather—crisp, cool air that kept you refreshed and never chilled.

London had changed so much over the last few years. Everywhere she had walked, there were buildings with craters, wrecked facades, and rubble where edifices had been. Yet the London spirit remained and not one person she spoke to complained about the war. Instead, she heard jokes and laughter and saw people who had chosen to not live in fear, to go on with their lives because the war was a part of life. Earlier in the day she'd had a meeting with one of the major banks of London. On her way there, she had seen a milk man making deliveries to the local banks and houses even though there had been a heavy attack the night before. She had spoken with several fire brigades putting out fires and cleaning debris; she'd had lunch near Borough market where the local vendors were still serving and singing. She had randomly met several priests outside St Paul's, again cleaning up the mess from the raids and laughing together. As she sat on the hill, she blushed because she was immensely proud to be from London. Even if they lost this war, the Axis would not break their spirit.

The whole point of the meeting with the bank had been to finalize her business and future. When the war started her dad had ran one furniture store and factory, but Owain had seen the potential that the war could have on his business. Besides that, his personal patriotism meant that he had wanted to find a way that he could contribute meaningfully to the war. However, it was Penny who had grown it into an empire. She was not entirely sure how she had even grown it so much, but as of Christmas she managed and owned a significant amount of land for numerous factories throughout.

But going to Trevanston at Christmas had made her realize that family was more important than money. For the last few months, she had accelerated her efforts to sell off all the factories and she now managed none of them. She had sold them all to injured soldiers and their families while she kept the land and ownership of the properties. Most of the men could not afford to buy the factories off her, so they had taken loans and Penny would receive a regular income. Before the war, these factories included tanneries, hat makers, and motorbike production.

The agreement was that the new owners had to continue the war efforts as per the government's request, but once the war was concluded, to revert to manufacturing their previous products. Penny had worked that into their contracts. All of the men were keen on the deals, seeing as how the factories were situated in their towns and villages. Jobs would be there for them, their friends, and families. A win-win for all.

She was wealthy beyond her wildest dreams and she knew she was set up for life. However, she made a promise to herself to remain humble and normal. Her dad was always humble, and she wanted to emulate him. She had not even told her mum about how much money she'd made so she continued to sometimes work on the factory line at her dad's factory, where she had started. They all knew her there and while she didn't want to let on that she had sold the factory, she had agreed with the new owner that she would work on the floor with the other women under the pretense of trying to improve processes. Deep down, she still wanted to do her part for the war and was not ready to walk away from the factory. With Mac and Owain gone, working here gave her needed solace and relief.

Just as the sun had set on the Thames, Penny got up and started to walk back towards her apartment, a forty minute walk away. She was interrupted almost immediately by the noise of the sirens. Penny did not exactly know where to go or what underground station to take shelter in. She scurried along the river until she saw the London monument. She knew there was a station near there. Her warden instinct kicked in and before she headed down the steps, she walked around the streets to try and find anyone else.

Families had set up homes around the area, just like the folks in her underground station. Bankers and businessmen were playing cards and drinking spirits in a corner. It looked like one big family gathering. One family offered her a seat with them and she found herself sitting with children around her. Despite the mass evacuation of children, plenty still lived in London and she loved their company. This station was one big curve so she couldn't even see around the corner. She had a comfy spot and she knew she would be in here for the night. As this station was closer to Central London than her local one, she could clearly here the planes flying overhead and the bombs going off in the distance. Penny wasn't scared though. She just closed her eyes and sat there calmly.

After a couple of hours Penny was feeling tired. It was only eight o'clock but it had been a long day. She was fatigued and hungry. When she started to curl up and drift off to sleep, a man ran down into the station screaming.

"Harry? Harry? HARRRRY!" It was an older man wearing an Airforce uniform. He ran from group to group, nudging people awake while yelling for Harry. At first, she thought he must be drunk but then she saw him and the desperation in his eyes. He came up to Penny and asked, "Have you seen an eight year old boy named Harry? He's my son and he's missing!" He was stammering his words. Penny jumped right up and said "No but I'll help you look."

Penny rounded up several other mums and they all searched every corner of the station. After about twenty minutes and with over a hundred people looking, it was determined that Harry was not in this station. The man started to break down and Penny consoled him.

"He was staying with his aunt in Cumbria but came back because his mother had died in a blast last week. I can't lose him as well."

"When did you last see him?" The airman told her how they'd been to St. Paul's Cathedral to mourn and then walked down by the river. He thought the boy was behind him but somehow lost him.

Penny knew that route as she had taken it herself. She calmly said to him "Stay here. I'll go to the surface and look. If he comes back, he will find you." She knew he would be in one of two places, either he had gone underground to another station or he was hiding on the street. Penny chose the streets and ran up the stairs and pushed open a chain gate and ran out.

The sirens were blaring and bombs were dropping nearby, so she ran back toward the river. She went down the steps on the bridge again and then along the river. A bomb dropped near her into the river and knocked her off her feet. She was grazed and bruised but ok. She roughly knew her way around and ran into a sign pointing her towards an underground station. This was a quieter station but she was still surrounded by people sleeping, including the priests from earlier. Instantly she saw him: a small boy sitting alone on the stairs.

"My guess is you're Harry," Penny said. The boy had been sitting with his face in his knees but looked up. His raggedy ginger hair was the same as his dad's and he was dressed as if he'd been at church. He slowly nodded. "I found your dad. He decided it would be fun to play hide and seek at different stations," she said jokingly while winking.

Penny did not want to risk taking the boy through the streets so she decided to walk down the tunnel back to Monument. One of the priests gave her a candle, a box of matches, and directions. Harry held Penny's hand tightly. They didn't speak much. The wind howled in the tunnel so she had to re-light the candle three times. The rats squealed around her and scurried indiscreetly. Meanwhile, she was terrified they'd run into a train. They walked on and eventually returned to Monument station. She was helped up the platform and brought Harry over.

The man ran over and embraced his son. News spread quickly through the tunnel and there were applause and cheering all around. After everything calmed down, the man hugged Penny and said thank you.

"Ma'am, my name is Jim. I don't know what to say. Thank you so much. How can I ever repay you?"

"Keep me company for the night. That'll be a good start."

They spent the whole night chatting. Jim was in his late forties and the same age as her mum. He was a squadron leader in the Airforce and had been a pilot for over twenty years. His squadron was based a few miles from London. Harry had fast become Penny's favorite human being. He talked passionately about football and told her who the best players to watch were. He reminded her of Mac and Eddie. He also spoke about America and how he wanted to go there and when Penny had told him of her trip there last year he thought of Penny as a god.

They all fell asleep but, in the morning, Jim got Penny's address and promised to stay in touch. The evening's events reminded her of Owain and how he died trying to save the little girl. Apparently, the apple hadn't fallen far from this tree.

CHAPTER 71

Rose had decided to bake some cakes on her day off and arranged to meet Clint at ten that morning. Together, they walked the five miles to the town centre for supplies. Clint had received a letter from Jill that morning and was in an exceptionally good mood. "When I get home and propose to Jill, promise me you'll come to the wedding?"

"I have never been off this island, let alone to America. How will I even get there," Rose asked.

"Where there's a will, there's a way," Clint said with a smile. They laughed and continued to talk about random things. He had suggested Rose make brownies.

"Brownies, Clint?"

"You don't know what brownies are? My God, another reason to get you to America!"

At first, she wasn't sure what he'd meant but after having it described, she'd decided that brownies were like chocolate cake, but she still wasn't sure. They strolled round the market and visited several of the local grocers, got the ingredients they needed, and headed back. In London they had to show their ration card for everything but with so many farmers growing vegetables and making food in Hemmington they always seemed to get what they needed. Plus, Clint had a different ration card for his regiment, so they were able to get all the ingredients with ease.

It was amazing just how much they had in common. Growing up, there was always a taboo about having a friend from the opposite sex but Clint and Rose were living proof that you could. Clint was a good man but there was no spark there; she didn't really love many men but there was something about Eddie's charm and confidence that always made her giddy. She was not sure if she would ever see him again. She hoped deeply she would. Hope was all anyone had now. Clint was obsessed with Jill and he spoke passionately about her all the time: about her looks, her background as a pageant girl (Rose had no idea what that was but politely nodded along as if she had), and her love of horses.

If the crossing was not so treacherous right now, Jill would have come over already. She had a ticket but the voyage had been rescheduled three times already. Just like Rose, Clint was a romantic at heart. *Would they ever see their loves again?* Lil constantly told Rose to get with Clint, that she should just be with him now and cease waiting for Eddie. That was Lil for you. That afternoon, the two of them gave out brownies to the nurses and children. The staff and patients eyed these new treats skeptically but were delighted upon their first bites.

Clint had a night mission, so he left Rose early in the afternoon. He was part of a six-man crew and their debriefing was scheduled for 1500. They all tried to get some sleep and food before boarding the plane at 1900. They'd flown together hundreds of times together and, although they were part of the American Airforce, they had been part of an RAF assignment. Their missions were to bomb key German cities. Tonight's mission was to bomb Hannover. It would be a trickier mission than usual. It was a longer flight than normal, and they'd be flying over several stations with anti-aircraft equipment. The precipitation had slicked the runway and reduced visibility. The crew had done it before though and boarded the plane. They went through the pre-flight checklist and received their clearance for takeoff.

The flight time to Hannover was about two and a half hours so the men passed the time poking fun at each other. Arthur Bryant acted hurt because Clint had not brought them brownies. "Hey Clint, if you don't cut it in the Air Force, you'll always have a job as a housewife!" Everyone laughed along with Arthur and Clint. The laughter died as they approached Hannover. They were coming up on their target, a construction site that their intel teams believed to be a cover for a Panzer development site. They rechecked their calculations, saw no hostiles below, and dropped their payload.

The explosions were always bigger than they anticipated. The blast always rocked the plane, creating a mild turbulence they'd learn to endure and—eventually—ignore. Everything went to plan, and they headed back. They swung low and cut an arc to return to England. They rarely spoke during the return flight. The clouds bunched up around the cockpit as the wings and propeller cut through.

They were twenty miles out from the French coast when they heard the roar of the Luftwaffe's engines. They all looked at each other gravely. One of the crewmen, Green, yelled for Clint to man the tail gun. The mist had not let up at all and the crew could only make out the fifty feet in front of the cockpit. From the port side, a steady stream of gunfire rocked them.

The sound of them bouncing off the hull left a ringing in Clint's ears. Clint ducked down low until it had stopped then jumped back on the gun to see if he could see any planes. They had been in situations like this before and being only twenty minutes from the English coastline now, they were all confident that they would soon be out of danger. In the distance, he saw a propeller and he started shooting ferociously. Guns were going off all around him as his comrades were returning fire. Then the gun fire came back and this time it was directly at Clint. He ducked again but the glass shattered around him. Bullets continued to whiz past. When it stopped, he got up and fired back, the wind now howling in his face. He heard the noise of a plane turning back. One of the Germans must've been clipped and turned around. There was a brief pause and the men checked on each other.

Everyone seemed ok. "That was a close one," Green said. As soon as he did, the bullets started again. Clint dove to the back again but caught a bullet in his abdomen. He lay on the floor for a minute unable to breath or speak. *God this hurts. Come on get up. The guys need you to man the gun. Come on get up come on get up!*

Despite the pain, he got up slowly on his knees and returned fire at whatever he could. The plane had been hit hard but was going to make it back to the base. Once they got near the coastline, the battle stopped, and the German planes headed back. It was then that the crew realized Clint was down on the floor. They dashed over to him and saw his shirt covered in blood. While they ripped open his uniform to assess his wounds, Green called out from the cockpit, "Guys—the landing gear is nonresponsive. I think the Germans damaged it on their last run. Strap in and brace for impact!"

Fearing that moving Clint would make his wound worse, they huddled around and covered him as best as possible. Arthur grabbed a morphine needle and jabbed his thigh. "Hang in there buddy. Rose and the gang will sort you out. Remember, you have a proposal to plan," Arthur said with a forced smile. Clint had a small smile and he thought of Jill their wedding. He moved his hand into his back pocket and pulled out three envelopes: one addressed to Jill, his mom, and to Rose. He held them in his hand as his eyes closed. They bounced off the tarmac a few times but Green managed to keep the plane upright. He had called in for an ambulance over the radio and it was waiting for them.

They carried Clint off the plane to the nearest gurney. The medic tried to revive him but got no response; he had passed away quietly. The wound was deep and there was little else they could've done to save him. The unit had been together for nearly two years and were like brothers. They didn't bother to hold back tears as the medic drew a sheet over Clint.

Rose woke to banging at her door. Lil and the others who were on the night shift had not returned home yet. She straightened up and opened the door in her night gown. There were three US Airforce members standing at her door. Upon seeing Clint's crew, she instantly knew the news. With tears in his eyes, Arthur told her what had happened. She didn't fully listen to what he was saying, the shock had taken way her ability to comprehend. Something about being hit in a dogfight. She was taught at an early age to show no emotion and had mastered it as a nurse, especially when it came to delivering bad news. She thanked the men, took his dog tags, the letters, and then closed the door without showing a flicker of emotion.

Once the door closed, she burst into tears. She had just seen him. She cried for an hour. By the time the other nurses arrived, she had cleaned herself up and hid the tears. She kept her stern face and told them of the news. They all hugged her as means to console but she told them she was ok. Eventually, she mustered up the energy to open the letter and read it.

Rose,

Thank you for making me so happy. I was so home sick before I met you and being with you made being away from my family so much easier.

I have a favor to ask of you. Please make sure that Jill and my parents receive their letters. Tell Jill and my parents I'm sorry. Follow your heart in life, as it is too short.

Clint.

Rose wrote to Jill and his parents that night and attached the letters to them. Over the next month, she cried every time she was alone.

CHAPTER 72

Mac woke up with a huge smile and some pep in his step. He was home on leave and did not have to report back for duty for at least a week. He'd been told that he may be on the docks for a while, given that the decommissioned ship was now safely back in the UK and the new ship he'd be assigned to was still out at sea.

His parents were still teaching and putting in long hours at that. He planned on being to the first one up but was surprised to find them up, dressed, and already eating breakfast in the kitchen. Despite the fact spring was here, there was still condensation on the windows from the cool night while Mac watched the steam rise from the kettle. They both hugged him. Long had gone the days where his dad had been tough on him while staying emotionally distant. Now, he embraced and hugged Mac at every opportunity. Mac had always been special to them, but when his twin brother passed away from pneumonia at the age of five, Mac had been watched over and cared for more than before. It had been just the three of them for the longest time and they all planned to keep it that way.

His parents were eating cereal and Mac poured himself a bowl and had a cup of tea. The conversation was great and lively, everyone smiling as they chatted. Mac had told them he was going to London today and would probably not be back for two days. His parents had grown to accept that Penny was now part of their family, so they invited her to join them on Sunday for dinner. Roger and Rebecca had taken more of shine to Penny and her mum, especially after they visited for Christmas but didn't want to let Mac in on how much. They all walked out of the house together and headed in the direction of the station before splitting and going their separate ways just as they approached the town.

Mac's parents lived down by the canal so the walk to the station was a long one. He walked at a brisk pace, calculating in his mind exactly how much time he had before the train got there, realized he had some time to spare, and made a stop along the way. He walked up past the Kings Arms pub and saw Bill. "How are you buddy," Bill said, stretching out for a handshake. Mac greeted him and said that he was going to visit his mum. "I see. Can you do me a favor and help me with these barrels? There's a quick pint in it for ya," Bill said. Mac agreed and with the barrels in the cellar now, Bill opened up the bar and poured them both a pint. Just as Mac sat down, Mugsy appeared out from the back of the bar and jumped up on Mac licking him all over. Mac was instantly reminded of Eddie who was inseparable from this dog and it was so great seeing Mugsy again.

They spoke for half an hour. Mac told him about what he had been doing but he quickly asked about Eddie. Bill shrugged his shoulders. "Last we've heard, he was in Burma. But that was months ago. Who knows where he's been shipped off to now," Bill said. Bill really missed his brother. He was proud of him and knew that most men had to fight, but he missed Eddie coming in the bar, lighting up the place with his charm and energy by being his cheeky self. Bill was much older than Eddie and they had only recently become close. Bill had fought in the Great War and knew full well the effects of combat.

They were so busy talking that Mac realized he was going to miss his train if he didn't leave so he said his goodbye and then jogged over. He got to the bridge overlooking the station just as the steam of the train appeared in the distance.

An hour later, Mac was in London and he found himself waiting for Penny. *Nothing's changed,* he thought. Eventually, he saw the squat figure of Penny bobbing and weaving through the morning crowd. He embraced her and they passionately kissed. Time stopped around them, it seemed like they'd never let each go from their tight embrace. "Mac, I have surprise you won't believe," Penny said. He halfheartedly started to follow her to a bus stop where they waited. Even though he felt like a new man, he still hated surprises. When they got off in West London, Mac could not help but smile. He saw football fans everywhere and that's when Penny told him that she'd managed to get tickets for today's Chelsea game. This wasn't any game; Chelsea happened to be playing Tottenham, a London rival and Penny had the best seats in the house. Penny didn't tell Mac that the Princess had given her the seats as a gift when they met for tea the previous month as she didn't think he would believe her. Before the game, they were treated to a sit-down lunch with a few others. Just after the teams came on the pitch, the stadium fell silent. There was a moment of remembrance for those who had fallen in service of their country. Mac bowed his head and took in the scene. There were thousands of fans here, a true spectacle. Mac was later informed that fifty-five thousand had crammed into the stadium. The atmosphere was electric and both Penny and Mac found themselves in the roar of the crowd chanting players' names and booing whenever Tottenham were awarded an advantage and a penalty. The match ended in a draw but was a highly entertaining game and Mac had loved every minute.

It was now the early afternoon and they caught a bus back towards north London. They decided to get off early though as they decided to and walk through London back to Penny's flat. Mac calculated it to be a was probably a five mile walk and would take them nearly an hour. Penny waved him off and said it would do them some good and give them the chance for some quality time.

They walked hand in hand along the Thames, passing locks and tranquil housing. Builders were everywhere. She told Mac that buildings would be destroyed and the next week the citizens would start to rebuild them. She called it the London spirit.

As they walked through Hatton Gardens, they came into the jewelry area and they stopped to look at some of the wedding rings. Mac was not very subtle and asked what type of ring she would want. As she spoke, he tried to memorize every detail she mentioned. The problem was that Penny was unsure of what she wanted. Out of the corner of his eye, Mac noticed a couple of men with dark, black, knee length jackets looking into a shop. Normally, Mac would not have noticed them but they stuck out like sore thumbs. Something in Mac's gut told him that this was not normal. *If you see a fox in your garden, you know it's up to no good*, he remembered his parents telling him. For the next several moments, Mac kept a close eye on them as he calculated what to do. It was two on one situation and he was not a fighter, in any way, shape, or form. His mind was in a frenzy and he quickly scouted the area. Mac made a judgment call and asked Penny, "Hey love, just look over your shoulder. What do you think of those two?"

"Who," Penny asked. At that moment, the men turned around and looked them straight in the eye. Mac screamed at Penny to run. As she sprinted down an alley, the men drew their guns on Mac and opened fire. *Isn't Germany the enemy,* he thought. He ducked behind a set of metal bins. Mac had been in multiple life or death circumstances over the last few years and had learned to let his training take over. In one movement, he picked the bin up and threw it at one man who staggered back after being hit squarely. His accomplice looked down to the ground at his friend and Mac pounced on him, knocking him to the floor and pushing the gun away.

Mac punched the guy a couple of times until the blood ran down and over the man's teeth. His eyes glazed over and rolled back into his head, so Mac stopped. As soon as he did, the other criminal threw him to the ground. He was on top of Mac and strangling him. While Mac fought him off, he couldn't help but think how he'd managed to avoid getting blown up at sea only to die at the hands of a thief in London. Several men came to the rescue and grabbed the man just long enough for Mac to escape. He got the bin and threw it again at the man, this time knocking him out.

"Wow—you saved us from being attacked. These men have been causing chaos, stealing from us to fuel their illegal racket for months." Two old men, the shop owners, stood above Mac and helped him up. They must have both been in their seventies, maybe even their eighties, and were obviously glad Mac had helped. Mac gathered his breath and told the men to grab a rope so he could tie them up. He secured them to a drainpipe so they had no chance to escape.

Penny came around the corner with a police officer. They both looked a little stunned at what had happened. The police took Mac's statement and then everyone else's.

"Now young man, you should really go down and see a doctor about your injuries. No sense in being more of a hero than you already are," the officer said. "All I want is a bite to eat," he replied. The two shop owners came out with a corn beef sandwich for him. They chatted for a while. Their names were Brian and Paul Chapman, brothers who had run this store since before the turn of century. Mac was amazed by their story and enjoyed their company. As Mac headed out, they told him, "When the time is right, come back to us. We will sort you out," they said with big winks while looking at Penny.

Mac stayed the night with Penny and as they fell asleep. "That was more of an adventure than any I've had at sea." With that, he winked at Penny before closing his eyes and nodding off. Mac spent the rest of his week between Trevanston and London. Penny still worked at the factory and he visited her most days. She'd come round to his parents' home on Sunday for lunch. Time passed quickly as he enjoyed himself at home. Mac's leave came to an end and he sighed deeply as he boarded the train back to the ports.

CHAPTER 73

Clint's death had hit Rose hard. She was struggling, barely able to work and found it difficult to keep up a happy face around the patients and kids. She now regularly smoked and didn't want to go out with the other nurses. Instead, she stayed at home and studied. She hoped to take the exams as soon as possible so she could leave the Yorkshire area. She wanted to leave and never return. She looked out on to Yorkshire downs, through the heavy wall of rain that fell on a miserable April day, contemplating the fact she might just sit in that exact spot for the duration of the weekend.

She had recently written letters to all her family. The best thing that happened that morning was that she caught the postman and received a letter from Penny. It read:

"Rose, I'm so sorry about Clint. I need a break from London. Why don't we go stay with your family in the valleys? Try to find a phone and call me if this will be possible for this weekend.

Love, Penny."

Rose had already thought about going back to Wales as her sister was back from nursing in France and this was just the perfect opportunity. Rose walked downtown and found a phone at the bank. She called Penny and they agreed to leave the next day. They would take a nice long weekend and catch up. She walked back to the bungalows that housed all the nurses and arranged for her shifts to be covered.

She only had two shifts in five days and they were easily covered by another girl who needed to go to a wedding the following weekend. Rose went to the train station and asked the train attendant how easy it would be to get to Cardiff. Luck struck twice as the direct train was leaving Leeds in a couple of hours. She packed up a few clothes and headed back to the station. She would work out the twenty mile gap to her family house when she got to Cardiff. She would surprise her whole family and Penny could join her tomorrow.

The train was relatively empty, so she studied for a bit and then just watched the English countryside. It was beautiful and she wondered how much had been damaged by the bombings. She heard on the radio that many cities such as Coventry and Leicester had completely been destroyed.

The train eventually pulled into Cardiff and there were sirens going off. She was one of three passengers on the train, so they stuck together and stayed at the end of the platform in the waiting room. The sirens continued long into the night and Rose found herself sleeping (and freezing) on a wooden bench. She had slept maybe an hour at most and looked a mess but didn't care. A train pulled in as she was leaving the station and from the distance a voice yelled, "Rose!" She recognized it at once and searched the crowd until she saw Penny's head bobbing between the crowd. She was small but glided through like a single bird flying through a flock of geese. They embraced and managed to get a lift with a postman to the village next to Rose's home. They got off the truck, walked the five miles in the Welsh countryside, chatted nonstop, and laughed the whole time. Eventually, they arrived and knocked on the door. Rose's mum answered and broke down into tears while she hugged them both.

Norman came to the door next. He was an older man and rarely showed his emotion. He had clearly aged in the last year or so and walked more slowly but Rose saw a rare grin on him and he hugged them both. He still remembered their near silent walk to the train station four years ago. There was a squeal and Rose's two sisters Gwenn and Patty came running in. Patty was now sixteen and had drastically grown up and her eldest sister was now nineteen. Gwenn had also been given a week off and had told Rose that she was also heading out again at the end of the weekend as well.

They all drank wine, played cards, and told stories of their adventures during the war. Penny had always been close to them; they visited each other several times a year for family holidays. She had always liked them, but she felt like part of the family tonight. Her uncle told her stories of her dad that she had never heard.

Despite them both seeming straight-laced and emotionless as adults, as kids they had caused plenty of havoc. One time when they were both teenagers, they had skipped school and caught a train to Cardiff. There, they got so drunk they couldn't figure out how to get home and stayed the night. The police were sent out to find them and they were spared no grief. Norman had worked with Penny very closely in the last few years and she was probably closet to him out of everyone.

That night Rose slept in her own bed for the first time in over a year. She fell asleep remembering the good times of her childhood. She felt wise beyond her years now. She'd left as a seventeen year old and had been scared to travel to London and meet Penny. Now, she was twenty-one, lived with nurses in Yorkshire, had worked hundreds of hours as a nurse, seen horrific injuries to children, and experienced death, bombing, and a whole lot more. She had seen more in her lifetime than her mum had experienced, and she was in her late fifties.

The next few days were full of fun. The whole family walked in the valleys. It had been a warm spring weekend, so daffodils were out in force and the paths to the waterfalls were easily accessible. In the evening, they ate home cooked meals including freshly caught rabbit and a cake baked with freshly laid eggs. Rose swore she could taste the difference with the eggs. In the evening, the sisters went to the local pub and gossiped all night. Rose had always been fond of Penny, but the war had strained their relationship. This weekend trip restored it.

Gwenn and Patty were naturally best friends, but Rose had finally become close to them. It was almost as if the war was over and they had no stresses in the world. She was so proud of Gwenn but could not believe her stories. Rose had decided that she would make more of an effort to be around them and the three of them stayed up the whole night talking. Rose eventually left Monday morning; Penny had left the night before but not before promising to visit Rose soon. Gwenn was to leave that afternoon.

That Monday morning was eerily misty, and her father had promised to walk her to the station as he had done four years earlier. Again, they walked in silence but when they arrived, they hugged, and her dad broke down into tears. "I love you so much. I am so proud of the lady you have become," he whispered. They hugged for a long time.

CHAPTER 74

Eddie had now been in the jungle with this group of men for several years. He had a set routine for his survival. At night when the bullets and bombs stopped, he dreamt of England. He fantasized about cooler weather, runs with Mugsy through Trevanston, and good beer at the Kings Arms Pub. In short, he dreamt of life back home. He had written several letters to his family but had not once received a response. *I'm sure they responded. It's just that daft mail service. They can't get anything right—in peace time or at war. Heaven forbid though, maybe they've forgotten me. Maybe they've written me off for dead. Oh God—are they dead?!?* In between bouts of maddening thoughts, Eddie spent time talking to the elephants and the villagers, playing football, and drinking beer.

In between missions (or in the infirmary), soldiers rarely saw any action. He told himself things could be worse. The local Burmese villagers adored the British men. Eddie's popularity seemed to have followed to the other side of the world; it was good to feel loved. He cared for his men and found that they all had many common ties. He found himself often thinking about his football mates, most of whom had died before the war had intensified. He particularly missed Mac whom he had not heard from in years. He told himself he'd write to Mac's parents tomorrow. Eddie smiled at this while he sat alone with his thoughts, sipping on a beer in the glow of a fading sun.

Aiden and Bond sat near to Eddie, in the shadow of the awning nursing some beers. Bond was still Eddie's commander, technically, but after what they had been through in Africa, Greece and now Burma, they were inseparable. The harrowing feats they performed and the danger they endured had formed the basis of a strong friendship. The three of them were the remaining survivors of that original unit formed in Wembley. They were some of the first soldiers stationed here. They'd arrived just after Wheaton and they had developed a connection with him. Wheaton had built this army of nearly ten thousand men from nothing and his dangerous, extreme tactics matched his erratic personality.

Most of the men didn't know him well and they harbored a great deal of skepticism and distrust towards him. The men felt he put their lives in too much danger, that all he cared about was winning at any price. Wheaton wanted to win; there were no doubts about that. That was his biggest and most admirable trait. He hated losing and would do anything to win the battle. Eddie admired that about him. They were at war. What else are you supposed to concern yourself with?

Eddie was busy rolling a cigarette with Aiden when Wheaton came over. He chatted to them for a few minutes, shared a smoke, and even told them a couple of jokes he had heard, before saying he had to catch a plane. "Must be nice," Eddie joked after Wheaton left.

"Maybe he's catching a plane to England. We should sneak on and get out of this hole," Aiden said sarcastically. Bond informed them about debrief he planned on having with Wheaton before he left. Wheaton was headed to the southern part of Burma for a leadership meeting with the Americans. Aiden and Eddie looked at each other and all three shrugged. *Just another day in paradise.* They said their goodbyes and Aiden and Eddie went back to duty.

The two men were near the airstrip on night duty. This meant they spent the night smoking and keeping their eyes open for enemy attacks. Although they had built a whole base here with thousands of men, many of them worried the Japanese would strike. Both Aiden and Eddie were now platoon leaders and they had assigned their units to walk the perimeter of the base. This afforded them some free time to smoke and sit.

The airstrip wasn't really an airstrip. It was more a flattened grassland that planes can touch down and take off from, but it was a nice change of scenery for them. Eddie looked out of his binoculars and saw Wheaton boarding his plane, with the propellers already whirring. "Hey, Bond's on that plane as well," Eddie shouted, watching him ascend the makeshift steps.

"Cheeky git," Aiden replied. "He didn't even say goodbye before heading back home." They both laughed.

Bond sat in the rear of the plane next to Wheaton and several other commanders. It was so noisy that he couldn't hear anything or even think clearly. He looked down at his dog tags. The letters were punched clearly into the metal: Francis Bond, Lt, blood type A. He had worn these for multiple years now. He balled them up into his fist and thought of his wife Molly. He desperately wanted to return home and start a family. He hoped one day to give them to his future child, assuming he returned home safely.

He had married her just before war had broken out and he had already been in the Army, so his fate was sealed. Now, he had multiple units reporting to him, many of whom thought of him as aggressive and hard on them. He knew this but he also knew himself. Deep down he was a family man; he hated this war and wanted peace. He longed to be at home but all he knew how to be was an army leader. The only place he could be one was out here. One day maybe the men, other than Eddie and Aiden, who were his two real friends, would realize that Wheaton and he designed their plans to save lives in the long-term. The short-term be damned.

The propellers started to whirl faster, and they were taxiing towards the end of the grass runway. Bond closed his eyes, hoping he could maybe sleep for the next few hours. Both Major General Wheaton, himself, and a few others were heading to other bases to review their conditions. He'd told Eddie and Aiden differently because he did not want the unit's morale to drop. Many of the men were ill with malaria and there were concerns and doubts about their ability to serve and fight in future missions.

Wheaton believed it was a case of homesickness and fatigue. All the men needed was a little motivation. Bond wasn't so sure, however. He'd seen firsthand how damaging these illnesses were and felt that better medical supplies were the surefire answer.

As soon as Bond closed his eyes, he knew something was wrong. There was a loud rumbling noise followed by a huge bang as soon as they got off the ground. The last thing Bond remembered was seeing a flame on the wing outside his window. He pulled out the picture of Molly that he always kept in his shirt pocket and kissed it one last time before closing his eyes.

Eddie had just returned from taking a toilet break when he heard the loud bang. He knew something was wrong and looked out towards where the plane had been. A wall of heat hit him from half a mile away. The plane was engulfed in flames and had crashed down on the runway.

Eddie and Aiden recalled their men and all of them sprinted to the scene, but it was just a fireball, they couldn't get any nearer because the plane was full of gasoline and kept exploding, its flames bursting higher and higher. Eddie slowly watched as the plane burnt in front of him. He was so helpless.

After a while, the base's emergency personnel managed to get water to the scene thanks partly to the elephants carrying large buckets of it, but it was too late. Black singed grass and metal debris were all that were left. Some of the men around Eddie cheered. *Wheaton had finally gotten what was coming to him. Serves him right working us so hard and risking our lives. Maybe now, HQ would call us all home.* Eddie stood there in disbelief. Wheaton had led them bravely into combat. Eddie knew he'd be missed but he was more devastated that he had lost Bond, one of his best friends.

CHAPTER 75

Gwenn remembered watching her sister from an upstairs window as she headed off to catch her train to London. Fifteen at the time, she'd never seen eye-to-eye with Rose, but she remembered bawling in her bedroom as her sister walked off, stern faced to London. Rose had always ben very shy and reserved so it had been amazing to see her sister head to London to be a nurse. She had believed she would be the one to stay behind in Wales and watch over the family. Ironically her departure had brought them closer than ever. Gwenn had wanted to follow in her footsteps since that moment she departed. Gwenn was the polar opposite to Rose growing up, she was loud and fun and had been really friendly with several local men who worked in the gunpowder factory her dad owned. She was often at the local pub and occasionally sang at the local community centre. Rose had only ever gone to the local pub at her father's request. Things had changed and now last month they had spent several days drinking together.

Gwenn quickly packed her bags on her final day, said her goodbyes and headed to the train. She was jumping with excitement at the opportunity to serve her country. Her father hugged her and wished her luck, he was worried that she was too laid back to survive war but as with Rose could not hold her back. Gwenn spent the day on the train from Cardiff to London and like her sister had met her cousin Penny.

That night, Penny took her to a local pub where they drank a whole bottle of port together. The next day, she headed to Folkstone and her new unit. She'd enlisted as an Army nurse and despite doing the basic training in Wales she would have to complete an additional six-week training program.

Gwenn loved every minute of it, she learned how to categorize patients, bandage them, triage them and even setup their wounds. The six weeks passed quickly. The sirens had gone off often, but the women would go into the air raid shelters and sing through the night. Upon completion, they would be heading to the battlefields in northern France near Lille.

Once they got there, reality started to sink in. She'd gone from a lovely furnished bedroom to a bunk bed to sleeping on a church floor. She was a mile from the battlefront and had been told to stay close to the medical centre. But the true horrors of war were impossible to ignore. Gwenn saw injured American soldiers coming in, holding the contents of their stomachs in their hands, their intestines looking like jelly on a plate. There were leg injuries so black and severe due to infection that she had to hold down a man while a surgeon amputated it. And of course, there were countless dead bodies.

Due to the graphic nature of their work, the nurses had become very close to another. Many of them were young like Gwenn and tried to bend over backwards for their fellow nurses and soldiers. She'd grown close with a nurse named Catherine Dixon, otherwise known as Dixie. She had a bubbly and vivacious personality, a mirror to Gwenn. She had come from Skegness, a beach town in Britain. Dixie had been out in Lille for nearly a year and had helped Gwenn's transition. The nurses were not meant to leave the hospital and church compound for their own safety, but Dixie had taken Gwenn into downtown Lille on several occasions to go to a boulangerie that still served amazing fresh bread and cakes.

It was the end of April and it was a rainy night. Gwenn had taken up letter-writing after her shift ended.

Nothing has prepared me for this, Gwenn wrote in a letter to Rose, exhausted after working nearly fourteen hours. She paused for a moment. I sound so bloody unhappy it might give the impression that I'm some sort of Moping Molly. Has anything good happened to put in this letter? Well seeing all the men recover as I make the rounds is pretty nice, uplifting actually. Plus the ones the ones that are awake enough to have conversation with always ask me to take them out. What a laugh. Yea, it'll be the three of us, you, me and your IV.

She took a sip of red wine and continued her letter.

I never realized the emotions war brings out of you. I remember you telling me in your letters, but I never quite understood what you meant. The feelings of patriotism, pride in our service, relief in helping the wounded and ill, the sadness at the death of those beloved and near and the anger at the sheer lunacy of it all. I can truly see how war can drive one mad, how it can extract all kinds of heartbreak, hatred and evil from a person's soul. I can only imagine how you feel after losing Clint, that must have been brutal on you.

Me and Dixie have made friends with a local family. Those poor things. Their home was destroyed by the Nazi's. They just laid waste to a two-hundred-year-old building, executed the husband and destroyed all their food. Dixie and I have been buying them at least of loaf of bread or and they've made the best vegetable soup ever for us! Anyway Rose, I wanted to know how proud I am of you. We're doing something great. I so enjoyed spending time with you, Patty and Penny and hope we can do more of that soon.

Love,

Gwenn"

Gwenn finished writing her letter and added it to the pile she had written that night to other family member and then got into her bed. Exhausted, she immediately fell into a dream. The next morning Dixie woke her. She'd been in a deep sleep and felt like she needed a few more hours. She checked her watch. It was five o'clock. "what's wrong" she asked while rubbing her eyes and getting her bearings. "Nothing. I was just told the sunrise today will be spectacular and thought you might want to join us a few of us." Dixie said. Gwenn and the six nurses all walked out together, down to the top of the hill, and sat their watching the sun rise while sipping on some coffee that one of the nurses had snuck out. It was spectacular and they all enjoyed it. The ground was still wet from the night before, but it added to the effect of the sunrise.

As they headed back to the town Gwenn piped up "you fancy seeing the Clermonts? I wrote to my sister about them yesterday and thought it would nice. " "Sure", Dixie replied, so they headed to get a load of bread and then up to the cottage. It was a big white cottage about a mile from the city and right near the battles. It had a thatched rood and the Clermont family had lived their for multiple generations. Despite the building being attacked you could still see the beauty of the old traditional country cottage. They arrived and the children rushed to see them.

"How are you?" the boy asked in his best English. Language was a barrier as Gwenn could only speak a little French and they could speak a little English.

The mum went and made breakfast for everyone, eggy toast. It reminded Gwenn of having fresh eggs with Rose and Penny the month before. Afterwards, Gwenn and Dixie played hide and seek with the kids. It was while Gwenn was crouched down next to a window that she heard the rattling and shaking. The treads and long barrels of the tanks were hard to miss; a Panzer unit was rolling through this way. They all ran down to the cellar as tanks approached.

The tanks eventually stopped outside the house and voices could be heard. Gwenn put her fingers to her lips to the children while above them, they heard the soldiers destroying the house. The cellar door opened fast and two men screamed and pointed the barrels of their guns at them. The kids screamed and everyone felt panicked. The Germans lined them up in front of the house and had them wait. The German soldiers were barking orders almost like they were arresting them.

Gwenn's confusion gave way to stark realization: this family was Jewish. Next, they shot the wife and she fell to the floor in one quick motion. They turned to the children next aimed at the little boy, now wailing and staring at the body of his mother. As the soldier drew his rifle, instinct took over and Gwenn jumped in front of the boy. The muzzle lit up and Gwenn's chest became a red splotch. It was warm to the touch. She fell to the floor, but Dixie couldn't help since she ran to be with the children.

Gwenn felt pain and numbness. The blood started to soak through as she lay there. Hopefully Dixie could keep them safe, then another roar began, and gunfire erupted all around while Gwenn lay there unable to move, not sure what was happening. In front of her the German tank exploded and gunfire continued. Gwenn felt herself wanting to just take a nap, she was tired after all and started to close her eyes. As she did a British man in uniform stood over her and said "she's still alive. The kids are fine." Gwenn was sure she was in a dream now as she was moving and could just see the countryside and then she was back in the hospital with her friends around her. She fought for some time but closed her eyes for that final sleep. All the nurses were distraught that they had lost one of their own and Gwenn had been a hero saving those children.

Several days later Rose was excited to see Gwenn's letter. After she read it, she felt immensely proud. About an hour later someone knocked on the door. It was a doctor she knew, and he told her that a call had come into the hospital. She fell to the floor in tears while he relayed the terrible news. Rose lay there and kept repeating, "Gwenn's dead."

CHAPTER 76

Although Penny had now retired from factory operations, she still felt an obligation towards helping the government officials. She'd already been a major contributor and aid but she was deemed vital to the war effort. She had helped to create the posters featuring women in key production and support roles on the home front. They'd been a major factor in the continued growth of civilian morale and support. She believed that without the women, Britain would have lost this war. She felt immensely proud.

It was a sweltering May afternoon and Penny was busy on the production line, affixing bolts to the seats. She glanced up at her father's office and felt odd. Only a few months ago, that had been her office and now it was occupied by Albert, the new owner. He was a great guy but she did often wonder if she had made a mistake. Perhaps, she should still be running the place? She paused and sighed and returned to the assembly line helping to roll out the seats for the planes. It had been a rough couple of months for her, Gwenn's death had really hit her and her family hard. She had seen her only a month before and then she had gone back to Wales for the funeral. Seeing her aunt and uncle so distraught made her miss her dad terribly.

The turnover of staff over the years at the factory had been high and Penny was embarrassed that she could not recognize at least half of the workforce there. However, that was a blessing in disguise as the newer women had no idea of her history so she could continue as she pleased.

She enjoyed the banter with them. Today's conversation was the classic "Marry, Shag, Kill". The current options were: the King, the Prime Minister, and the leader of the Opposition Party. Penny was amazed so many chose to kill the king and she stayed quiet for most of the conversation. The looks on their faces if they ever knew that she'd met all three. The conversations helped the days go by. The standard workday had grown to twelve hours, with a first and second shift, at the factory. Penny had heard the women complaining of hunger, so she secretly arranged for a baker to come every day and provide canned corned beef sandwiches, soup, and bread.

It was a joy seeing these women so happy. Typically, after her shift she would either go to her flat for a bit, then she would man the streets to ensure people were safe before going underground during air raids. Some nights, she would go to the local pub with the women for a few drinks. Penny had secretly paid the barman to cover all their drinks. "The drinks are on the house. Thanks for your hard work," he would tell them.

Penny left the girls early as she had other business to attend to. She still did other work with the government, which she relished and tonight happened to be one of those nights. She was heading to the war room and she duly obliged. There was a lot of hustling, bustling, and noise. This wasn't unusual but Penny had become an expert in reading people's eyes and she knew something big was about to happen. She was ushered into a new room where she was sitting with several other women, all in silence. She desperately wanted to break the silence and sat there looking through her handbag until she spotted something in the corner of the room.

There was a small King Charles spaniel puppy sitting on a blanket in the corner. It looked so helpless. Penny went over and looked into its eyes. She knew instantly that he was scared. She sat down on the floor and started to rub behind his ears. The dog perked up and nudged his head onto Penny's lap. One of the security detail walked into the room "Don't get too comfortable with that one," he said to Penny. "Came into the kitchen soaking wet. We dried him off to see if the owner would arrive but it's been two days and we have been told to get rid of him tonight." Penny was shocked at the callousness of it all. "No!" She hadn't meant to scream like that, to catch everyone's attention. Even the dog looked up at this sudden noise. "I'll take him," she said. The dog seemed to understand and buried his head even more into Penny's lap and then cheekily looked up at the man as if to say he wasn't moving from that spot. "Fine. One less thing we have to deal with," he snorted. He addressed the room now, explaining that they had all been picked to conduct a film interview where they would wish the soldiers good luck and hoped that they hurry home. Penny was up at the front of the room so she went first. "To my man Mac in the Royal Navy and all the other naval folk, I want you to know we miss you at home, but you are doing a valiant job for the sake of the country and we appreciate your efforts. We love you loads!" Penny had insisted that they hurry through this so that she could get back to her new friend and that nothing had happened to him.

She returned to an empty room and the dog wasn't there. *Damn,* she thought*, where had he gone?* She looked around the room and couldn't see the dog anywhere. Starting to get frantic now, she asked the other girls in the room if they had seen the dog. They looked around and tried to help Penny but others just continued talking and ignored her completely. They were far too excited to be movie stars. Penny rolled her eyes at them and then continued looking. She was panicking that someone had thrown him out.

She found a door that was ajar and decided that this must be where the dog went, she hoped and hoped that no one had taken the dog to destroy it. She would be heartbroken if that happened. She walked down the corridor, offices on either side of her and a small group of people in each. She wasn't an idiot and these people were strategizing about something. As she walked past one room and she saw a map of France and the words *Omaha, Utah, Juno, Gold,* and *Sword.* As much as the curiosity was eating inside her, she was focused on finding the damned dog.

She turned a corridor and she heard a lot of people chatting in one room and so headed in there. She heard the distinctive heavy breathing of a dog. She walked in, ignored everyone, and starting crawling in between feet trying to find the dog. Finally, she saw the tell-tale wag. She desperately crawled to the tail and grabbed the dog, who was now sitting on two black, shiny shoes. "Gotcha," she said in relief.

The commotion had made everyone in the room stop talking, a few even gasped. Penny looked up to see who was the owner of the black shoes and found herself gasping. Staring down at her was the Prime Minister. "Man's best friend, unless he does something disastrous like interrupt a top-secret meeting," he growled. Penny apologized profusely, still in disbelief of what was going on. Then she quickly rambled to the Prime Minister that she was Owain's daughter. That caught his attention and then apologized again. It turned out that the Prime Minister had a soft spot for dogs and for Owain so he said, "Make sure you look after him." With that, he turned his back and started the conversation again.

Penny knew it was time to leave and picked up the dog, carried him under her arm, and made her way out of the building. That night, she fed him and got him a leash.

The next day she took him to the factory where she asked one of the men to engrave a piece of scrap metal with his name. "What's his name, then," he asked as the dog licked his face. "Winnie," she replied.

Winnie and Penny instantly became best friends and he was found in the factory with her or jumping on the other workers, he slept with her in the underground and was never far from her side.

CHAPTER 77

It was the end of May and Mac was back in New York. The first time he'd visited New York it was almost a fun experience; the city was bustling and America hadn't joined the war yet. In the last few years, he'd gone back and forth across the Atlantic more times than he can remember. He'd been at Pearl Harbor, which up until that day was his favorite memory of America. The beaches and relaxed way of life was something he could relate to. He had been to numerous other states and had travelled across the country via train. On his last voyage, a seventeen-year old kid had been beaming at the idea of travelling America thanks to the Navy.

Mac now despised the travelling. Even though he liked parts of America, he would be content living at home. He longed for the war to be over; he had been in it for four years now. He still clung on to the few memories of home, especially after his latest visit but his life was now consumed by the war. He did some mental math and calculated that twenty percent of his life had been involved in this calamitous event.

The only good thing was that he'd moved from ammunitions to leadership training. On this particular ship, he was now on the Captain's deck in charge of all weaponry. His experience and training had made him a perfect candidate for this position. If—when—they were under attack, at least he'd to be the one directing the guns and weaponry instead of being cooped up with all the munitions. He was also working for Captain Pollack again. Captain Pollack was a great man; he'd been a Captain since the twenties but was a humble man and appreciated Mac for asking questions and getting stuff done. They stood together on the huge carrier, watching thousands of

Americans board. Mac knew better than to ask questions, but he knew there was some kind of massive operation in play if all these men were being routed to England. They were to set sail and had to have the men in Southampton in eight days.

They all finally boarded and Mac went on deck to clear the ropes, raise the anchor, and watch as the ship was led out by tugboats. The New York skyline quickly became a distant haze as they set sail across the Atlantic. Mac's new role also meant that the operations of the ship, including the guns, were running smoothly and efficiently. Once they were at full speed, he did a search around the ship, checking on all the guns, nests, and munitions depot before returning to the main deck. Despite being overcrowded with men everywhere lining every corridor, the deck was eerily quiet he returned. The ship glided through the ocean with great ease but abruptly rocked to its port side. They'd just made contact with a German mine. The Germans had laid mines down throughout the Atlantic and although the allies had new technology to detect them it wasn't always effective. When a ship got near one, some would detonate. The loud explosions and the water that erupted with it often stirred the men into a frenzied panic. Mac had become desensitized to them.

He'd been on ships long enough to experience these near misses and he had also seen ships sink as a result of them. The problem was the lack of control. It was like walking blindfolded through a snake pit, not knowing when something will attack. After that near miss, the coast was clear. Several days later, they could see the English coastline. As they pulled into Southampton, Mac stood next to the Captain and thanked him for getting Mac and the crew home safely, then Mac thanked God. Mac had a ritual now to pray every time he left port and thank God when he arrived. He had done this when he was left to die on the deck and felt, somehow, that someone had looked out for him.

The American soldiers marched off the ship and Mac was due to take several days off. He was hoping to see Penny and his family before heading back over the Atlantic. Captain Pollack had trained Mac some more throughout that voyage and had mentioned to him that he would put in a recommendation for Mac to be promoted to Captain. Mac was pleased that his hard work was being recognized and that it was soon to pay off.

He was heading off the galley when someone shouted his name. The Captain was looking for him, a young sailor said. Mac headed back and the Captain told him about a sudden change of plans. They were reassigned to a new ship that was headed towards France. Part of a top-secret and highly important mission. Something about storming the beaches. Inside Mac was livid. It sounded dangerous and risky. Mac wanted time off, but he duly obeyed. What choice did he really have?

It was sunset and he had to report back tomorrow. *So, just one night in England,* he thought Mac weighed his options: take the train to Southampton, arrive in London late, spend the night with Penny or take the train to Trevanston to see his family. Unsure of which he wanted, he found a hotel and asked to use their phone. He dialed Penny's factory and a man answered. She was out, he said. *Damn. Trevanston it* is. He headed to the station and just missed the train. The next train wasn't for another three hours. He was hungry and tried to find a café near the station. He lucked out and found one. After settling inside at a table, he ordered egg and chips. As he was sitting there, he noticed nurses sitting at the table near him. He recognized one of them, but could not remember from where. He racked his mind for several minutes, trying to recall the face and it finally hit him.

"Rose," he asked. She looked up and scrunched her face in confusion. "Mac!" They embraced and Rose introduced her friends. He was relieved to find a familiar face. They chatted about everything: their stories, the war in general, and, of course, Penny and Eddie. Rose told Mac of Gwenn's death with teary eyes and said the last time she saw Penny was at the funeral, but had also had a great time with her the month before. He decided he'd spend the night with Rose and her friends. They stayed in the café until closing. There were no air raid sirens, so they could talk in peace. It was a fun evening and Mac was grateful for company. Rose and the other nurses had a curfew at eleven, so Mac accompanied them back to their quarters. They had informed him they were shipping out in the morning to France. Mac was smart enough to know that the large presence of American soldiers, the extra nurses, his time off being cancelled, and his reassignment added up to something big happening. He said good-bye to them and walked back alone, wondering what all these factors were leading to. He found the officer's quarters easily and fell asleep quickly.

CHAPTER 78

For the past month, Penny's factory had shifted from just manufacturing aircraft parts to odds and ends like mannequin dummies. The factory girls had a real laugh about it and they had taken to posing with them for seductive and comedic pictures. They'd also made new weapons. Their most recent one being a flamethrower. One of them joked that with a hose like that; she'd take it and use it to water the gardens.

That got a big laugh. A lot of factories openly communicated with one another about their production numbers, lines, and plans. Inter-factory competition had ceased for the time being. They were all focused on a collective effort to manufacture and provide support to the wartime effort. Penny had caught wind of another factory making parts for boats that could land on beaches and highly maneuverable tanks. Other factories Penny owned had been making parachutes and waterproof guns.

She was aware of a large-scale operation that was being planned. Ever since her encounter in the War Ministry's office, it now seemed that things were coming into play. Penny's factory had been asked to deliver these dummies to an Army base about an hour from London. She and Winnie loaded up the truck and set off. It was a nice change for Penny. She looked comical, her short frame barely peeking over the wheel and steering column of the truck.

Winnie was loving life. He and Penny had formed a great bond and he enjoyed running around the factory every day and snuggling next to Penny in the underground at night. Today, he shoved his head out the window, tongue hanging about and barking with glee at passers-by. He was living his best life. The journey took several hours and it gave Penny time to reflect. Despite being a city girl, she had cultivated a love for the peace of the countryside. She was heading towards Trevanston and thought about Mac and how they would move there together when—if—this war ended. She never imagined a life post-war without Mac. Penny missed him desperately.

Lorraine had come along as well. She needed to keep busy and was more and more involved with developing and advancing women's rights. It was a tremendous campaign and she was passionate about it. Plus, it kept her mind off being a widow. Lorraine also loved the countryside and was enjoying time with Penny and Winnie.

Once they got into the city, they took several wrong turns due to Lorraine's poor map reading. They even drove the wrong-way down some streets. Luckily, there wasn't much traffic and Penny managed to maneuver the truck through narrow streets. Eventually, they arrived at the Air Force base. They showed their credentials and were escorted in. There were men in uniform all around them. British, Canadian, and American and they all seemed to be very professional with stern looking faces as they loaded trucks, planes, and cars.

A couple of British men helped Penny and Lorraine down before quickly and efficiently unloading their truck. It all happened in the space of fifteen minutes and Penny was a little disappointed she would be heading back so soon, not knowing what this mission was about. Just as she was heading out, she saw a familiar face. Much to the annoyance of the squad of troops, she stopped the truck, jumped down, and ran towards a group of men.

"Jim," she shouted, interrupting the conversation. A tall man turned around and it was indeed Jim, the man who had lost his son that night in the underground. "Penny, what on earth are you doing here," he said, startled to see her. They quickly hugged and Penny explained she was dropping off some supplies for the RAF.

"Any idea why you guys need dummies," Penny asked. Jim was a senior officer in the RAF and she saw hesitancy in answering that question but he slowly responded. "There is an imminent attack on the Axis forces and these are going to be dropped from planes as a decoy," he answered. Penny somehow knew he was hiding more information but didn't want to push it. At that point Winnie started barking and Penny had almost forgotten about the dog and her mum. She grabbed Winnie and her mum stepped off the truck. Winnie was super excited and started jumping up at Jim. Luckily, he was a dog lover.

He looked up and saw Lorraine. Jim had only recently lost his wife, but he was mesmerized by Lorraine. She was an elegant lady and her rich hazel eyes highlighted her face and body.

"Err, I'm Lieutenant Jim Crowthorn," he stammered in a deep voice. Lorraine could not believe how beautiful this man was. He had tidy red hair, was tall, slim and dressed perfectly in his blue suit. She extended her hand. "Lorraine, the pleasure is all mine," she responded. Jim composed himself a little and knelt down to Winnie.

"Why don't you all join Harry and me for dinner tonight? He is still down here for a bit, being educated on the base. He would be delighted to see you Penny. I promise it won't be a late night as I have some important missions this week." Penny wanted to get home but was surprised that Lorraine responded for both of them with an affirmative.

"Great. We'd be delighted," she said while staring at Penny, who simply nodded in agreement.

"Ok—perfect! Park here and walk down to the _Queen Anne_. It is the local hotel and pub. I will meet you there in about an hour".

Penny didn't know what had just happened and felt a little uneasy not being in control. Still, she walked down the street next to the city walls that were built hundreds of years ago as a defense for the Romans. Penny and Lorraine sat at the bar and didn't really talk. Penny had a port, Lorraine a Gin and Tonic. Not long after they had arrived, Harry and Jim walked in. The boy sprinted over to Penny and gave her a huge hug.

"Guess where I was the other week," Penny winked at Harry. "The Chelsea game!"

"No way! The papers said that was their 'Game of the Year'."

Penny mainly talked to Harry and he showed her what he was learning at school. He was teaching her how to calculate percentages while Jim and Lorraine in deep conversation. Penny kept watching them out of the corner of her eye.

They were flirting with each other in an awkward way. Penny found it really cute and let it play out. It was getting late and Harry had to go to bed. The ladies had to get home too, so Jim walked them all back and took Lorraine on a separate walk. Penny said goodnight to Harry and promised to write him. Penny jumped into the truck and Lorraine sat there, smiling broadly.

"Thank you for that evening. Jim is lovely man and I am going to see him again next week after his missions," Lorraine said. Penny shook her head and just smiled back at her mum.

CHAPTER 79

Mac, Captain Pollack, and many other leaders from the Navy were all in a large hall located on the Isle of Wight. They'd all been instructed to dock their ships around the island and head to the meeting. As Mac looked out of the windows, it was a dreary night. Even though they were in the middle of summer, the sun had long disappeared and the dark cloud stood lowly over the horizon. Mac glanced around the room. There had to be at least one hundred men, representing thirty to fifty ships. This had to be a big operation. He'd noticed some American uniforms as well, which he recognized from his time in America.

There was a lot of chatter going on and a clattering of teacups as the men drank the tea provided. Captain Pollack leaned over and in his broad Yorkshire accent said "'Ere we go." He pointed to a skinny man walking in followed by several young cadets bringing in portable blackboards. The man began to speak and the room went silent.

"Tomorrow, you will all embark on one of the largest land and sea operations the British Navy and British Army has ever witnessed along with our comrades from Canada and the USA." The audience in the room gasped, cheered, and sat motionless after hearing the news. The man explained how the troops were going to attack five beaches while planes would deploy parachutists. Everyone else would provide support from their ships, after having docked not too far from the beachheads.

The blackboards flipped and detailed diagrams showed the stages of the attack. Mac was assigned to the HMS Belfast, the same ship he and Captain

Pollack had been on earlier in the year. After the very detailed plan was revealed, Mac felt uneasy. It seemed that an awful lot of casualties were going to happen based on the diagrams and briefing. He was not filled with hope.

The HMS Belfast was to be the ship leading the battle and their job was to attack and clear the beaches before the landing crew went in. The main problem they faced was getting near the beaches. Because of the shallow water and the anti-air encampments on the shore, they were going to be attacked hard and fast by the Germans stationed there, not to mention their ships and aircraft. The presentation ended and Captain Pollack ordered Mac back to the ship. They walked the half mile back and during that time, they went through a checklist of necessary tasks. Mac's primary job was to ensure that the ship was fully stocked with weapons and ammunition. He had already completed this earlier in the day, so now he had to raise the gun roosts so the gunners would have a clear line of fire on the beach heads. Despite it being the middle of the night, Mac ordered the men to raise the angles of the guns to what he estimated would be a clean shot.

They were due to depart at midnight but the storms had delayed them. The boat rocked as the rain swept over them. It was a warm evening in of June and the rain was actually refreshing. Mac did not want to get soaked so he stood on the top deck under an awning. He watched the wind whip across the deck. He looked at the stars and thought of home. It had been years since that January evening with his friends and Penny, when they had looked at the stars in Trevanston. He missed Penny and would do anything to be with her right now. Recently seeing Rose had reminded him of her. He didn't even know if Eddie was still alive, but he knew many of the team were now gone.

As he had walked around the boat, it had dawned on him that he was now four to five years older than some of his comrades. He would have graduated university now if he had stuck to his original plan, although the irony would be that he would probably still have wound up being enlisted. Mac finished his chocolate bar and headed back inside. He fell asleep almost immediately, the rocking of the ship soothing him.

A day later at midnight, the ship was let loose onto the seas. The men had slept much of the day and the night sea was much calmer. Despite the years of service, Mac had travelled through the English Channel only a handful times. After about an hour, he could clearly see the white cliffs of Dover glistening in the moonlight. There was such a fear that the Germans would spoil the plans by finding the fleet that all their lights were cut off. They sailed in the pitch black but the stars and moon shining on the white cliffs gave them the necessary light. He waved goodbye to England and turned to face the wine dark sea.

After three hours of sailing, the boat stopped. In the distance, Mac could see other ships and he peered through his binoculars. There were the beaches. They seemed so quiet and undisturbed, like a picture from a postcard. The sea splashed on the shore, the sandbar looked untouched. Mac knew that the picturesque quality would not last. His mind started to wander and he calculated how far the beaches were and, therefore, how far back the German tanks were probably located. He felt the wind and tried to calculate the right angle that the guns needed to be at.

He moved around the ship and worked with the gunners to ensure each of their angles were correct. As he got to the last gun, Mac gave the gunner the angles and waited for confirmation. The gunner responded in the affirmative but something was different. The voice was familiar but Mac couldn't place it. He heard some laughter and saw a familiar face peer down at him. It was Herbie.

"As I live and breathe, Herbie—it's you! How'd you manage this? "

"Got transferred last night with the storm. One of your men was sick." Mac embraced his good friend and promised to catch up after battle. *This had to be a sign of good tidings,* Mac told himself.

At 0500, the alarms went off and the whole ship awoke. Mac bellowed to the gunners at the front "FIRE," and huge booms echoed around. Fireballs lit up the sky as streaked towards hidden bunkers. Mac could see sand explode everywhere as mortars landed on the ground. He saw fires starting and, much though he loathed war, there was something beautiful about this.

For ten minutes, there was a constant barrage. Mac's ship and the others bombarded the beaches. After a while, they felt the job was done and they stopped. Silence filled the air but only briefly. Suddenly, the guns from the Panzer tanks fired back.

Mac and his ship were under siege. An airplane flew low and pelted the ship with machine gun fire. Mac took cover and ordered the men to get down but it was too late for some of them. Several men lay wounded on the deck. None of them moved. There was a scream for a Medic but Mac ran over first to the wounded. He flipped them over to see if anyone were still alive. The third body he ran to was Herbie. He was dead. Mac had no time to process this. He focused and ordered the runners to load the guns and then followed them down to the ammunition room. Mac ran up himself and took hold of Herbie's gun. *Lead by example*, he thought. The battle intensified and lasted a good hour. Mac had to twice take some of his commanders down to the medical unit due to bullet wounds and the whole ship deck was drenched in blood.

As the sun broke, the fighting intensified and became even more complicated as Mac's ship lowered hundreds of small boats with Canadian and British soldiers who were to land on the beach. They had to ensure that their troops were not caught in the crossfire. All morning, Mac was out on the deck and constantly relocating guns and acting as a runner and loading them. He was doing everything he could and he was exhausted. A bomb landed next to the boat, right on the side of the ship where he was standing. He heard the bang and was swept off his feet. He assumed that he was done for. He lay on the deck soaked, until someone grabbed him and pulled him to cover. He recovered and got his bearings while whispering a small prayer.

Eventually the battle ended as afternoon rolled in. Ships were deploying men and thousands of small boats with men crammed in them heading towards the beaches. All around Mac, the men were helping each other. Water along with bread and jam was handed out and Mac gladly took some along with a cup of tea. He helped clean the deck and reload the guns, just in case. He headed to the Captain's area and Captain Pollack handed him some binoculars. "Remember this day son. Remember that you were a part of history." Mac looked through to see men breaking on to the beaches and guns firing everywhere. He was tired of making history. He thought of Herbie and the others that were killed and injured today. *When will this end?*

CHAPTER 80

Rose was woken up by flickering lights. She was in a three story building that housed all the Army nurses. She had been sleeping in a small bed in the corner of the room with about twenty other nurses. She got her bearings, put her glasses on, and looked out of the window. It was pitch black. She looked at her pocket watch, 0400. *Damn*, she thought, *I hardly got any sleep*. There'd been a request for nurse volunteers to assist with the front line and Rose felt it was her duty to do so after Gwenn's death. She volunteered and had been on this mission for only two weeks now.

"How you feeling Rose," a small young lady next to her asked.

"I'm alright Maud. How are you?"

Maud was only seventeen and had looked nervous last night so Rose had spent a few hours talking to her. She made an effort to highlight the fun times, no matter where you found them, as a means to lighten the mood.

They both went to the washroom, shared a soap, and got into their uniforms. They lined up outside the house and their matron, who went by Captain, marched them down to the docks. Even at 0430, the port was bustling with people. Everyone was scheduled to get on boats. Rose and Maud had to maneuver through soldiers, sailors, and other nurses. Rose had overheard American voices and thought of Clint.

Eventually, they boarded a boat. Rose realized at that moment she had never actually been on one before and started to panic. There was limited lighting but she could hear the waves slapping against the boat and felt it rock. She was surrounded by women and felt very claustrophobic. Maud and Rose found some space on the side of the boat next to a railing but as the ship set off, it rocked further which made Rose queasier. She had to close her eyes to cope.

The sun started to rise as they approached France. All the nurses were called together. They were told to head directly to the front lines, the beaches. There were two medical tents and the women were split into handling both tents. Rose and Maud were both in Tent A, which would be about half a mile from where the men had landed. They were to run to the tent in case of danger but the beach they were landing on should have been cleared.

The boat jolted upon landing. They landed a short way from the beach, so Rose had to jump into the water and freeze from the waist down. She trudged to the tents along with Maud and about twenty other nurses. The smell of death instantly hit her. She looked around and all her patients were lying on temporary beds and stretchers.

"You two," a male medic bellowed at Rose and Maud, "Men are coming in all the time. You need to make quick decisions. If they are no hope, put a black line on them using this marker. If they have minor injuries, fix them up and move them into the tent onto the left so they can be moved out. If the injuries are serious, put a red mark and try to fix them." He held up some vials and handed them each a pack of them. "This is morphine, use it wisely". Then he held up another few vials.

"This is penicillin. It's a new wonder drug that cures bacterial infections. Inject both of these in their thighs, then bandage them up. We only have a limited amount, so I'll repeat myself use them wisely. Any questions?"

Rose and Maud didn't speak, still processing everything he'd said.

"None? Good. Get to work." Rose had heard of penicillin from Dr. Wessex and had a brief memory of the old doctor she used to visit. With that, Rose was thrust into action. She naturally knew what to do and she moved over to the far side of the tent. Maud followed behind like a lost puppy.

Rose went over to the first bunch of men coming in from the battlefield. The first solider had a huge gash through his thigh and Rose could see his femur. Maud turned away and almost threw up. Rose asked the man, "Where's the pain?" The man shook his hand towards his thigh and also his chest. Rose opened the shirt and saw shrapnel under his skin. Maud went to inject penicillin and Rose stopped her hand.

"No, this man needs other medicine." Rose calmly got her black pen out and drew a line on his arm.

"Just rest up, I will go get you some more medicine." She held the man's hand and rubbed his face. They walked away and Rose whispered to Maud. "Save the drugs for those who need it. That man will die soon." Maud looked distraught but understood.

For the rest of the morning, Rose quickly worked into a chaotic groove. She had walked around her area, spoken to all the men and categorized them all. She was covered in blood, smelled of decaying bodies, and she was exhausted. Walking on the beach had really worn down her feet and she was hungry. She found a lady giving out spam sandwiches and she grabbed a couple for herself and Maud.

They sat on the beach and briefly looked at the waves. It was a peaceful moment. Maud looked distraught and so they spoke about their families. Rose felt tears well up as she spoke about Gwenn. Maud mentioned that her mum was also a nurse and had encouraged her to enroll. Rose started to head back and she slowly walked over the sand, pondering on how exactly she'd wound up on a beach in France, nursing injured British and Canadian men. She could hear explosions in the background.

"A German got them with a flame thrower," Rose overheard. She got to work quickly. When she looked out on the battlefield, she saw other men struggling but no one helping them. She abandoned her post and she sprinted out to the beach to go help them. She got to the men and saw they all had bullet wounds.

"Woman, get down," a man screamed. "A sniper has a sight on most of us." Rose knelt down and attended to several of the men. She tried to bandage up the easy fixes.

"What's your name," she asked one man.

"Adam Nelson, ma'am," he replied. She suspected he was younger than her and new to combat.

"Lucky miss," he joked as Rose bandaged an arm wound. The bullet had gone straight through and he seemed ok.

"Thanks again," he said and stood up. Instantly, Adam was shot in the head and Rose was covered in blood.

She just stood frozen. Rose tried to process what had just happened while Adam lay on the floor, twitching uncontrollably as his head bled all over the sand. Rose continued to mend all the men for the next thirty minutes. She guessed she'd treated at least a dozen soldiers and they were all grateful. She felt something hit her shoulder. Rose was tough so she ignored it and went to help the others until she felt some dampness on her shoulder. She put her hand on her shoulder and pulled it back, it was covered in blood. She'd been caught in the crossfire. She lay down with the other men and felt light headed. Everything suddenly went to black.

Rose awoke and thought it had been a dream. She felt as if she was floating but others were moving her. She looked down and then panicked.

"Stay calm," a voice told her. She looked up and Maud was holding her hand. She slowly moved her head and saw that she was going towards a boat. She closed her eyes again and someone whispered "She should make it, don't black line her." Her final vision was seeing Maud heading off the ship and back to the beaches. The next time Rose woke up, a bright light flashed down on her. She looked at the white ceilings and knew she was a hospital.

"You are in Basingstoke General and you are going to be ok," a nurse said. Rose was in pain, but managed a smile.

She spent the next two weeks in the hospital and was a terrible patient. She loved working in hospitals but hated staying in one. Penny had come to visit her and it had been good to catch up with her; she'd even got to see Lorraine and Lil. Eventually, she was discharged and Penny had bought her a train ticket to Wales. The feeling in Wales was now slightly different with

Gwenn gone. Seeing her parents and having home cooked food was nice. Summer disappeared and Autumn began. The nights became longer and Rose made a full recovery. It was time to head back to England and move on with the next chapter of her life. *I'm never going back to the front lines,* she thought.

CHAPTER 81

The news had reached Eddie and the men in Burma. The D-Day landings were a success. It had been a good and necessary morale boost. The Germans were in retreat and that meant the war was nearly over. But the war they were engaged in seemed far from over. For several months now, the Japanese had tried to attack and penetrate India. They progressed and reached a town called Kohima.

Although a small town, it had tremendous value to military supply chains. If the Allied forces couldn't hold the Japanese back, they'd be giving up access to supply routes, a train depot, a port, and an airstrip. Eddie and his unit were located about one hundred miles away from Kohima but they knew that road and town well. When they had first arrived in Burma, they had set up their base near there on the Indian side of the boarder. A call had come in, they had to move out and up to Kohima to help secure the town.

So, Eddie, Aiden, and five hundred men marched northwest towards the town. When they first arrived at Kohima , there were no roads and it was all jungle. At least now, roads had been built which made the walk bearable. But it was still torture to march over this terrain, especially in the heat and Eddie's feet felt like sandpaper had ripped through the skin. He was exhausted, hungry and tired from the march.

The only thing that reassured Eddie a little was that they had met an American regiment along the road who had also been called in to support. They had tanks and other heavy-duty weapons. Eddie had not seen a tank in several years but it made him feel more confident and at ease marching towards the enemy. In the evenings, certain men would take guard and the rest would sleep around the tanks while drinking American bourbon and singing British and American songs. Eddie and Aiden had become a hero to everyone around them as they had been in Burma since Wheaton's first campaign and because they had both also been in Dunkirk, Africa, Greece and now all of Burma.

"How the hell are you two alive," an American asked.

"Pure luck," Aiden said with a smile. "That's why they called us 'The Cats'. We have nine lives!"

After five days of hiking, they arrived on the east side of Kohima and were met by Lieutenant General Mills, the officer in charge. He asked for Eddie and Aiden to lead their men through the back of the town, which was where the enemy was approaching. There was a former British ambassador's house at the top of the hill and they needed to ensure the Japanese did not pass that house.

Eddie and Aiden looked at each other. They were used to certain death situations and they knew this was, yet again, a tough mission. *Why couldn't we be the men twenty miles from the battle,* Eddie thought to himself as they finished a smoke and rounded up the men. They found the British building. It was glistening white and looked typical of what a Lord in England would live in, nestled on top of a hill and built to stand out. They hatched a plan to approach the building at night, ideally under the radar of the Japanese soldiers. The Americans and the tanks were to stay at the bottom of the hill until given the radio call, then they'd drive up to provide support.

Eddie and Aiden had British soldiers with them, along with Indian soldiers and they all sat around singing as the sun set before their mission. Eddie sang "When you go home, tell them of us and say, for your tomorrow, we gave our today." Eddie had to admire these Indian troops; they'd been fighting bravely in this area for months with only limited weapons and were seriously outnumbered. They had a good spirit about them despite all that.

Nighttime hit and everyone became sullen, serious, and focused. His Indian colleagues led Eddie up the hill and they surrounded the compound in the pitch black of night. He tried to just focus on the five yards ahead of him and took each step slowly. He was used to snakes and other creatures now but did not want to disturb them. Out of nowhere he got smacked in the head by a tree branch and knew he was bleeding onto his face. There was nothing he could do about it now, but it wasn't a good start.

They got to the front of the house. No lights were on and, in Eddie's mind, this was not a house but a palace. An Indian man whispered "This is what all Englishmen live in right?" Eddie had to laugh. He was used to tight Victorian street housing where rows of streets were all next to each other. Trevanston had one manor ten miles from the town but Eddie had never been inside. Eddie couldn't even imagine living in this house—his whole family could live there.

Eddie went left and Aiden went right, each with about two hundred and fifty soldiers. In the yard, there was a large lagoon style swimming pool and beyond that Eddie could see trees and a low wall. Apparently, the Japanese were about a mile further down. Eddie was torn; he didn't want to fight during the night, especially when he had no idea about the scenery. But at the same time if he sat there until morning, he would be a lot more visible and the element of surprise would be gone.

While pondering this, Eddie pointed up and indicated a third problem. The skies opened up and the rain just poured down. Aiden came up with the idea to go into the house. This was an embassy house and they were warned not to go in but camping out in the rain wasn't an option. They went up to the house, Aiden broke a window, climbed in, and guided the men in. They all settled in for the night; many of the men, Eddie included, slept whenever they got a chance. It was peaceful, listening to the rain pound down on the windows around them and Eddie slept in a bed for the first time in years.

Eddie was woken up to gunfire. He looked out the nearest window and saw that the skies were still grey, the rain was still coming down hard, and gunshots had started to come close to them. They smashed some of the windows, especially on the top floor, and started firing towards the source of the gunshots. Eddie quickly realized that this was stupid. The enemy was randomly firing at them and they were firing into space. Eddie and Aiden got together and decided to first try the men at the bottom the hill over the radio. There was crackling and interference through the radio but no response.

"So, let me get this straight," Aiden started. "According to reports yesterday, there are about two thousand enemy soldiers about half a mile straight ahead of us shooting at this house. We were ordered to come here and protect this house that is not even being lived in. We have about five hundred men and are outnumbered four to one. We left hundreds of Americans down the bottom of the hill because they were going to be our support but then a monsoon happens and we can't get hold of them.

"Yep," said Eddie with a grin and he offered Aiden a roll up cigarette. "That pretty much sums it up."

"Oh, and if they take this house, they take this town and disrupt our supplies," Eddie added.

Some of the men had binoculars so they peered out towards the woods hoping to see anything. Of course, they couldn't, especially with the fog. Eddie went to a window and could make out the hill they climbed; it looked a lot steeper in the light while mud gushed down it. The Americans had a bunch of supplies so Eddie handed out a few candy bars amongst the men and the water in the house miraculously worked. He and Aiden positioned the men around the house and then they waited. If he was an enemy soldier, he would wait until nightfall and then attack and that was exactly what happened. No sooner had the sun set, although it had never really shown itself, the gunfire started.

Gunfire was coming from two locations and all the men ducked down. Windows were smashed but there was no damage to personnel. But there was movement happening at the front of the house and a ton of the enemy soldiers were marching towards them. They opened fire and felt they had hit some, but the gunfire was two way and Eddie saw a few men getting hit. He needed to preserve the lives of his men as they were outnumbered already. He called his medic to treat the injured quickly and quietly.

The firefight continued for most of the evening with a few casualties for Eddie's men but they held the enemy off. As sunrise happened for the second day, Eddie's men reported that the Japanese had now made base just behind the swimming pool and had actually dug trenches. Eddie could not see them because of their positioning. The second evening came, still with no word from the men they had left at the bottom of the hill and so Eddie braced himself for another attack. This time, however, it was more fierce than before. The Japanese were smart and threw several grenades into the water of the swimming pool to make a distraction and then fired mortars and guns from other directions. The Japanese had surrounded the building and were closing in fast.

After several hours of fighting, things were getting worse for Eddie and Aiden. They were running out of bullets and the Japanese were now several hundred feet from the house. Eddie had been in too many battles but knew this was a bad one, so he quickly found a corner and wrote a letter to his mum, saying how sorry he was not to see her again. He pocketed it, hoping someone would find it, and post it just as the Japanese entered the building.

Eddie ordered the men to fall back upstairs and Aiden's team covered one side of the stairs while Eddie's had the other. Grenades were thrown into the building and there were squeals of pain as men who were still downstairs were killed. Eddie and his men opened fire and for a moment were able to hold them off, with the enemy retreating. But that was short-lived and the Japanese gathered momentum entering the house.

It was probably another hour of fighting where the men bravely fought the Japanese from entering upstairs but that had started to break. Eddie ran forward to the first enemy on the balcony, he smashed the butt of his gun into the face of one guy and then used his bayonet to stab the other. He looked down distraught. These soldiers were younger than him and were doing their job. He should have been playing football with them, not killing them. Others followed him, including Aiden, and together, they pushed twenty men down the stairs, but they kept coming. Eddie saw Aiden fall to gunshots, he seemed to still be moving, then Eddie was doing face to face combat again, head-butting one man and stabbing several more. Just as he turned, he knew he had made a mistake and was stabbed on the side of his ribs. He winced, and was then stabbed in the back. He fell down hard. A Japanese soldier walked over him, gun pointed at him, but there was something in the soldier's eyes, a kind of mutual understanding and fear.

He just walked past Eddie, actually moving him out of harm's way and then continued on.

Eddie lay there, not sure what had just happened. The soldier could have killed him but didn't; maybe he knew he was dying anyway. He could feel his shirt was soaked with blood. Maybe he didn't want to kill and, if that was the case, why was he fighting people who also didn't want to fight. Eddie had been on the floor for a while, he assumed hours but he had no idea. There was still fighting all around him. Out of nowhere, there was a huge boom and then another. Eddie recognized the noise—it was the American tanks and, eventually, Eddie heard American and British voices. He passed out at that point, knowing at least his body was safe.

Eddie woke to sun in his eyes. He was lying on his back and he tried to get up but his chest felt like an elephant was on it. He slowly looked around to check his surroundings. He was outside for sure. He was on a bed in a tent. Someone rushed over; it was an American.

"Woah there, take it easy," he shouted.

"Where am I," Eddie wheezed. He'd had a seizure but it was over. They had moved him from the floor in the ambassador's house to a stretcher in the Med Tent.

It was explained to him that the seizure was over and he was in a medical tent. He got up and walked around, ignoring the advice of the medic. The stench hit him quickly. To the left of him was a bunch of dead bodies being covered up. Eddie counted the bodies and stopped after he reached one hundred. Many of them had been under his command. Tears streamed down his face. *I let them down,* he thought. He got his bearings and realized he was down by the swimming pool and American tanks and soldiers were all around him.

As he walked by the house, he saw a bunch of Japanese prisoners being held captive. The Americans had captured these men. Eddie spotted the man who had spared his life in the battle. He walked over to him and asked the Americans if he could talk to him. They didn't object. They were guessing Eddie was going to kill him. Who were they to object to a revenge killing? Eye for an eye, as they say.

However, Eddie had another intention. They walked together until they reached a clearing and they could look out on the valley. The man looked scared. Eddie calmly sat down and pulled out a cigarette. Eddie got out some matches. They sat there and smoked in silence. The pain through Eddie's chest was almost unbearable but smoking relaxed him.

Eddie calmly pointed to himself and said "Eddie."

"Kensho," the man said. Eddie raised his hands and showed five fingers four times and then one finger, indicating Eddie was 21 or at least he probably was, he had no idea what day of the week it was. Kensho responded with a seventeen. "Neither of us should be here, this is a screwed up war." Kensho couldn't understand what Eddie said but acknowledged the feelings. Eddie could tell, the feeling was mutual.

Kensho opened his pocket and showed a picture of a baby. Eddie understood and smiled. They shared one more cigarette and then Eddie said "Go." But Kensho refused. He said one word only, "honor." Eddie knew that the Japanese culture meant that Kensho could not run away. He had to stay and face the consequences. Eddie admired that so they walked back together. Kensho got back in line with prisoners to the utter surprise of the Americans.

Eddie went over to the American Captain and spoke a few words. "No more killing," was all he said. The American Captain outranked Eddie, but he could see Eddie's emotions and ordered his men to round up the prisoners and take them to a nearby base. Eddie headed back to the medical tent and heard someone shout.

"You're not dead yet?" He turned around and saw Aiden. The men awkwardly embraced. Their injuries made it painful and all Aiden could say was "I need a beer."

CHAPTER 82 -1945

Roger and Rebecca had been in Bletchley House for several years now and had managed to keep it a secret from most people, thanks to their alibi of being school teachers. The school they worked at had been informed that they were helping out another school in London. There was no confusion. Most surprisingly, Mac still had no idea. Christmas had come and gone. It was a cold January morning with frost all over the grounds.

For Rebecca, she had really enjoyed being part of the war effort. She was an immensely gifted mathematician and this was her calling. She had also loved spending more time with Roger. Because they didn't own a car, they cycled to work most days and even picnicked on the Bletchley estate in summer.

Roger was still very much suffering from post-traumatic stress from his experiences in the First War and hearing about the battles and news from the European Front had not helped his recovery. He was around good people and had tremendous support, especially from Rebecca but his tough exterior though was easily cracked and he missed his son dearly. He hated how his only son was battling and in constant danger. He would have done anything to swap places with him but he knew the world didn't work that way. Throughout the years at work, they had gone through a range of emotions. There had been long evenings where they desperately tried to crack the German codes and they had worked until midnight with no luck knowing they'd have to start again in the morning. They were completely frustrated. However, in recent months, they had cracked at least some of the codes which had bought a sense of euphoria and camaraderie to all that worked there. Now they seemed to be winning the battle and were able to strategically intercept German warships.

Despite the frost, they still cycled to Bletchley. The frost had melted a little, so their commute to work was muddy. Mud had splashed their ankles but neither of them cared. The sun was still rising when they arrived at a quarter to eight. The guards knew them now, but security was still very tight. They still had to show their passports before being allowed in. After grabbing a tea, they settled into their desks and started plotting activities. Their leader had insisted on regular breaks due to their intense and strenuous work. By eleven o'clock, they had had multiple teas and Roger needed a well-deserved toilet break.

Despite the secrecy, Roger was constantly amazed at what was discussed in the loo and as he sat in a cubicle reading the morning *Times*, he overheard two men in deep conversation. "Yes, it's tragic but sometimes we have to let the Germans win so that they don't know we are on to them." One man with an accent from Manchester stated. Roger thought he knew the man but wasn't sure, however his ears pricked up. "But to knowingly let them attack an Atlantic battleship with all those innocent men onboard when we can prevent it seems like a tough pill," the second man with a southern accent said. Roger had no idea who that was. Roger was intrigued and wanted to know what ship they were talking about. His heart sank as the first man mumbled, "God speed to the men on HMS Rockingham." That was Mac's ship!

Roger finished in the bathroom and dashed to find Rebecca. He was all flustered when he found her in the kitchen area. She knew something was wrong. Suspecting he might be having a post traumatic episode and knowing that the whole office constantly had their eyes on him in a distrusting way, she pulled him into a small cleaning closet.

"Ok, what's wrong hun," she said in a reassuring and calming tone while rubbing his shoulder. Roger just kept repeating Mac's name. He was shaking and sweating, so Rebecca sat him down and let him breath. The cleaning closet was a little claustrophobic but eventually Roger calmed down and then was able to reiterate what he'd heard in the bathroom. He could see shock wash over her face and the energy drain from her eyes. Rebecca was normally more composed than this. She was the sensible one out of the two of them. She was livid now and sprinted into the main command room with Roger in tow. She walked right up to the Admiral on duty, "You need to inform the Rockingham now of the impending German boats," she screamed and the whole room suddenly looked at her.

The admiral tried to grab her arm and pull her into a room. That was the wrong thing to do. Roger jumped in and got in his face. "Get your hand off my wife right now!" Rebecca was grateful Roger was standing up for her, but knew that him beating up the admiral wouldn't help. The admiral had been a friend of theirs, especially Rebecca's, for several years and cared about them. He stared into her eyes and she could see remorse looking back at her. After a long moment of silence, he calmly spoke. "We cannot change any protocol here. We cannot let the German's take back any advantage we have. You are well aware of this." Rebecca's emotions got the better of her now. "My son is on that ship! You are sending my son to his death; I beg you—warn them!"

There was a long silence and the admiral felt the eyes of the whole room on him. Everyone was aware of what was going on and no one had complained before. This time, though, it was personal. He could feel the tension in the whole room. He had a great deal of empathy but orders were orders and he knew what to do. He breathed in deeply and calmly spoke again.

"I am truly sorry, but you know the protocol. I feel that your time here at Bletchley is over. I will have these guards escort you and Roger out. You'll have honorable discharges and go back to your old careers. Your country thanks you for your service." He had already motioned for the guards to come over and they were now standing directly behind Roger and Rebecca.

Roger was a calculated man. He knew the fight was over. Rebecca did not initially and screamed at the room. "You can all save my son and hundreds of other men. Their blood is on your hands." It was a desperate plea and the room, most of whom were their friends, stared at their shoes. Roger tapped her on the shoulder and simply said "Let's go, let's hope God can take care of our boy."

They left the building and got their bikes, cycling home in silence. They sat at their dining room table all night, not eating anything, not saying anything.

Neither slept, either; they just hoped now. After Roger and Rebecca had been escorted out, Admiral Adams ordered his staff back to work and then went and sat in his office. He poured a whiskey and slowly drank it while replaying what he'd heard with the words "You are sending my son to his death," resonating in his head. He was a man who never let his emotions waiver but he shed a tear for his friends in private. *War was cruel,* he thought, *very cruel.*

CHAPTER 83

D-day was now a distant memory for Mac. It had been over six months since that day and from all the press they'd seen, it had been a huge success. The Allies were now taking the offensive in France.

Since then, he'd been on Atlantic duty which had been relatively easy compared with the convoys earlier in the war. He had not even seen a gun fired in over a month. Mac had a three days break over New Year and returned home to be with his parents. He told them that he was number three on a ship called the HMS Rockingham. He still worked with Captain Pollack. He had briefly also got to see Penny. He adored her and wanted to just spend the rest of his life with her. That was his only focus. But to do that he needed to do his job well and that meant the task in hand. He boarded the ship, met with the Captain, and they set off to New York.

He could see his breath, thanks to the crisp cold air on the deck. He had his uniform and gloves on but he could still feel his bones rattle and shake. He completed the rounds on the deck, checked all the guns, and made his notes before heading downstairs to the ammunitions room, then up to the Captain's deck to report. He informed Captain Pollack that everything looked good but he was a bit worried about the guns being iced over and not functioning.

Mac went down to the mess hall to grab dinner as the ship set sail. After five years on these boats, he was used to the diet of corned beef, mashed potato, and some vegetables at least twice a week. He was sick of the food and vowed never to eat corned beef after the war. He sat with a few men from the engine room, one of whom happened to be from a town near Trevanston. He was a young kid named Ben Moon and he had just turned eighteen. This was his first ship and Mac wanted to tell him to leave the boat, that he should forget about the Navy. But he didn't and knew that he had no choice, it was a crime to run away. He told him that he'd had a wild adventure so far, seeing a lot of the world and that the battles were exciting.

Mac did a final ammunitions check, ensured the gunners on duty had gloves and hot cocoa as they were going to be on deck for much of the night, and then he headed to his mess. He had the top bunk in the large quarters with only a few other leaders and he liked that. He liked not chatting. He took the picture of Penny out of his pocket and fell asleep just as the engines started churning. They set sail from Plymouth out onto the Atlantic.

Several hours later, Mac was woken up by a loud thud that threw him from his bed. He picked himself up from the floor, slightly bruised and battered. The ship was in trouble. Alarms started ringing and just as he started to run down the corridor towards the ammunition room, another loud thud threw him onto the ground again. This time, he'd cut his head on the metal walls. He checked the wound. It looked like it wasn't getting any worse so got up and sprinted to the ammunition room. His colleague was already loading the guns from within the room and also sending people with trollies to go load the guns.

"We're under attack," the man screamed. *Obviously*, Mac thought. The sailor had the ammunition room under control, so Mac headed up to the deck. As soon as he got there, panic erupted. Men were screaming everywhere, to his right and in the middle of the ship a fire was raging. To his left, men were hoisting down life boats. As Mac peered down toward the front of the ship, he could see that the nose of the ship was heading into water. *Oh damn. We're sinking.*

Mac paused a moment, closed his eyes, and tried to gather his composure. He asked himself, *what needs to be done, how do I save as many lives as possible, and how do I survive?* He breathed in and out slowly for thirty seconds, then decided on his plan. As a leader on the boat, he was responsible for saving lives, even if that meant he would die. So, he ran towards the fire. The ship had water cannons already in place and he helped several men take control of them. They sprayed water on the fire before it grew into an uncontrollable fireball. When a ship is sinking everything seems to happen in slow motion. He remembered studying why the Titanic sank at school and the theory was that it bobbed around for an hour before going down.

Mac saw that the front of the ship was now submerged into water. That will no doubt cause the rest of the ship to sink, he told himself. He remembered the ship's map and which lower desks were at risk for flooding first. The engine team were on the lowest deck so he grabbed a few men and headed down the stairs. He found the engine room with men still working, fueling fires and trying to fix machines. He found Ben, who looked naïve and unaware of what was happening. "Ben, who's in charge?" Ben pointed to a man Mac also knew called Mike Kingsley, a real brute of a man. Mac gasped due to the immense heat and grabbed of his shoulder. Out of breath, he wheezed "This ship is going down. The front is submerged and we have to evacuate." Mike was a huge rugby player from Newcastle and the idea of failure never occurred to him. Mac cut him off and ordered the evacuation. Mike stared at Mac and knew that this was a losing battle.

Men dashed past Mac including Ben and the other guy and Mac struggled to fight his way through the crowds as he headed to the Captain's deck. He found the Captain right in the middle of the command area. The ship was now starting to submerge and Captain Pollack had tears in his eyes. Captain Pollack simply said "Get the men out and get out of here." He turned his back on Mac; he knew that was the last conversation they would ever have. Captain Pollack was traditional in every sense of the word and he was going to go down with his ship.

Mac went down to the life boats and relief struck him as he could see one hundred boats now in the water and he also saw two other ships coming towards them and he assumed they were Allied boats coming to their rescue. The irony struck him that throughout the war, he'd been sinking ships and almost enjoyed it. He had survived many battles but now he was going to get sunk, just off the coast of England.

Mac got in line for a boat and noticed Ben again with the same guy he had evacuated with. Mac looked closely and saw they were holding hands. Mac walked over to them. "We meet again," Mac smiled and the lads quickly separated their hands. There were about forty men to a boat. When Mac jumped in, the boat was released. Mac was actually more scared about being in this rescue boat than he was on the main boat. They were floating in a sea of mines and they were in the freezing cold water of the wintery Atlantic. Mac had calculated in his mind that the other ships would be with them in thirty minutes if all went to plan.

Mac closed his eyes as they floated and thought of Penny and his parents. From a distance, an explosion was heard, followed shortly by screams. Mac briefly opened his eyes to see some of the crew being flung into the air and land in the cold water. *Those poor bastards must've grazed a mine.* Then after a few minutes, his boat started rocking and a commotion came about. Mac sat up and went to investigate.

"What the hell are you doing," he screamed. One of the men was strangling Ben. "Sit down! If we move suddenly, we'll hit a goddamn mine!" Mac was the most senior officer on this boat so the man stopped.

"This faggot and his boyfriend were hugging! It's disgusting and we should throw them both overboard." Mac looked at Ben and saw all the fear in his eyes, and made a decision.

"I told them to hug. Just like I'm telling all of you to do so you can keep warm."

"Nah, he's a poof." Mac remained calm, otherwise he'd blow Ben's cover even more.

"I am the leading officer here. I made that decision and I encourage you to do the same." The man put Ben down but mumbled, "Haven't heard the last of this," and then slouched into the boat.

Less than an hour later, they were being hoisted onboard another ship. It was a huge carrier and it was tricky getting the men on board since they had to climb rope ladders. As Mac climbed up, he was handed a cup of cocoa and he could see the man from before already talking to an officer. Mac sighed as two petty officers came over to talk to Mac, Ben, and the other boy. The two of them were being taken away.

"Is what this man said to be believed?"

"Depends what he told you," Mac replied. "As I explained on the boat, I instructed those two to stay close to keep themselves warm."

"He said they were hugging and groping."

"I didn't see that. I simply saw men trying to survive in the freezing weather."

"You know that it's a criminal offense, being homosexual. It is also a criminal offense for an officer not to report it." Mac again sighed.

"I am well aware of the responsibilities of being an officer. I have been in this war for nearly five years and have more battle time than either of you. I am taking my captain accreditation next month. Why would I jeopardize that and everything I have fought for to defend a kid I don't know?"

That seemed to have gotten the point across and the petty officers took Mac's details before being done with it. The next day Mac was back in England, and disembarking at Portsmouth. He knew the city well now and he had been advised to go to the training base where he was to be reassigned a boat. As Mac was walking off the boat, someone tapped him on the shoulder. It was Ben. "Err officer, I just wanted to thank you for the other day. You literally saved my life." Mac winked at him and said "Men die in this war every day. No one should die for love. Just be more careful next time." With that, Mac kept walking to the mess hall before heading off on his next mission.

CHAPTER 84

The war had been wearing people down so many people for years and Rose appreciated that. In some sense, she had been really lucky, she had escaped with minor injuries. Her injury from last year had been serious enough to keep her out of work for over six months, but minor in her eyes as she had made a full recovery with just a small scar to show for it. However, the last few months had been tough for her and she currently sat on a park bench in Watford reflecting.

Losing Clint was a blow to her. Even though she had only known him for a year, they had become good friends. He had made her laugh and had taken her out of her shell. Losing Gwenn was devastating for her, she felt partly responsible because she had followed Rose to war. She had been to Wales twice now to bury a family member but with Gwenn it was a lot more real. She had liked her uncle and felt sorry for Penny and Lorraine but she had grown up in Wales and only seen them a few times a year. She had played with Gwenn every day as a child. She had gone up into the waterfalls and hiked with her, stolen apples with her, and now she was gone. When Rose left Wales five years earlier, she had felt this huge sense of adventure. She was getting out of Wales and doing her part for the country.

Now, all she wanted was for this war to end. She had enjoyed the winter in Wales. She spent it recovering. It had almost been as if no one had left and nothing had changed. She would walk round the waterfalls daily, pick fresh eggs, and help her mum and dad. It was like the war didn't exist. Yet the war had impacted them and there was no Gwenn now. The pictures on the wall were a constant reminder. It was February and she was now back in Watford. She'd been assigned to work as a general nurse at the hospital. She had loved her time at Watford before and felt this was where she was going to be happiest. But as she sat on the bench watching the trees return to life, she became anxious about returning.

She felt alone and scared for the first time since she could remember and part of her wanted to go back to Wales and just be with her family. She had written to several people to inform them about her new location, including Edith. At least she'd see a familiar face. But there was still a nervousness about starting over again. Finally, after sitting on the bench for an hour, Rose forced herself up and walked to the hospital.

As she walked in and headed towards the nurses' quarters, someone jumped up behind her.

"Hello stranger," a voice shouted. Rose jumped nearly as high as the ceiling. She turned around and standing in front of her was Lil. Rose did a double take.

"What are you doing here," Rose stammered.

"After your last letter to me and after what you've been through, I thought I would come back here as well. Besides, there are a lot more handsome men here than there were in Yorkshire." Rose paused for a moment, then hugged Lil and murmured thank you in her ear as tears streamed down her face.

"Don't be showing emotion now. That's not the Rose I know. Come on, I will get you settled. There are others excited to see you as well."

Rose followed Lil to the nurses' quarters and saw several other nurses she had trained with. Jenny, Rita, and of course Edith came up and gave her a big hug. "Welcome back to the family," she said and that's exactly how Rose felt. Her anxiety had disappeared in a second and she felt right back at home where she belonged. After getting settled, she was thrust into action, putting casts on broken bones within an hour. She was back working with children and she loved that as well. They were always so happy.

The next several weeks flew by and Rose had not stopped at all. When she had an evening off, she was studying for further nursing qualifications or had been taken out to the local bars with the nursing crew. She worked long hours but that helped her forget everything else. The hospital was constantly busy and with London still being bombed, they were taking an overflow of patients from north London in. Rose arrived one morning for a six o'clock start and Lil was just finishing up her shift.

"Whoa, what a busy night. We have a ton from the bombings last night. Good luck," she said. Rose did her rounds and checked in on all the children, adjusting meds, and taking temperatures. Nearly all of them had adults, normally parents or grandparents, so she would update them on the patient's status. But she came across twins and there was no adult around. She assumed they had gone somewhere, so she checked on them. They were a girl and boy, both with mousy brown hair and with sparkling blue eyes. No more than seven or eight, you could tell they were twins based on their eyes and the shape of their cheeks.

She went over to the boy first, checked his file and saw his name was Colin. "Hi Colin, I'm Rose. This file tells me you have some cuts and bruises, anything else hurt?" Colin looked scared and just touched his ribs. Rose gently prodded him and asked him to breath. Based on the sound, she was fairly sure he had a collapsed lung. She went to the girl next and her name was Gwenn. Her name made it difficult for Rose to focus. She had to wipe the tears from her face and act professionally. She told the girl how much she loved her name and that she knew someone incredibly brave once also called Gwenn. Gwenn had a broken arm and leg. Rose cleaned under the casts before setting out.

She had an instant affection for both of these kids and about an hour later after she had finished her rounds, she went back to check in on them. Still no parents to be found. So, she asked another nurse, "Do you know who brought these two in and who's looking after them? The nurse looked at her with a look of sadness.

"A local guy bought them in after a ton of bombings. They were found in the rubble of their house after lying there for days. Their parents died in the blast and no one has been able to find a guardian. Rose hated hearing this but it was part of the package with her job. Social services would be called and they would either find foster parents or she would go into an orphanage. Rose checked in with the twins as often as she could, changing shifts, and giving up her chocolate rations to them. The first day neither really spoke to her, the second day

Gwenn spoke a little to Rose but really only to tell her where she was in pain or that she needed to use the bathroom. Rose persisted and by the end of the week she was playing games with Colin and Gwenn. They hugged her whenever she came to see them. Gwenn had even called Rose her best friend. This was exactly what Rose needed.

This routine continued for about a month. Rose had also roped in others to come see these kids. Lil had swung by a couple of times and had provided them with oranges, having said she knew a man who could get them. She later told Rose she was dating a pilot who had made regular trips to Africa. Penny had also come to visit these kids, bringing them toys and talking to them for hours about football. Colin loved that Penny had gone to the game last year and Penny had promised to take him to a game. Rose had promised Gwenn that when they went to football, she would take her to see some of the London museums.

Then in one quick swoop it was all changed. After her rounds one day, she came into the room and found a representative from Child Services there. Rose spoke with the rep outside and asked what would happen to the children. The woman coldly said, "They will be put into a children's home and hopefully someone will take them." Rose looked upset by this. She had no experience of children's homes and had heard that the war had made thousands of children into orphans. She just couldn't imagine them in such a place. "Is there anything anyone can do," Rose said, sound nervous and desperate as her voiced rose one octave while speaking. The child services representative could see there was genuine affection here, so she lowered her voice and said, "Unofficially, if someone had a good home for them then I am sure the paperwork would get pushed through."

Rose couldn't care for them herself but she wondered if maybe she had an answer here. She asked her matron if she could have the day off and telegrammed Penny to meet her in London. Then she jumped on the next train to London with Colin and Gwenn. Penny met her at Euston station.

"What's up," she asked. "I need three train tickets to Wales, but I can't afford it. I want to take them to Wales." Penny stared for a moment, unsure of what to say. She already had an idea and without saying a word, walked up to the ticket counter and purchased four first-class tickets to Wales. "If we are going, we are traveling the fun way." Penny smirked at Gwenn.

The kids had never been on a train. They had grown up in a poor part of London. A first-class cabin was something truly special for them. They loved the whole train journey, looking out the window, and seeing the countryside. They arrived in Wales and got the last bus to the village.

They walked up the pathway with Gwenn hobbling a bit. After answering the door, Rose's mum looked at them in disbelief. She hugged Rose and Penny. "What are you doing here," she asked.

"Mum before I tell you everything, this is Colin and Gwenn," she said. Anne introduced herself but winced when Gwenn introduced herself. Anne still grimaced and teared at the name so she changed the subject by calling Patty and Norman to the door. None of them could believe what they were seeing and embraced everyone.

Rose's mum made tea and brought out cakes. Rose told her the story and she ended by saying, "I thought you might like some company. Maybe they can live with you for a while." This was the first time Colin and Gwenn had heard this news and they were a little shocked so Rose spoke to them.

"I will come visit you all the time and you can come visit me." Colin finally spoke to Norman and asked, "You like football?"

"I do but I will also teach you rugby," he said with a grin. That was that. Everyone got on a train the next day and after another week, the paperwork was complete. Colin and Gwenn were moving to their new home in Wales.

CHAPTER 85

Penny was out walking Winnie around Hamstead. She loved to explore new areas of London and enjoyed the fresh air. Winnie loved being outside and had his tongue out. His tail was wagging, but he was clearly cold. The trees were starting to bloom but there were still very few leaves on them. There was a brisk wind sweeping through the park.

Penny was wearing a woolly hat and did not care for the weather, but she felt good being out and about. Her impromptu visit to Wales was a couple of weeks ago and as promised she had written to Colin and Gwenn. They had also lost their parents, so Penny felt a connection with them.

It was amazing how peaceful London could be, despite the fact the city had been totally annihilated by war for the past five years. There had been a period about a year ago when the bombings seemed to lessen but now they were more frequent and destructive. This had not been helped by the fact that the Germans had created a new weapon called the V2 rocket or the doodlebug, which was much larger than previous bombs and much more powerful. Penny had seen whole building and houses turn to rubble just the other day.

As always, London carried on and Penny would see Frank the milkman most mornings delivering milk with a smile on his face. People continued to go to work as normal. Penny often went to the movies just to see the news reels and it was always positive. Always about how the Allies had taken this town or won this battle and that they were winning the war but Penny had to wonder how much more London and England could endure.

She had seen five years of this now and despite the London spirit, there had to be a breaking point. As she walked, she wondered when and what that would be.

Penny reached the top of a hill and had a fantastic view of London. The sun was setting and the clouds were coming in. Penny was going to be on warden duty that night so she knew she had to head back. On the way to her flat she popped into a pub called The Cricketers that was near her flat. She knew the landlord and ordered a glass of port and some dinner. There were still strict rules on rationing but the Nick the old land lord and his wife made the rations go a long way. This pub had hops in the wooden ceiling and you could tell it had been around for a long time—it smelled old.

But Nick was always welcoming and made people feel at home. Winnie calmly sat at the bar greeting all the guests and eating scraps where he could. Normally, the pub was quiet but on this evening, it was fairly busy with soldiers who had located themselves in one corner of the bar, drinking shots. Penny sat there and read the papers, ate her dinner, and relaxed. This was her one day off from the factory and she enjoyed every moment of it.

As she was reading The Times newspaper, she paused at a picture. There staring at her was a picture of Eddie. The story was about how British, American and Indian soldiers that were outnumbered but had held off a huge Japanese attack. Eddie had aged dramatically and looked thinner but it was clearly him. She wondered if his family knew of this or if Mac saw it. She ripped the page out and thought that when she left she would frame it for Mac and try to buy other copies to send to the Hartley clan in Trevanston. She had not seen him in a while and it made her smile to know he was still alive.

Suddenly the sirens started. Penny knew she had to get her warden hat and gas mask on and start manning the streets. She gave Winnie her leftovers on the plate which he ate in a matter of seconds. Technically with rationing, wasting food like that was frowned upon but Penny did not care.

A loud explosion went off right over the pub and the whole building shook. Nick shouted to Penny and the others in the pub.

"Quick, come on, it's already started. Get down the cellar." Penny was hesitant but then a second explosion knocked her off her feet and a couple of the soldiers picked her up. "Let's get you downstairs," they said with a strong cockney south London accent. About fifteen people in all went down the ladder to the cellar and sat there in near silence. A couple of the men had matches and Nick had a candle. His wife, Maggie was already down there. She had baked a sponge cake and hastily shared it with everyone.

The fifteen strangers at first sat there in near silence before one of the men started singing and they all joined in. Nick had all of his supplies down in the cellar so they started drinking and telling stories. The men had recently been fighting in Belgium and were now on break. One of them had even gone to the same school as Penny. They were all slightly older than Penny and it was fascinating to her to hear stories of the professions they had before the war. One was a policemen, another a banker, and another was a welder.

For several hours, the explosions happened all around them. A few times they could tell it was close because the bar shook and they could hear glasses falling everywhere. Eventually, Nick looked at his watch and said "Rise and shine everyone it's six in the morning." Penny had not slept at all but Winnie was fast asleep snoring on her. Nick's pub had been hit and where she had been sitting not twelve hours earlier had now disappeared, replaced with a big hole. Everyone looked at each other, they were so lucky to have survived that. Nick looked close to tears and Maggie just looked in shock. Penny thanked them again and whispered "I'm so sorry." Nick looked at her through watery eyes and told her thanks.

Penny and Winnie walked the streets, but all around her was rubble. She wanted to help, but firemen and other men were already clearing it up. She wanted to check on the factory and the people there. Suddenly Winnie stopped in front of a block of rubble and refused to go any further. He started barking and spinning around. "What's wrong," Penny asked, but he wouldn't move. It was then Penny realized they were standing over the rubble of a church and Winnie had noticed something wrong. Penny took a look and under the rubble she could see that multiple families were stuck. She screamed down "I'll get help." A man just nodded at her. Penny ran as fast as she could to the firemen, got them to the scene, and everyone started to move bricks.

After an hour, they had pulled out four adults and six children. They had been really lucky as a wooden beam had fallen at such an angle that it had a created a cove for them, but what was even more lucky was that their cove could have collapsed at any moment. The man thanked Penny and then everyone thanked Winnie who had saved the day. He was given bacon rations and everything.

It had been a long day for Penny and she was exhausted when she eventually got to the factory, but more bad news hit her. The factory had been damaged and it was decided it needed to be closed for a few days. There were no injuries thank God. Penny worked with the owner for a while sorting out next steps and then went home.

She got to her flat and desperately needed sleep, but her head was spinning with everything that had happened in the last few hours. After thirty minutes of failing to fall asleep, she grabbed her checkbook and Winnie and headed back out. First, she headed to the factory and told the new owners that they can use her for a credit line and the women were to continue receiving payments. Then she headed to the church that was destroyed and left a check with a note. It read "Fix your church and keep the faith going." Next, she went to the fire brigade who had helped the night before and told them she was buying them all lunch.

Finally, she went to Nick's pub. She found Nick sitting on the rubble, looking really low. She quickly wrote him a check and said, "I will fix the pub for you and pay for all damages as long as Winnie and I can keep having dinner there." Nick was lost for words, no one had ever been that kind to him. He hugged Penny for a long time and then she headed back.

It was now the late afternoon and fatigue suddenly hit her. She could hardly keep her eyes open, she wanted to sleep so badly but as she neared her flat the sirens went off. She popped her warden hat on and headed back out to the streets. She forced herself awake and guided people into the tube station. Finally, she headed underground and to her little area where she fell asleep with Winnie on her lap. She felt good about what she could do with her new wealth.

CHAPTER 86

Everyone in England seemed to be around a radio as a special news announcement was due to be broadcast in less than an hour. Rose had just finished her shift but had decided to stay around the hospital with the other nurses. All of them, including Edith, were in the nurses' quarters.

Penny was in the factory and production had halted since they all had gathered to listen round the two radios that the factory had. There was a keen sense of excitement. Many had already guessed what the news would be based on the recent newsreels but they needed to hear it. The announcer came on the radio and everybody heard the Prime Minister's voice.

"Today Germany has surrendered, their leader found dead. Our brothers from the Soviet Union have taken control of Germany. The war in Europe is over."

Penny could not hear anything as huge cheers erupted around the whole of the factory. It was a large space, so the noise echoed all around and was made louder with the men and women banging on the machines. Winnie was initially scared with all of the loud noises but soon realized this was a happy noise and joined in the euphoria. Winnie barked and howled along with the cheers. Penny hugged everyone, literally everyone on the floor and she thanked everyone for their hard work. Then she looked up to her father's old office which was sitting deserted since the new owner was on the floor celebrating. She went up to the office, opened the wooden door, and sat in her father's chair. She quietly broke down into tears. They streamed down her face and memories of Owain came flooding back. She had missed him every single day since he died, but at least now she knew his ideas and help in building airplanes and weapons had saved lives. He helped win the war. *Rest in peace,* she thought. The door opened and the factory owner, Albert came in and hugged her. He thanked her for everything.

Rose was wrapped up in the moment. Nurses all around her were cheering and crying. Many including Rose had lost loved ones throughout the years and now it was over. There was a lot of hugging between them and then all the nurses decided to celebrate with everyone in the hospital. Rose found herself dancing along the wards celebrating with injured soldiers, children, and anyone she could find. She had never felt so happy in her entire life.

There was a queue for the hospital telephones but Rose managed to send a telegram to Penny. She left on the next train with Lil and a few other nurses who had also just finished their shifts to London. She got into Euston station and all around her were celebrations. The crowds were crazy, but standing at the end of the platform along with several other women was Penny. They saw it each other and hugged intensely, tears streaming down both their faces. Then some of the other nurses Rose had travelled with grabbed them both and they all headed towards Trafalgar Square.

The walk took thirty minutes and everywhere they went people were hugging and dancing. Penny found herself hugging an eighty-year-old man who had just left his house and Rose with three children. Once at the square, police had stopped all traffic and there was a street party to end all parties. People were in the fountains and alcohol was being shared by everyone. Neither Penny or Rose had ever experienced anything like it. Rose thought back to when she first came to London as a teenager. She was shy, didn't talk to many people, and she definitely didn't drink alcohol or smoke. Now here she was, drinking gin from a stranger and smoking like a chimney. The party lasted most of the evening and as it wrapped up, Penny and Rose agreed they would meet the next day and travel to Penny's mum's place. They would see her and Jim before heading to Wales to see the family. Penny was excited to see the twins anyway.

She left and fell straight asleep on her bed. Rose caught the last train back with the other nurses and she had already arranged for her shifts to be covered over the next few days. The wave of emotions hit her on the train journey home and without notice, she burst into tears. She thought of her uncle, of Gwenn, of Clint, and all those who had all died in the war. Then she thought of Eddie; she just knew he was alive somewhere, but he was still fighting and silently prayed she would see him again.

Penny awoke the next morning with a sore head and was running late. She dashed with Winnie to go and meet Rose at Liverpool St train station. She was surrounded by bankers and others in suits. She managed to find Rose amongst the crowd and they boarded the train together. Jim picked them up from the station. He seemed a different man from when Penny had met him that first night in the Tube station. He seemed relaxed and happy and not at all uptight. He told the girls how excited he was to just spend time with Harry and Lorraine and not fly anymore missions.

Lorraine was at Jim's station house and she hugged her niece and then gave the biggest hug Penny had ever had. Jim told them that he did not need his car as he was still on base and so he lent it to the girls. Together, they drove down to Wales.

Rose's family was surprised to see them and even more surprised to see them turn up in a car. In fact, half the village stopped and stared at them when they arrived. The twins ran out and gave Rose a huge hug. She spent that whole evening learning hop scotch and playing card games with them. Penny had built a close bond with her youngest cousin Patty, so they spent time chatting about the hot film stars. Norman had shot a pheasant which they prepared for dinner with all fresh grown vegetables.

They spent two days in Wales walking around, enjoying the fresh air, and just relaxing. Winnie loved it. It seemed a whole weight had been lifted from everyone's shoulders. They drove back smiling. Rose had bought a ton of vegetables and fruit and brought it back for all the other nurses.

The following weekend, Trevanston hosted a massive town party. The Hartley family had organized it as always but everyone had been involved. They had put tables and chairs throughout the streets and everyone had collected each other's rations to cook massive pies, cakes, and other treats like sausage rolls. Bill and Charlie had constructed a miniature stage at the end of the street and several of the town had agreed to play live music. The Kings Arms pub would be providing the alcohol and they had stocked up well. News had travelled fast about the party so Penny turned up with Jim, Harry, and her mum to help celebrate. She had already written checks for Bill and Dorothy as her new wealth could help cover the cost.

Penny also went to visit Rebecca and Roger. They seemed happy and they were keen to be part of the celebrations. School was already out for the year but Roger had informed Penny he would be headmaster at the primary school next year and was looking forward to it.

Penny had grown really fond of them over the last few years. Rose was on a double shift because she had taken time off for Wales. Since others had wanted time off, so she did not finish until nine that night. She thought she would pop up to Trevanston anyway. Edith had informed her of the party and she travelled with her. She was glad she did as the town was all out, partying in the streets. She hugged everybody and felt totally at home here. *Finally, life was really good*, she thought.

CHAPTER 87

Mac was stationed in New York, a city he had become familiar with over the years. The docks were always busy and bustling. The city itself was bigger and had more things happening than London even. It was a warm sunny morning in June and Mac was due to set sail that evening back to the UK. He was on a small destroyer ship and was second in command, having now completed part of his Captain's training.

He doubted he would ever be a captain, though. There were more qualified captains ahead of him in the pecking order than there were ships and more importantly, he still loathed the war. He loathed fighting and becoming a captain would have required a complete attitude reversal. He took the exams because it was suggested he did so and it had meant a few weeks in England. He took it as a compliment that at only twenty-two, he was being touted as a Captain.

As always, he had passed the exams with flying colors and he even had recommendations from the men who worked under him. *It would be just my luck to wind up getting promoted, captain the smallest ship in the fleet, and get sunk on my first voyage,* Mac thought.

On this day, Mac had an afternoon off, so he decided to walk around the city. More people drove cars here than in London and the walk from the docks to the city was actually a fairly long one. Still, Mac was able to see construction workers building these "skyscrapers" and take in the scenery on his walk. New York was full of skyscrapers including the biggest in the world, the Empire State building. Mac headed towards that and felt he would explore the surrounding area. He had been walking for a good three hours before he could tell he was near to the Empire State building but a strange thing happened as he got closer. He heard cheers in a local bar, then a local clothing store, and then people came out on to the street. Mac quickly asked "What happened?" An American woman screamed "Germany has surrendered! The war in Europe is over!" Mac fell onto one knee, scuffing his uniform in the process, tears streaming down his face. He felt so indescribably happy.

For a moment Mac felt extremely alone. He wanted to be with Penny, his parents or even Eddie, to remember this moment together. Failing that, he wanted to be with other British men and women. Being in America was great but they had not experienced the same torture as everyone in England. Mac kept thinking about Eddie in that moment.

Mac never really had many friends, being a bit socially awkward. He was currently standing in New York alone in a bedlam of celebrations and excitement because he had decided to walk and be on his own. Eddie on the other hand, had always been his friend, he had encouraged him to be part of the football team, to socialize, and leave his comfort zone. Hell, if he didn't leave it voluntarily, Eddie would push him out. *Eddie, are you out there celebrating like the rest of us? Are you even alive?*

Mac decided to head back to the port. He assumed the ship would still be setting sail that evening and he also assumed others would be celebrating and he should be there. He turned around and headed back in the direction he came.

His journey however was severely hampered, as people were flooding the streets from every direction. Music had started playing from some buildings and there were men and women just dancing on the streets. Reels of paper were also thrown from buildings in celebration, America really did know how to party. For a moment, Mac got into the party mood. He found himself drinking Whiskey and Coca Cola a stranger had given him. *that tasted really good,* he thought. He found himself dancing on the streets a little and even smiling. But in the back of his mind, he remembered that he had to get back to the ship, so after hours of maneuvering through crowds, he ended up at the docks. Mac returned to the boat and realized he was one of the first to return, even the Captain wasn't on the ship.

Mac went through and checked the whole ship, so that it was ready to sail. The ship was part of a convoy and they had to ensure three American supply ships made it to England. They carried American Army pants, uniforms, corn, and other food. Not sure how useful the uniforms would be now, but the food was still vital to the UK, so Mac wanted to make sure the convoy disembarked on time and as planned.

Mac checked all the guns, the ammunitions, the sonar, and then headed to the deck. More and more men came back on board, all saluting him as they passed with tickertape paper stuck to them. Mac cringed, thinking how unprofessional they all looked but at the same time he couldn't help but smile. It was great to be around happy people for the first time in a while. Eventually, the convoy set sail with Mac's boat leading the pack. The ships were like a flock of birds flying south for the winter all in unison. Mac had traveled this route many times and knew what it entailed but this time the ships seemed to be going faster. He could almost see England already, even though they were several days away.

For the next few days, the crew behaved as they should. They were still on duty after all; the war was still happening in Asia and Mac suspected he might have to go there next. They still had a mission and had to behave, although Mac had to be the bad guy the first evening when he caught three men drinking whiskey and beer on the deck and mooning other ships. All of them had been sent to duties below deck. Just as Ireland was in their sights, reality hit. Mac had been watching the sonar and realized that they were heading into a minefield.

He diverted his ship and got on the radio. "Convoy, sharp port turn," he bellowed down the radio. However, one small ship did not obey and went straight into the minefield. Seconds later, there was a loud explosion and a huge wave was seen ahead. Mac knew instantly that the boat had been hit and he calculated there were about sixty staff on there. The ship was sinking fast and smoke bellowed from the wreckage. Mac went out on deck and looked through his binoculars. He could see men swimming for their lives and screaming for help.

"We have to go help them," one of the younger men said.

"No son we can't, it's too dangerous for us," Mac coolly responded. It was weird that he would've said the same thing a few years ago. The mood on the ship immediately changed after that and when they finally docked in Plymouth, the men got to unloading all the supplies and were released. Mac looked up at the stars that night and hoped he was finally free.

CHAPTER 88

Eddie and Aiden were yet again thrust into action, but this mission seemed to be of vital importance. Eddie was hoping it would be his last battle. Since the battle of Kohima and the subsequent recuperation, they and their units reported to a new Lieutenant called Farringdon. They had marched south with him. Eddie was reminded on the march's first day that Burma is at least three times the size of England. They were marching down muddy roads and through the jungle.

They had set off over a month ago and the march had been excruciating on Eddie mentally and physically. He had sores all over his feet, his shoulders ached from carrying heavy bags, and the sun on his neck had been intense. The good thing was that they were with American soldiers who seemed to be well armed and the Americans had perfected the supply drop, so the troops weren't starving. The other good news was that the enemy's size had dwindled due to other battles throughout Burma. They hardly encountered any enemy forces. The occasional night time battle ensued but nothing that really bothered Eddie these days. He was more worried about the tigers and the snakes than the enemy.

They had marched for such a long time that when they arrived at their destination, all the men were completely drained. They arrived at a town called Rangoon. It was a crucial port town and was vital for supplies. The Axis and Allies had raced there in order to stake their claim and solidify their position. For years now, the British and American troops were hampered because they had to fly in supplies and drop them in place. Having a port would mean supplies could come more easily and in greater amounts. From there, they could be quickly unloaded to waiting trucks and vans and dispensed to different locations much more readily. The race to get there was because of the weather. The monsoon season was about to start again and if that happened, the Allies would struggle to secure the town.

The Japanese were also aware of this and had sent extra troops to ensure the port survived until the monsoon. Eddie, Aiden, and the men were sitting several miles away from the city, awaiting further instructions after spending a month rucking there.

Eddie rolled a cigarette and lay down as the sun set. It had been a clear night and he was able to see the stars. His mind wandered to his home. He hoped that if he got there it would be the same, the people would be the same, but he knew that was just wishful thinking. Everything always changes. Aiden sat down next to him.

"Where've you been," Eddie asked.

"Nature's toilet," Aiden winked and rolled a cigarette too. Aiden and Eddie had been through so much that they were more than best friends. They had made plans for life after the war.

Aiden was a huge Liverpool fan and felt that Eddie should move to Liverpool or Ireland with him so that he can toughen up. The next morning, they broke into formation, mentally prepared themselves, and went to attack. This was a massive operation, so other units had been expected to hit the city first. They were to storm it from the back. They ran in and encountered a few lone gunmen that were easily taken care of. There were no signs of other hostiles or any signs of battle for that matter.

That changed when they just entered the city limits. The Japanese held the high ground, so Eddie and his men found themselves hiding behind debris and shooting up. Things quickly changed when American tanks destroyed the buildings the Japanese were entrenched in.

Soon, the city was captured and Eddie had wished the whole war was like that, hardly any action or a need to reload the gun. Rangoon became his new home. A unexpected monsoon along with the recent battles had damaged the port town, so he and his men spent a good couple of weeks fixing the port and ensuring supplies were delivered. Eddie's life was great now; he'd found comfortable places to sleep, wasn't under any attack, and they had even found beer. Fixing the port reminded him of home. Some local builders had hired him as a helper when he had given up school at fourteen, so he was fairly handy. But seeing the ships come in nearly every day reminded him of Mac. Every day he hoped he would see the British Navy arrive instead of the American supply ships. Maybe then, he'd see his good friend.

The heat was unbearable, even with the monsoons and rain. By lunchtime each day, they had finished their work and relaxed at their makeshift base or at the bar. Long gone were the days of training exercises for Wheaton. Back then even when you had an afternoon you still had to do reconnaissance missions or last minute drills. The new leaders didn't care about how the men spent their time; instead, they advised that the men regain their health before their return.

Eddie had a potbelly from the amount of beer he had consumed and his poor diet. He mainly consumed fruit, vegetables, and rice. Although the other day he had stumbled across an old farm near the base and had somehow managed to barter for some chickens. They had cooked them on the base, much to the delight of the men.

Eddie decided one morning to go for a run. It cleared his head and he always used to run in Trevanston. He ran down the hill into the city, which still had a few American men staggering home and a few women trying to sell their services. He ran past all of that and kept running through the city and back up through the mountains. He knew this was dangerous with enemy snipers potentially still around but he didn't care. He needed to be free. He paused at the top of a steep hill out of breath. He noticed another small village to his left. The men and women were starting to farm the crops around them. Eddie went over to introduce himself.

Initially, they were scared but he helped two women carry their bags of tools to where they were working. It was the little gestures of kindness that made the biggest difference now. As he turned around, he noticed the view. The sun was rising above the ocean and the small cliffs; it was beautiful and he just watched it until it fully sat in the sky.

He headed back to the base and heard a loud commotion. He grabbed his knife, thinking that they were under attack and he used whatever energy he had to sprint back to the base. As he got closer, he realized the sound was cheering and he ran up to someone.

"What's happening," he asked.

"The war in Europe is over. Germany surrendered!"

Eddie hugged the man and went to find his unit. For the next half hour, he was shaking their hands and hugging all of his men. Eventually, he found his brother in arms Aiden and they hugged. For a while, there was a feeling of levity in the camp. But that feeling quickly soured. At lunchtime, one of the Generals made a speech to all of them.

"It's true—the war in Europe is over. Germany has surrendered. Our battle is not over, however. The Japanese are still very much at war; our efforts to repair this port are crucial, so we can advance and take control of this country." Eddie and Aiden finished listening to the speech and rolled up cigarettes before heading down to the dock.

"I'm going to die in this godforsaken country," Eddie exclaimed. They had both had experienced down periods over the last few years and both had helped each other bounce back. So, this time it was Aiden's turn.

"We are the cats. We'll be alright. Besides, I need to take you to a real game of football at Liverpool."

"We should just sneak onto a boat and runaway," Eddie stated.

"And go where, America? These boats are heading back to a place where they know nothing of football and play something called baseball. No thanks." Eddie laughed and agreed.

Less than a week after the end of the war in Europe, the whole unit was told that the port was in fine shape and they needed to march back north to assist other units still in battle. Eddie rallied his men and he and Aiden led the procession through the town and back through the village. They were the elite soldiers after all and now they were the most elite, actively fighting men in the British army.

CHAPTER 89

Eddie and his men had marched for days. The monsoon season seemed to have ended or at least they had not experienced one for at least a week. However the terrain was still difficult to maneuver, with muddy banks and wet dense jungle. Eddie was exhausted, so much so he could barely walk let alone tell you what day it was.

To make matters worse, they were supposed to have received a food and supply drop yesterday, but when they got to the spot, there was nothing. They'd become accustomed to food drops from the Americans, so this discrepancy was a blow to their morale. They still had water bottles from the last drop but with no food and the continued marching through the jungle, Eddie, Aiden, and their men felt exhausted and were ready to quit. As one of the leaders, he had to set an example so he just marched and focused on the journey. Typically, they would march during the day and then camp out at night. Sleeping was tough as the jungle was crawling with creatures and insects and you couldn't see the enemy.

The good thing was that before they departed from Rangoon, they'd received news that the enemy had retreated significantly so they'd only had one minor battle. There were about one thousand soldiers with Eddie and Aiden, so it had been a quick battle and uneventful for Eddie. He had stayed out of the gun fight. In the distance, Eddie saw what he thought was a thunderstorm. The sky was darkening, flashes of light streaking across the sky. He hoped they were near the base because walking in the rain would be terrible. Then again, he had seen something similar the other day and it had not materialized. The navigator had predicted that they were close to the base on the Indian border. They should arrive by nightfall. They were about to set up camp but the navigator was convinced they were close. So, they continued marching into the darkness and the unknown. Eddie had felt at least one snake slither past his leg and he just hoped he didn't tread on one. He didn't want to die from a snake bite after everything he had been through. The only hope he had left was that if the war in Europe had ended, maybe a ceasefire would be declared in this war. He could go home.

Up ahead, they heard noises. Eddie, Aiden, and all his men were on alert, guns and bayonets at the ready. But they saw lights and heard the voice of another British soldier.

"We've got an incoming platoon." They'd made it. Eddie and his men had no energy but they managed to jog into the base. Weirdly, they arrived to cheers.

"Where've ya come from lad," a big commander with a bushy grey moustache asked Eddie.

"Rangoon, sir," Eddie said while trying to catch his breathe.

"Oh, you boys are the Chindits! We were expecting you three days ago. When you hadn't appeared, we assumed the unit must've been attacked."

"Yes, sir. We're the Chindits and no sir, we weren't attacked."

There was still cheering and celebrations going on even after all of Eddie's men were in the base. *How odd,* he thought. They were all given tobacco, water, and local rice dishes which they devoured. Finally, Aiden asked the question which was on everyone's mind.

"Sir, why the celebrations? We get it—we made it here but it feels a strange, sir." The man paused a moment and then smiled. He stood on a crate to address the thousand men assembled before him.

"I didn't realize. You haven't heard the news. The enemy surrendered today and the war is over." Chaos erupted all around Eddie. Men cheered, cried, and threw other men into the air. Eddie took a couple of steps away from his men and lay on the floor. He stared at the sky and cried. He had gone through hell and had made it out the other side. Now—he could go home. That evening no one slept. Men fired their guns in the air, they drank American whiskey, smoked, and celebrated. Eddie acted like his old self and was the life and soul of the party. He was making jokes and dancing with people. Technically, they were still on duty but no one really cared that night. After that, for the next week, Eddie and his men were waiting for their next command, so they sat around the base and ate. Eddie even found a football and, after a couple of days, found his energy to kick it around with a few others.

Later that week Eddie, Aiden, and a few others were playing a quick pick up game of football with jackets for goalposts when a commander came over. Eddie knew the party was over for them.

"Hartley and Doyle."

"Yes, sir," they said, both at attention.

"You've been asked by the highest-ranking officers to go back in. Your mission is to retrieve the dog tags of the fallen soldiers and create at least temporary graves for them." Eddie had been collecting dog tags throughout and had many in his bag.

He believed it was important the family members to at least know how their loved ones died. But at the same time, he wanted to go home and not collect any more. The next day, they set out and marched about thirty miles. They got to their coordinates. A weird feeling overcame Eddie; this was where they'd found the camp and had been in that huge battle several years before. It was so different in the light years later.

Eddie and the men got to work and found several fallen men in a rain laden ditch. They turned them over for their dog tags but hadn't expected the decomposition to be so advanced. Their faces were rotted out completely. Eddie quickly put his hand in the water, turned the body over, and got the tag. There were hundreds of men and they spent the whole day doing this. That evening Eddie started to feel ill. Aiden had also fallen ill with a nasty bout of diarrhea. Eddie was experiencing chills and sweats. He'd been in the jungle too long to know what was happening. They must have caught malaria or something from the water. He went to order an evacuation but collapsed and passed out. When he came to, he was on stretcher being carried out of the jungle and heading back to the base. Eddie still had chills but felt a lot better. "Stop, stop. I can walk," he said and he jumped off the stretcher. "Just need water and rest," was all he said. He walked the few miles back to base to recuperate. He felt light-headed and nauseated but he didn't want to waste a stretcher. "Where's Aiden," he asked one. A man pointed up ahead. Aiden was holding his stomach and Eddie jogged up to him.

"Want a stretcher?"

"Are you kidding? A little stomach bug isn't going to get me. Maybe we can get some more time to recuperate when we get back."

There was a medical tent at the base and Aiden, Eddie, and a few others went there to get checked out. The doctor ran some tests and wrote some notes.

"Both of you have malaria and maybe something else. Did you drink the water?"

"Maybe a little on the hike from Rangoon but nothing on the way back," Aiden replied.

"Look Doc, we're fine. Let us rest and we'll finish our mission tomorrow," Eddie interjected.

That night, however, their health deteriorated. Eddie started to have sharp cramping pains in his stomach and Aiden started to vomit. The next morning, the Lieutenant came to both of them. "You men are going home. We'll arrange a train down to Rangoon and from there, the American Navy will take you back to Europe." For a moment, Eddie was frustrated by this decision. He wanted to finish the mission he had been tasked to do, but then he realized he was going home. He closed his eyes and silently rejoiced. His war was over and he was finally going home.

There were about ten men all with similar illnesses and all of them boarded the train. No one spoke to each other and the train stank. The smell of vomit and excrement loomed and the heat was unbearable. They were in a metal train cart designed to carry concrete. Aiden looked terrible and Eddie was gradually feeling worse. Seven hours later, they arrived at Rangoon and an American was waiting for them. The men hobbled onto the ship, were put in quarantine quarters, and ordered not to leave. There were no beds, just a bare floor but they'd all slept in worse conditions. They were to travel to Malta, a week's journey. From there, they were headed to England. The ship medic investigated each man and told them all to drink plenty of water, try to eat, and sleep whenever they had the chance.

Eddie had not slept well for years but given the pain he was in, he slept most of the first two days on the boat. The sharp pains continued but the water's undulation helped him and he felt slightly better. The men all around him were suffering, most of all Aiden. He'd grown weaker and paler every day. The fact that his body was rejecting any food didn't help his condition any. On the fifth day, Eddie sat by his dear friend. He could hardly breath. Eddie banged on the door and after no response, he left the quarantine and walked up to the doctor's office. After being shouted at for leaving, Eddie grabbed the doctor and headed back. The doctor gave Aiden pain medication and an IV drip of water.Eddie sat next to his friend and whispered

"It's time to get better bud. We've got that Liverpool game to go to."

"We had a good run mate. Go enjoy your life," Aiden whispered as he leaned over. He closed his eyes.

"Don't you die on me, Aiden; after all we've been through, you can't die now," Eddie said. Aiden was gone and refused to wake up. Eddie spent the rest of the trip lying next to his friend's body, he was too distraught to move.

All his friends from the football team had died in front of him years before. He had seen others die whom he had great affection for, including Captain Bond. He'd even lost his dad at a young age but with Aiden it was different. They had spent every day together for the past three years. They had helped each other through rough times, through near death experiences. Now, he was gone and Eddie was alone. The rest of the men tried to cheer Eddie up but he was inconsolable. He simply sat there in silence. When they arrived at Malta, he carried his friend off the boat. Eddie would be on a boat to England but he couldn't accompany Aiden's body. Eddie, despite still being weak, carried his friend's body to a beach off from the docks and let his friend float out to sea. Plans had changed; Eddie was told he'd be in the hospital for the foreseeable future.

He desperately wanted to return home. He was back in Europe and the war was over. He was so close! But his weight was dangerously low and his health had deteriorated. Until he had a full recovery, he was not going anywhere. Eddie couldn't sleep. He just sat in a hospital bed, staring at the ceiling, and thinking of Aiden. He thought of Mac and Rose; he hoped they were ok but he suspected they were all gone as well. He just wanted his life to end. *Everyone's gone, so what's the point of keeping on?* He cried so hard and had no idea what to do.

CHAPTER 90

Mac had to spend several months docked in Plymouth. He had to ensure the ship was ready for action in case the war restarted. He had telegrammed Penny but had not been able to get hold of her for several weeks. He had written his parents and they knew he was safe. Even though the war was over, it was not over for him and the men were anxious to return home. Mac found it very hard to motivate his men because he felt the same way. He was so close to total freedom but orders were orders. To combat the dip in morale, the Navy had planned for career advisors to come and talk to the men about their plans after the war. The advisors were met with a mixed response but Mac was quick to take advantage of this. It was sunny Tuesday morning and Mac was meeting with his career advisor. Mac was surprised when he walked in.

"Lt. Kelly—what a surprise! What are you doing here?" Lieutenant Matthew Kelly had been in charge of the ammunition depot during Pearl Harbor. Evidently, he had been injured and moved over Career Advisory, but he remembered Mac and had made time to meet him on his first trip to Plymouth.

"Good to see you survived the war," he said while shaking Mac's hand.

"You too, sir," Mac replied with a smile.

"What can I do for you?"

"Well sir, I read in the *Times* that there is a huge shortage of teachers and headmasters now. The government is keen for children to start back in school and my parents are teachers. I know how to teach and, sir without being arrogant, I have very excellent grades. I know I have to still be in the Navy but I would like to be reassigned to the academy in Dundee, Scotland where I can train new recruits and also attend Dundee University to get my teaching certificate."

Mac paused, realizing he had spilled his whole plan to the Lieutenant within five minutes of seeing him. Lieutenant Kelly, paused for a moment, read through Mac's file in front of him, occasionally raising an eyebrow here and there. Mac wanted to say something but didn't know what to say. The silence was killing him. "You raise good points but here's the thing, the navy will probably still need you here on leadership duty for at least a year." But then the Lieutenant came across something on Mac's file and tapped his finger.

"What happened here," he asked. Mac looked at the file and it was the incident with the kid Ben Moon, who was caught holding hands with another man. *Damn,* Mac thought, *do I lie or not?*. He started to sweat.

"Exactly as it says in the file sir," he finally replied. "Two men were accused of being homosexual but all I saw were two sailors keeping each other warm when rescued from the cold sea." Lieutenant Matthew Kelly paused again and brought his fingers to his lips.

"Well between you and me, I personally believe that what goes on in the bedroom stays private. It doesn't matter who you share a bed with and I have told my nephew that. He recently told me of a man who literally saved his life by not informing others on him after his ship was sunk. You might know him. Does the name 'Ben Moon' sound familiar to you?"

There was another long pause as Lieutenant brushed his blonde moustache. Mac had no idea what he was thinking. "I have not forgotten about you pulling me from the bus in Pearl Harbor and I think you did save Ben Moon's life. That means my family is indebted to you. Oh, by the way, we do desperately need teachers, let me put in a few words for you and see what I can do." With that they shook hands, Mac not quite sure on what had happened.

The next week Mac was notified that his request had been approved and he was to be relocated to Dundee and, assuming he accepted, he could also study at the university. Mac was so grateful. What was even better was that he had three days off before having to report to the Dundee training camp. Mac only had one thing he needed to do in that time. He packed his bag and jumped on the next train to London. Six hours later, he was there. He pulled into Paddington at sunset and he caught a train to Trevanston, got home, and surprised his parents. Both had tears streaming down their face when they saw him and more tears flowed when they heard the news he had. He stayed the night with them, enjoyed some home cooked food, but at breakfast the next morning, he told them he had to leave. They understood and promised to visit him in Scotland.

He walked to the train and bumped into Bill at the local Trevanston bank, who yet again persuaded him to have a beer together. They sat down for a quick drink and Mac filled him in briefly before running to catch the train. Bill had become a brother to him over the years and wished Mac the best of luck. He boarded the train and was off, back to London.

He went to the jewelry store he had previously visited with Penny and hoped the owners remembered him. Brian opened the door and instantly beamed a smile, his old yellow teeth in full display. Brian was the older of the two brothers and looked frail, but held out his hand and Mac shook it. "I hoped we would see you again. Please come inside." In the back room was Paul and he also looked very frail but straightened his tie and then shook Mac's hand with glee. Mac went through his requirements and both men came up with different options. He finally decided on the item and said his goodbyes to the brothers. He promised to stay in touch, but he was on a tight agenda so had to get going.

Mac headed around to Liverpool St station and then caught yet another train. There was a huge RAF base several miles away from where he got off and he decided to walk to that base. One local man had given him directions and he walked up a steep hill and then down some country lanes. He finally saw some barbed wire fences and followed it round to a base entrance. He was exhausted and looked a mess, his uniform had mud all up the legs from the lanes but he didn't care. At the checkpoint and a little out of breath, Mac asked for Lorraine. At first, the guard denied all knowledge, but Mac pleaded and explained the situation and the guard relented and made a phone call. Five minutes later, a soldier came down in a Jeep and asked Mac to get in. He did and he was driven to the living quarters. Jim answered with Harry and both looked a little startled to see this stranger in naval uniform, but Mac explained who he was and he was welcomed in. He sat down and spoke with Lorraine and then they told him to stay the night on the sofa and he reluctantly agreed. He and Harry spent a good couple of hours talking about football.

Mac had fallen asleep and awoke before the others. He quickly left, leaving them a brief note. He headed back through the country lanes in the darkness and back down to the station and caught the milk train back to London and was at the factory before the sun was fully in the sky. Then he waited.

Penny arrived a little after nine o'clock. She was skipping in her beat and didn't even notice that Mac was waiting for her. Mac came up behind her and grabbed her which startled her so much, she turned and hit him. He didn't mind as he knew time was of the essence. Mac spoke quickly, told her how he was going to study to be a teacher, told her how he had to move to Dundee for at least six months so he can do intense training to be a teacher. Mac breathed and Penny promised that she would come to visit and she was excited he would be in the UK. Mac then said "I'm glad. You can come and visit. But do you know what's even better? That you would be my wife," and as he said that he got down on one knee.

Penny burst into tears and instantly screamed "yes!". She jumped into Mac's arm. All the workers in the factory had appeared and they started cheering. They embraced and Mac was so relieved that his plan had worked.

Mac and Penny spent the day together just enjoying London before Mac had to catch a train Scotland. They embraced at the station before Mac boarded the train. After several weekends at college and training the new recruits. Penny came to visit. Mac seemed happy and Penny was excited to be his fiancée. The war had created some distance in their relationship but now they were going to be together forever.

CHAPTER 91

Penny was excited to meet Rose. It had been a while and there was a great deal of news to share. For once, Penny was actually at Euston station early and was at the end of the platform when Rose's train pulled in. Rose had been working a lot of shifts and very long hours recently as many of the nurses had quit after the war. The hospitals were desperately still trying to hire new recruits.

Rose had actually just finished a shift and had no sleep so was hoping this would be a short trip with Penny. However, she was excited to see her and catch up. They had grown closer over the years and they were family. Penny had written her a letter insisting they meet. The tone of the letter made it seem that Penny was in trouble.

The train pulled in and through the steam at the station, she could still see the city was bustling, men in uniform still dominated the station as well now as a growing number of men in suits. Rose pushed her way through the crowds and saw Penny standing at the end of the station in a bright red coat and her signature crimson lips.

"So great to see you," Rose said and they hugged. As they separated, Penny put her hand on Rose' shoulder to show off her new ring but she played it cool. "What's new with you," she said moving her hand in front of Rose but she did not understand the reference and started talking about work and the shifts.Feigning interest, Penny smiled and thought of a different tactic.

"I have heard of this place that's like a spa, but they just focus on your hands. She waved her hand in front of Rose again, who still did not get the hint.

"That may be nice. I've never done a spa, but I don't have that much money."

"Oh no worries," Penny said, now given up on subtle hints.

"How about we go wedding dress shopping!"

Penny showed Rose her ring.

"What!" Penny then told her the whole story of Mac surprising her at the factory and how they were to get married as soon as Mac was done with training in Scotland. Rose beamed with delight and hugged her cousin.

She and Mac had been together for such a long time, it was inevitable they would get married if they survived the war, but Rose was delighted that it was now officially happening. They met Lorraine for scones and tea at a really posh hotel. Lorraine had organized it and Rose felt very under dressed. There were lots of ladies dining, smoking, and enjoying jazz music from an American band. They ate cucumber sandwiches and other finger foods. Rose could not believe they cut off the crusts, especially with rationing still going on but gladly ate three rounds of sandwiches, three scones and two cakes. They also drank so much champagne that by the time they left, Rose and Penny were both feeling giddy.

The hotel was not far from Park Lane and Hyde Park, which was ideal since the bridal shop was on Park Lane. It was a bright sunny day and Penny had a bit of sweat on her brow after a ten minute walk. Rose was a little confused as they were outside what appeared to be a white town house. "Are we at the wrong address," she asked Penny, who just grinned and knocked on the door.

After a brief pause the huge black door opened and a tall slender woman with charcoal black hair and a pale complexion stood there. Rose was a little intimidated by her until she smiled.

"Alright—which one of ya is Penny?"

Penny responded and they all entered. She'd had told Rose that the Princess had told her about this place and made a few calls to introduce her to Ellen Dunsworth, the seamstress and bridal outfitter for the Royal Family.

The champagne flowed again and Penny kept going back to try different dresses. She had not found anything after an hour, but the three of them were having fun. Eventually after a couple of hours, Penny was starting to get frustrated that no dress fitted her. Ellen searched and found one more but Penny sat in the changing room staring at it. She hated how the other dresses squeezed on her.

It looked great though. *What hell. One more dress isn't going to heart. Besides, I'll just pick the one I like and have Ellen alter it an obscene amount. That'll be good enough.* She mustered up the courage to try the dress on and instantly she knew it was right. It fit in all the right spots and hugged her, not squeezed her. She walked out and the everyone's faces lit up with happy surprise. She did a little bow and walked off to some applause and wolf whistles. It was like she was getting a standing ovation at a play. She could not hide her delight and that smile stayed for the rest of the day.

The women all departed now. Rose headed back to Watford on the train lightheaded from the champagne. Penny and her mum walked back arm in arm to their family house. Lorraine made tea and they stayed chatting until nearly sun rise. It had been a great bonding experience for them both and they fell asleep in the same bed.

CHAPTER 92 -1946

Mac had spent just seven months in Scotland, but he'd endured all four seasons. He was focused on finishing his qualifications while the summer was in full swing. The University of Dundee and the Navy had both been cooperative with Mac and he had managed to complete his teaching degree in record time. Mac felt exhausted from it all, he had been up at 0600 every day training new recruits, running drills, and generally keeping them in shape. Every afternoon he had finished at 1500 and raced over to the evening lectures. He then spent most of his evenings studying and doing coursework.

Even when he had leave, he was busy. It felt like he was constantly doing something. He had a quota of teaching hours to complete in a classroom, so every eight weeks he would find himself teaching in a local primary school. Any weekend off, he found himself on a sleeper train down to London and seeing Penny or doing wedding planning.

Mac could see the light at the end of his tunnel. He had one final exam and one final piece of coursework, then he would be done with the course. Assuming he passed, he would be able to apply for primary school teaching roles. They had also been in peace time for over a year, so the Navy was happy to discharge certain members.

Mac had an exit interview on Monday morning. He'd caught an overnight train from London, spent the evening with Penny and left her at Kings Cross. He had slept for a few hours on the train, and he now watched the sun rise over the Scottish hills. There was a morning dew and a light dusting of frost on the ground. The steam from the train drifted into the crisp sky as the train pulled into the station. Mac walked in uniform to the Naval base which was thirty minutes away. Mac enjoyed these walks, strolling through downtown and admiring the shops and city being rebuilt. He would admire the ships in port as he walked down the docks. He was mostly happy that he wasn't on those ships anymore. There was a small part of him that missed the camaraderie of the men and even missed the adrenaline while he was under attack but his hatred for the war and being trapped on the ship remained unchanged.

Mac arrived at the base and walked through the sea of new recruits. He entered the interview room and waited. He stood to attention and saluted the three officers that walked in, all of them with files in theirs hands that bore his name. He was slightly nervous now, seeing how thick their files were.

"Lieutenant MacPherson—you have an impressive record," the middle officer said as they all sat down. He was a tall and had high cheek bones and a slightly unshaved face. His deep voice boomed through the room.

"You have six years of service."

"It's closer to seven, sir," Mac responded with a nervous laugh.

"I see. And while we are still on heightened security, you want to leave?"

"Yes sir. As you can see, I have represented my country to the best of my ability and—I believe—exceeded the expectations placed on me. Now, I'd like the opportunity to educate the younger generation. That is a mission I would be better suited for at this time." Mac was expecting a longer of an interview and more of an interrogation. The man in the middle simply stood up and said, "I have two young children. If you can teach them as well as you have served our nation, I know our children will be ok. You are honorably discharged from the British Navy."

He saluted Mac and shook his hand. The three men filed out and thirty minutes later, Mac had all the necessary paperwork completed. He was leaving the Naval Training Centre for the last time.

A week later, Mac walked into the University Hall and sat down for his final examination. He felt confident about it and was not nervous at all, surprisingly. He had already guessed what type of questions would be on it and he knew he'd passed before he'd even left.

He picked up the last of his belongings and met Penny at the station where they embraced and boarded the train. They arrived in London and stayed at Penny's apartment that night. Within a couple of weeks, they had moved into their new house and Mac had received an offer to teach at a primary school in Trevanston. Now, the next goal was to finalize the wedding. Mac had not forgotten about the war and still woke up with nightmares, seeing sailors drown or explosions going off but he was loving life again. His dad had actually been the biggest help as he could finally talk about what he experienced in the First World War and what had helped him.

His relationship with his parents was stronger than ever and it felt great to be near them. He happened to be down at the Kings Arms one night when Bill and Charlie were talking about a new football team starting up. "I'll coach it and I'll even wash the shirts, so long as the Pub's being advertised on them. But we need players," Bill said.

"Christ, Eddie might eventually come home and he can be captain again," he said. A couple of young lads were at the end of the bar playing darts and overheard the conversation, "We'll play," they said. Mac thought they looked fourteen at most, but quickly took down their details anyway. The concept of the new Trevanston football club had started. Throughout the next week, Charlie had enrolled his apprentice butcher, some school kids, and even the local policeman who was sixty-three. The new football team was born.

Penny played a crucial role for them. She reached out to all the local villages in the areas and soon Trevanston had a schedule of games. Every game started with the local priest, who was also a player for Trevanston, saying a prayer for their fellow brothers in arms whom they'd lost during the war. Every town and village was the same. Many of their men were now gone. Many mothers were without sons, many wives were without fathers and husbands.

The local teams helped start a sense of community and became a reason to rebuild towns and communities. At their games, people brought picnics, shared blankets, and created a sense of comradely. Come rain or shine, the whole village would attend. For Trevanston's game against local rivals Ashcoe, nearly two hundred people attended. Mac, who was now Captain of the team, felt an immense sense of pride and unity.

His leg and stomach injury prevented him from playing at a good standard, but he could still carry on. As he took in the scene and an apple while warming up, he was preoccupied with Eddie. He was still missing and he had always been the heart of the team and the village. *He would have loved this*, he thought. Both of Eddie's brothers and sisters were there as well as his frail mum Dorothy, who had Mugsy sitting on her feet.

They were on the sidelines and were waving him over. Dorothy did not look well and was sitting on a bench, with a stick in hand wheezing but the family were clearly coaxing him over. Mac walked over and Dorothy said "So good to see you Mac. Oh, you and Eddie loved this team. We all miss him." Mac didn't know how to respond, so he nodded and stayed quiet. No one had heard from Eddie in over a year. They assumed the worst.

"You should write him" she mumbled.

"I'm sorry? What did you say?"

The family nudged him and smiled. Dorothy searched through her purse and pulled out a ratty piece of paper and gave it to Mac. He couldn't believe it! Eddie was alive! It was brief but Eddie was alive and in Malta. It was postmarked two weeks ago and Mac could tell by the tone that he was not in a good place, but he was alive and that was the most important thing.

Mac wrote a letter to Eddie that night. Penny called in a favor from her government friends and two days later it was in Eddie's hands. He opened the letter and it read.

"Old friend,

I hear you're safe in Malta. I'm glad to hear it. Every day, I've thought about you and looked at the stars to see if you will come home, if we'll be home together. The last I saw of you was a picture in the paper. I hear Burma was horrendous. Sorry you had to experience that. I too have had quite an ordeal for the past six years and you certainly owe me a beer or two for convincing me to enroll with you! However, the war is over now, your brothers and I have started a new Trevanston FC but it needs a captain and more importantly (to me at least), Penny and I are engaged and get married in two weeks. I need you as my best man. What can I do to get you home?

Mac"

CHAPTER 93

It had been a tough time for Eddie. He had left Burma over a year ago on that fateful boat journey and he'd seen Aiden die in front of him, something that still haunted him. Things had gotten worse for him after that. He'd thought he'd gotten over his illnesses but a week later, he collapsed in the hospital and was confined to bed rest. The diagnosis was Dysentery, malnutrition, and Jungle Fever.

He would sweat, not eat, feel sick, and continue to lose a dangerous amount of weight. Eddie had seen the exact same symptoms in himself as he had in Aiden and knew he was dying. Part of him wanted to just die already and join his friend. Something nagged at him though, preventing him from giving up. The hospital was swamped with injured men arriving from all over Africa, Asia, and elsewhere. The staff had decided to move Eddie into what was known as "the Death Wing" on Christmas Day. The chaplain read him his last rights while Eddie wrote several goodbye letters and was prepared to die. The hospital nurses cared for him but many of the doctors and staff had given up on him.

There was something nagging him at the back of his mind. *Go home.* He'd promised Aiden he would go home. He kept thinking of his family in Trevanston and Rose. So, instead of doing what was expected, he got a little stronger and achieved small mile stones every week. He was able to eat, to walk, and gradually recovered by himself.

That was only half the battle, though. Depression had taken over and he was discharged to another hospital for observation. He had been so close to ending his life, but something in the back of his mind kept him going. Today was different. He had received some mail. The letter was stamped only three days ago which was odd. Nothing ever turned over that quickly. He turned the back of the envelope over and saw Mac's name. He could hardly believe it and read it again to make sure his eyes weren't fooling him. He quickly ripped open the letter in his bed, his clumsy fingers struggling with the thin paper. Eddie smiled hard. Mac was alive. He and Penny were getting married.

He read it again and that was enough for him. He decided in that moment he was going home. How amazing that one letter changed how he felt, the feeling of euphoria that sparked his reinvigoration.

What Eddie didn't realize was that he couldn't just leave and catch the next ship home. Eddie had no intention of ever serving the Army again, but if he just ran away, he would be charged for absconding and declared AWOL. Eddie decided to find an officer at the base who could help him get discharged. He ran to the officer's quarters and asked to speak to any available officer. It just so happened that an officer appeared at the gates in his Jeep as Eddie was trying to get in. The Jeep pulled over and the officer stepped out.

"Hartley! I don't believe it," the man boomed. Eddie squinted in the sun and then finally saw that the officer was Captain Jenkins, a unit commander who'd been stationed in Burma with Eddie. The Liverpool accent was unmistakable. He said, "Good to see you! So good to see another brother survivor!" Captain Jenkins now had a huge ginger beard and had he put on weight since they'd last seen each other, which was the battle in the prisoner camp, where Eddie thought Jenkins had died.

Despite that and the fact that Eddie now had more scars on his body and face, they still recognized each other. Eddie was amazed how small a world it was. Jenkins asked Eddie why he was there. Eddie opened up and explained how he'd ended up there and how he now wanted to get home.

"Well, it's Major General Jenkins now. Let me see what I can do." Eddie was invited into the base and went down to the officer's quarters where he ate food and kept to himself. After a couple of hours, Jenkins returned.

"So, it seems you have served for six years. You've been in more battles than most, even more than me. Because of your distinguished record of service, I'm pleased to say that your request for an honorable discharge has been granted, should you still wish to leave." Eddie wanted to hug his old friend and cry but he forced himself to salute Major General Jenkins. "Thank you, sir," he said with pride.

With that, Eddie was out of the army and now, he had to get home. He managed to get a pack of smokes from another soldier and he ate another meal before leaving. He had left all his personal belongings in Burma before being shipped out to Malta. He had his dog tags, some English pounds, and shillings that he always kept in his boots. Jenkins had arranged a lift for Eddie to the port but warned him he was on his own to get home from there since there was a wait to get on British Naval vessels.

Eddie had regained some of his confidence and decided to walk down the docks. He was looking for an opportunity and it didn't take long to find one. Down on the fisherman's side, he found a bunch of guys kicking a football and he decided to go join them. He started playing with them and realized he was playing with Frenchmen. The language was a problem but after some time playing, he told them he wanted to jump aboard. They managed to work a deal where he would fish and work for them if they dropped him off in Marseille.

That evening they set off and Eddie was given instructions on how to fish. He'd never done anything like it and he was up all night throwing slimy fish into nets. The seas were rough and Eddie was nearly swept overboard several times. Despite the work, the men all had a great evening and afterwards were busy drinking wine and singing. Eddie found himself as part of the crew and was shaking hands with them all several nights later when they arrived in Marseille. Jacques, one of the crewmen, had even helped Eddie get a train to Calais.

Eddie stank of fish, so no one wanted to sit next to him on the train. That suited him fine and he fell asleep. He woke up hours later in Calais. He could practically see home. He knew there'd be boats going back to England, and so he decided to find a military unit of some sort. There was a tank unit coming back from Poland and as luck would have it, they were from Ashcoe. The men thought he was homeless at first, given his dirty clothes and aroma, but he charmed them into sharing some of their clothes with him. He finally managed to shave and showered in a makeshift stream just near the sea. One man had even lent him some cologne so when they finally snuck him into a tank, Eddie looked (and smelled) like a new man.

They boarded the tank onto a boat. Eddie climbed out to be on the front of the ship. It was night and he was cold, only wearing a white t-shirt and green trousers. He didn't care though. The moon shone down brightly and, after waiting a while, he could see the white cliffs of Dover. By the moon and the stars, Eddie could make out the coastline. Finally, he was back in England!

CHAPTER 94

It was the morning of the wedding and, as always, Penny was running late. She'd stayed at The Staffordshire Hotel in Trevanston the night before but snuck out to have a few last minute drinks at the Kings Arms with Bill and a few others. She'd woken up with a slight hangover and was late for her make up appointment. Winnie had luckily awoken her by barking at others in the street. It was nine o'clock and the wedding was at noon. She had not even started to get ready.

Rose had arrived yesterday and was already seated with her mum, sister, and Aunt Lorraine. They were getting their makeup done when Penny walked in. They knowingly smiled at her and said nothing. Downstairs, Rose's dad was busy entertaining the twins at breakfast. Colin and Gwenn were full of excitement at being in a wedding and had already spilt porridge over themselves.

Mac had stayed with his parents the night before. They had a roast beef dinner and with some red wine. Charlie had delivered a huge piece of beef from the butcher's. "don't worry about the rations," was all he said with a wink. Mac could have stayed at his and Penny's house but felt it nicer to stay with his parents. In a strange way, even though he had not lived with them for six plus years, he felt closer than ever to them. Both were proud of him becoming a teacher and the conversation the night before had included classroom planning, how they never used the cane, and some of the joys they'd had. Mac was excited to start his career in a couple of months. They'd also spoken of marriage and about Penny, with both parents reminiscing about the Christmas they'd spent with her.

After breakfast Mac went for a brief run. Eddie had always mentioned how he ran every day to clear his mind, so Mac decided to follow in his friend's footsteps. He ran through the park where a memorial was being built to honor the lost. He remembered all of the football team and knew he was the only survivor in the town.

He got back to the house, bathed, and went over the day's schedule. It was a fifteen-minute walk to the church, he needed to be there at a quarter to noon, but he didn't want to be sweaty so he would put on his suit precisely at ten 'til eleven and leave at a quarter past. He wasn't planning on missing anything.

Eddie arrived in England to see the sun rise over the bustling port of Dover. *I'm finally home. I can't believe it! I made it out!* He disembarked, marching with the tank division, and was met with cheers from locals welcoming them home. Eddie looked a little out of place, wearing just his white tee while the others were clad in their uniform. The Salvation Army was there handing out cigarettes, cups of tea, and chocolate bars. Eddie gladly accepted it all, eating his chocolate in one bite and lighting a cigarette. He took a long drag and slowly exhaled, watching the smoke rise above him. It was the best damn cigarette he'd ever had. He said goodbye to the tank unit but promised them a game of football in the future.

"You should come to Trevanston. My buddy started a football team and we'd be game to play you!"

He walked from Dover's docks to the station. It was over a mile long and Eddie just took in the scenery, the green grass freshly cut, the cricket team practicing, the birds chirping, and houses with fresh laundry hanging off the lines. He was indeed back.

He got to the station and saw that a train was about to depart. He dashed over the bridge and caught it. The conductor walked past and Eddie searched his shoe for his last shillings. The conductor was an older man— possibly a veteran—who just waved the money away as he calmly said, "Keep it son, you earned it." Eddie thanked the man profusely and sat amongst his thoughts. *Gee, I must have made some money from this bloody war. I hardly spent anything in Burma, plus I had some socked away at home.*

He left the figuring of sums for another day; instead, he watched the train glide through the Kent countryside. There were several others in Eddie's car but it was mostly empty. Eddie had noticed that one man was reading a paper and by the time the train pulled into Gravesend he had finished.

"Sir, do you mind if I read your paper," he asked. The man just nodded and turned away. The first thing Eddie noticed was the date. *Damn, today's Penny's and Mac's wedding.* He still had the letter and he reread it to confirm the time. *Noon at Trevanston church.* His watch had broken in the last battle in Kohima, he still wore it since his mother had given him it.

"Sir, one more question—do you happen to have the time?"

"Just about half past seven," he grumbled. *Perfect, I might be able to make it on time.* As he was getting into Orpinton, the train stopped. There was a downed tree limb on the line so they were going to be delayed. *Perfect.* He became antsy as the train sat and he decided to get out.

The conductor and his mate struggled to move the branch, so he went over and helped them move the cumbersome thing. It was heavier than it looked. Some more passengers disembarked and offered a hand and eventually they threw it off the tracks. Once back on, Eddie made some small talk with them. They were part of the RAF. *I wonder.*

"Where'd you boys serve?"

"Biggin Hill," one man responded.

"No way! I was there years ago." Eddie and the men had several mutual connections and that broke the ice.

Eddie spent the last thirty minutes of the journey remembering and swapping stories, thinking back to the nights in the pub with the Airmen when he'd his broken arm. One of the air men told him he can get the underground up to Euston. So Eddie said his goodbyes, they wished him luck and he was on his way to Trevanston. Eddie arrived at Euston and had to wait an hour for a train. It would depart at ten am and the ride would take under an hour. He might just make the wedding after all.

Penny finished her make up and started to get her dress ready. Rose and Lorraine were getting ready with her. As Penny put on her dress, Lorraine started crying, Penny looked so beautiful. Penny still could not believe that the princess had recommended the royal seamstress. So many women were getting married that there was year-long waiting period for any and all dresses. Many resorted to just borrowing family dresses. Penny looked gorgeous. She owned the room despite being the tiniest one in it and her dress sparkled as the midday light shone in.

The hotel was a five-minute walk from the church and just across the market yard. Penny was hoping to arrive by car so that she wouldn't damage the dress. There was only one problem, Jim was late. At ten 'til noon, she picked up her train and vale and marched to the church with her bridesmaids and wedding party and Winnie who obediently trotted along next to her. Lorraine was worried that Jim wasn't there, but could not focus on that right now. Penny walked across the street as others were arriving at the church and she got cheers from the locals.

Mac was exactly on time and left the house on schedule. He walked down the street and up past the lock on the canal to the church and was there to meet the vicar. Mac had asked Eddie's brother, Bill, to be his best man, given that Eddie wouldn't be there. Bill met him at the church several minutes later. Mac had never seen him in a suit, but he looked remarkably clean cut, as if he were a lawyer. They all waited at the front of the church. People started to trickle in and several came up and shook Mac's hand. His former school teachers and other locals were proud to be there and Mac was grateful they'd made it. All of the new football team were sitting on the wooden church pews.

He wasn't surprised that the whole village was there. People had expected rain but it was a beautiful sunny day but with a cold wind. As it picked up, it could be heard through the church. Mac was amazed with the turnout. Many of his fellow comrades weren't able to make it but Matthew Kelly and Ben Moon had turned up. Most of the guests were the factory owners and female assembly workers.

Of course, the train ran late and Eddie arrived at Trevanston station at ten to noon. He was so pleased to be back home but he had no time now. He had to get downtown but it was a thirty-minute walk from the station. Eddie sprinted up the stairs and started running towards the town. He didn't care about the odd looks he got, so long as he made it to the ceremony on time.

As Eddie ran, he saw a man in distress with a car broken down on the side of the road and a small boy in the back. Eddie initially ran past but something told him to stop. He turned around and approached the man. "What's going on," Eddie said panting.

"No idea," the stranger said. Eddie had some knowledge of cars and understood basic mechanics from the days at the RAF base, so he looked up under the hood and instantly knew the problem.

"Your hose is loose," Eddie said. He jiggled it and tried to catch the thread. Some of the residual pressure spat oil at him, covering his shirt. He tightened it and asked the man to try the ignition once more. He got in and the engine turned over nicely.

"Any chance of a lift," Eddie asked.

"Of course," the man replied.

"Name's Eddie. You are...?"

"Jim, and this is Harry in the back" the man replied as they sped off to the church.

Penny was ready to enter the church with her mum walking her in. She thought about Owain. She wished he was there, walking her down the aisle. It had been years since his death but she still thought of him every single day. The doors opened and the music started, Lorraine kissed her, and they walked down the aisle, Rose in tow holding the dress.

Penny was trying to take it all in, all the family members, factory workers, locals including all the Hartley's, her family, and Mac's at the front. At the very back, there was a girl standing next to an Army man with a big hat. Penny realized the Princess was there. All of the owners she'd done business with were there, along with Nick and Maggie, the bar owners from London. They were seated next to Lil and several of the other nurses who Penny also knew through Rose.

Mac's parents greeted and kissed her on the cheek. Mac stood beaming. He had a tear in his eye and could not contain himself. He pulled back Penny's veil and whispered to her "I love you." She whispered the same back.

The priest gave a nod and men at the back closed the wooden doors. The whole church boomed as the first hymn was sung. Mac was trying to take it all in, looking around the room, so many familiar and unfamiliar faces. The priest started the ceremony with a prayer and went through the vows. Penny kept staring up at Mac, thinking how lucky she was, his big dark brown eyes staring back at her. The ceremony was coming to an end and finally the priest said, "Before we confirm this marriage, does anyone object to these two being wed?"

"I do," someone shouted from the back and the room gasped. Mac couldn't believe it, he clenched his fists, looking for the voice that had spoken. He stared at the back of the room in disbelief. Eddie and Jim walked in.

"I object to my best friend getting married before I can congratulate him," Eddie shouted.

He ran down the aisle, slapping hands with people in the pews, stopping to kiss his mum and sisters along the way and getting a huge lick from Mugsy. He winked at Rose and then hugged Penny and Mac.

"I love you guys. Sorry I'm late. I've been a bit of a mess today." The church roared in laughter and happy surprise.

That night the party was in full swing at the Kings Arms. Eddie had easily fallen back into his old self—telling stories, dancing, drinking, and just having fun. He could not believe how a little love from his friends had freed him from such a dark place. Just as the night was ending, Rose grabbed Eddie and kissed him.

"I have wanted to do that for so many years," she said to him. Her father gave her a worried smile, but said nothing. Eddie beamed at her and took her hand. They walked towards the exit of the bar and Eddie found Mac and Penny. He put his arm round them all and they headed out. Somehow, they all knew where to go. They took the same walk that they'd done a little over six years ago, laid down in the exact same spot, and stared at the stars.

"I love this view. Seems to me that stars really do guide you home," Eddie whispered and they all smiled.

The End

Made in the USA
Lexington, KY
17 August 2019